Praise for *The Highlander's Bride*

"Another winner from Forester... Her wonderful medieval romance is driven by strong and appealing characters... Exciting adventures keep readers captivated, while the lovely romance enchants and delights."

—*RT Book Reviews*, 4.5 Stars

"Amanda Forester weaves a simple plot into a gorgeous tapestry...in this beautiful romance."

—*Foreword Reviews*

"Forester keeps the effortless plot moving at a swift pace. Readers will be mesmerized from the very first page."

—*Publishers Weekly* STARRED Review

"All the trappings of an old-fashioned romance with some delightfully feminist twists...an exciting setting and period in history, fabulous clothing, and an action-filled plot, but the greatest joy of *The Highlander's Bride* lies in the lead characters' relationship."

—*BookPage*

"Colette finds depths and strengths she never knew she had… And an adventure is always more fun with a beautiful man in a kilt beside you."

—*Heroes and Heartbreakers*

"A passion–filled drama…heart, laughter, and adventure."

—*Harlequin Junkies*

Also by Amanda Forester

Medieval Highlanders
The Highlander's Sword
The Highlander's Heart
True Highland Spirit
The Highlander's Bride

The Campbell Sisters Novellas
The Highland Bride's Choice
The Wrong Highland Bridegroom
The Trouble with a Highland Bride

Regency Romance
A Wedding in Springtime
A Midsummer Bride
A Winter Wedding
If the Earl Only Knew

My
HIGHLAND
Rebel

AMANDA
FORESTER

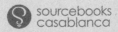
sourcebooks
casablanca

Published by Sourcebooks Casablanca, an imprint of Sourcebooks, Inc.
P.O. Box 4410, Naperville, Illinois 60567-4410
(630) 961-3900
Fax: (630) 961-2168
www.sourcebooks.com

Printed and bound in Canada.
MBP 10 9 8 7 6 5 4 3 2 1

To Edward, who always sees me as my best self.

One

Highlands, 1362

CORMAC MACLEAN SNUCK OUT OF THE MONASTERY, Aristotle in one hand, Marcus Graecus in the other. He was not stealing, just borrowing the scrolls until such time as it was convenient to return them. Had the good brothers of St. Finan's Monastery allowed him to read the scrolls in their extensive library, he would not have had to help himself. So really, if you thought about it logically, it was the monks' fault he had to steal.

Cormac slipped noiselessly across the cobblestones of the monastery courtyard to the gate. It would be locked at this time of night, the wee hours before dawn, but Core was accustomed to overcoming obstacles. He stuck Marcus in one side of his wide leather belt and Aristotle in the other. He reached up and began climbing the wrought iron gate in smooth, fluid movements. A few moments more, and he would be free.

"Stop, thief!" a black-robed monk shouted at him from across the courtyard.

Cormac hoisted himself up and over the gate with renewed vigor. It was time to disappear into the night.

"Open the gates! We must catch the thief!" shouted the determined monk, running toward him. The church bells began to ring, waking the good brothers from their slumber.

Cormac ran down the road and then veered to the north into the moors of the Highlands. He would cut across country and lose them in the thick mist of the coming dawn. Cormac settled into a loping stride, his long legs carrying him far from the monastery. 'Twas a shame what a man had to do to get a little education.

⁂

She had always wanted to have an adventure. That was her first mistake. Her second was to set off for a little privacy in the thick fog of the Highland morning.

Lady Jyne Campbell tramped along the cold ground of the Highland moor, trying to retrace her steps back to camp. She could not have gotten far. Could she? She considered calling out to her brothers for help, but rejected the idea. She wished to show her clan that she was capable of taking care of herself. Admitting she had gotten lost in the fog was not going to help her cause.

Being the youngest daughter, Jyne was accustomed to being bossed about by all of her fourteen siblings. And not just any siblings—Campbell siblings. Her eldest brother was David Campbell, laird of the powerful Campbell clan. The Campbell brothers were tall, broad-shouldered, hardworking, and a formidable foe to their enemies. The Campbell sisters were statuesque, brave, bold, and ready to stand shoulder to shoulder with any man to defend the Campbell clan, or against any clansman who got out of line. Jyne's mother had borne fifteen children, and not one of them had the audacity to die in childhood. No, frailty was not allowed in the Campbell household.

All except Jyne. She had been born a little too soon and had always been small. In childhood, she was prone to illness and had a delicate constitution. Being of questionable health during her formative years, she was never chosen to travel or join her clan in anything beyond the castle walls. Though her dreams were as big as any of her siblings, she had to content herself with listening to the stories of others and making herself useful about the castle, while the other siblings returned with wild tales of their exploits.

It was hardly fair, for she was not even the youngest sibling. Her younger brother, Rab, held that honor, yet at eighteen, he was treated as a man. Though she was twenty years old, she was not given the same freedoms. But Rab knew better than to be sickly and grew up just as strong and tall as any of his elder brothers. While Jyne remained…just Jyne. Though no one ever said it to her face, she knew that within the Campbell clan she was considered the runt of the litter.

Jyne paused a moment, straining to hear sounds from the camp. She had been so excited when David had finally allowed her to travel to see her dower lands at Kinoch Abbey that she had not slept well and had risen early to care for her morning ablutions before the rest of the camp was awake. And now, she was lost.

No, not lost, just momentarily disoriented due to the fog. She was sure if she continued just a little farther, something would start to look familiar. She would rather search for hours than admit to her over-protective brothers she had gotten lost in a bit of mist.

She continued walking in the thick gray fog, which blanketed the rugged landscape. The moor was damp and boggy, and she hoped to avoid having wet feet for the rest of the day's journey. She hummed a bit to herself to keep up her spirits. Sometimes she dreamed of being caught up in some great moment of crisis. Her castle would be besieged, and elephants would burst through the gates. Everyone would panic, but she would somehow stand bravely against the onslaught to save the keep. Of course, she had never actually seen an elephant, but she had heard the stories of Hannibal and his elephants, and thought that if she were attacked by them, she could be brave. Then maybe her family could see her for something other than sickly little Jyne.

She strained to see ahead of her in the fog and stepped onto something she thought was firm ground, but suddenly wasn't.

"Oh!" She fell forward into a bog, gasping as the cold, muddy water engulfed her to her thighs. "Oh, no!" She struggled, trying to find firm ground to drag herself out of the treacherous moor, but everywhere she touched was made of cold, wet mud. Her efforts were rewarded only by her sinking into the bog a few inches more.

The freezing sludge seeped through her clothes and held her fast, like an icy claw. The smell of rotting swamp gas made her gag. Her heart pounded in her throat, along with the remnants of her last meal. She had heard stories of people getting trapped in the bog and never returning.

She clenched her teeth to stop them from chattering. Should she call for help? The thought of the looks on her brothers' faces to find her stuck in the bog shut her mouth. She made another try for solid ground, straining her reach for a crop of grass.

She could almost make it. Her fingertips brushed tantalizingly against the stems of the grass, but there was nothing to grasp. She could not reach solid ground. Her efforts had only caused her to sink another few inches as fear slithered down her spine. Nothing she could do was going to get herself out.

"Help! David? Rab? Help!" Her pride was gone. She only hoped her brothers would hear her before *she* was gone. "Can anyone hear me?"

She had expected her siblings to come running as soon as she called. She could not be that far from camp. Could she? She listened for footsteps, for any hint that help was on the way. She heard nothing.

Panic surged within her, tinged with frustration. The one time she actually wanted her brothers to hover over her, and they were nowhere in sight. She made another lunge for solid ground, but the more she moved, the farther the bog sucked her down, and soon she was up to her waist, panting with exertion and sheer terror.

She closed her eyes and screamed with all her might, "Help! Heeeeeelp!"

"Here, lassie, take my hand." A man, a stranger to her, flung himself onto the solid ground and reached out his hand over the murky bog. She grasped it, and he began to back up slowly, pulling her from the quagmire. He pulled hard, but the swamp resisted, as if unwilling to release its prize from its cold clutches. Finally, he wrenched her from the deadly swamp, and she collapsed beside him on firm ground.

"Thank ye," she gasped, not sure if she was trembling from the fear of coming near death or the frozen chill of the mire still permeating her bones.

"Are ye hurt?" asked the stranger. He was a tall, lanky lad dressed in the plaid kilt of the Highlander, belted at the waist and thrown over one shoulder. He had a wild mop of unruly brown hair and glinting dark eyes. He was armed with a bow and quiver of arrows and had several scrolls stuck into his wide leather belt.

Her teeth chattered. "N-nay, just relieved to be out o' the bog."

The stranger stood up and took her with him, easily lifting her to her feet. "Ah, lass, ye're chilled to the bone." He pulled her close and wrapped the ends of his plaid around her, warming her with his own heat. She melted into the comforting warmth and safety of his arms.

Jyne sighed. She had a vague feeling she should not be enjoying an embrace with a total stranger quite so much. She was simply thankful to be out of the bog. At least that is what she told herself to explain why she rested her cheek against his chest.

"Thank ye. I dinna ken what would have happened to me if ye had'na come along," said Jyne into the man's chest. "Ye must have been sent by the angels to save me."

The man laughed. "Angels? That would be the first time anyone said that about me."

Jyne looked up at him. He had a decided jawline and sharp cheekbones. His face was almost angular, but attractive. His dark green eyes gleamed in the early morning light. He was a tall, trim man who looked to be in his early twenties. Perhaps it was her brush with danger, but she decided he was the most handsome Highlander she had ever seen.

"Then I am glad to be the first to say it to ye. Ye truly are my hero." Jyne's voice trembled with sincerity.

"I'm nobody's hero." He tilted his head with a sardonic smile.

"Ye are to me. I am Jyne and much in yer debt."

He shook his head. "Ye owe me naught."

She touched her hand to his cheek, and he tilted his head toward her, leaning closer.

"Unhand my sister!"

Jyne jumped away from the stranger and turned to see her brother, Laird of the Campbells, emerging from the mist.

"David! 'Tis well. He was helping me."

"Exactly how was he 'helping' ye?" David Campbell glowered at her, his legs planted shoulder-length apart, his arms folded across his chest. Behind him was Rab, copying his elder brother move for move.

Jyne took a step away from her brothers. It was not that she was afraid of her eldest brother, but David Campbell was built on a large scale and had decided notions of how his sisters should behave. He was never cruel or mean about his dictates, but he expected and received absolute obedience. He was a tyrant to be sure, but a benevolent one. She glanced down at her muddy gown. No hope to convince him she was capable now.

"I…I got caught in—"

"'Twas my fault," the stranger jumped in. "I wasna looking where I was going in the fog, and I ran into this lovely creature and knocked her into the bog. For my clumsiness, I humbly beg yer forgiveness."

Jyne stared at the formidable stranger. He had lied for her. He had *lied* for her! Not that she condoned falsehoods, but in this case, it was tremendously kind.

Jyne could not let his act of kindness go undeclared. "Ye're too kind, but truth is I fell into the bog, and this man rescued me from the mire."

"Then I owe ye my thanks," said David, still skewering the stranger with a deadly stare.

"No trouble. Happy to be o' service."

Jyne could not fail to notice that the stranger stood his ground against her imposing brother.

A faint voice floated across the wisps of mist. "Stop, thief!"

"What was that?" asked Rab, looking about for the author of the voice.

"Sounds like someone else is in need o' my help," said the stranger quickly. "Must go."

"But I dinna know yer name—" called Jyne, but he was already gone. Jyne stared at the place in the thick fog where the stranger had disappeared. Who was this man? Her first embrace with a man not her kin was with a stranger who had saved her life and vanished into the swirling mist. She trembled with the excitement of it all.

She turned slowly back to her brothers to find equal looks of disapproval. "Ye're covered in mud," observed David. "Come back to camp and change. We are headed back to Innis Chonnel."

"Wait, we are returning home?" Jyne hustled after her brothers as they led her across the moor.

"Aye," said David. "We got word this morning that the demon warlord, Red Rex, has struck a hamlet south o' here. We need to get back to the castle and prepare a force to march out to face this threat."

"But what o' the journey to my dower lands?" Jyne was crushed. Her expedition could not end now, not when it was only just beginning. "This is the first time I've ever left the castle."

"Nay, surely not," said David, frowning at the thought. They emerged back into camp, where David had led them unerringly. He did not get lost in the fog.

"But it is. I never have any adventures." Jyne gave voice to a complaint she had often felt but seldom shared. She wished it hadn't sounded childish, but she was tired of playing the role of the dutiful youngest sister.

"Ye're covered in mud, and I found ye in the arms o' an unknown Highlander," Laird Campbell accused. "That is adventure enough. Now, change yer kirtle. We leave shortly."

"I could take her to her dower lands and return her back home," volunteered Rab. Jyne smiled at his support, though she knew he had his own reasons for wanting to accompany her.

"Aye, that would be better for us all," Jyne agreed.

"For I warrant ye can move much faster wi'out me slowing ye down."

Laird Campbell frowned again, considering the request. Jyne held her breath. Kinoch Abbey was north of their location and should be well out of any danger.

"All right then, but, Rab, ye best look out for her. Dinna let her wander off alone. Take her straight to Kinoch Abbey and then back to Innis Chonnel. And, Jyne, I ne'er want to find ye again in the arms o' some strange Highlander."

"Aye, David," Jyne acquiesced. She was in full agreement. If she ever ended up in the arms of that mysterious stranger again, she most definitely wished David not to interfere.

She gazed again in the direction her intriguing stranger had gone. Her adventure had just begun.

Two

"Stop, thief!"

The monk behind him was certainly determined. Cormac would have made a clean escape had he not stopped to assist the delightful young lass out of the bog. She was a lovely thing, slender, with high, regal cheekbones, blond hair plaited under her veil, and bright blue eyes. In truth, he would have stopped to help anyone stuck in the moor, but the beauty of the damsel in distress had made him linger.

His enjoyment of the rescue had dissipated with the appearance of her kin. Even worse, the persistent monk must have heard voices and followed the sounds to him. It was not good, but still, not the worst day he had ever had. Cormac plotted a course through the treacherous moors and ran swiftly until his lungs burned with every painful breath. When he could run no farther, he paused a moment to catch his breath and listen carefully.

The sun had made an appearance, turning the mist to orange. Soon it would fade away into a bright Highland spring day. Core heard no footsteps or anything else that might suggest he was still being followed. He took a good, deep breath. His escape had been a little more difficult than he had expected, but still, he had gotten away with it.

Of course, he had nowhere to go except the last place he wished to be. With a sigh of resignation, Cormac turned his course back to the thieves' camp. He snuck back into the camp with caution. The men were enjoying the recent plunder of a conquest. Like the cunning of a cat, their leader knew when to move on, and had led his band of thieves, thugs, and mercenaries quickly and quietly to their current location to the north, to enjoy their ill-gotten gains without the unpleasantness of Highland justice.

Cormac climbed over a crumbled part of the stone wall surrounding the abandoned tower house that was the temporary home for the warlord and his followers. The muffled shouts and coarse talk of the men floated to him from inside the main keep of the tower. Core had no intention of joining the revelry. Instead, he sought out a relative measure of peace and quiet in one of the crofters' huts, which were built against the berm around the tower. Alone with his scrolls, even if it was in the dirt of the abandoned hut, was much preferable to the company of the thieves' den.

With a wariness born of experience, Cormac scanned his surroundings. Assured he was alone, he entered the hut and pulled an old sack off a wooden box, examining the contents within to ensure everything was as he had left it. He checked his equipment, materials, and notes, and breathed a sigh of relief. It was all accounted for. He put Aristotle aside for some light bedtime reading and unrolled a scroll of Marcus Graecus. He was sure it contained the information he needed to succeed.

Cormac had worked long on his experiments. He was close; he knew it. Scanning the text, he found a piece of new information. A quiver of excitement hummed through him as he began to read. This might be the missing piece he needed to make his experiment work. Then he could show everyone the true benefit of gaining an education. It would be a fine day when his unusual proclivities toward book learning would be respected rather than mocked.

"Thought I would find ye here."

Core jumped at the unexpected intrusion. He tried to roll up the scroll before it was noticed by Bran, the surly brigand standing before him, but it was no use. Core had been caught red-handed with contraband. Bran towered over him with a scowl, his large brown mustache almost completely obscuring his mouth.

"What's that ye got there, Core? Good thing we didn't find ye wi' books; ye ken how he feels about reading books."

Dubh, a heavyset man with a slightly confused expression, entered the hut. He rubbed the top of his bald head with a meaty hand.

Core didn't bother trying to explain what a scroll was. "What do ye want?" He eyed a window for escape.

"Red Rex wants ye."

Red Rex. Core's heart sank. Nothing good could come from being called before the warlord. The mere mention of his name struck fear in the hearts of decent folk. Truth be told, it struck even greater fear in those who followed him. Those closest to him knew well why he should be feared.

"Why?" asked Core, though he doubted he wanted to know.

"Dinna ken. Dinna care. He said to bring ye, and so we will. Ye coming?" There was a hopeful glint in Bran's eye, as if he wished Core would make a run for it just so he could chase him down.

Core considered his options. He could run, but if Rex wanted him, there was no hope for success, especially with Bran and Dubh on his tail. Core had tried it before. It had ended badly for everyone.

"Aye, I'll come by an' by." He surreptitiously stuck the scrolls in his belt behind his back, hidden by the end of his plaid that draped over his shoulder. He grabbed another from a stash under a crate and shoved it in his belt to the side.

"Ye'll come now." Dubh pounded his fist into the stone doorway. It was the stone that crumbled.

"Aye," muttered Core with a sigh. He had dealt with Red Rex before; he could do it again.

He followed Dubh and Bran into the abandoned tower house Red Rex had chosen as his temporary base of operations. The stale, fetid air was the first warning of the dangers that lurked within. Core walked carefully over slick, molding rushes that smelled as bad as they looked. The hall reeked of human waste and neglect. There was no thought to cleaning it. The men were content to pass a bottle of whiskey to numb the pain rather than improve their lot. Within the hall, disreputable men slouched along the walls, drank at the tables, and generally added to the stench of desperation.

"But I dinna care for him," cried a young lady with fiery red hair, standing before the notorious warlord. "Ye canna make me—"

"Ye'll do as ye're told. Ne'er defy me again, or I'll cut out that sharp tongue o' yers!" raged Red Rex. True to his name, the warlord had flaming red hair that stuck out at all angles and spiked down into a large, bright red beard. He wore a red-and-black great plaid and a leather arming doublet studded with iron spikes protruding from his chest in an ominous manner. About him, he wore a bearskin cloak, giving his already monstrous form even greater proportions. He was larger than any man had a right to be. Core suspected somewhere in his genealogy must have been the fabled giants of old.

"What is this?" Core asked Bran in an undertone.

"One o' Rex's daughters dinna care for the groom he picked," replied Bran.

"Why?"

"Because he's a ruddy bastard, that's why."

The young lady opened her mouth to respond, thought better of it, and snapped her mouth shut, stalking out of the room with a fierce look and tears in her eyes. If this was the way the man treated his own daughter, there was no hope for Core.

"Ah, Cormac, how good o' ye to visit our happy gathering." Red Rex sat down in a large chair draped with animal skins and motioned him forward.

Core stepped closer with a hesitation he attempted to conceal. "Ye wanted me?" He maintained a benign, slightly bored demeanor before the warlord. The man had no patience for fear. He wished to avoid the warlord's ire, but if Red Rex had set his sights on him, he had best make his peace with God, for he'd be seeing his Maker soon.

The warlord slowly pronounced the crime. "I heard ye snuck into a monastery."

Core's heart sank. How had Rex found out so fast? "Got hungry. Stole a loaf o' bread," said Core, hoping the unforgivable sin of visiting the monastery would be dismissed as petty theft.

"But that's not all," Rex said with a decidedly evil smile. "Ye took some scrolls. Precious ones, according to our poor friend." The warlord waved his hand, and two of his men marched out a monk in black robes. The prisoner's hands were tied behind his back, and a noose hung from around his neck. The man's short black hair was shaved on top in the symbol of piety of monks. Unlike most men who were brought before Red Rex, this man stood tall, and his jaw was set.

Core's shoulders slumped before he could remember not to react. This must be the monk who had chased after him. The man must have gotten caught by Rex's men. Poor soul. The monk looked determined to end his life with a courage Core did not wish to share.

Red Rex stood, his massive form dwarfing those around him. Even the brave monk took a step back. "I ken why ye went to the monastery." The colossal warlord stalked toward Cormac, murder glinting in his eye. "Ye were there to read." Core's indiscretion was stated with such ominous loathing that the entire hall quieted, shocked by the horrific turpitude.

"Ye can learn things in books that may be helpful," Cormac began to explain, holding his ground.

"Silence! No good can come from squinting at little marks on paper like some bald-headed monk." Rex gave the monk a shove, and the man fell to the floor. "Being raised by those alms collectors made ye scrawny."

"I doubt the ability to read made any difference on my stature," Core returned. It was a foolish thing to argue with the warlord.

"Insignificant worm! How dare ye challenge me?" Rex grabbed the scroll from Cormac's belt and held it over the fire.

"No!" cried the monk, struggling to stand again with his hands tied behind him. "No, kill me instead. Do not destroy the scroll."

Red Rex smirked at the man. "Ye'd give yer life for naught but ink on a page?"

"Yes, I would," said the monk, brave to the end.

"Then ye're a fool!" shouted Rex, making everyone flinch. "And I have no use for fools." He dropped the scroll into the flames.

"No!" shouted the monk, but it was too late.

Cormac watched helplessly as the flames licked along the edge of the scroll until it suddenly burst into flame.

"Kill the monk," said Rex over his shoulder as he returned to his throne-like chair. "Better yet"—he turned back to Cormac—"have Core do it. Ye've been here too long, supping at my table, wi'out earning yer keep."

Someone pushed a sword into Core's hand, and the

men holding the monk pushed him down to his knees. The monk turned his sad blue eyes to him, then slowly bowed his head.

Core's heart pounded. Kill the monk? What was he going to do now? "I canna kill this monk," said Cormac, his head scrambling for some explanation. He could not outfight Red Rex, so he must outthink him.

"What did ye say?" Red Rex drew his mighty claymore, the ring of steel on steel as he drew it from the scabbard resounding ominously through the silent hall.

Core took a breath, clinging to the facade of a cool demeanor. "I said I canna kill this man, for now that ye burned the scroll, he is the only one alive who knows the location o' the treasure."

"What treasure?" Rex narrowed his eyes.

"The treasure I went to the monastery to steal," said Core, warming up to his story. "Ye ken that the Templar knights came here years ago. Some say they brought a treasure wi' them."

Men in the hall nodded and moved closer to hear Cormac's story. Rumors of the Templar treasure had been the stuff of many a fireside winter's tale.

"Dinna the McNab clan find a chest o' Templar gold?" called out one man.

"Aye, they did. Warrant there be more," said another, rubbing two dirty hands together.

"O' course there be more," said Core confidently. "And this monk knows where. Why do ye ken I stole the scroll? And why do ye ken he followed me all the way here to get it back? Because it was a treasure map, that's why!"

The hall exploded into eager chatter as the men

shared the excitement over the prospect of finding treasure. Red Rex remained silent for a moment, pulling at his red beard.

"Where be this treasure?" demanded Red Rex. "Be it in the monastery?"

"No!" The monk struggled to his feet. "It is not there. It is…it is—"

"It is somewhere near the Kinoch Abbey," said Core, thinking fast. He had passed the abbey before and knew it was abandoned. The monks had lived there before moving to the larger St. Finan's Monastery.

Red Rex speared him with a fiery glare that seemed to melt through Cormac's lies. Core braced himself for injury, but instead, Rex gave him an awful grin. "Fine, take yer monk and find me this treasure. But understand this, 'tis time for ye to live the life ye were born to. Ye will prove worthy to me, or I swear by all those Saints who winna help ye, that if ye disappoint me again, I will put to the flame every book, every scroll, and every damn brother in that worthless, damn monk-house. Ye ken me, boy?"

"Aye…Father."

Three

"Do ye think ye have enough stuff?" Lady Jyne smiled at her brother. "I always heard 'twas the lady who wished to take the entire contents o' the castle wi' her."

Rab scowled and trotted beside her on his magnificent warhorse, giving a tug on the reins of his pack animal that followed along behind. The packhorse was burdened with chests and all sorts of arms and armament, such that it rattled and clanked behind him. To be fair, one of the chests was hers, but most of the gear belonged to her younger brother. Rab would have cut an admirable figure, sitting tall on his impressive warhorse, his back straight, his chin up in typical Highlander defiance, but the clanking of the palfrey following him did diminish the overall presentation.

"Canna leave it by the side o' the road," said Rab testily. He'd been thrilled when David had agreed to let him escort Jyne that morning, for he had planned to attend the spring tournament along the way. The emergence of Red Rex, however, caused David to ban the excursion to the tournament. No jousting, carousing, and charging in the melee for Rab.

"Do ye intend to sulk the entire way to Kinoch Abbey?"

"Aye, that I do."

"As long as ye have a plan."

Rab relaxed into an easy smile. He was too good-natured a lad to let Jyne's teasing bother him for long. In form, he was similar to all the men of the Campbell clan, tall and broad. Unlike some of his more serious elder brothers, he had sandy brown hair, light brown eyes, and a pleasant nature.

"Och! How lovely." Jyne pulled up on her mount to stop at a particularly attractive viewpoint along the road, turning her face to the warming sun. The wind played with the heather, and it flowed like ocean waves across the rolling hills. After spending her life in a castle, everything was new and fresh to her eyes.

"Do move along, Jyne." Rab dug his heels into his charger and clanked on ahead of her down the road.

"Ye must think this a lovely view." She turned to Donnach, the Campbell guard, who rode silently behind them. Though they passed through Campbell lands, and David expected no trouble on this stretch of road, still he had sent Donnach with them.

Donnach gazed over the swaying purple fields and gave her a grunt and a quick jerk of his head, which Jyne chose to interpret as something of a nod. He was a seasoned warrior, tall of stature and large of frame. His bushy black eyebrows and full black beard gave him the appearance of a permanent scowl. Though taciturn in speech, Donnach was one of Campbell's most trusted warriors.

"Do ye wish to see yer dower lands or no'?" called Rab ahead of her.

Jyne gave her mount a quick kick and followed her brother. She was excited to see her dower lands for the first time. David had purchased the abandoned abbey and the land around it from the Church to be given to her upon her marriage. The land bordered the large Campbell holdings and was a good investment to increase his domain. David had hired men to repair and repurpose the old abbey, though for the past year, the work had ceased.

Jyne took a deep breath, thinking on what might have been. She would have been married now and living in Kinoch. David had arranged a marriage for her with the fifth son of Laird Douglas. She had met her intended twice and had been content in the match, for he was young and lively…until he died of the plague.

With his death, work on Kinoch Abbey had stopped. Jyne had mourned him, though she knew him but little. She had mourned the loss of her future dream. In recent months, David had felt it was time to find her a new groom. Nothing had been decided, but David had planned the journey to Kinoch Abbey to see what was left to be done, which Jyne felt was a good sign that he was thinking about her future once more. It was not that living with her numerous kin was onerous, but until she married and ran a household of her own, she would always be treated like a child.

By midafternoon, they entered a lush green valley, and she breathed in deeply the scent of heather and cherry blossoms. The fields were overrun with wildflowers, and on the far side of the valley rose a quaint abbey with one circular tower. Surrounding the abbey were cherry trees, pink and fluffy in bloom. Down the center of the valley ran a little brook, chattering at them as they rode by.

"Och, 'tis a lovely sight. I've ne'er seen anything so bonnie." Jyne grinned at Rab and Donnach, but it was not returned.

Donnach rode forward. "Is that smoke rising?"

Jyne frowned. A tiny spiral of smoke rose from the abbey. "I thought the place was deserted."

They rode forward cautiously, Rab and Donnach ahead of her, surveying the situation. Other than the wisp of smoke, there were no signs of life. The tall stone wall around the abbey and the wall walk above it appeared to be relatively new and in good repair. Jyne did not doubt that repairing the guard wall would be the first thing her protective brother would do.

They dismounted at the abbey wall, walking the horses through the open gate into the outer ward, a large field around the abbey. "Hello there," called Rab. "This be property o' the Laird Campbell. Show yerself!"

No one answered.

"'Tis all right. We mean ye no harm," urged Jyne.

"We are here, or what is left of us." An elderly man, hunched and spindly legged, emerged from the main keep of the abbey, leaning heavily on a staff. "Forgive us, for we dinna ken this was the property o' the Campbell."

"No harm done," said Jyne kindly. "But what mean ye by what is left o' ye?"

"I am Alasdair from the clan Ranald. The great plague came last fall. It struck hard. It struck fast. Right in the middle o' the harvest. Those that were no' needed to bring in the grain, the old and the verra young, they were sent here to this old abbey to try to avoid the coming sickness. It was months before we heard anything. When our kin finally returned, they told us the plague had claimed many victims."

As he spoke, Jyne noticed children appearing in the doorway that led into the main keep. Their clothes were worn, their faces thin. Jyne's heart melted for these poor souls, seemingly abandoned by their people.

"So many of our clan were gone," the old man continued. "Those that were left claimed their children and took as many as they could, but there were too many o' us to feed. In the end, we chose to stay here so as no' to be a burden and to care for the wee ones as best we could. We dinna ken this abbey to be o' use to anyone. We can move on, if it be yer wish."

"Nay, I beg ye would stay as our guests. I am Lady Jyne, sister to the Laird Campbell, and these are my dower lands. Ye are now under the protection o' the Campbell."

Rab and Donnach simultaneously cleared their throats, and Jyne felt she must have forgotten something.

"Och, we invite ye to swear yer fealty to the Campbell in order to secure his protection," she added.

"Aye, m'lady, we would so swear. And thank ye for yer kindness." Alasdair's face broke into a sea of wrinkles as he tried to smile. "I've been praying for a miracle, and the good Lord sent ye to us."

His praise warmed her heart. At last, she was able to help others.

They entered the abbey into what had once been the main sanctuary and now had been converted to a great hall. On the west side was the circular tower, with stone steps leading up to the floors above. A large hearth had been added at the far side of the hall and the pews replaced with a raised head dais and long tables with benches in the middle of the hall. Jyne could not help but smile. This was a place that could feel like home.

They walked out of the hall into a central courtyard, around which the square abbey had been built. This had been the inner cloister for the monks and still held a peaceful air. Jyne mentally planned where she would plant her garden and fruit trees. A well in one corner was a good sign that the keep boasted its own water supply.

The elders came slowly out into the courtyard to swear their fealty to the Campbell clan. Jyne accepted them with grace, while Rab stood guard and Donnach searched Kinoch and the surrounding area to ensure all was well. Donnach returned and gave them a nod to let them know the grounds had been searched and nothing amiss had been detected. These were simply people who needed her help, and she was more than willing to extend assistance.

"Let us send Donnach back to Innis Chonnel to bring provisions, and we will tend for these people as best we can until help arrives," said Rab, who was never slow to offer aid.

"Why no' do this task yerself, my brother?" Jyne stepped near to him and put a hand on his sleeve, whispering in Rab's ear. "There is no danger here, and it doesna appear that these poor people are in emergent need. Why no' return home by way o' the tournament? I'm sure it will be all right."

"Are ye certain it will be well?" Rab's eyes shone with intensity. Jyne knew she had tempted him with the true desire of his heart.

"My good man"—Jyne approached Alasdair— "what is the state o' yer affairs? Is there anyone in need of urgent medical attention?"

"A few are ill, but their needs are chronic. We got none on their deathbed as yet."

"Do ye have food to last ye the next few weeks?" asked Jyne.

"We've been rationing well enough. We dinna have plenty, but we have enough to sustain life for a while yet. What we truly need is the fields to be plowed for us to do the planting, for it is already past time for seeds to be in the ground. We do have seeds, but no' the strength, I fear. That is, if ye will allow us to stay here this year, m'lady."

"O' course ye must stay," said Jyne with a smile, turning back to Rab.

Rab's eyes danced with excitement. "Are ye certain? Can ye manage for a week or so on yer own?"

"I am sure. This is a lovely place, and I would like to stay here above all else. Besides, Donnach will stay as my guard, though I doubt he will be needed. Bring back some men to plow the fields, for Alasdair is right, 'tis past due." Jyne's mind took a happy detour, dreaming about being the mistress of Kinoch, bringing in the harvest, before returning her attention to Rab.

"Now go and enjoy the tournament. I will enjoy ye more when ye're no' fractious." Jyne gave Rab a smile, which was returned in full.

"Ye're the best sister a lad could want." He squeezed her shoulder and quickly prepared for travel, leaving the traveling chest behind with her. Rab jumped nimbly into his saddle and waved them a cheerful good-bye, not hesitating in his departure, lest she should change her mind. He trotted out the open gate, his packhorse clanking along behind him.

Lady Jyne waved her brother good-bye, then turned and smiled at the children's faces that watched her from doorways and from behind barrels and along the sides of walls. With the removal of what must have appeared to be a fierce Highlander, they crept closer.

"How are ye, my dears?" she called to them.

Suddenly, she was barraged by children, at least two dozen of them in varying ages from barely walking to nine or ten years old. Her benign question was answered by multiple children at once, all talking in a happy cacophony, and all wanting her attention. She smiled down at them. It was fun to be the eldest for a change.

This was an even greater adventure than anything she had anticipated. Here, she was something more than David's littlest sister. Here, she was needed. Here, she could do some good work. Strange, but she felt like she had finally come home.

"Would ye like to give me a tour o' Kinoch Abbey?" she asked and was soon escorted about by a swarm of happy children, all vying for the attention of the new stranger. She was shown the chambers in the tower, the former chapter room with ornate carved woodwork, and the former refectory. The southeast corner held a storeroom with a trapdoor down to the abbey's crypt. Fortunately, the children moved on quickly, for that was one place she did not wish to explore.

The east side held small, individual cells that formed the dormitories for the monks. Work had begun to tear down some of the interior walls to form rooms more suited for a keep, but the work had clearly stopped abruptly, and many of the small cells remained. She paused for a moment, staring at a moment of time: the time her fiancé had died, just one more victim of the great plague, and all work on the abbey had ceased.

"Come on! Here, there's more," urged a young girl, pulling her forward.

Jyne was dragged back into the present. She smiled at the exuberant lass and followed her and the other children past the exterior door that led to the postern gate, to the northeast corner where a small chapel remained for the use of the keep. The children ran ahead of her and, after a few minutes, ran past her once more. Following them into the kitchen and out a newly added door, she found herself once again in the great hall and realized the abbey structure formed a large loop around the central courtyard, much to the amusement of the running children.

Jyne breathed deeply, content with all she saw.

"We tried to keep it as we found it," said Alasdair, leaning on his cane.

"I would hardly know ye've been here," exclaimed

Jyne. "There is work to be done to make this a proper keep. I wonder if the children might be enlisted to help."

"Aye, m'lady, we are yers to command." Alasdair gave her a wrinkly grin.

Jyne returned it. She was excited to get started. In truth, she had no interest in returning to Innis Chonnel. She began to set everything to rights, organizing the children with their boundless energy. Soon, new rushes were laid in the great hall, fresh cloths were placed on the wooden tables, and supper, thanks to Donnach, who had returned with a successful hunt, was roasting in the hearth. Jyne walked about, satisfied that all was going well.

Kinoch Abbey was hers now. After all the disappointment of the past year, she was finally home.

❧

Cormac saddled a horse and packed as quickly as he could, taking all his precious gear with him, before his father could change his mind. If the monk had any sense, he would run away as far and as fast as he could. Core's first thought was to follow suit and take to flight. Perhaps this time his father would not find him. Maybe he could go someplace no one knew him, and he could gain a position as a scribe.

It was a pleasant dream, but he knew better than to be tempted by it long. Red Rex would never be played the fool. His reaction to Cormac's betrayal if he tried to run would be the thing of nightmares. Besides, Core could not let the monks be at risk. He must warn them somehow. And of course, the destruction of all those lovely books was unthinkable.

Cormac had not gotten far down the road when the thunder of hooves on the ground behind him drew his attention. Bran and Dubh emerged from around a bend, riding hard to catch him. Behind them were about twenty more men.

With a groan of resignation, Core pulled up and waited for them to overtake him. "What do ye want?" he asked brusquely. They were the harbingers of doom and destruction.

"We've been sent to go with ye," Bran told him in a grave tone. "We are to make sure ye dinna take more than yer share o' the treasure."

"Rex said to follow ye and make sure ye dinna run off," Dubh said, giving an unnecessary explanation. Red Rex was certainly no fool and trusted Core no more than Core trusted him.

"We found yer misplaced monk." Bran gestured behind him, and the monk came into view. He was riding a horse as well, but was tied by the wrists to the saddle. Core stifled a sigh of disappointment. He had gone to considerable trouble to save the monk and had hoped the man would have been able to get away. Luck was not on Cormac's side today. It was not an unusual circumstance.

"How thoughtful," Cormac muttered. "Looks like we're all going to Kinoch Abbey."

Four

CORE AND THE MEN HIS FATHER HAD SENT TO BABYSIT him rode hard their first day of travel, spent a cold night on the ground, and then were back up and moving early in the morning. Bran pushed them to keep a brisk pace, though Core hardly knew why they were rushing. For his part, he still had yet to figure a way out of his present untenable situation.

In theory, his father's men were supposed to be serving him, but Cormac had no illusions that the men with him had any loyalty other than to their own desires and a slavish devotion born of abject fear of his father. If Red Rex demanded something be done, it was done. So when Rex told Bran and his men to go with Core, they did it. But while they served his father with blind allegiance, they would not serve him.

This mission was about making Cormac do what Rex wanted. It was about showing Core that his master was Rex and that he could be forced to do anything and everything his father wanted. Despite having abandoned him as a young child, now that Core was a man, Rex wanted to fashion him into an image of himself. Core had no doubt this was only the beginning of his education in how to be as wicked and as brutal as Red Rex himself.

Cormac glanced back at his riding companions. The monk glared at him. Bran scowled at him. Everyone looked like they wanted to hurt him. Core sighed and hastened his pace. The sooner he got to Kinoch and found something resembling a treasure, the better. Though how he was to make that unlikely event come about, he did not know.

He needed to keep his wits about him and devise a plan. His quick thinking had kept him alive this long, and it would not fail him now. At least…he sincerely hoped so.

Core slowed a bit to allow the monk to ride up beside him. If anyone knew anything about Kinoch Abbey, it would be him.

"Ye and yer monks lived at Kinoch afore they moved into St. Finan's, no?" asked Core, careful to keep his voice low.

"Yes," answered the sullen monk. He was a young man with short, black curly hair and slate-blue eyes.

Cormac lowered his voice even further. "I dinna suppose there is a treasure at Kinoch Abbey?" It was worth the question.

"No." The monk glared at him. "And now, because of this story you told, you have put not only the entire library but all the brothers at risk!" Though he spoke perfect English, his accent branded him an outsider, probably from somewhere on the continent.

"I saved yer miserable life," countered Cormac. "Have ye no gratitude?"

Instead of expressing his thanks, the monk narrowed his eyes in a disapproving manner. "You put us all at risk of death because of your thieving ways. Did you want to sell them? Is that what this is all about?"

"I wanted to *read* them," growled Cormac at the sting of an old wound. "But I suppose that seems impossible to ye."

"Highly improbable," responded the monk with infuriating superiority.

"Ye monks, ye're all the same. Judging that which ye know little about," muttered Core.

"And what do you claim to know of our way of life?" the monk asked in a voice like ice.

"I know I was raised in a monastery until they discovered the name o' my father and kicked me out on my arse." Core could not speak the words without feeling the familiar stab of pain.

The young monk beside him was quiet for a moment. "Whatever your mistreatment might have been, it does not excuse theft. An irreplaceable scroll was lost because of you!"

Cormac reached into one of his saddlebags and produced the two scrolls. He couldn't resist a smile. "'Twas a blank scroll cast in the fire." Core was his father's son, and he could be as crafty as the old bastard himself.

"Oh, you saved them." The monk's eyes widened, and he attempted to reach for the scrolls, forgetting his hands were still tied to the saddle.

"I've no more desire to see the library destroyed than ye do," said Core in an undertone. "But know that my father does not make idle threats. So if ye'd no' like to see yer books made into a funeral pyre, ye need to help me."

The monk's blue eyes flashed steel but dimmed into resignation.

"Tell me o' Kinoch. Did ye leave anything o' value behind? Why did ye leave it?"

"Kinoch Abbey was old and too small for the needs of the growing community of brothers. Laird Campbell offered a good price for the land, and we used the money to build the larger monastery."

"Kinoch is old. Mayhap there is something o' value? Any out o' the way places something may have been left behind?"

"No, only the crypt below the abbey, but there you will only find the dead."

"Is there anywhere a person might have hidden something? Any secret doors?" Cormac had to find something.

The monk shook his head. "The postern gate on the north side is hard to find, but you will find no buried treasure at Kinoch."

It was not what Cormac wished to hear. He was still chewing on forming a plan when the party came to a pleasant valley with a brook prattling its way down the middle. At the far end of the valley sat Kinoch Abbey, its stone walls warmed in the orange light of the setting sun. It would have been an agreeable sight had it not been for his unwanted traveling companions.

"Look!" cried one of the men behind him. "There's smoke rising from Kinoch. Someone's got there afore us!"

"They're trying to steal our treasure!" growled another.

"Ye'll be needing this, then," said Bran, and one

of Red Rex's horned helms was brought forth and slammed on Core's head. It smelled like whiskey and the armpit of a cave troll.

"Ye're too kind," said Core, muffled through the repulsive helm.

"To war!" shouted Dubh, and the men galloped forward, with him carried along at the fore, the unwilling leader of the charge.

Cormac cursed with every bump of his mount, the heavy helmet pounding down on him with every jolt. He was being attacked more from his own headgear than anything else.

Core knew Kinoch had been abandoned and expected any squatters who might have strayed there to flee as soon as they saw them coming. He certainly hoped they would move along fast, for with his father's men in full charge, things were about to get unpleasant. Instead, the gates of Kinoch Abbey swung shut as they approached, and all was barred when they arrived.

Cormac groaned inside the heavy helm. Now he would be obliged to besiege Kinoch, for there was little hope of turning aside the intentions of the brigands now that they thought a Templar treasure was inside the gates.

"Charge the gate!" shouted Bran, and the men took up a terrifying war cry and galloped to the gate. It was a fearsome display, but largely pointless, since the gates were barred.

Core dug in his heels and galloped after Bran, gaining the advantage and turning him and Dubh aside to get their attention. If they were going to do this thing, at least they could do it well.

"Out o' my way!" snarled Bran.

"Quick, to the side," shouted Core, remembering what the monk had said about the side gate. "We must guard the postern gate before they send a runner for help."

Bran frowned but slowed down. "Ye think they'll send a runner?"

"Would'na ye if ye saw us coming?" The last thing Core needed was more people joining this party. He took off to the north side of the walled abbey, with Bran and Dubh following him. Flowering cherry trees lined the walls, streaming pink and white petals down on them in a cheerful but guilt-inducing welcome, considering their intent. Around the side, the shrubs and brush were thick and overgrown, forcing them to slow their progress. The helm was a hindrance in the trees, so Core tossed it aside, hoping to never see it again.

At a flash of movement ahead through the trees, they all stopped. As Core had suspected, a man on horseback and another smaller cloaked figure emerged from the side of the castle.

"Well, I'll be damned," muttered Bran.

"I'm sure ye will. Now quick, after the man. I'll get the other." Core sent Bran and Dubh to intercept the runner, while he dealt with the smaller figure.

The figure of a woman.

⤝⤞

"We'll find a way to repay ye." Alasdair wrung his tam in his gnarled hands. He followed Jyne as she took account of the storeroom. "We found things well stocked. I confess we have helped ourselves to yer larder, and for that, I humbly apologize."

"Ye had but little choice," said Jyne sympathetically. Fortunately, when construction had stopped at Kinoch, the workmen had left the stores behind.

"Aye, but it dinna sit well wi' me, just the same. We rationed so we could make the provisions last till the harvest. If we could get the fields planted, that is."

"When my kinsmen return, they shall see to it," reassured Jyne. Though Alasdair's wrinkled face continued to show concern, she could not help but enjoy the presence of the Ranalds. She had finally been given the opportunity to serve as the chatelaine of her own keep.

Since her arrival at Kinoch, it had been a time of firsts for her. The first time she had sole control to manage her own household. The first time people looked to her to make decisions. Even the first time she had slept in a bedchamber by herself. It had been strange to try to sleep without hearing the gentle breathing—or outright snores—of any number of sisters, cousins, and nieces. When she had finally drifted to sleep, she had happy dreams of running through fields of heather toward a handsome young man who might have looked suspiciously like the Highlander who had saved her from the bog. She woke with a smile on her face.

Jyne had spent the day getting to know her new people, taking stock of her new domain, and organizing improvements. She even made a tincture, as best she could remember from her sister-in-law's teachings, to help an elderly man with gout. Finally, she had a place where she could be mistress.

Jyne stepped sidewise to continue counting sacks of flour, careful not to knock over her new friend. A little orphan named Ina had taken a liking to her and had rarely let go of her skirts, following her about all day. Jyne gave the young girl a smile. The lass hid behind Jyne's skirts but did not let go. Jyne finished counting sacks of flour and went on to taking inventory of the whiskey.

"We drank only a wee bit o' that," said Alasdair, giving his tam another twist. "Only what was necessary to preserve life."

Jyne smiled at him. "O' course." It was a rare Highlander indeed who didn't feel a drop of whiskey now and again was essential for the preservation of life. She continued with her inventory. The Ranalds had been frugal to make the provisions left at Kinoch stretch as far as they had.

"M'lady! M'lady!" A young boy scurried up to her as fast as he could. "We're under attack."

Jyne's tranquility shattered like glass. "What say ye?"

"'Tis the Red Rex!"

"Nay, 'tis no' possible. Red Rex is far to the south. Laird Campbell has gone to find him."

"Then who be marching at our gates?"

Jyne turned to Alasdair for a possible explanation, but he appeared as stunned as she felt. Jyne picked up her skirts and ran to the wall walk surrounding the abbey, followed by Donnach. There must be some mistake. Or maybe it was her own kin returning early.

Breathless from sprinting across the courtyard and up the stone steps to the wall walk, Jyne squinted into the setting sun. On the far side of the field were two dozen warriors galloping toward them at great speed. Her heart sank with the realization that these warriors were not her clan. The leader wore a giant helm with demonic horns.

"By the saints," exclaimed Donnach in a grim tone. "'Tis the Red Rex!"

Jyne watched the approaching riders in shock. Fear squeezed her heart with an icy grip. What was she to do now?

"Bar the gates!" shouted Donnach.

Jyne stared mutely at Donnach. Where were her brothers to protect her when she needed them? A small hand clasped hers. She looked down to find Ina holding her hand, her eyes wide in terror. The child's fear shocked Jyne out of hers. Somehow, she needed to protect these people.

"Donnach, ye need to ride back home and let David know what's happened." Their only hope was to send for help.

"Nay, I canna leave ye. Yer safety is my responsibility."

"I shan't be safe for verra long wi'out reinforcements. One of us has got to go for help." Her heart pounded with the rumble of the approaching riders.

"Aye." Donnach frowned with concern. "Ye come wi' me then."

Jyne shook her head. "I would only slow ye down. Ye ken I'm no great rider. We'd both be caught. Ye need to go. Quick, before they are upon us!"

The gates clanked closed, and some of the boys managed to lift a thick log to bar the gates. Jyne was grateful the wall had been one of the first things that had been repaired. She glanced back at the raiders swiftly approaching. She needed to act, and fast.

"Listen, all o' ye." She ran down the wall steps. The elders and children gathered around her, wide-eyed and pale. "We need to set guards on the walk, at least such that it appears this fortress is not entirely unprotected."

"One o' the storerooms has a bunch of old armor in it," volunteered one of the girls.

"Verra good. The taller lads and those able-bodied of our elders can pose as warriors. We just need to keep them at bay until help arrives. Is there another way out?" she asked Alasdair, who had hobbled after them and joined them on the walk.

"Aye, the postern gate."

"Good." She turned to Donnach, who was still shaking his head, the permanent frown of his whiskers even more fierce. "Ye must go for my brother before it is too late. Ye're our only hope. We need Campbell."

Donnach's shoulders hunched in defeat, and he gave a quick nod. He ran to saddle his courser while Jyne grabbed a bow and a quarrel of arrows and followed Alasdair, little Ina still clutching her skirts. She desperately hoped Donnach could escape, for the attackers were so close, she could hear the thunder of the hooves drawing ever nearer.

"Ina, please stay with Alasdair." Jyne took Ina's hand and gave it to Alasdair, who pointed them in the right direction, unable to keep up with their sprinting pace.

They ran around the far side of the abbey to a narrow walk that ended in a thick oak door banded with iron bars. Donnach wrenched hard to loosen the old, rusted door, while Jyne held the reins of his mount. The sound of approaching hooves suddenly grew silent.

"Och, they be at the front gate. Ye must fly, Donnach!" Jyne led the courser out of the small gate, for it was not tall enough for a man to ride through. She held the horse's head while Donnach mounted, her hands trembling with the reins.

"Stay safe, and bar the door, or David will have my head!" Donnach kicked his steed and raced away through the woods.

"Godspeed!" she cried. She watched for a moment as he disappeared into the trees. She turned to run back into the gate but stopped short, her heart frozen in fear.

A shadowed figure stood between her and the safety of the abbey. In his hand was a knife, the setting sun glinting off the naked blade.

Jyne gasped, a scream in her throat, until she caught a glimpse of his face. It was none other than the man who had yesterday pulled her from the bog.

"Jyne?"

Five

JYNE STARED AT THE MAN WHO HAD SAVED HER LIFE and wandered shamelessly through her dreams. He was her hero.

And he was sneaking up on her with a knife.

He appeared quite taken aback to see her and stared at her openmouthed. She took advantage of his surprise and nocked an arrow, pulling back the bow and aiming right at his heart. She did not let fly but stared at him, unsure.

"What are ye doing here?" she demanded.

"Och, I wish I knew," he muttered to himself. "Easy now, lass. I mean ye no harm." He slowly sheathed his knife.

"Then why creep up behind me with a knife?" Jyne demanded, her heart pounding, unsure if he was friend or foe.

"I…" He ran a hand through his already wild hair, making it stick up in places. "I do apologize if I scared ye. I…I am a wanderer. I saw these wicked men approach and feared they would do the abbey harm. I came to the side to warn ye." The man's words seemed choppy, as if he was nervous or unsure of what to say. Of course, she was threatening him.

"Who are ye?" asked Jyne, relaxing the bowstring ever so slightly.

"I am Cormac. My friends call me Core." He gave her the faintest of smiles.

"And what do yer enemies call ye?"

"Ah, that I could'na say to a lady." His smile widened, and something within her melted. His unruly hair fell over one eye, and he had more than a day or two of stubble on his jaw. The effect was dangerously alluring.

Jyne lowered her bow. "I am sorry. I feared ye were with those men."

A flicker of emotion passed over his face, but was hidden in a smile a moment later. "That would be most unfortunate."

"Is it true we are attacked by Red Rex?"

"No' Rex, but his son."

"No doubt he will be even worse," said Jyne, her current worries pressing down on her.

Core sighed. "Aye, ye dinna ken the half of it, lassie."

"I am glad ye're here. I know I am already in yer debt, but I would ask ye for more. Would ye help me again?"

"I've said before, I'm no hero." Cormac shook his head with a rueful quirk of his lips. "Go back to yer prodigiously large brothers. They can keep ye safe better than I."

"But they are no' here. 'Tis only I."

Cormac frowned and stood a little taller. "They left ye alone? What were they thinking? Ye need to get out o' here. Come quick wi' me, and I'll find ye a safe place to hide."

"Hide? Nay, I canna leave Kinoch."

"Och, lassie, ye must. I have seen what these men can do. Ye'll no' be safe here. Ye must come wi' me now before ye're seen." He reached out and grabbed her hand and began to lead her into the forest, but she wrenched her hand away and stood her ground.

"Nay! I canna leave. There are only elders and children here, wi' me as their only protector. Will ye no' help us defend Kinoch against these evil men?"

Core's shoulders slumped. He turned back to her with a slightly desperate expression. "Only elders and bairns?"

"Aye. So ye see why I canna leave."

Cormac closed his eyes and gave something of a groan. "They are yer kin? Why would ye be here alone?"

"They are no' kin—"

"Then leave them."

"Nay! I canna abandon them!" Her heart pounded in her chest. She could hear the war cries of the brigands who had reached the front gates. The temptation to run away with the handsome man before her was so great she could taste it. Her hands shook, not with fear, but with the effort it took not to run.

He stood before her, a deep frown etched on his face, as if he was wrestling with an internal struggle.

Jyne walked up to him and put a hand on his sleeve. He stared at her hand, clean and white compared with his dirty tunic, but did not speak. This close, she could see he was breathing hard. She moved her hand to his chest, placing it over his heart. His breath caught, and he looked down on her with dark eyes burning with intensity. The air crackled between them.

"I ken ye to be a good man."

Cormac shook his head slightly.

"Ye have a good heart."

Core's face hardened, as if her words hurt him. "Nay, ye dinna ken who I am."

"It doesna matter—"

"It *always* matters."

This man was Jyne's only potential ally. She was not sure who he was, but she knew he had helped her before, and she needed to convince him to help her again. "It does not matter to me now. Please, please will ye help us?"

A resigned sigh escaped his lips. "Aye." She was about to thank him, but with a twinkle of mischief in his eyes, he continued before she could speak. "For a price."

It was her turn to frown. She dropped her hand from his chest. Maybe she had been wrong about him. "A price? My brothers can pay ye—"

"Nay, yer brothers have naught that I want. Ye need to pay me."

"I have nothing of value—"

"A kiss," he blurted out the words, his eyes wide as if he was surprised he had said them. He schooled his features into nonchalance. "A kiss."

"Ye wish to kiss me?" Her pulse quickened.

His coloring heightened. Was the man…blushing?

"Ye want for me to kiss ye?" she asked.

He nodded his head vigorously.

He was right. This man was no hero. And yet… he was the only man available who could possibly help her. Besides, if he did help her, his life might be cut short. Should she not offer him one last request? She rationalized the shocking request, for she was not immune to the powerful draw between them.

She stepped even closer and noted the veins in his neck thrumming with a rapid pulse, much the same as her heartbeat. She put a hand on his shoulder and stood on tiptoe. She breathed in his masculine scent, and her heart raced even faster. Slowly, she leaned toward him. He remained frozen, which gave her confidence.

She pressed her lips on his cheek, thrilling with the feel of his harsh stubble, lingering a moment before withdrawing once more. All the while, he remained motionless.

"Now will ye help us?" Her voice was breathless.

He nodded. "I will help ye as I am able," he whispered.

"Thank ye." She stepped back, unsure what to do now. It seemed like they had been talking forever, but in truth, it had been only a few minutes. The sounds of the war cries once again assailed her ears. They could not dawdle here.

"Please, ye must come in to the abbey before they catch us." Jyne showed him the door on the side of the wall, hidden behind some thick brush.

Cormac blinked twice, as if awaking from a dream. "Nay, I can help ye more from outside. I will try to disrupt them as best I can, while ye defend the keep. Focus on defending the main gate."

"I will." She stared at him for a moment, then stepped up to him and pressed another quick, warm kiss on his other cheek. "I fear one kiss was insufficient payment for my request o' ye. I hope ye consider yerself well compensated now."

He placed a hand over his cheek as if to keep the kiss from fading away. "I have been given beyond anything I deserve."

"Then make sure ye earn it!" She smiled at him.

He returned the smile before the look of concern returned. "Go now. Get inside. Stay safe."

"Thank ye. Wi' yer help, all shall be well. Ye've given me reason to hope!" She gave him one last smile before running back inside, locking the postern gate behind her.

Kinoch Abbey was under attack, her life and those around her were at risk, but she could not wipe the smile from her face. Despite the gravity of her situation, all she could think about was her first kiss.

Her first kiss.

⁂

Cormac smiled at the lovely Jyne as she retreated into the gate. Her blond hair was plaited in one long braid that fell over one shoulder. She turned and glanced at him once more. Her face was flawless in the cool twilight. Her blue eyes were large and framed with long eyelashes. One look at her, and he was lost.

She gave him a hopeful smile and closed and locked the gate. He continued to smile at the closed door before coming to his senses. What was he doing? He leaned back on a tree trunk, then turned and hit his head on the tree a few times. Maybe it would knock some sense into him.

He truly was a despicable man. Red Rex should be

pleased; he was every inch the bastard his father was. No, Core was worse. At least Rex did not pretend to be an ally and then stab you in the back. His father preferred the more direct route of stabbing you in the eye. At least you could see it coming.

Whatever his wishes, Core was the villain in this scenario. He needed to play out his role. And yet, one thing was certain. He would do his utmost to shield Jyne from harm. But how could he protect her? Oh, and the monks, and the books too…

Core took a deep breath. He needed to think clearly. This was a tight place, but he had been in difficult situations before. He had always been able to reason his way out of them. He just needed to focus, something made difficult by the fact that her kisses still tingled on his cheeks. And was that perfume she was wearing or just the fragrant smell of a clean human being? She was a lovely lady…

Think! He needed to think. He inspected the small oak door further. He might be able to breach it. If his father could see the potential of his experiments, the power of alchemy, then maybe Rex would forget all about the treasure and his threats to burn the books of the monastery.

Cormac smiled to himself. He grabbed his discarded helmet and headed back to his men. For the first time since being called before his father, he felt like he had the beginnings of a plan. Maybe with some luck, he could redirect his father's men away from Kinoch and the bonnie Jyne and whatever poor people she was protecting.

It was a slim chance. But it was all he had.

Six

Cormac returned to the brigands who were preparing to take the abbey. Kinoch was surrounded by a thick wall, but was not prepared for battle like a proper fortress would be. Darkness settled on the valley as the last ray of sunlight vanished behind the horizon. Core could barely make out dark figures on the wall walk, but he knew one of them must be Jyne.

Core sighed. Jyne was in more danger now than when she had been on the moor. Walls could be breached. The men of Red Rex had no end of unpleasant methods of doing so. They could rush forward with ladders and swords drawn, use a battering ram to break down the front gate, or even use a catapult to toss in rotting animal flesh to induce sickness in the inhabitants.

The men were hungry for a fight, itching for it. They were ill suited for any civilized society and had spent their whole lives learning to be as dangerous and disagreeable as possible. If they took Kinoch in battle, the people inside would die. Rex's men would not show restraint for children or elders. Even worse, Core shuddered to think of what they would do to Jyne.

"I love it when they bar the gate," said a wizened old warrior with one eye and a perpendicular tooth that appeared to be trying to escape from his mouth. Considering the rotting stench of his breath, Core did not blame the tooth at all.

"Want me to cut down a battering ram?" asked a husky warrior who looked quite capable of uprooting large trees with his bare hands. This was the type of hulking brigand his father had hoped for in a son.

"I have a way inside. A way to take them all by surprise," said Core to the men. "Just get their attention for a wee bit. Dinna attack before I give the signal."

"Why?" asked Bran, returning from his errand.

"I need dark and no distractions to work my magic."

Bran raised an eyebrow, utterly unimpressed.

"Faith, man, stop questioning me, and do as ye're told. Did ye get the runner?"

"Aye, o' course." Bran pointed to Dubh. He rode forward, holding the reins of a horse with a man draped over the saddle.

"Is he dead?" asked Core with some anxiety, particularly because he guessed Jyne would be displeased if the man were killed.

"Nay, but his head will feel it in the morn."

Core was relieved. "Keep him out o' sight."

Bran shrugged but complied. Core wagered he was being tested. He needed to impress these warriors; then maybe all the treasure nonsense would be forgotten.

"Keep their attention, but dinna attack until ye hear my signal," commanded Core.

No one gave him much regard, and the warriors continued to prepare to break down the gates.

"If ye break something, ye might destroy a clue to finding the treasure," added Core, pleased that this time he had gotten their attention.

"What's yer signal?" asked Bran.

"Just give me some time, and I'll open the gates," said Core with a cheeky grin, hoping he could back up his words of pure bravado. He grabbed the unpleasant horned helmet and plunked it down on his head. It would not do to have Jyne see him fraternizing with the enemy.

The steel helmet was designed more for intimidation than practicality. It entirely encased the head, with only small slits in which to see out, effectively hiding the wearer's face from view. On either side of the helmet, large horns protruded, with tips that had been sharpened and dipped in bronze. He could see little, hear less, and the horns on either side of his head made him unstable and top-heavy.

"Ye have yer orders. See it done," Core commanded Bran and then turned to the monk before Bran had a chance to react. "Ye're wi' me." Core slashed through the bonds on the monk, setting him free.

The monk glared at him. "Why should I go with you?"

"Ye'd rather stay wi' them?" asked Core in an undertone. Core grabbed some of his equipment and held it out to the monk for him to carry.

The monk glanced around at the battle-hungry men and took the crate of equipment, recognizing Core was a safer option than remaining behind alone. The monk made no attempt to hide his displeasure, but followed him to the side of Kinoch Abbey without further complaint.

"Where are ye from?" Core asked, deciding to learn more about the monk beside him.

"I once was known as Luzio of Florence," said the monk in an accent Core could now identify as Italian. "When I joined the brothers here, they changed my name to Brother Luke. And you? You said you stole the scroll to read it?"

"Aye."

"But…why?" Brother Luke glanced back at the illiterate company Core kept. They had started drinking, carousing in a manner that was loud, fierce, and profane. Why any of their number would wish to read was a legitimate question.

"Bad habit, I suppose," muttered Cormac, keeping low to the brush to avoid being detected by those on the wall above.

"A habit acquired from being raised by monks?"

"My mother died young. My father was not the sort to nurture a child."

Brother Luke snorted at Cormac's gross understatement. "So he gave you to be raised by monks?"

Core shook his head, remembering. "I was tended by a crofter's wife for my early years. Then my father decided I was old enough to join him. I was a disappointment and could not keep up. So he left me. I wandered about for a time until I came to the monastery."

"How old were you?"

"About six."

Brother Luke sucked in air through his teeth. "That is young."

Cormac shrugged, stepping down on some thick brush for Luke to pass. "I stayed there until ten years later, when Red Rex found me again, and the good monks decided I was not worth the keeping."

"So you decided to become a brigand." Brother Luke's judgement was clear.

"Nay, do ye take me for a fool?" Nobody sought out Red Rex. "I ran for a while, searching out other places to hide, but he always found me."

Core had thought briefly about the church as a refuge. The thought of learning and copying scriptures all day was agreeable, but the price of forgoing female company for the rest of his life was hardly appealing. Though it was true that members of the fairer sex had not taken much interest in him, he had taken a great deal of interest in them…from afar, where it was safe. But still, he knew enough about himself to know that celibacy was not a condition in which he would choose to live for the rest of his life, even if it was a condition in which he found himself currently.

"After my birth, Rex had naught but daughters," continued Core. "Some say 'tis a curse for his wicked life. I might agree. Trouble is, that leaves me his only heir. He is determined to see me a warlord like himself or kill me in the process."

Somehow, Core needed to prove himself to his father. It was the only way to get the man to let him be. Core had tried to prove that learning could be beneficial. After learning of the new weapon used by the English in the wars in France, Core had plunged into the study of alchemy.

"That cannot be easy," said the monk with more compassion in his tone than Core expected.

Core turned to him. "'Tis not."

They reached the side of the abbey, and after a bit of searching, found the postern gate. Core would never have been able to find it had Jyne not shown him first.

"What are you doing?" asked the monk as Core unpacked his equipment by the small door.

"Using alchemy to good effect," said Core. He did some calculations, then did them again, using the new bit of knowledge he had gained from his read of the scroll. This had to work. He had to show his father that he could do something no one else could. His studying had revealed to him the fascinating effects of black powder, which the English had learned from the Chinese. Core had attempted to conduct explosive experiments with black powder that he had hoped would be of interest to his father. Unfortunately, something had gone wrong in the proof, and his grand experiment had fizzled instead of impressed. This time it had to work.

"You wish to use the science of the black powder?" asked Luke, his eyes wide.

"Aye."

"I shall not let you!" Luke surprised Core from behind, knocking him to the ground and holding a knife to his throat—a knife Core had no idea the monk had.

Core struggled until he felt the cool of the man's blade on his neck.

"What kind o' monk are ye?" gasped Core, his pulse beating against the man's blade. One twitch, and his life was forfeit. This monk not only had drawn a hidden dagger but knew how to use it.

"Not the kind to underestimate."

"And that excuses murder?"

"And what are you doing?"

"I'm trying to take Kinoch wi'out anyone getting killed," explained Core as calmly as he could with a blade hovering at his throat. "If I dinna breach this gate, Rex's men will go through the front, and they'll no' be kind about it."

Luke paused a moment, then cursed in Italian and let him go.

Cormac rolled up and stared at the militant monk. "Who did ye say ye were?"

"Who I am is not your concern," said Luke in a chilling tone. "I suppose you will demand my dagger now."

"Nay, keep it. Glad to know ye can look after yerself. Only dinna use it on me, if ye please. Now either help me or be off wi' ye."

Luke sighed so loud, it was more of a growl. "How can I help?"

"Hold this for me." Core handed him a glass bottle and began to measure his ingredients carefully. He did a few more calculations and a bit more mixing until he felt confident that it would work. At least, it was the best he knew. Never mind that his experiments thus far had been underwhelming; this time, with his new calculations, it would work. It had to work.

"Why not do this at the front gate?" asked Luke.

"I need to mix it just right and place it by the door. Folks have a tendency to pour boiling oil on ye if they ken ye're trying to breach their gates." Core carefully placed his experiment next to the oak door.

"Good point."

"Ye back away now. Take cover," Core instructed the monk. The other reason Core didn't want anyone to see what he was doing was that if he was unsuccessful again, he did not wish there to be witnesses. He was tired of failure.

"Cormac."

At the earnestness in the monk's voice, Core turned to where he stood.

"If what you say is true, and you were asked to leave the monastery only because of your sire, that was wrong. I offer an apology."

Core stared at him, surprised by his words. "It was long ago." He shrugged as if it was of little consequence, but no one had ever apologized to him before. Brother Luke's words were a balm on an old hurt.

"And thank you for trying to help save the brothers."

"I'm doing it for the books. Why this sudden kindness? A few minutes ago, ye were trying to kill me."

"I have seen much, and I know the power of what you hold in your hand. Should you die, I did not wish to have the guilt of words left unsaid."

So the good monk thought he was going to kill himself. That was encouraging. Core carefully laid the charge. He lit the fuse and watched the spark crackle as it raced up the powder line, until he suddenly realized he was too close.

He sprinted into the woods, recognizing that he should probably have considered where he was going to hide. He ran for a moss-covered boulder, when a huge explosion sent a concussive blast into him, sending him flying behind the rock formation. He lay there for a moment, eyes closed, alternating between elation that his experiment had finally worked and apprehension that he had done himself harm in the process.

He slowly sat up and took a mental inventory of

himself until he was satisfied that there was no major damage done. He peered over the boulder at the smoking chasm where the postern gate used to be. It had worked. It had truly worked!

Brother Luke emerged from behind a tree, his mouth open wide in a stunned expression. He crossed himself. "Holy Mary, you did it!"

"I did it! I actually did it this time! Och, this changes everything!" Cormac slammed the foul-smelling horned helmet on his head and charged into the smoking cavern.

Kinoch Abbey was his.

❧

Lady Jyne nocked an arrow, careful to keep herself out of the line of fire from their enemies. The marauders had gathered for a frontal assault. Fortunately, they were not a large party, only about two dozen men. Unfortunately, that was two dozen more men than she had.

Jyne glanced around at her "soldiers" who gathered on the wall walk, their pale faces illuminated by flickering torches in the dark night. Alasdair had found a rusty helm and stood beside her with a bow she was not sure he could even draw. Several of the elder children stood on the gate in random pieces of armor and helms that were much too large for them, trying to appear older and more formidable than they were. They could do little if the brigands actually attacked. Two of the elder matrons set a large cauldron of oil on an open fire. That would be the weapon most likely to actually do damage, though Jyne doubted scalding oil would be enough to keep these rough men at bay.

Her only hope was to hold out until Donnach returned. Since she had not seen his dead body thrown before the walls, she assumed he had gotten away. Though it had taken the better part of a week for her to get to Kinoch, she reckoned if Donnach rode through the night and was able to change horses often, he could reach Innis Chonnel in two days. It would take two more days for the Campbell warriors to return, and she would be safe. She only needed to hold out for four days.

An ominous shout came from the raiders below. She prayed she could last through the night, let alone four days. Her one consolation was that Cormac was out there, somewhere, and would help her protect Kinoch. She was not sure what he could do, but she felt sure she could trust him to render assistance.

Another shout rose from the men below, followed by mocking insults. She had longed for an adventure, but she now had more excitement than she had ever wanted. Staying within the protective gates of the Campbell castle suddenly did not feel like such a bad thing after all. Standing brave against marauding hordes seemed so much better when dreaming of it by the safety of one's own hearth.

One of her young soldiers reached out with a small hand and clasped hers. Jyne looked down at Ina, whose wide eyes were staring at their attackers. The marauder's insults were profane at best, and Jyne had to check the impulse to yell down at them to watch their language, for children were present. She smiled down at Ina, trying to reassure her.

Suddenly, a huge, thunderous crash shattered the

relative peace behind her. It was as if lightning had struck the side of the abbey wall near the postern gate. Everyone froze. Even the marauders outside their gates were shocked into silence. Ina squeezed Jyne's hand, and the small movement brought her back to her senses. These people were relying on her. They needed her.

"Stay here and guard the gate. I shall see what the matter is," she called to Alasdair, who was still staring open-mouthed in the direction from which the loud sound had come.

Jyne ran down the open stone stairs and across the courtyard, slowing to creep cautiously toward the source of the noise, her hands shaking with fear. Dust filled the air, and she could see nothing before her. She squinted into the swirling, murky chasm illuminated only by torchlight. Her heart pounded in her throat. What could have possibly caused this?

She edged closer, holding up her bow, willing her hands to stay steady enough to shoot. A dark form approached. At first it was nothing but shadow, but then a tall black figure emerged, with two large horns on either side of his head like a terrible demon.

Jyne was frozen, unable to move, unable even to scream. She was filled with the desire to run away, but she remembered Ina's hand, warm and sticky, pressed up against her palm. She must protect these people.

She raised her bow and let fly, aiming directly at the beast's head. The arrow glanced off the warlord's helmet and landed limply on the ground. She hardly had time to register her failure before the intruder was upon her. The bow was ripped from her, and a firm hand grasped her shoulder.

"Stop!" demanded the invader in a deep, throaty voice.

She kicked him in the knee instead and tried to spin out of his grasp and run, though she had nowhere to go. He hissed in pain, but she was not able to break free from his steely grip. In an instant, he drew his knife and pressed the flat of his blade against her cheek. Her heart stopped and then pounded again in terror. This was it. She was going to die.

He walked her forward, toward the main gate, and she had very little choice but to go in the direction he silently demanded. Her pulse thumped so loudly she could feel it in her ears. She glanced around at her ragtag band of defenders, consisting of the too young and the too old.

"No," she mouthed to Alasdair as he made to raise a sword. There was nothing they could do against this warlord, and she did not wish anyone to come to harm for trying to protect her.

"Lay down yer arms and open the gates," demanded the warlord. "Obey me, and she will be spared. Continue to resist, and all shall perish."

Jyne wanted to yell at her people to save themselves, but where could they go? With the warlord already in the courtyard, they were caught between him and his friends outside. There was no hope for escape. Ina, standing on the wall walk in the oversized helmet, shed silent tears that ran down her cheeks.

The warlord motioned for a few of the lads to open the gates, and they slowly did so. Jyne's heart sank. What was she to do now?

The marauders rushed in with great whoops and hollers, brandishing weapons like the demons they were.

"Harm none of these simple folk, for we need them," commanded the warlord. It was of little comfort. What was the warlord going to do with them?

The warlord released her, and instead of running away, she spun to face him. "We have surrendered to ye, as we have no other choice, but that does no' mean that ye need to act like a pack o' wild jackanapes. Can ye no' see ye're frightening the wee ones?"

"Send them away," commanded the horned demon.

Jyne was prepared to fight against anything the man wanted, but she quickly saw the benefit of removing the children from the scene. She nodded to a few of the women, who quickly gathered up the children and hustled them into the main keep, Ina's eyes large as she was dragged away.

"Now ye have what ye wanted. Take what ye want and be gone." Jyne backed up as she spoke, not wanting to be anywhere near the large warlord. With his demon helm and thick bearskin cloak, he had the appearance of some fell creature from the bowels of hell.

She backed herself into another raider, and she jumped away from him. The foul-smelling man ran his eyes up and down her body with a sneer, such that she had a sudden desire to wash off the filth of what his expression suggested.

"Mayhap I'll take ye as my spoil of war." The brigand reached out for her, but the helmed warlord suddenly pulled her behind him and stood tall against his fellow marauder.

"This lass is mine!" bellowed the warlord. "None shall touch her but me."

Seven

CORMAC GLANCED AROUND WITH SOME ANXIETY, having to turn his head back and forth to see out of his ridiculous helm. He needed to protect Jyne and her people from his father's men, without seeming weak before them or letting her discover who he was. He was sure any chance at another kiss would be dead and buried if she knew it was him beneath the helm.

Now, all he needed to do was to show Bran and his men the gaping hole where the postern gate had been only a few minutes before. The raiders would be so overcome with his extraordinary achievement in alchemy that they would forget all about the treasure and escort him home as a hero.

The men would then share the amazing tale with his father, who would be duly impressed with his son for the first time in his life, hailing his remarkable achievement. All other concerns would be forgotten, and the monk could scurry back to his monastery, his library safe. Core could sneak back to Kinoch Abbey, convince Jyne the departure of the brigands was due to his bold interference, and enjoy the sweet reward he would undoubtedly get.

At least, that was as good a plan as he could devise. He glanced at Jyne, a mistake, since she was seething at him. He had no doubt that if she could manage it, he would be impaled at the end of a pike.

"Let's tear this place apart, stone from stone!" cried one of his men. The others hollered after him and raced around the outer ward like wanton, headless chickens, bent on destruction.

"My men, follow me, for I have something o' great import to show ye," shouted Core.

The men cheered and raced to him, no doubt expecting him to produce the treasure. Core grabbed Jyne's hand and took her with him. He did not trust his men enough to leave her unprotected in their midst. The only way to keep her safe was to keep her within arm's reach. The look of disgust on her face was enough to let him know his efforts were not appreciated. It was of little consequence. Nothing could reduce the thrill of his triumph.

"As ye know," began Cormac, "I have been doing experiments in alchemy."

"All can me?" asked Dubh, scratching his head.

"Red Rex told ye to quit that nonsense," growled Bran.

"Then I have disobeyed him," said Core boldly. "For ye see the results." Core stepped over the stone rubble and pointed to the hole where the gate used to be. Beside him, Jyne gasped.

The men stared in silence at the hole. The gaping wound in the wall was still slightly smoking.

"So ye found a hole in the wall. Good for ye. What did ye want to show us?" Bran asked.

"I dinna *find* a hole in the wall. I *made* the hole in the wall," cried Core. "Do ye no' see? My experiments finally worked!"

The men stared at the smoking hole. "But where is the treasure?" asked one of the men.

"But this is better than a thousand gold bars," cried Core, exasperated that his men did not see the potential of his discovery. "Why, with this, we can breach any wall we wish!"

The men glared at him.

"Nothing's better than a thousand gold bars," growled one man.

"Looks like this here hole's been here a while," said another.

"It's still smoking!" cried Core. "There was a gate here, wasn't there?" He turned to Jyne for support.

Jyne crossed her arms and said nothing, skewing him with a glare so laced with malice, even his father would have been proud.

"How is this going to get us the treasure?" asked Bran.

Core ground his teeth from within his helm. This was not working the way he planned. "Do ye no' see? I harnessed lightning and struck the wall! Ye've heard the English have done this, no? Now we can fight like them!"

"That's what the English say. All them Sassenach are liars," said one man.

"Nay, I've seen the cannon wi' my own eyes at the battle o' Crecy," argued another man.

"Ye're a liar too!"

"I'll cut out yer tongue, ye bastard!"

"Stop!" roared Core. "I harnessed the power o' the black powder. I'm the first Scotsman to do it. I ken ye all heard the thunderclap."

"We heard something," said Bran slowly, disbelief clear in his tone. "Why dinna ye show us this lightning o' yers."

"Well…that is…I need time to prepare more o' the powder."

"Powder? Och, wee lamb, ye need to grind some more flour?" mocked one man, and the rest of the men laughed.

"Can this powder o' yers lead us to the treasure?" asked Dubh.

"We can use it to our benefit," Core muttered, defeated.

"Where do we start?" asked one man.

"Mayhap the wench knows where it is."

"Let's put it to her." A thin man with long, slimy hair grabbed hold of Jyne's other arm.

"The lass is mine!" roared Core. "Besides, she knows naught. Can ye no' see the poverty o' these folk? If they knew where the treasure was, they would be living like kings."

The men grumbled, but this was at least logic they could understand. Finding treasure spending treasure. This made a good deal more practical sense to them than lightning that rained down from heaven.

The men walked into the main keep. Core slowly followed, his plan a smoking pile of ruin, much like the hole in the wall.

"Ye best find this treasure," Bran said, walking by,

"and fast." He rapped the hilt of his sword on Core's helm, sending a loud ringing tone reverberating through his helmet. Core wished to remove it, but one glance at Jyne reminded him he needed to maintain his secret.

Life was about to get even more difficult.

⤜⤛

Jyne's heart raced in fear, or maybe anger. How dare this warlord breach the walls of her domain and then claim her for his own! She could see he had wished his friends to be impressed by his handiwork at the gate, but she had no interest in helping him.

"What do ye want? We have no treasure. There can be naught for ye here," demanded Jyne as she was marched back to the courtyard. She may be the smallest of the Campbells, but she was still a Campbell.

"The hour grows late. We request food and drink," said the warlord.

Though his tone was low and ominous, she could not help but be surprised by his words. He *requested* food? Should he not demand it?

"As ye wish," said Jyne, considering that feeding the men may be the easiest way to appease them until they moved on. Perhaps they only wanted shelter for the night and would leave tomorrow, once they realized there were no riches here for them. She could hope.

"Let her go!" Alasdair came charging toward them, sword in one hand, cane in the other. "By clan Ranald, ye winna hurt Lady Jyne as long as I can draw breath."

"That winna be long," laughed one of the marauders, easily tripping the man. The brigand grabbed Alasdair's sword and held it above him for a death strike.

"No!" screamed Jyne, trying to run forward, but she was caught by the leader in the horned helmet.

"Stop!" commanded the leader of the brigands. "We need them alive to serve us, unless ye fancy making yer own victuals."

The brigand stopped midstrike, but snarled at them.

"Tell yer clan to serve us well and no' attempt aggression, or I swear they shall not live to see the morn," said the horned leader in a harsh whisper. Jyne was not sure if it was a threat or a simple statement of fact. Either way, the result was the same.

"Aye, we agree." Her arm was released, and she ran forward to help Alasdair Ranald rise. "Are ye all right? Can ye stand?"

"Aye, m'lady. I am sorry I failed ye."

"Nay, ye have been braver than is wise. But now is the time to be wise, aye? Please tell yer people to comply wi' the brigands, and hopefully they will move on soon."

Alasdair's wrinkled face collapsed into a picture of concern, but he nodded his head in agreement.

The raiders stormed into the main hall, making a good deal of noise and being as obnoxious as they could, but at least none of the elders had been harmed. The attackers threatened and terrified, but were content to let the elders run about and prepare them a meal.

Jyne gave some commands and moved toward the kitchen, but the warlord grabbed her hand and held it fast. He marched through the center of the great hall, dragging her behind him. He claimed the center chair of the high table as his own and pointed at the chair beside him for her to sit.

She had no choice but to sit beside him and watch as

the elders were forced to serve the marauders, bringing out ale and whiskey to appease the voracious drinking habits of the men. The great horned leader sat at the high table, smugly surveying all that was before him. At least, Jyne assumed he was smug. He refused to remove his helmet, so she could not see his face.

"Dinna forget yer guest," said one of the men in a mocking tone, and a monk was brought forward and made to sit next to her.

"Ye travel wi' these men?" she demanded of the monk.

"It seems I do," replied the monk with an accent that branded him a foreigner. "Though not of my own volition." He was a young man, wearing the black robes of the Dominican order.

Jyne turned to the warlord sitting on her other side. "Ye would capture a man o' God? A man in holy orders? Have ye no shame?"

"Apparently not," replied the warlord. He sounded a little disappointed in himself.

"This goes beyond all bounds, even for such a loathsome creature as yerself. Have ye no fear o' God Almighty? Ye need to release this man immediately," Jyne demanded before she remembered she was trying not to antagonize the leader.

The warlord turned to look at the monk, causing Jyne to duck to prevent being speared by one of the treacherous horns.

"Ye're free to go," the warlord told the monk.

Jyne stared at the warlord in surprise. Had she just convinced the warlord to do as she said?

Jyne turned back to the monk. "Do leave before he changes his mind," she urged. *And get help for us.*

The monk scowled into his ale. "He knows I cannot leave."

"Has he threatened ye if ye do?" she whispered to the monk.

"Not him…but I do not wish to concern you in my affairs. You have enough to worry yourself with at the moment."

"He is despicable."

The monk paused. "There would be few who would disagree with you, though perhaps all cannot be seen at first glance."

"You defend him, Brother…?"

"I am Brother Luke, and I am no defender of these men, though perhaps it is not the well who need the doctor but the sick."

"These men are beyond any hope of salvation," she said bitterly.

"No one is beyond the redemption of God," replied the pious Brother Luke.

"But only if they choose it," snapped Jyne. These men knew nothing of salvation. It was undoubtedly uncharitable, but these were not the men with whom she wished to share eternity. It was bad enough to have to share the great room with them. It gave her some consolation to know she would not have to look at the faces of the marauders in her heavenly reward.

The food was brought forth, and the men were pleased with the roasted venison. Jyne was dismayed to see it disappearing into the bellies of the attackers. The meat could have fed her newly accepted people well, but now their share was divided with a pack of ravenous wolves. The more food the raiders ate, the more Jyne was concerned by how much of their limited food resources were being wasted to serve their attackers. These men were like locusts, using up everything around them and then moving on, leaving devastation in their wake.

Her warlord attacker was strangely quiet during the proceedings. He did not engage with the other raiders but instead remained silent, surveying all. The huge, horned helmet could not be comfortable, but still it remained on his head.

At one point, he even raised his chalice to his lips but met with the clank of his helmet. Jyne expected that he would take off the impractical helm. He put his hand to the helmet, as if to remove it, but he turned toward her and apparently changed his mind.

He attempted to shove little bits of food through the grate on his visor, which could not have been effective. It was only the fear of antagonizing him that kept her from asking what he was doing. Was he truly going to go through the feast without removing his helmet? What was beneath the helm that made it impossible for him to take it off?

Through the feast, the horned man said nothing, though his comrades laughed and caroused, growing louder and more intolerable with every chug of whiskey. Since there was no entertainment, they decided to amuse themselves by cursing and throwing insults at each other, chasing each other about the room, and seeing who could hurl knives, spears, and random pieces of furniture the farthest.

Through it all, the great warlord said nothing, ate nothing, and drank nothing. Who was this man?

Eight

CORE WAS MISERABLE. THIS SHOULD HAVE BEEN HIS greatest triumph. His experiment with the explosive black powder had finally worked! He had blown right through the postern gate. He had demonstrated that all his study and all his careful science could be beneficial in the new manner of war. His men should have been impressed. They should have been astounded and amazed and run back to his father to tell him the incredible thing he'd done. But no, Core's plan, like so many others, had failed.

To make matters worse, Core could not figure out how to take off the helm without giving himself away to Jyne. The helmet also seemed to garner some respect from his men, not much, but at least they had let him be during their meal. He was not sure if it was respect or, more likely, that they did not care.

So he kept the helmet on and sat at his own feast, his stomach rumbling, unable to eat. The delicious scent of food wafted through the slits in the visor, causing his stomach to complain more and more, yet he couldn't figure out how to eat without taking off the helmet. And he couldn't figure out how to stay in the good graces of Jyne if he took off his helmet. And he couldn't figure out why her good opinion mattered to him anyway. He grabbed a chalice of wine and tried to drink some through the slats of the helmet, spilling wine down his front and soaking his doublet.

He groaned at the absurdity of his situation.

Although…he forced himself to look on the brighter side. His experiment had worked. He had taken Kinoch without getting anyone killed. The bonnie Jyne could not look in his direction without a glare, but at least she was alive and unmolested. Considering where he had been a few hours ago, that was something.

Jyne's kisses still warmed his cheeks. Yet, if she ever found out who he was, she would never kiss him again, never speak to him again. No, this was one secret he had no intention of ever telling. Somehow, he could make this work. He would find some sort of treasure, appease his father, then return to seek his reward with Jyne. This was only a minor setback.

His stomach grumbled again. When he could take no more of watching other people eat while his own stomach rumbled, he stood at the table. "Good night, my good men," he called out to his father's soldiers.

They paused in their raucous games, silence creeping over the main hall. Then they suddenly all burst into peals of laughter. Had he truly just wished them a good night and called them his good men? At least they couldn't see how his cheeks burned at being embarrassed by his genteel behavior and polite turn of phrase.

"I take this wench as my prize for conquering this castle!" he said, trying to recover from his faux pas before the warriors. He grabbed Jyne's hand and dragged her up beside him. This brought a cheer from the men, or possibly a jeer. Jyne glared death at him.

He marched out of the great hall and up a spiral stone staircase, never letting go of her hand, dragging her along behind him. He went up a few stories and stopped, realizing he had no idea where he was going. He paused on the landing, trying to figure out what his father would do in this case. Probably nothing that Core would ever contemplate doing. Cormac made a horrible warlord.

Jyne wrenched her hand out of his, glaring at him, her arms crossed. She appeared to be considering ways to injure him, for she scowled at him with intense loathing, with an occasional slight half smile, as if she had just devised some new torture to make his life a misery. She needn't have tried so hard—his life was already rather miserable.

He cleared his throat. "Take me to the master's chambers."

Jyne narrowed her eyes at him. "Ye'll no' hurt these people. There are naught but elders here."

"What is that to me? Ye'll take me to the master's chambers now!" Whenever his father made a demand, people generally wet themselves and scampered off to obey him with all due haste. Jyne merely scowled at him in a manner so fierce he almost took a step backward.

"I will take ye to the master's chambers and…and stay wi' ye if it be yer wish, but I will have yer word as a Highlander that these people winna be harmed in any way." She held her back straight, her hands clasped before her, her knuckles white with the effort. Her lower lip trembled as she made the offer, which only made her that much more beautiful. Truly, he had never seen a more stunning woman in all his life. She was offering herself to him for the protection of others. She was an angel, which could only make him a demon.

"I so swear, no harm will come to these people." He spoke reverently, truly, for he would do anything she asked. She blinked, staring at him, surprised. He cleared his throat. "I care naught for these people. They can do as they wish as long as they stay out of my way. Now take me to the master's chamber. Nay, take me to yer chamber!"

She raised one thin eyebrow and raised her hand to point at the door they were standing before. Core opened the door and strode through it. The room was a bit sparse, but had a comfortable feel. The main thing he noticed was a large bed with a richly embroidered canopy about it. He took a few more steps toward the bed. The large bed. The large bed where he and Jyne could… He shook his head and only succeeded in worsening his headache as the heavy helmet wobbled on his head.

He turned to Jyne, who very slowly inched into the room, leaving the door open for a quick escape. Wise lass. "Ye would give yerself for the protection of others, Jyne Ranald?"

Jyne raised her chin. "I am not a Ranald. I am Lady Jyne Campbell, sister of Sir David Campbell."

Core froze. It was fortunate that he still wore the helm, for she could not see how his jaw dropped at the unfortunate news.

"Laird Campbell?" he asked in a voice an octave higher than his previous question. Dread ran a frozen finger down his backbone. The Campbells were well known in these parts. The Campbells were well known everywhere.

"Aye. Kinoch Abbey belongs to the Campbell now. He will come for me, make no mistake, and I will enjoy seeing ye drawn and quartered for yer crimes!"

Core swallowed hard. He had attacked the sister of David Campbell. He was dead for sure.

❧

The imposing warlord stood before her, silent and inscrutable in his iron helm. Jyne remained in the doorway, casting the occasional glance toward the stairs. Maybe she should make a run for it. Yet if she did, what would happen to the people she was determined to protect?

She looked again at the stairs. These people were not even her clan. Their own clan had left them behind, these elders and children. Clearly, they were not worth much to anyone. She was the daughter of Laird Campbell. Why should she sacrifice herself for these people she had only just met? She could run to the stable, grab a horse, and fly back home—back where it was safe, back where everyone treated her like a child, back where everyone knew she was not capable of handling situations such as the one before her.

She took a deep breath and stepped farther into the room. She was a Campbell, and the Ranalds needed her. She would run from no one. She glared at the warlord, for even if she could not see him, he could see her. She did not wish him to guess his presence made her heart pound against her rib cage. He was a tall man, but his exact proportions were difficult to determine beneath the large cloak of a bearskin draped over his Highland plaid.

"My brother will kill ye." She was simply stating a fact.

The man before her sighed audibly. "Aye, I ken it."

She was surprised by his easy agreement on this point. "Who are ye?"

He stood tall before her and spoke in a low, gravelly voice. "I am the Fire Lord, son o' Red Rex."

Jyne took a shaky breath. She wished to mock the presumptuousness of such a title, but she had seen herself how he had destroyed her gate with thunder and fire. Yet no matter how impressive his skills, her brother would come for her. "Ye must leave here now, Fire Lord. If ye do, my brother may spare yer life."

"I canna leave." He sounded as displeased to say it as Jyne was to hear it.

"Why not?"

"I must finish what was started."

"What have ye started? And what is this nonsense about a treasure hidden in the abbey?"

The warlord started for her, and she backed out of his way, toward a corner of the room. To her surprise, he walked past her and drew the heavy oak door closed with a bang. "What do ye ken of a treasure here?" he demanded.

Her heart pounded so hard, she feared it would be heard across the room. "I ken naught. The first I heard o' the tale was from the lips o' yer men."

The Fire Lord's shoulders drooped at her response. "There's no treasure here? Naught that could be seen as treasure?"

"Nay. And even if I did find treasure, I would hardly give it to ye." She was determined not to be bullied.

"Not even if it meant I would leave?"

"I may have a few coins." She rummaged through her pockets. If she could pay him to leave, it was worth the price. "Would this do?" She held out a handful of small coins.

The warlord glanced at her meager offering and shook his head, causing him to have to steady the heavy helmet with both hands. She wondered what he was hiding beneath the helm. Why did he not take it off? Was he so hideous that he needed to conceal his face? Perhaps he had experienced a grievous injury, and his scars were so repellent that he could never show his face again. Or maybe he bore the scars of the pox. Or maybe he was just being an arse.

"There is no treasure here, naught o' value," she repeated. If only he could be made to believe it, maybe he would move on.

"I hope that's no' true." The warlord turned away from her.

She tried talking sense to the man. "But it is true. Ye need to leave now. Ye've already eaten through most of our stores. Ye should move along. Leave before Laird Campbell returns."

"I wish I could," was his muttered reply.

"What do ye mean? Are ye no' the leader o' these men? Tell them to be gone!"

He made a low, snorting sound from inside the helm and changed the subject abruptly. "Why are ye here, Lady Jyne Campbell, sister o' the Laird Campbell?"

"These are my dower lands," she informed him boldly. "We have come to inspect the property."

"And have ye a groom, Jyne Campbell?"

She took a breath before responding. "I was promised to be married, but he died. The great plague."

The warlord made no response, and she continued. Somehow, it was easier to speak to someone when she could not see his face. "I had only met him a few times, but still, I mourned him and what might o' been. We were to be wed this spring."

"So ye traveled here to see yer would-be home. But who are these people to ye?"

"Their clan was overcome by the plague, and these poor folks were left behind."

"So they are no' Campbells?"

"They have sworn fealty to the Campbell, and they are under my protection!" She put her hands on her hips and stood her ground. After all, she was a Campbell. She might be the runt of the litter, but she was a Campbell nonetheless.

The Fire Lord took a step closer. "Ye would sacrifice yerself for these people ye only just met?"

"These poor folks have suffered enough. I will help them if I can."

"Ye help them, for ye ken what it is to lose. They lost their kin, and ye lost yer affianced husband."

Jyne blinked at the man. She had been prepared for him to attack her, not bring tears to her eyes by reminding her of her lost future. "Aye," she answered softly.

"I am sorry for yer loss."

Jyne was confused by this warlord. Was he playing at some cruel jest with her? She had expected to be dragged into the room and ravished senseless. She gripped the handle of her knife where it was hidden up her sleeve. She fully intended to gut the man if he tried anything more than a firm handshake.

Instead of attacking her, he offered sympathy? What nonsense was this? Still, he had taken her home by force, eaten through her stores, and called her a wench—grounds for murder if there ever were any. She crossed her arms once more and stiffened her resolve. There could be no sympathy for this man.

"If ye had any true feeling, ye would take yerself from here and stop terrorizing elders and wee bairns. Have they no' suffered enough? Ye should be ashamed o' yerself." He took a step toward her, but she continued.

"Ye attack innocents—women, elders, children. There's no glory in that. Ye're naught but a worm, preying on the weak and the helpless, because ye're too cowardly to take on anyone who would give you a fair fight. Ye're a loathsome creature, and I despise ye!" She expected him to fight back, but he said nothing.

They stood together in the silence of the chamber, with nothing but the flicker of a single candle illuminating the room. It was unnerving, and her hands trembled. With the helmet hiding him from view, she could not read his facial expression to predict what he might do next. She may be confused by his inaction, but she knew he was a dangerous man. Anyone who could call upon lightning to strike a hole through an iron door was treacherous.

"Ye should be ashamed o' yerself," she repeated. This time, it came out almost as a whisper, yet it bounced off the bare stone walls of the tower chamber.

"I am."

"What did ye say?"

He cleared his throat. "I am tired o' yer fractious, arguing tongue. Come here, wench." He added the last as an afterthought, purposely designed to insult her.

Her legs suddenly felt like jelly. She glanced at the door leading to the stairs. It was closed but not locked. She could make a run for it if she could get her legs to hold her.

"Remember, it was ye who offered yerself to me."

She hated him. With every ounce, every fiber of her being, she hated him. She had tried to do something noble to protect those who could not protect themselves, and he made it sound all very sordid, as if she had wanted to give herself to him. Yet now she was bound by the deal she had made with this devil.

Slowly, she forced her feet to move closer to him, shuffling toward the lingering shadows where he stood. She stopped when she was a foot away from him. She tried to peer between the slots of the helmet to see the man within, but in the dim light, she could see nothing of his face, which she was convinced must be a mangled wreck of pure evil. Her fingers clasped around the knife hidden in her sleeve. When he reached for her, she would stab him in the gut…or maybe just a little bit lower.

"Ye'll stay here tonight. Dinna attempt to leave." The Fire Lord stomped to the doorway, leaving her confused in his wake.

"Where are ye going?" She regretted the words as soon as they left her lips.

"Miss me already, my bonnie lass? Ye females are such a fickle breed. Nay, I dinna desire ye tonight. But remember, I have claimed ye, and none shall have ye but me!"

He jerked the door closed, leaving her alone in the dimly lit bedchamber. With a clank and a heavy click, she knew she'd been locked inside.

She wrapped her arms around herself to keep from trembling. She hoped Donnach would return soon with her clansmen.

Nine

"Just kill him."

"Nay, where's the fun in that?"

Cormac raced down the tower stairs to the great hall, where he found yet another problem. The man Jyne had been sending to get help had been revived and tied with his arms stretched wide to an upended table. The men were taking turns throwing knifes at him, presumably seeing how close they could come before they killed him.

Though he was being used for sport, Core knew the man's life would be short-lived. Rex's men might allow elders to live to serve them, but they would not trust an able-bodied man. No, this man they would kill.

"Enough, just be done with it." Core strode into the room, pulling off his helm. It was a tremendous relief.

"Done trying to impress the lass?" sneered Bran.

Core ignored the older man and strode directly toward the grim face of the Campbell warrior. Core took out his knife with a flourish. The man's jaw set. He was a brave one. Core hoped he was also smart.

Core put a hand on his shoulder and moved in close, lunging at the man like he was going to stab him.

"Play dead," Core hissed in the man's ear.

The man's eyes narrowed in uncooperative defiance. Why did everything have to be so difficult? Core knocked him on the head with the crossguard of his dagger, and the man slumped against his bonds. Core jabbed his knife forward, as if he was stabbing the man, his large bearskin cloak hiding the subterfuge from his men. Core wasted no time in cutting the man free, and he collapsed forward in a heap where none could see the lack of blood.

"Aw, ye ruined our amusement," complained one man.

"Nay, we still got the monk. Tie him up 'til he tells us where the treasure is!" said Dubh.

The men cheered and moved toward the monk, who was still sitting at the table where Core had left him. Of course, there was no way the monk would have been allowed to leave.

"Stop!" commanded Core. "I tell ye he doesna know where the treasure lies."

"But ye told Rex—"

"I ken what I told my father. He doesna need to worry over details. Truth is, the monk doesna ken the location o' the treasure but can translate some texts that do. Dinna harm him, or we'll ne'er get our hands on the gold." Core spoke quickly, as Dubh had already dragged the monk to his feet.

Dubh gave Core a pout and shoved the monk back down.

"Get my things and put them in the top chamber

of the tower," Core commanded the monk. "I will be taking the master's chamber. The rest o' ye sorry lot can fend for yerself."

"And what if he doesna want to help ye?" asked Dubh.

"O' course he doesna want to help me," replied Core. "But he will, or I will send him down to ye to help motivate him."

This gained Core several smiles of approval. The men of Red Rex enjoyed being motivational. Core gave Brother Luke a nod. The monk left the room with Dubh following behind to ensure cooperation.

Core surveyed the large form of the collapsed Campbell warrior with disapproval. Of course he had to be a large man. Core bent down and pulled the warrior up and over his shoulders, grunting with the effort to stand. The warrior was as heavy as he looked, but Core was uncommonly strong for his size. His unfortunate parentage was good for something at least.

"What are ye doing?" demanded Bran, blocking Core's escape.

"I ken ye like the smell o' rotting flesh when ye eat, but I dinna care for it. I was going to toss his carcass outside, unless ye'd rather do it."

Bran stood aside with a shrug, and Core staggered into the inner courtyard with the man. He hoped Jyne would appreciate the backache he was going to have for saving the man, though of course she could never know.

He struggled his way across the courtyard, satisfied at least that the man was still breathing, though it would have been easier had he played along. Now where was he going to hide the body?

❧

Jyne was determined not to sleep. She didn't know when the warlord would be back to do whatever it was he had in mind to do to her. She did know before he got a chance to do it, she'd poke a few holes in him for his trouble.

Despite her best efforts, she found it impossible to keep standing in the middle of the room after such a tiring day. She sat on the bed, refusing to loosen her gown for fear the warlord would return and see it as an invitation.

The candle gutted, leaving her in complete darkness. She shivered and resigned herself to huddling under the blankets, just to keep warm. She slipped the knife under her pillow. She intended to be waiting for him, but her eyes refused to stay open.

At some point in the middle of the night, she was awoken by a slight tapping on the door. She sat bolt upright, fumbling for the knife. Her heart beat in her throat, but she was ready to defend herself.

Instead of the odious warlord barging in her bedchamber, the slight tapping came again. Maybe it was Alasdair or one of the children. She jumped out of bed and ran to the oak door, her bare feet cold on the stone floor.

"Who is it?" she whispered, pressing her face to the door.

"'Tis I, Cormac. Are ye well, m'lady?"

Relief flooded through her. Cormac had returned. "I am well, but that bastard locked me in here."

"Let me see what I can do."

Jyne waited, listening to soft clanking at the lock

until the door jerked open. She stepped back to allow him to enter, which he did quickly, closing the door softly behind him. He carried a small lantern that emitted a muted yellow glowing light. In the soft light, his face appeared a chiseled perfection, angular but handsome. She had never seen a more attractive man.

"Thank ye!" She wrapped her arms around his broad shoulders and hugged him tightly. She jumped back a moment later, realizing what she had done. She should not embrace a strange man; however, since she was being rescued, she felt she had earned some latitude.

"Are ye well? Did he hurt ye in any way?" He touched her shoulder and ran his hand down her arm until he was holding her hand.

"Nay, I am unhurt. He just scared me a bit. Then locked me in here. I was fearful he would come back." Her heart beat fast, though she was not sure whether it was from the awful memory of the warlord or because the Highlander before her gently squeezed her hand.

"I hope he was no' too frightening." Cormac's warm eyes were ones of concern. "Though he is a rather terrifying figure. I canna blame ye if ye were scared o' such a man."

"Nay," answered Jyne, her confidence returning. "He tried insults, then he tried kindness, but I saw through his lies. In truth, he was more annoying than frightening."

"Annoying?" Cormac seemed disappointed. "This mighty warrior, the Fire Lord himself, strikes through the postern gate using a science bordering on the magical, takes over the abbey in a matter of minutes, locks ye in the tower, and ye find him merely annoying?"

"And rude and ill-mannered," added Jyne.

Core looked slightly mollified. "Aye, rude and ill-mannered, he is that, indeed."

"But how is it ye've come here? How were ye able to get in?" she asked.

"Picked the lock," he replied, as if it was no great feat. "Returned and found a massive hole ripped through the postern gate. One o' the elders told me ye were locked in the tower. I came as quick as I could."

"'Twas verra brave o' ye to come."

"Aye, thank ye for noticing."

Jyne broke out into a smile, and Cormac returned it. Though he was a tall man, he moved with an easy, graceful manner. In the orange light, his unruly hair, fluid movements, and days' stubble on his face gave him the appearance of some wild, fey creature, possibly from the race of ancient faeries of old.

They were still holding hands, and Jyne had no desire to let go. It was Cormac who cleared his throat and stepped away.

"Let's get ye out o' here. I've found a safe place to hide," said Core, turning to the door.

"Nay, I canna go. I made a deal with the warlord that I would stay here, and he would'na harm the Ranalds."

Core frowned. "What makes ye think he will keep his word?"

"I dinna ken if he will, but I do know if I break his bargain and people here are hurt, I could never forgive myself." She wished to run away with Cormac, or fly back home, but she could not leave the elders, and especially the children, not now.

"I canna leave ye here unprotected. Ye must come

wi' me. I found a crofter's hut where we will never be found. I shall protect ye." Cormac's dark eyes glinted in the soft, warm light of the lantern in a manner that made her knees weak.

Jyne hesitated. She wanted to hide away with this man more than she should. It took considerable resolve to shake her head. "If he comes back, I shall be ready for him. I am not entirely unprotected." She revealed the knife she had up her sleeve.

Cormac's eyebrows shot up. "Wh-what are ye going to do wi' that?"

"Whatever I have to."

"Well now, glad it dinna come to it." He shook his head with a rueful gaze. "But please, m'lady, let me take ye from here where ye can be safe. I shall even carry on the resistance here and look after these people until the ruffians move on."

"Aye, let us resist these wicked bastards." She liked his thinking, but she could not seek her protection at the risk of others. "We must stop these brigands, or the people here will have naught left to eat. What good does it do to protect them from the sword, only to sentence them to starvation?"

"Starvation?" Cormac gave her blank look.

"Aye, ye've no idea how much food those sons o' knaves ate tonight. I fear these poor people will have no' much left in their larder after those locusts devoured all."

"Oh." Core continued to stare at her with an expression she could not read. "I had no' thought o' that."

"I doubt those ruffians thought about it either.

They winna care until the food runs out." Jyne gritted her teeth. "They have lost too much, only to have their demise come at the hands of a bunch o' greedy thugs."

"But these folk are no' yer kin." Core tilted his head to one side, as if thinking on a puzzle. "I doubt yer brother would want for ye to put yerself in harm's way."

Jyne sighed. Cormac was right. "True. But are we no' called upon to care for our neighbor? Is that no' what ye're doing? Neither these people nor I are from yer clan, yet ye returned to help us."

Cormac shook his head. "I am a selfish being. I only returned for ye."

Her pulse began to rise. "Because o' the kiss?"

His eyes danced. "Aye."

"Are ye to be my hero then?" She gave him a small smile.

"I tell ye the truth, m'lady. I am no hero." His eyes were sad, and they drew her closer.

She rested a hand on his shoulder, and she went on tiptoe to whisper in his ear, "Are ye sure?"

His cheek was so close to hers, she could feel his warmth, yet he did not turn toward her. "I'm sure o' naught when I'm wi' ye."

She kissed his cheek, breathing in his scent, earthy and raw. "And now?"

"For a single kiss, I'll be anything ye wish, if ye let me." His voice was reverent and sent shivers down her spine.

She turned to him, their cheeks touching for a moment. She wished to kiss him on the lips, but he did not move, allowing her to choose. Would she kiss him? "Och, well now." Jyne stepped back, more because she didn't want to than because she did. This was getting out of hand.

"So ye'll help me?" She took both his hands in hers and gazed up at him. She was flirting. For a cause, but flirting nonetheless. What would her brother say if he knew? Probably a lot of something she did not wish to hear.

"Aye, if ye wish it." His eyes were large and black in the soft orange light.

"Thank ye." She gazed into his eyes for longer than she should, sending ripples of an emotion she could not readily name through her. She looked away, trying to remember the thread of the conversation. "Together we will defeat this warlord. Together we will see him dead."

"Aye…dead." Once again, Cormac's face was inscrutable. He ran a hand through his wild hair, making the brown mass stick up even further. "Or perhaps we could simply run him off."

"I think he ought to die." Jyne was clear about right and wrong in the Highlands. This warlord had stolen the food off the table of children. He needed to die.

"We shall do our best. He is a clever and worthy foe."

"Then we shall have to be more so. Like ye, how ye picked the lock. However did ye learn?"

Core shrugged and changed the subject. "But how shall we combat such a foe?"

"I ken a few things about herbs, taught to me from my brother's wife. If ye can bring me certain plants and I can manage to get into the kitchen, I can make a special brew. Since these bastards wish to eat all our food, we shall let them gorge themselves to death!"

Cormac stomach rumbled in response. He paused for a moment and then said with a sigh, "'Tis a goodly plan."

❦

"Dinna eat the food today," Cormac advised the monk the next morning.

Brother Luke raised his eyes over the scroll he was reading, one of the ones he had retrieved from Core. "Why not?"

"Because Lady Jyne is going to poison it."

Luke's eyes flew open. "She will poison the food? With what?"

"She named some plants for me to collect for her. Had me leave them for her in the kitchens. Not sure what she will do wi' it."

"When did you speak to Lady Jyne?"

Cormac sighed and sat down beside Brother Luke before the fire of the private solar Core had adopted. His story of how the monk needed quiet to translate documents to find the treasure had worked in allowing him to escape the drunken antics of the band of thieves. Brother Luke had made himself comfortable in the large solar they now shared one floor above the lovely Jyne.

"I tried to get Jyne to leave Kinoch last night so I could get her to safety," explained Core.

The monk raised a suspicious eyebrow. He was right in his mistrust. Cormac had planned to sequester Jyne away in a small crofter's hut. It was for her safety, naturally, and if she chose to express her gratitude with a friendly embrace, or more, who was he to refuse?

"Whatever my hopes in that regard," admitted Core, "she would no' come wi' me."

"She is a good lady. I like her."

"Instead, she recruited me to lead the rebellion against the raiders."

Luke frowned. "So you are helping her to remove yourself from Kinoch?"

"Apparently so." Core shrugged.

"This will not end well for you. You should tell her the truth, sooner not later."

"The truth? Have ye gone mad?"

"When do you plan to tell her?"

"Umm…never!"

"She will find out."

"Not unless ye tell her." Core glared at the monk.

"You should not deceive her."

Core saw his carefully constructed lies falling apart. "We need her. She might be the key to finding something resembling a treasure here. She will talk to me as Cormac but not as the son o' Red Rex."

The monk shook his head, but there was indecision in his eyes. "She will discover the truth anyway at some point, and woe to you when she does."

"I dinna like to brag, but I am quite adept at keeping secrets." He'd had a lot of practice at it.

"*Testis falsus non erit inpunitus et qui mendacia loquitur non effugiet,*" muttered Brother Luke.

Cormac was not sure if Luke intended him to understand the Latin, but after being raised by monks, he could easily translate the verse from Proverbs: *A false witness shall not be unpunished: and he that speaketh lies shall not escape.* Core paused, for he knew what the monk was telling him was right. Yet to tell Jyne the truth at this point was unthinkable.

"Think verra carefully before ye say something to her that canna be unsaid. The lives o' yer fellow brothers are at stake," reminded Core. It was no doubt uncharitable to remind Brother Luke of Red Rex's threat, but he was desperate.

Luke frowned at him. "I despise you."

Cormac sighed. "Ye're not alone in that sentiment. What o' the sick needing the doctor and no one being beyond redemption?"

"I am beginning to think Jyne had the right of it."

"I fear ye may be correct." Core sighed again. "She's the sister o' Laird Campbell."

Luke stared at him for a moment, eyebrows raised, before returning to his scroll. "You are dead."

"I know."

Ten

JYNE CAREFULLY MEASURED WHAT SHE HOPED WAS THE right amount. She had been surprised by the Fire Lord this morning, who wrenched open her door and demanded that she report to the kitchens to prepare food for the warriors and stay out of the main hall to avoid his men. She did not appreciate being commanded to do anything, but she actually had no complaint with either of the requests.

"Are ye sure ye ken what ye're doing, m'lady?" asked the old cook. She was a generously proportioned woman with gray hair piled on top of her head, known to all as "Cook."

"Aye, Lady Isabelle taught me how to do this," said Jyne with a confidence she did not entirely feel. Truth was, her sister-in-law had shown her many of her healing potions and other herbal remedies. There were potions for colic, balms for burns, tinctures for headaches, and rubs for congestion. There were also all manner of special drafts—some cured pains, some gave sleep, some induced labor in a woman expecting, and others delayed it.

Isabelle had shown them all to her at one time or
another when they were needed. Jyne was certain—
mostly certain—that she remembered how to do this
particular brew correctly. She held the crushed herbs
in her hand, trying to recall the right proportions.
Isabelle always made it look so easy.

"Ye're sure?" Cook raised a gray eyebrow, as if
she could see through Jyne's facade to her worried
thoughts beneath.

"Aye, dinna fear. I ken what I'm about." Jyne
smiled with false bravado. Turning away, she closed
her eyes and tried to bring to mind what Isabelle
did to make this potion. She had seen it a few times.
Difficulty sleeping was a common enough complaint.
It had to be just right to bring sleep, but not so much
that it killed. Despite Jyne's brave words of wanting
to kill the warlord, she did not actually wish to do
anyone harm.

She simply needed them to leave.

"What is the plan?" whispered a familiar voice.
Cormac ducked his head and entered the low doorway from the outer ward into the kitchen.

"I found the herbs ye brought me." Jyne smiled
at him. She could not help herself. She was finally
seeing him in full daylight, and she took a good look.
He was tall and trim with a great plaid of green and
black pleated around him and thrown over one broad
shoulder. His eyes were a dark green, and there was
an aura of mystery about him. She still did not know
where he came from or even his clan, but she surprisingly found that when he gave her a half smile, she did
not care in the least.

"Did I find what ye needed?" he asked.

"Aye. But ye should'na be here," chastised Jyne, looking around to see if any of the Fire Lord's men were about. "Someone could see ye."

Core shrugged in a manner she found both brave and endearing. "I wanted to make sure ye were all right and see how I could help. Is that the poison?" He pointed at the jar in her hand.

"Aye. This will put them all into a sleep."

Core raised an eyebrow at her. "Sleeping wi' the angels or just sleep?"

"I doubt any o' these men will be let through the gates o' Saint Peter. But nay, I dinna intend to kill them. At least, not if I dinna have to." She stirred the potion a few more times.

"And when they sleep, what do ye intend to do to them? Kill them?"

"Nay!" Tricking a man into drinking a sleeping potion and then killing him while he slept did not hold with her sense of Highland justice. "I thought we could drag them to the dungeon and lock them up."

"Got no dungeon here, m'lady," interrupted Cook, disappointing her plans.

"A jail cell perhaps?"

"None o' those. Just the crypt below wi' the dead."

"Doubt it would be big enough for all those Highlanders," said Core hastily.

"How about an out o' the way storeroom wi' a door that locks?" asked Jyne.

Cook smiled, revealing a few missing teeth. "That we have."

"'Tis no' a bad plan." Core rubbed his jawline. He

was freshly shaved, and Jyne had the sudden, disturbing desire to touch his cheek. She had kissed him with stubble; she would like to do it again when he was clean shaven.

Jyne cleared her throat and turned back to her work, absently mixing in a few more ingredients before pouring it into several large pitchers of ale. "I'm glad ye're here, for ye can help me drag the men after they fall asleep. Some are prodigiously large." These were Highlanders. They grew them large and rough around these parts.

"Aye, their leader is certainly a powerful enemy." Core nodded sagely, with a keen glint to his eye.

"I was thinking more of some o' the larger men."

Cormac's shoulders sagged, but only for a moment, before his air of casual nonchalance returned. "But what shall ye do wi' them in the storeroom, once ye got them all in there?"

"I shall wait for help to arrive."

"And what help is coming?"

"My brother, Laird Campbell, will come for me, along wi' several o' my brothers and his armed guard, if I ken them at all. They shall make short work o' these knaves!"

"Will they now? How…reassuring." Core gave her a forced smile. "Well now, must be going. Canna be caught by these bastards, pardon me for saying so, m'lady." Cormac took a step closer but glanced around, noting that they were not alone in the kitchen. He gave her a hasty bow and slipped out the kitchen door, back into the courtyard.

"Aye, stay safe," she called after him, wishing he

would stay close. She felt more confident with him near. She took a deep breath. With or without him, it was time to start her plan in motion.

∼

Cormac raced around to the far side of the abbey, making sure he stayed out of sight. He was so accustomed to avoiding his father, his actions were not unfamiliar. He stared up the tower. Fortunately for his desire for stealth, thick vines had grown up the gray stones.

He climbed up the tower without incident and pushed open the shutters and climbed inside the solar, startling Brother Luke.

"What are you doing?" demanded the monk.

"Climbing up the tower. Canna have people see me go into the solar o' the Fire Lord."

"Fire Lord?" Luke raised an eyebrow.

"That's me now," said Core boldly.

"How…understated," replied the monk.

Core ignored the mockery. "Decided to stay in here?"

"Thought it best to avoid the poisoning." Luke returned to his scroll.

"Probably wise." Cormac donned his padded arming doublet, thick bearskin cloak, and huge horned helm to transform himself into the Fire Lord. He could not see the effects of his costume, but he hoped it was duly intimidating, though Jyne never appeared much cowed in his presence.

"'Tis time to rescue my men from Jyne's sleeping draft. I hope they will appreciate it," said Core.

"They won't," replied Luke without even looking up from his reading.

He was probably right. Cormac walked down the circular tower steps and strode into the main hall like a king.

"My friends," Cormac addressed the surly bunch of men before him, none of whom looked anything like a friend, "please follow my example and dinna eat or drink anything that is laid before ye today."

"Dinna drink? Ye might as well tell me no' to breathe," shouted one of the men.

"Ye dinna eat. We need our food like a man."

"He would'na ken anything about that," called out another man with no effort to lower his voice.

Cormac took their abuse with unruffled calm. It was all as he expected. "As ye wish." It was certainly not his idea to poison his men, but he could use it. Once again, he had a plan.

"Just because ye canna eat in that ridiculous helm doesna mean we should starve," growled Bran, stalking up to him. "Where is this treasure ye promised us?"

"We are working on it."

Bran ripped the helm off his head and glared at him. Core's heart raced. He was in the middle of the great hall without his helm. If Jyne should look out of the kitchen door, he would be seen, and everything would be lost.

"Where is the treasure?" repeated Bran in a low growl, his face inches from Core's. The man was about his same height but had at least a good two stone more muscle than him.

"We are working on translating the texts," fabricated Core. He needed to think fast before he was caught by Jyne or strangled by Bran. Though he hated the helmet, it was shocking how exposed he felt without it.

"What texts?"

"The scrolls, the ones I stole. They have clues, but it takes time." Core glanced at the kitchen door, his heart in his throat. She could walk in at any second.

"Give me the monk. I'll make him work faster."

"Nay, I need him to think clearer, no' faster. Ye canna be o' help in this matter unless yer Latin is better than mine."

Bran scowled at him. "Where's that wench o' yers?"

Core's blood ran cold. "She's nothing to you."

Bran gave him an evil smile. "She's the only halfway decent thing to look at around here. Ye think ye can keep her all to yerself?"

"I'll gut anyone who lays a hand on her," growled Core with a vehemence he had never before experienced.

Bran merely smirked. "Ye can try."

"Dinna underestimate me. Now let me be about my work." Core grabbed the helmet from Bran's grasp and slammed it down on his head. He needed to get away before Bran saw how his words had impacted him. Core glanced again at the kitchen door and, to his relief, saw no trace of Jyne. He attempted to walk away, but Bran held his arm with an iron grasp.

"Wear that helmet as much as ye like, if it makes ye feel stronger, but ye'll ne'er live up to yer father's name." Bran strode off, leaving Core to chew on his words.

Every hour he stayed at Kinoch with these men put Jyne at risk. Core knew he would never be his father, nor did he wish to be, but nobody defied Red Rex. Gaining the same blind obedience from these rough men would be impossible.

Elder matrons began to enter the room, bringing food and drink into the hall. Core's stomach rumbled. It was going to be torture again, smelling the delicious food and not being able to eat.

Core watched with a smug satisfaction as his men ate and drank. Served them right for not listening to him. All was going according to plan until Jyne herself entered the hall, a bottle of tainted ale in her hand. Men who had not given the elderly serving ladies a second glance turned to look at her, all eyes following her movements through the hall. She was not safe here.

What was she doing here? He had told her to remain out of sight. Was that Cormac or the Fire Lord who had said it? He couldn't quite remember, but he knew one of them had.

"Get back to yer chamber," he growled at her when she approached.

She flinched—slightly—but he saw it. He despised himself for making her uncomfortable. She leveled him a glare that told him she agreed with his opinion.

"Ye demanded food and drink. I canna serve ye from the kitchens, can I?" She poured him a healthy amount of the ale she carried. He had no doubt it was tainted heavily with her special potion.

He leaned closer to her and put a hand on her sleeve, speaking in a low voice that reverberated in an ominous fashion from within the helm. "These men dinna ken the meaning o' restraint. Get back to the kitchens wi' ye, and dinna put yerself in their company again."

Her lips parted slightly, and she stared at him, perhaps wondering if he had given her a warning or a threat. It was a little of both.

"Aye," she whispered.

Cormac watched carefully as she made her way back to the kitchens. One of the men stood up behind her, a leer on his face. Cormac's empty gut clenched as the man reached out to grab her. Quick as lightning, Core grabbed his *sgian dubh*, the hidden knife all Highlanders carried, and threw it before the man, sticking it point down in the table between the man and Jyne.

The man stopped and turned back to Core, a look of surprise on his face. Core was not known to start a fight, but he would protect Jyne with everything within him. She had paid for his protection with a kiss, and he would honor it.

Core walked boldly to the man, glad he still wore the monstrous helm, silently daring him to continue. Whether due to intimidation or surprise, the man cursed and sat back down. It was not the deferential respect afforded to his father, but still, it was a retreat.

Smiling at his success, Core retrieved the knife from where it was stuck in the table and replaced it in its hiding place in his boot. He had a win; it was time to withdraw.

"This food tastes like swill! I will not eat it, nor should ye!" Core pounded his fist on a table as he had seen his father do many times. It did not quite resound with the same ferocity, but he was, after all, still learning the ways of being a warlord.

Jyne had reached the door of the kitchen and turned back, scowling at him. It did strange things to him, that glower of hers. He felt warm in odd places. He cleared his throat to focus back on his current role. He was a ruthless warlord.

"I am returning to my chamber, and I'm no' to be disturbed!" He strode from the great hall and up the stone steps. As soon as he was out of sight, he ran to his chamber, removed the ill-smelling helm, and took a deep breath of fresh air. He shrugged off the large bearskin and the padded arming doublet and changed back into his regular attire.

Brother Luke hardly afforded him a glance. "Even if I keep your unholy secret, she will find out."

"Not if I can help it."

"It is wrong to deceive her so."

"Aye. I'm an evil warlord, ye ken?"

"Are you?" This time, Brother Luke gave him a long, appraising look.

Core sighed. "'Tis what my father wants."

"And what do you want?"

Core shook his head. "Ye dinna understand. What my father wants is what will happen." Core took a breath and blew it out. He did not wish to think on these things, but he was a practical lad, and he knew his fate. "I may be able to hold him off for a while, but eventually I will become like him, or he will kill me. There is no other option."

Eleven

WHETHER HE WAS A WARLORD PRETENDING TO BE A rebel or a rebel pretending to be a warlord was getting a little confused in his mind. Either way, Cormac wanted to return to the kitchens to witness what would happen to his men. Spending more time with the lovely Jyne was an added benefit.

He opened the shutters and climbed several stories down the ivy-covered tower. He had been sneaking in and out of places for most of his life. While some men stood their ground in a fight, he preferred to disappear when things became difficult. Picking locks and scaling down walls was second nature to him now.

He was down the tower in mere seconds and around to the kitchens, striding into the back door with a certain confidence. Jyne rushed up to him directly in a manner he liked quite a bit.

"All the men drank from their mugs o' tainted ale, but I dinna ken if that Fire Lord drank his. He's gone up to his solar and doesna want to be disturbed." A little crease formed on her brow between her bright blue eyes.

"How soon will the sleeping draft take effect?" Core asked.

"I made it extra strong. They should be slumbering soon. But what if the warlord should return? He will find his sleeping men and take vengeance out on us." She looked around at the elders and children helping in the kitchen, clearly concerned for their welfare.

"Dinna worry so. Take some food and drink. I warrant the warlord went to his chamber because he was beginning to feel the effects of yer potion. I doubt verra much we shall see him for hours." Cormac was very confident in this.

They sat at an old oak table and broke bread together. Cormac found goblets of wine for both of them and some food for a meal. It had been long since he had filled his belly, so he ate hungrily of the bread and the hearty stew before him. Jyne must have been reassured by his confidence, for the little crease on her forehead disappeared, and she began to eat and drink with him.

He liked this, sharing a meal with her. He could almost block out the sound of his men carousing in the great room next to them. She was a beautiful lass. She must have been thinking of other things when she'd gotten herself dressed this morn, for her veil was not securely fastened, causing her long, straight blond hair to fall out before her. The color of those errant strands was like gold. He longed to reach out and touch it. She absently brushed a lock of hair behind her ear with a careless finger, causing him to pause in his eating. Her blue eyes sparkled at him, and he noticed those blue eyes had flecks of hazel green.

A disturbance erupted in the dining hall, and one of the elderly matrons ran back into the kitchen.

"What is the matter?" cried Jyne, rising to her feet. "Are they no' getting tired?"

The woman placed a hand over her bosom, her eyes wide. "Nay, they're getting randy!"

"Pardon?"

"I had two o' the men say they thought I was a vision o' loveliness. Three done laughed so hard, they fell from their benches, and four others started a brawl o'er the right way to eat stew. They've gone mad, they have!" The matron threw her hands up in the air.

Before Core could make any sense of this, another elderly clanswoman, with thinning gray hair and a large goiter, shrieked as she scrambled back into the kitchen.

"What happened to ye?" asked Jyne. She ran to the elderly woman and helped her to sit on the bench she had just vacated.

"I dinna ken they're about. One man dropped to his knees and began to recite poetry, or at least something like it. A few others started dancing, wi' no music—wi' each other! Another one demanded my hand in marriage. To me! What sort o' mean-spirited shenanigans are these hooligans up to?"

Jyne's face was one of complete loss. "Is this some sort o' game?" she asked Core.

"If it is, 'tis unknown to me." Cormac had seen quite a bit of rough play from his father's men, but he had never heard of anything like that.

Core and Jyne peeked inside the great hall and were

astounded at what they saw. Several of the men were having a heated argument as to which of the elderly servers was more beautiful. Some were dancing to no music. Some were running around the room, batting at the air, as if trying to catch invisible fairies. Others were fighting while laughing hysterically. Jyne and Core stared at each other.

"Why are they acting this way?" Jyne met his eye. He realized they were standing very close as they peeked into the hall. Her beautiful blue eyes widened, and she flushed, her cheeks a rosy hue. Her lips were the color of pale pink rose petals and appeared so soft and inviting, he wished to lean in for just one taste. She was beautiful. Truly beautiful.

"I dinna ken." He had to remind himself to answer her question. It was the truth. He had never seen the men act in such a manner.

"Oh!" Jyne suddenly gasped. "The potion. It must have made them mad."

Core couldn't help but laugh. "Ye made them all act like fools? Och, I wish my father was here to see it!"

"Who is yer father?" she asked, turning her innocent blue eyes to him.

He realized in a flash he had made a slip. "No one. Just he would think it amusing, is all," he said hastily. "Will the potion make them tired or just mad as imps?"

Jyne slapped a hand to her forehead. "Och, I'm a dunderhead, I am. Too much ale wi' it can make a man lose his senses."

"Ye gave my men something to make them witless?"

"Well I… It wasn't what I intended… Wait, *yer*

men?" She raised an eyebrow at him, and he knew he was in trouble.

"My men? I…I have no men." He attempted nonchalance. It was not a natural state.

The little furrow between her brows reappeared. "But I thought I heard ye say—"

He kissed her.

It was the only thing he could think to do. The only thing he wanted to do. He was drawn to her by a power he could not deny. He embraced her and allowed his lips to melt onto hers. He did not have much experience in kissing, but he pulled her closer and deepened the kiss, waiting for the inevitable slap. Instead, she wrapped her arms around his neck, pressing herself against him and returning his ardor with a passion that lit an explosion within him. He did not care that his men were making fools of themselves next door. He did not care if the entire kitchen staff could see them. He had to kiss her.

Finally, she pulled away, her breath coming quick and fast. "I…I…" She glanced around, noting that everyone in the kitchen was staring at them. "Och, I fear ye are also under its spell. Ye must have drunk the tainted ale."

He was not under any such spell, for he had drunk wine, not ale, and his feelings for her had begun the moment he had pulled her from the bog. She could not be unaware of how he felt about her. Did she truly think he was under the influence of the potion, or was she trying to give a plausible rationale for the kiss to those in the kitchen? He was not familiar enough with the workings of the feminine mind to know. He hesitated for a moment but felt it best to agree with her. "Aye, it would seem so. Is there an antidote?" He fervently hoped not.

She shook her head. "It will wear off in time."

He nodded and turned to spy once more on the commotion in the great hall. At least the kiss had distracted her enough from remembering what he had said. He also was having difficulty attending to what he ought; instead, he was thinking of situations where he could kiss her again.

"I wish I knew what I did. I've ne'er seen a potion so powerful," commented Jyne.

"It must be, for those bastards to start spouting poetry."

Her eyes sparkled, and mischief tweaked up the corners of her mouth. He wanted to kiss that mouth again. "It should not be long now. They should fall asleep soon. At least, I hope so. I wish Isabelle was here."

"Isabelle?"

"She is my brother's wife and a skilled healer."

Cormac shrugged. "I'm sure it will be fine." He peeked once more into the great hall. Already, some of the men were laid out on the benches or curled up on the floor. "Look, I think it is taking effect."

"Truly?" Jyne moved to enter the great hall, but he put a hand to stay her.

"If those men are randy due to yer potion, I hate to think o' what they might do for a right lovely lass. Might throw them into apoplexy or start a riot."

"Right lovely?" She spoke the words softly, looking up at him through long lashes.

Something of a chill, but a whole lot warmer, coursed through him. He cleared his throat. "No' safe for ye out there."

"If ye say so." She gave him a wide-eyed smile.

His mind went blank for a moment. He smiled in return.

Core glanced out into the great hall where Dubh was reciting a sonnet, or at least he was trying to. It started with poetry and ended as a dirty limerick.

One matron returned from the hall with a smile. "I got four offers of marriage and five offers of something I canna say in polite company," she said with a twinkle in her eye.

"Mayhap we can step outside to discuss what is to be done now?" asked Core, wishing to have a more private audience with Jyne without the bustle of the kitchen workers.

Jyne nodded, and he followed her out the side door into the sunlight of a fine spring day. The sun caught the gilded strands of her long hair, turning them to pure gold. He stared, transfixed, before remembering himself.

"Do ye wish to drag them to the storeroom?" asked Core, not particularly relishing the onerous task. His back still ached from the exertion of saving her guard last night.

Jyne sighed. "Aye, but I am worried about the Fire Lord. I am almost certain he dinna drink the ale. How could he, wi' the helmet on? He could return from his chamber at any time. If he finds us carting his sleeping comrades into a storeroom, what then?"

"He would attack, no doubt."

"Och, I hate to think all this trouble was for naught, but I do not wish to give him any excuse to make trouble for these people or for us."

Core nodded in agreement. His plan would work better if his men were not locked in a storeroom. "Will they return to normal when they wake up?"

"Aye, the potion does not last long. Like all illusions, it will eventually dissipate." She turned her face to the sun, her skin bathing in the golden rays.

"Good. Verra good." He did not know exactly what to say. He wanted to kiss her again. He needed to kiss her again. He wished to say something along the lines of *be quiet and kiss me*, which, potion or no potion, could hardly be an appealing enticement toward romance.

"Ye're verra good." He leaned down to kiss her, but at the last moment had a rush of conscience that prevented him from doing anything more than brushing his lips against her cheek. "Forgive me."

"I understand. The potion." Her eyes were wide, like bottomless blue orbs. She pushed a wisp of hair behind her ear again with a delicate finger. She had an ethereal, otherworldly quality, so much so that if she suddenly sprouted wings and flew off like a fairy, he would hardly have been surprised.

"Nay, ye must ken I drank none o' yer brew, yet I have surely been bewitched." Her eyes met his; her face was unreadable, her lips slightly parted. She was irresistible. He drew her into his embrace and kissed her, expecting her to pull away. Instead, she pressed her lips against his, kissing him with a sweet passion he thought he would never experience. Her arms wrapped around him, her fingers threading through his hair, and he could not resist. He held her close. She might be petite of frame, yet no one had held him more in their power.

When the kiss finally ended, it took a moment or two to open his eyes once more, forcing himself to come back to earth.

"Forgive me. I take liberties," he murmured.

"Aye, ye do." And she flashed him a smile that made his heart stop.

"I…I should no' be out here in the open."

"Aye, do take care." Her brow furrowed in concern. All he could think was that she looked adorable, even when worried.

He took his leave and ran away, chastising himself for going too far. He needed to think clearly, but something about being in the presence of Jyne Campbell made that quite difficult. He was not sure what sort of game they were playing or whether he was winning or losing, but he did know she was trouble to him.

And all he could think of was when he could see her again.

∽

Jyne stared at Cormac as he walked away. She had kissed him. *Kissed* him. She'd kissed Cormac!

She was not under the influence of any spell or potion. Yet when he looked at her, gazed deep into her eyes, her knees went weak, her heart began to pound, and all her intended no's just faded away. She knew she was not supposed to go about kissing men, especially men she had met on the moor, about whom she knew nothing. What was she thinking? This was so unlike her. Maybe she had taken a swig of her own medicine.

Jyne returned to the kitchen and began to pace. She was not one for self-deceit. She had kissed Cormac because…because…she wanted to. She wanted to very much. Before this momentous day, she had never before been kissed. The thought of pressing one's lips against someone else's had seemed a bit strange and not at all something she would enjoy. She had been wrong. Very wrong.

Cormac was a handsome man, with his angular cheekbones and strong jaw. He was muscular, yet not in the bulky manner of her brothers. No, he was strong in his own way. This was not even his fight. He had no ties here, not to the land or to her clan. He could just walk away anytime, yet he had stayed to help her. He was an honorable man to be sure.

Jyne smiled to herself with a sudden realization. All of her sheltered life, she had wished for the ability to show her worth. She had wanted the chance to show her clan that she, too, could be capable and brave. She had also secretly desired to fall in love in some wild fashion, as many of her siblings had done.

Whether she liked it or not, she had finally gotten her wish. She had embarked on a true Campbell adventure!

Twelve

CORMAC ABSENTLY SCRAMBLED UP THE IVY WALL AND slipped into his solar chamber with a smile that never dimmed. He feared he might have a goofy grin on his face for the rest of his life. He should be thinking of what to do next. Instead, all he could think of was kissing a certain lass. She was wonderful. She was beautiful. No one had ever kissed him like that.

He stared at the horned helm, discarded on the floor. If she knew that Cormac and the Fire Lord were the same, she would despise him. And most likely impale him on one of his own horns. He had won her kisses only because he had pretended to be someone other than who he was. Of course it could never last. Eventually, her kin would put a stop to it. With any luck, he would be long gone before they did.

Trouble was, now that her kiss was on his lips, he doubted he could ever forget it. She had treated him with more kindness in a few short hours than his father or any of his ilk had ever done in a lifetime. Perhaps she could be convinced to run away with him. They could flee to some distant land where his father would never find them…and she would never discover his deceit. He would have no complaints waking beside her every morn. He definitely would have no complaints taking her to bed each night.

"Cormac."

He could wrap his arms around her and—

"Cormac!"

Core's delightful dream shattered, and he blinked at Brother Luke, who was glaring at him.

"Aye?" asked Core, wondering how long he had been lost in his daydream.

"I have been trying to speak with you, but you have done naught but stare at the walls with a stupid grin on your face. What happened down there?"

"Nothing!" Core was too accustomed to covering his tracks to do anything but lie. "All is well. The men sleep. Jyne is well. No problems at all."

Luke raised an eyebrow. The man was no fool. "I am glad to hear it, but what of your plans? How will you get a treasure to save the monastery? You have not forgotten, have you?"

Forgotten? No. Devised a plan? Alas, also no.

"Have a plan. Working on it now!" More lies.

"What is this plan?" Brother Luke was not easily convinced.

"Um…well…we could…"

"You have no plan."

"Something will come to me. Something always does."

"I do not need to remind you that a library of irreplaceable books and the lives of over twenty good brothers lie in the balance."

"Aye, I know it." Core sighed and ran his fingers through his hair, pulling a bit to focus his attention. He needed to get himself together. He had to prove to his father he was a bloodthirsty warlord who did not care for anything but a lust for power and destruction, or Rex would burn the books—all his wonderful books. And of course, saving the monks would be good too, though they were not half as welcoming to him.

Books had always been there for him, giving him companionship when he was young and alone. They had opened his mind to new ideas and perspectives. They had provided him the clues to unlock the mysteries of alchemy. They had not judged or abandoned him when the truth of his unfortunate parentage had been discovered. Many times, they had been his only friends. Truth was, he would give anything to save that library.

In order to gain his father's approval and stave off the attack, he first needed to earn the respect of his men. Thanks to Jyne, he now had an idea of how to do it.

"The first thing I need to do is get the attention o' my men."

"The men who treat you with utter disrespect." Brother Luke showed no mercy in his observations.

"Aye, those men. And to do it, I'm going to need yer help."

Brother Luke frowned. "I'm not going to like this, am I?"

Core smiled. "Ye might. What do ye ken o' alchemy?"

A few hours later, Red Rex's men were beginning to wake, rubbing their heads and complaining of a terrible ache. It was all the better for him. Core glanced toward where Brother Luke had hidden himself behind a tapestry. This had to work.

"Ye all will swear yer fealty to me!" declared Cormac.

"Ye want me to do what?" growled Bran. He rubbed his head and had a difficult time opening his eyes more than a painful squint.

Cormac scanned the great hall, making sure all the men were accounted for and trapped within. He had shut and barred all the doors of the great hall so he could have some privacy with these men. He was the son of Red Rex. It was time to show them exactly what that meant.

"I demand ye to swear fealty to me."

"Piss off!" growled Dubh to the grumbles of agreement of the men.

"Feeling ill? I dinna care. Ye'll swear fealty to me now!" Core's pulse was elevated for speaking so boldly to these men, men he knew could kill without a second thought. He almost wished he had worn the horned helmet to give him the appearance of authority. He took a breath and reminded himself the point was for the men to see him as their leader, not his father.

Bran snorted and took to his feet, the first of the men to do so. Even hurt, he was dangerous. "Who are ye to ask such a thing?"

"I am the one who holds something ye prize, and when ye swear yer oath to me, it will be returned to ye." Cormac leaned back in the master's chair on the dais.

"What item?" asked Dubh.

Cormac merely smiled.

"I'm in no mood to play wi' ye, lad," snarled Bran.

"I'm no lad. I am the son o' Red Rex, who I'm sure will be interested in how ye were subdued by a few old serving wenches."

"Ye'll ne'er get the words out o' yer mouth," roared Bran and reached for something hidden in his boot. Except it wasn't there.

"Looking for this?" Cormac held up the hidden knife, the *sgian dubh*, the sign of the Highlander. To have it taken from a man was a great shame. Taking a man's sword or his horse, or even his tam or his boots was one thing, but taking a man's *sgian dubh* was taking his dignity.

Core lifted a canvas bag from the floor and plunked it on the table with a metallic clatter. He had a bag full of them from all the men. He smiled at the sullen men and leaned back in his chair. "Ye will swear fealty to me, or I will give these all to my father. I'm sure he'll be interested in knowing how I came to have them."

"Ye canna defeat all of us," growled one man. "Give that back, ye filthy—"

Cormac jumped to his feet, giving the signal to the hidden monk. "I am the one and only son o' the great Red Rex. Defy me, and ye will feel the wrath o' the Fire Lord!"

Explosions rang out, with loud bangs in each corner, filling the room with sulfur smoke. The men jumped and held their hands over their ears, huddling together in fear. It was helped by the headaches they all seemed to be experiencing, which must have worsened with the noise, making them all wince in pain. The effects were only a mere pop of black powder, enough to make a loud noise, but not enough to hurt anything. Of course, the men didn't need to know that.

"Ye will bow before me and swear yer fealty. If ye do so now, I will grant the return o' yer knives. If not, I will count ye among my enemies, and we shall do battle. Now, who is with me?" Core waited and held his breath.

Nobody moved. The smoke slowly settled, and still no one said a word. Finally, Dubh trudged forward. "Ye're the son o' that bastard fer sure," grumbled the large man, and he swore fealty.

The next to come was a tall, blond-haired man with one eye. Next was a bald man with a ginger beard and enormous forearms. One by one, the men came forward and swore their fealty to him until only Bran was left.

Bran walked up to Core slowly. "Ye surprised me today," he grudgingly admitted. "I do solemnly swear my fealty to ye, but ye've a long way before ye're a match for yer father."

Core nodded at the battle-hardened warrior and returned the man's knife to him. To gain Bran's allegiance was something. To keep it was another.

All in all, it went as well as he could have hoped. Core strode through the great hall, the men giving him nods of respect as he passed. He paused at the door and donned his horned helm before unbarring the doors. The helmet still smelled, but he didn't mind so much. Today, with the help of Lady Jyne and the good Brother Luke, he had defeated his own army. It was a good day.

Thirteen

JYNE WAS NOT ONE TO BE DISSUADED BY AN INITIAL setback. The sleeping draught had not worked as she had planned, but there must be another way to remove the unwanted marauders from her home. It was time to strike once again. Trouble was, Jyne had no idea how to oust the warlord and his motley followers from Kinoch Abbey. She paced back and forth in her chamber. After the debacle with the sleeping potion, she wasn't sure what to do next.

Making things worse, she had a difficult time concentrating on the problem at hand when her mind kept returning to her time with Cormac. She sighed and leaned against the cool stone wall, remembering his kisses. She had never felt such a lightness, a warm joy that spread throughout her entire body. He made her feel wonderful. Had it been momentous for him too?

What if it wasn't?

What if it was?

Jyne groaned and began pacing her chamber once more. She needed to forget about Cormac and focus on her current problem. She needed to get the Fire

Lord and his knaves out of Kinoch before one of the elders or the young ones got hurt. She needed them out before *she* got hurt. Though the Fire Lord had left her alone last night, she had no guarantee he would do the same tonight.

A loud bang and a popping sound startled her out of her troubled musings.

"By all the saints, what was that?" she gasped. She ran down the spiral stairs in the direction of the sound. Had the Fire Lord used his dark arts to rip another hole through a wall of Kinoch? Was anyone hurt? She ran faster.

She reached the large double doors to the great hall, but they were shut. A small crowd of elders and children was gathered around the door.

"What happened in there?" Jyne asked Alasdair, who hobbled forward, a gnarled walking stick in his hand.

"I dinna ken. The doors are locked from the inside."

Jyne heard shouting coming from inside the great hall, but could not tell what was being said. "Who is in there? Are any of our people in danger?"

"'Tis the Fire Lord and his wretched band what's in there," said Cook, wiping her hands on her apron. "I saw them all go in, but none so far has come out."

"Mayhap the Fire Lord has rained down fire on himself and tore himself to bits?" suggested one of the matrons.

"It would surely serve him right, but I fear we canna hope for such luck," replied Jyne. "I think we should get the wee bairns hidden back away."

"Awwwww," sounded a chorus of children.

"'Tis for yer own safety," chided the elderly matron.

"But we've done naught all day but sit around. We want to play!" complained a child who looked to be about four years old.

"I dinna want to go back there. It's haunted!" cried another child.

"And if these wicked men kill each other, they'll surely turn into more ghosts," said a lad with a glint in his eye.

"What is this about it being haunted?" Jyne asked the matron.

"'Tis naught but their imagination," she said, walking over to her. "Actually," she added when she was close enough to whisper without being overheard by the children, "I have heard it too. We took the children to the refectory to sleep and stay out o' the way o' the men. 'Tis next to the storeroom, which holds the trapdoor what leads to the crypt below."

The matron paused, looking about to make sure none of the children were close enough to hear her words.

"What happened?" prompted Jyne.

"I heard such noises, I could'na account for them. There was banging and pounding and cries of a banshee. Och, it raised the hairs on the back o' me neck, it did."

"Did ye go down into the crypt to investigate?"

"Lord love ye, nay, Lady Jyne. Why would I wish to meet wi' a ghostie? Have we no' enough problems of our own?"

"Aye, ye're right, o' course," replied Jyne, not sure what to make of the tale.

The doors to the great hall flew open with a bang, and out strode the Fire Lord himself, his face concealed as always with the large, horned helm. The elders and children scurried out of his path. The man pointed at Jyne.

"Why are ye here? I told ye to stay in yer chamber or the kitchens," thundered the Fire Lord.

Jyne raised her chin, defiant. "This is my keep, and I'll go where I wish. Besides, I heard such a loud noise, I feared ye had torn another hole in one o' my walls."

"Ye are mistaken. For this is *my* keep. And ye belong to *me*."

"How dare ye!"

The warlord ignored her gasp and turned his attention back to his men, who crowded around the doorway of the great hall. "This wench belongs to me. If any o' ye touch as much as a hair on her head, I shall call down my fire and rip ye apart until ye're wearing yer entrails like a hat. Is that clear?"

The marauders all nodded and mumbled, "Aye, sir," showing more deference than ever before.

"Bran." The Fire Lord addressed a tall, muscular man. "Dubh." He turned his attention to an overfed man, his sheer size intimidating. "I'll have yer word on this."

"Aye," the men replied, giving him a glare but complying with his request. Satisfied, the Fire Lord strode with confidence up the spiral stone staircase.

When he was gone, Jyne was faced with the glares of the warlord's men. Any trace of deference was gone, and she hoped they would follow the warlord's commands in his absence.

"Take the bairns away," she whispered to the elderly matron.

The matron nodded and motioned for the children

to come with her. Jyne could detect some silent reluctance on their part, probably due to fears of ghosts and ghouls. After some hesitation, they all followed the matron away from the main hall.

An older man with a brown mustache and a powerful presence, whom the Fire Lord had addressed as Bran, walked up to her. She took a step back, then another.

"Dinna fear. I winna risk my entrails by harming ye," said Bran in a low voice. Though his words should have been reassuring, his tone was one of warning. "I ken it was ye that tainted our meal. I'll have no more o' that nonsense in our food and drink. I may no' be able to harm ye, but if any o' my men get so much as a bellyache from our victuals, I'll cut off the heads o' all those in the kitchen, starting wi' that cook and going down to the youngest scullery maid. Ye ken me?"

Jyne swallowed hard. "I understand."

There would be no more plots with the food.

The men filed out into the courtyard, and Jyne retreated back to the relative safety of her own chamber. She put a hand to her chest and took deep breaths until she could no longer feel her pulse beat in her ears.

That man would kill her people without a thought, without remorse, and without any difficulty. What match were a few elders and children compared to a demon like that? She hoped they could hold out until her brother could return, though it would be at least another three days before anyone would come. Could they last that long?

A soft rap sounded on her door. She opened it a

crack, then opened it wide to allow Cormac to enter. Her heart began to beat loudly again, though for a much different reason. He had returned!

"Forgive the intrusion, m'lady." He gave her a hesitant smile. "I heard the loud blast. I feared for yer safety."

"Thank ye for yer kindness. I am well. It was only the devil warlord and his demon army. Destroying things must be their idea of amusement." She gave him a tentative smile in return, wondering how it was that she could ask him the question she needed answered. Trouble was, it was not the sort of thing one could ask a man.

"Well…I am glad ye are well." He stood awkwardly before her, much unspoken between them.

"Aye, thank ye."

Silence descended upon them, and Jyne struggled to find a safe topic of conversation. "Are ye…feeling well?"

"Aye. Verra good. I…I hope I dinna offend ye earlier today in the kitchen. I fear I took liberties."

"I was no' offended," she murmured.

"Yer brother would'na agree."

The mention of her brother had a chilling effect. Though she wished for his presence to help her, once he arrived, he would see to it she was never again alone with Cormac.

"My brother is protective."

"He should be."

Heat coursed through her at the veiled compliment. She stood awkwardly before him, not knowing what to say.

"Mayhap I should go and let ye be," said Core slowly.

"Nay, please continue to help us. We need to think of another plan to get them to leave. We canna use any further potion on them. Too dangerous. One o' those devils threatened to kill the cook and everyone else who worked in the kitchens."

Core's face darkened. "Bastard," he muttered. "I'll not let that happen. At least," he amended quickly, "I'll try not."

"I dinna ken where we would be wi'out ye. Thank ye so much for yer help," said Jyne with much sincerity.

"I fear I have no' been much help to ye at all."

"Och, but ye have. Ye give me hope. I feel safe when I'm wi' ye. I know I can trust ye."

Core's face brightened for a moment, then a cloud passed over his sad eyes. "I dinna deserve yer trust."

"Why? Because our first plan dinna work?"

"Nay."

Jyne swallowed on a throat suddenly gone dry. "Because ye kissed me wi'out gaining permission first from my brother and laird?"

Core sighed. "Aye, something like that."

"Well, my brother is no' here yet. Ye can ask him when he arrives."

Core shook his head sadly. "I canna do that."

"Why not?"

"I…I just canna speak to yer brother."

Jyne's disappointment was palpable. He was telling her he would not be a suitor for her hand. At least he was being honest in his intentions, though she took no comfort in it.

"I see."

"I'm sorry. I will just leave ye be." His voice was contrite, but Jyne noticed he did not leave.

"Nay," said Jyne, feeling a rise of determination that was new to her. She was a Campbell after all, and she still had a mission to do. She was called to protect the people of Kinoch, and this man could help her do it.

"Nay?" he asked in a tone that was almost hopeful.

"Nay," she repeated with growing certainty. "Ye promised to help me for a kiss. Well, ye've received yer kiss. Now 'tis time for ye to live up to yer word and help us."

Cormac's eyebrows shot up in surprise and then settled into a smoldering half smile. "As ye wish."

"Now then." She took a breath, trying to turn her focus away from his dark green eyes to the matter at hand. "We canna fight them directly. We canna poison them. Somehow, we need to make them wish to leave."

"Little hope o' that, I fear, when they are under the mistaken belief that there be treasure here. If they could only find what they seek, I'm sure they would leave." He gave her a hopeful look.

Jyne shook her head. "There is naught here that anyone would consider a treasure."

Cormac sighed and sat down on the stone bench by the window. "That is most unfortunate." He propped up one long leg and leaned an elbow on it in an image of a man in thought. Jyne was instantly drawn to his casual demeanor. It was difficult to focus when she was unchaperoned with a man in her bedchamber.

"There has to be some way to make them leave."

Jyne paced back and forth, trying to clear her head enough from the day's events to think cogently. She was having a difficult time focusing on anything other than the kiss that bound him to her. And her to him.

Exerting great mental effort to think of something other than his surprisingly soft lips, she thought back over the events of the day, trying to find some weakness. The men ate, caroused, made loud noises, threatened elders and young children…

She certainly hoped the youngsters would stay out of sight and not leave the refectory, even if they were afraid it was haunted.

"Wait! I may have an idea. Do you think those men may be afeared o' ghosts?"

Fourteen

He had tried. He had tried to do the honorable thing. Core had told her there was no future together. He had offered to leave, even if he had not been able to make his feet comply. But no, now it was she who demanded he stay and help her.

Cormac smiled to himself. He should have felt some shame in demanding a kiss in return for his assistance, but he could not bring himself to feel any ounce of remorse. He had kissed her. He had enjoyed it. And he hoped to do it again.

He wondered if he could demand more of her charms for further assistance. Was that going too far? He thought about it a moment. Probably. Did he care? Probably not. He had the disturbing suspicion that he was becoming like the father he had resented and feared his whole life.

Cormac brushed the unwanted musings aside and focused instead on the new plan Jyne had devised to remove the men from Kinoch. Core sat at the high table, surveying the men as best he could through the slits of his helmet.

As punishment for not listening to his advice before, Core decided that his men would have no drink for the evening meal. Thus, he had the pleasure of sitting at the raised dais while his men quietly ate their portions and cast about fierce but forlorn looks. The men were clearly still reeling from the aftereffects of the potion, for they moved slowly and spoke softly.

The purpose of making his men abstain from their prized libations also helped Jyne in her latest plot to scare away the men from Kinoch Abbey. He doubted her little plan was going to work, but he was happy to at least give it a try, for he would be pleased to leave Kinoch Abbey, almost as much as she would be to see them go.

Jyne approached him from the kitchens. She had taken some time with her appearance, and wore a sage-green kirtle with a sleeveless surcoat of embroidered cream. Her hair was swept back in a modest veil, but her blue eyes shone brightly. This was part of the plan she had devised with him—at least it was a plan she had devised with Cormac. In this role, he played the evil warlord.

"I have come to offer entertainment for ye and yer men," said Jyne boldly. Core could not help but admire her courage to stand before these men. He hoped they would honor their pledge to him and not attempt anything untoward. She stepped forward with a calm he did not share.

"What entertainment do ye bring, wench?" His words sounded harsh in his ears. He would certainly never wish to speak to her in this manner, but he felt he must maintain the appearance of a ruthless chieftain or face the loss of the newfound respect of his men. He needed their allegiance, or she was in danger.

"I offer a story, a tale of murder and intrigue that may be of interest to ye and yer men, especially since the tale is one that happened here at Kinoch Abbey and is the real reason why the monks abandoned the abbey."

Core was impressed. She had proposed a story that would be of interest to his men. Without their ale and whiskey, they were a sad-hearted group and appeared eager for any distraction from the misery of sobriety and the pounding of their heads.

"Then tell us this tale, lass." Truly, he could not continue calling her a wench. Even evil warlords must have their limits.

Jyne boldly strode forward to the middle of the hall. She paused a moment, and all voices hushed until all that could be heard was the occasional soft pop of the fire in the great hearth. "Many years ago, this fair land was owned by a man who did not deserve his good fortune. What many have now forgotten is that this hall was originally built as a fine keep by Laird Archibald for his new bride. Unfortunately, the Lord Archibald was a man of infamous temper and poor moral character."

Jyne paused, and her audience waited for her to continue. Men of infamous temper and poor moral character were quite familiar to them. "The Laird Archibald wooed the fair maiden, Lady Joan, reciting poetry to her and playing skillfully on his lute. He ingratiated himself to Joan's father and brothers, for not only was Joan the fairest maiden o' the land, but she also had a dowry that would make any man who wed her as rich as a king. Though Joan was wary o' deceitful suitors, Laird Archibald courted her with genteel manners and kindhearted actions, but he was entirely false.

"As soon as Lady Joan and Laird Archibald wed, he revealed his true nature. He treated her with cruelty and contempt. He dinna allow her to see her family. He was disrespectful to her before his men and the servants, and even brought women o' ill repute to sit beside him in the great hall, while she was left, crying, in the tower alone.

"Perhaps ye've wondered why Kinoch Abbey has only one tower. Well, when this keep was first built, there was another tower, a twin to the one that still stands. In this tower was Lady Joan's chamber, where she lamented her ill treatment at the hands o' this ruthless man.

"After several years, Lady Joan had borne Laird Archibald no children, for there was no love in the marriage, and as punishment, he was denied heirs. Laird Archibald was enraged and decided to murder his wife in order that he might wed another.

"Joan was warned o' his nefarious plot by a faithful servant. She determined to leave her ruthless husband, but on the night she planned her escape, she was betrayed, and Archibald locked her in her tower. Lady Joan ran up to the top of the tower, trying to flee from her husband. The night was dark, and a storm broke, raining down hail and sleet upon poor Lady Joan's head. She stood brave to the last in a shimmering white gown."

Though storytelling was not a common entertainment for the men who followed Red Rex, they all leaned forward, eager to hear her. Core did too, for he dearly loved stories.

"The wicked Laird Archibald reached the top o' the tower and advanced upon her. Lightning flashed and glinted off the blade in his hand. His eyes were blood red with the lust for murder. She stood boldly before her killer." Jyne began to act out the story, bringing her words to life. Core stared, utterly transfixed.

"'Dinna do this evil thing ye have in yer heart, husband,' Lady Joan said boldly. 'For if ye do, ye shall most certainly face judgment.' Joan was brave to the end, but the man was half-crazed with the evil that resided in his soul. He pounced upon her like a beast, striking his dagger deep into her chest. She closed her eyes and breathed her last."

Jyne clutched her hands to her breast as if she had been struck down and paused for dramatic effect. His men were silent, eager to hear the lurid tale.

"Suddenly, a flash illuminated the night sky, and an angel from above came down to take the hand of the good and faithful Lady Joan, guiding her soul up to her divine reward. The evil Laird Archibald was not repentant, even in the face of a messenger from heaven, and cursed his wife even in her death.

"'For yer evil deeds,' commanded the angel, 'ye shall be condemned to walk the halls o' this keep forever more.' With a roar of thunder, lightning struck down Laird Archibald. The force of the fiery blast ripped stone from stone, the tower crumbling to the ground.

"After the death of Laird Archibald, strange things were said to happen, for the man, so evil in life, was denied entry to either heaven or hell and was forced to walk the floors of his keep, dragging the chains of his evil deeds, never allowed a moment to rest.

"In time, the story o' this evil laird was forgotten, and the keep was turned into an abbey. Yet on certain nights, the monks still heard the clanks of the ghost's chains and the moans of him begging for a mercy that he will never find. Sometimes, if a wicked man enters this place, the white lady herself will return and touch the man with the cold finger of death. Wanting a more peaceful home, the monks moved away, leaving the haunted keep o' the wicked laird abandoned."

Jyne smiled at her audience, the men utterly rapt in the story that she told. Core himself was amazed and, if truth be told, a little frightened by her tale. He was glad he knew that the supposed history was merely a product of the fertile imagination of Jyne Campbell. He had never been more attracted to a lady.

"I hope ye have enjoyed my tale. Have a good night." Jyne walked serenely out of the great hall, leaving the low rumblings of men behind her.

Highlanders were known to be a superstitious lot. Dealing with ghosts and ghouls was not something to be trifled with. Jyne had chosen her fearsome story well. Still, these were Red Rex's men. They were accustomed to frightening things—*they* were frightening things—and would not easily be scared from a place by a ghost story.

"Well, men," Core said bravely. "I hope ye'll no' let the story o' this keep frighten ye away from yer dreams."

"Is it true, the story she tells?" asked one of the men.

"Aye, it is, lads, or at least that is what I've heard. I dinna wish to tell ye before, for fear ye'd no' come.

But I suppose 'tis only fair ye ken the truth o' this place. Why else would it be so abandoned?"

"But there were folks living here," commented one man.

"Aye, the verra old and the verra young. They have the protection o' the white lady. I think it best ye no' do anything that might antagonize her, ye ken? Well, to bed, men." Core strode up the stairs to his chamber, smiling to himself as he went. He changed back into his regular garments and waited until the appointed time before rapping at her chamber door.

"Ye were amazing!" he pronounced as he walked inside the chamber.

"Did ye hear me?"

"Aye. I hid in the kitchens and heard every word. How did ye create such a tale?"

Jyne smiled at him and shrugged her delicate shoulders. "I do love a good tale. I put together pieces o' several stories. I fear it was quite ghastly."

"All the better. That should put the fear in these bastards. It was completely imagined, ye say?" he asked, just to make sure.

Jyne laughed at him, a merry sound. "I dinna scare ye, did I? Rest assured, it was all a story. I was often sick as a child and spent much time lying on my pallet while others went out to play. I amused myself by making up stories."

"I used to love reading stories when I was young." He stepped closer to Jyne, unable to stay away. "I was not sickly, but there were no other children, so I had to amuse myself. Stories were to me a window into a greater world."

"Aye, that is how I feel too." Her eyes were kind in the candlelight. "Were ye an only child?"

"I was raised in a monastery. The monks fed me, taught me to read, but were not much for games."

"I was the youngest Campbell daughter. I wished to play wi' the others, but I was always too small or too weak. So I made up stories instead."

"I would love to hear those stories." He was completely sincere. He had been drawn to her for her beauty and innate kindness, but a storyteller? That was a true gift.

He realized he was holding her hand and did not even remember taking it. Or maybe she had reached out to him. It felt so natural that he had not noticed.

She gave him a small smile. "Nobody has ever been much interested. Or mayhap I have no' shared them wi' anyone."

"I hope ye might be convinced to share them wi' me."

She looked down, and he suspected a blush. "I do hope it shall scare away the Fire Lord and his men, especially after tonight."

"Is there more to this plan o' yers?" he asked.

Jyne released his hand and rubbed hers together. "Och, aye, there is. Ye'll help me?"

"I'm yers to command." He smiled at her. "What is yer plan?"

"I plan to make a little ghostly racket."

"Ye're a devious one, Jyne Campbell. I like that in a lass."

Fifteen

"DID YE FIND ANY CHAINS?" JYNE WHISPERED TO Cormac. She held wooden shoes in her hands and had a few items in her pocket she felt might serve their ghoulish purpose for the evening. Despite the seriousness of her situation, she could not help but feel a tremble of excitement to be conducting her plan beside her new friend.

More than a friend.

"Aye, some chain mail ought to do," responded Core, and Jyne had to think hard to remember the string of their conversation. She needed to stop falling into a dreamy reverie and focus on their task, or they could both be in danger.

"Verra good. Now we just need to figure out where to hide." Jyne followed Cormac as he slipped noiselessly down the circular stairs of the tower. He moved as silently and as gracefully as a cat. Clearly, he had practice in the art of sneaking about.

"I ken a good place," he said. "Brother Luke told me that there is a passageway between the courtyard and the barracks where the men are sleeping. It was the old passageway of the converts from the abbey days. The workers had begun to seal it up, but I think there is a small space we can crawl through to it."

"Ye talked to Brother Luke?" Jyne was instantly concerned. What if the monk revealed their plan?

Core stopped, his back to her. He paused a moment before turning to her. "Aye, I felt he could be trusted," he said in a hushed tone.

"But he is staying wi' the Fire Lord. What if he reveals us?" Jyne whispered furiously.

"He winna do that. He has no more love for these men than ye do."

Jyne was confused. "But how did ye even meet wi' him? I dinna think he ever left the solar."

"He must have. Otherwise, how could I have seen him?" Core hedged. "We should really get moving before someone hears us."

Jyne followed him into the central courtyard. It was a cold, cloudless night, the white stars scattered across the night sky, sharp and clear. A half-moon hung low in the sky, casting a pale light on the courtyard. All was silent.

Core kept to the shadows along the edge of the building. The raiders had been an unusually quiet and downcast lot without their usual drunken carousing and had turned in early. They had taken up residence in the old cells for the monks, which had been in the process of being renovated. The old dormitory was located on the east side of the old abbey, next to where Jyne's fictional tower had crumbled.

Core turned and pressed a finger to his lips to admonish her to move more quietly. She thought she had been noiseless, but apparently not silent enough for the master before her. He paused for a moment outside the dormitory. No sound could be heard above the occasional snores of the brigands.

Core slowly unlatched the door and moved in without making a sound. Jyne was impressed. She attempted to follow suit but received a sharp look from him when her slipper scuffed along the floor. She shrugged her shoulders to let him know she was doing her best.

They moved forward carefully into the antechamber before the dormitory. There should have been another door leading from the small chamber to the sleeping quarters, but it had been removed, so they were visible if anyone stuck their head out into the main corridor and looked down the hall. Jyne's breath quickened. What would these men do if they found them sneaking into their barracks at night? Torture? Death?

Jyne's pulse raced. It was one thing to plan in the relative safety of her chamber. It was another to actually follow through with real, dangerous men.

Core motioned to her, and she followed him to the corner where some wood planks leaned against the wall. Core kneeled down and crawled behind them and disappeared. Jyne waited for a moment, for there could not have been more than a few feet of space under the planks.

A snort and a grumble from one of the men had Jyne ducking down to crawl behind the planks with Core, space or no space. She was surprised to find, first, there was no Core, and second, there was a hole in the wall. It looked like it had been a passageway at one time and was being closed off. This must have been the passageway of the converts!

Jyne crawled through, having to pull her skirts along, and was able to stand up once she reached the passageway. It was pitch-black, for neither of them had brought a candle. Jyne felt around, trying to determine the dimensions of her location. It appeared to be a long, narrow hall. If she stretched out her arms, she could touch both sides of the cold stone walls.

She waited for a moment but could hear nothing. Where had Core gone? Had he left her there alone? "Core?" she called in a loud whisper.

Suddenly, strong arms wrapped around her. She cried out in surprise, but her mouth was instantly smothered in a demanding kiss. It was either a very affectionate ghost, or Core had returned to kiss her senseless. If that was his goal, he was doing a good job of it. Her body pressed against his, and her ears buzzed with a happy tingling. She knew her brothers would not approve of such goings-on, but alone in the dark with a handsome Highlander—how could she resist?

He broke the kiss, but remained holding her close, whispering so softly in her ear, she could barely hear him. "Ye must remain quiet."

"If I dinna, will ye kiss me again?" she whispered back, but apparently not quietly enough, for he kissed her again.

Her body melted into his, and she savored his kiss, giving back to him what she received. Delighting in the novel experience, she found she enjoyed kissing very much, and when his hands moved up into her hair, she enjoyed that too.

Finally, for no other reason than she was becoming light-headed, either due to the amazing sensations he was creating within her or from lack of breath, their lips parted, and she rested her head on his shoulder, still warm within his embrace. She realized how lonely she had been, living within her brother's castle, serving others. There were always many needs to tend, with many people about, but she had kept a little to herself.

Now she experienced the thrill of the desire of a man. He wanted her. He enjoyed kissing her as much as she enjoyed kissing him. It made her feel powerful and bold. And yet, he had made it clear that when her brother arrived, he would be gone. She feared heartbreak when it came time to part.

With that unsettling thought, she pulled away enough to whisper in his ear, "We should do this."

Core nodded, his cheek rubbing against hers. He released her, and she wrapped her arms around herself against the sudden cold.

The sound of chains being dragged slowly across the stones echoed through the narrow chamber. Core must have been dragging the mail across the floor.

"What's that?" asked one of the warriors on the other side of the wall. "Hey, did anyone hear that?"

"Wheesht!"

"Shut up! Trying to sleep!"

"Wait, I hear something too."

Jyne slipped on her wooden shoes and began to walk slowly, pounding her foot down and then dragging it along the stone floor to create an eerie scraping sound.

"What is that noise?" asked another man.

"'Tis the ghost!" cried a man whose voice sounded like the large Dubh.

"'Tis not a ghost," roared Bran. "'Tis probably some o' the wee ones, playing a prank. Quick as ye can, run around and catch the buggers, and we'll give them what for!"

All the men now seemed to be awake, and the loud pounding of their footsteps could be heard running around to the other side of the wall, while she and Core remained hidden in the passageway in between.

"There's none here!" called a few of the men from the other side of the wall.

"Probably scared them off," called Bran. "Go back to bed."

Jyne took out a broken handle from an iron pot and ran it along the wall, making a horrible scraping noise that might have sounded like a blade being drawn across the wall.

"W-what the hell was that?" cried one man, his voice shaking.

"Who be making that noise?"

"There's none on this side."

"There's none on the other side, either," called back some others as the men walked around both sides of the narrow passage.

"'Tis the ghost!"

"'Tis not a ghost," demanded Bran.

Suddenly, a loud racket was made from the kitchens, with the sound of pots and pans being clanked together.

"It's the tricksters again. Get them!" cried Bran.

With a whoop and a holler, the men raced to the

kitchens, giving Jyne and Core the opportunity to leave their hiding place.

"I hope the lads winna be caught," whispered Jyne as she crawled out of the passage and was helped back to her feet by Core.

"They be swift lads. They ken how to make a racket and race back around to the refectory through the great hall. They'll be fine. Now, scream."

Jyne shrieked with what she hoped was unearthly horror. Core had chosen the place well, for the sound echoed down the halls in both directions, making it difficult to tell where the sound originated.

The men hollered back at the noise from the direction of the kitchens. They sounded scared. Jyne smiled at Core, enjoying herself despite the fear of getting caught. Core returned the smile with a mischievous grin of his own and grabbed her hand as they ran back to the refectory, where they had planned to take refuge among the youngsters, but the door was locked.

"They must have forgotten to leave it open," said Jyne in a hushed tone. The sounds of the warriors were drawing nearer.

"Quick, in here," said Core, and they rushed into the storeroom, closing the door behind them, casting them again into complete darkness.

"Oh," said Jyne, tripping over something. "I canna see a thing."

"Where are ye?" responded Core softly from a different part of the storeroom.

"Over here," replied Jyne, perhaps a bit too loudly, her mind focused on the kisses they had shared. It seemed like another excellent opportunity.

"Och, hide!" whispered Core so softly, she could barely hear him.

"What?"

Before he could answer, the door was wrenched open, and Bran and Dubh stood blocking the doorway, lanterns in hand. Bran was wearing nothing but a kilt, revealing rippling muscles. Dubh, on the other hand, wore nothing but a tunic stretched over his wide belly. The fabric barely covered what it ought, and Jyne turned away quickly, not wanting to see any more of Dubh than she already had.

"There! I told ye this was naught but a trick. That is yer ghost, our unwelcoming hostess," declared Bran. He turned to her with a snarl. "Ye have some explaining to do!"

Jyne quickly scanned the room, but Core was nowhere in sight. He must have been able to find a hiding place in time. Jyne squared her shoulders and faced Bran and Dubh. She had witnessed her brothers get out of tight situations too many times not to know what to do. When caught red-handed—deny and blame!

"*I* need to explain? I was awoken from my slumber by banging and hollering. I came to see what the matter was and heard an unholy cry. It sounded like a woman being murdered, it did. If ye have hurt any o' the elders, I swear I shall see ye face justice for it!"

"We dinna hurt anyone," said a wide-eyed Dubh. "It was her what screamed, the white lady!"

"Dinna let yerself get caught up in a fanciful tale!" demanded Bran. "This witch is the only unholy creature here. She told us all a frightening tale and thinks to make us look the fool by clanking a few chains and screaming like a banshee. Why else do ye ken she's standing in the dark in the storeroom?"

"I was pushed in by ye!" declared Jyne. "I ran down to see what was the matter and then one o' yer men pushed me in here. At least I thought it was one o' yer men. I felt two icy hands on me back."

Dubh shuddered as if he too could feel icy fingers run up his spine.

Bran opened his mouth to speak, but his words were drowned out by three distinct clangs of metal against metal.

"W-what was that?" asked a quivering Dubh.

"'Tis no' me," declared Jyne, for it wasn't. "Ye can see for yerself I dinna make that noise. What is it?" Jyne was impressed that Core had the presence of mind to make some "ghostly" noises to distract them.

Bran shook his head. "She must have someone else wi' her here." He strode boldly into the room, standing on the trapdoor. "Show yerself!"

Three clear clangs sounded again. This time it sounded clearly like it came from underneath. Bran jumped back off of the trapdoor, his hand on his knife. Jyne also backed away from the trapdoor, standing close to Bran and Dubh as if she was more afraid of the ghost than them.

"T-that way leads to the c-crypt," stuttered Dubh.

"'Tis a trick. There is no such thing as ghosties," said Bran, but he sounded much less sure of himself.

They all backed away toward the door.

"She must have one o' the young ones down there," said Bran.

"Are ye daft? None o' the elders or young ones would be out on a night like tonight," declared Jyne, warming to her story. "Try the door where they are. It be locked. That is the only way to stay safe. For this be the one hundredth year since the wicked laird murdered his wife. 'Tis no' safe to roam about."

Dubh dashed out of the storeroom and tried the door to the refectory. "'Tis locked," he called. "I'm going back to my cell and lock the door!" His heavy footsteps ran back to his sleeping quarters, and his loud voice rang out clear. "The only way to stay safe is to lock yerself in. Ye must lock the doors against the ghost o' the white lady!"

Bran scowled at her and shook his head. A slight sound over his shoulder startled him, and he spun around, knife in hand. A large orange cat padded by on soft paws. Bran snarled at her but turned on his heel and stormed back to the barracks.

Jyne stood watching until all was quiet. Core joined her, touching his shoulder to hers. "Thank ye fer helping me," she said, gently leaning into him.

Before Core could speak, three distinct tones of metal on metal came from the storeroom.

"What was that?" Jyne gasped.

Core slammed the door of the storeroom shut and dragged her out into the pale moonlight of the courtyard. "I dinna ken. There are no true ghosts here, are there?"

"I...I dinna ken."

"I'll walk ye back to yer chamber," said Core.

"Aye, thank ye." She suddenly wished to be back in her own chamber again, where it was safe.

It was hard to be anything but happy when Core held her hand in his, but what had made that sound? She recalled the matron had said she also heard noises in the night.

Was the abbey actually haunted? A shiver crept down her spine until Core wrapped an arm around her and pulled her close. She breathed deeply. Whatever enemy she faced, at least she did not face it alone.

Sixteen

THE NEXT MORNING, CORE WOKE AFTER A DEEP SLEEP. Sleep in which a certain Highland lass was featured prominently. Putting fear into his father's men, who had belittled and threatened him since his arrival in their midst, was more rewarding than he had anticipated, and he slept better than he had in months. He still had situations to resolve, but he had already accomplished more than he expected, so he gave himself leave to feel optimistic.

"Things went well?" asked Brother Luke in a tone that conveyed disapproval.

"Aye," said Core, belting on his great plaid. "Dubh was terrified. Bran was too, but he'd rather face a thousand banshees than admit it."

"I understand the goal of Lady Jyne was to frighten off the men. Have they left?"

"'Course not. The men o' Red Rex winna turn tail just because of a wee little ghost."

"Then it was a doomed exercise from the start." Brother Luke turned back to the scroll, his feelings on the matter clear.

"They winna leave, but we've put the fear in them."

"I understand how scaring your own men may bolster your status, but how does this help the objective of finding a treasure to prevent the destruction of irreplaceable texts and the wanton murder of dozens of God's holy men?"

The monk's words were like ice water dumped on Core's head. He turned to Brother Luke slowly. "At least I am trying to do something. All ye've done since we got here is hide in this solar and read Aristotle. I would'na be in this mess if ye had'na gotten yerself caught and I was forced to make up a lie to prevent ye from being killed. All this trouble and pain o' coming here is to try to save yer precious monastery. If ye ken a better way to do it, I wish ye'd get off yer arse and get to it!"

Brother Luke set down his scroll and slowly stood. He stared at Core, his face inscrutable.

"Come to think of it, ye ne'er even thanked me for saving yer life, ye ungrateful sod," accused Core, giving voice to his anger and his frustration at the sad truth that he was no closer to finding a solution to their problem. "I should've chopped yer head off and saved myself all this bother!"

Cormac stormed to the door and wrenched it open.

"Cormac," said Brother Luke. "Thank you."

Cormac paused in the doorway, then stepped back into the solar and closed the door. It was not what he was expecting to hear.

"There is truth in what you say," continued Luke. "I hope I am not beyond accepting rebuke if I am in the wrong, even if it comes from an unlikely source."

Even in Luke's concession, there were little barbs.

"Well, thank ye for that. Just remembered I'm Cormac, so I need to go out the window." Core walked to the window and opened the shutters to climb down the outside of the tower so his true identity would be kept secret from Jyne.

Core could no longer meet Brother Luke's eyes. He had felt for a moment that he had the upper hand, but it was difficult to feel morally superior when you were sneaking out a window.

"*Qui diligit disciplinam diligit scientiam qui autem odit increpationes insipiens est,*" quoted the monk with the ease of a man who had studied the scriptures his whole life.

Unfortunately for Core's peace of mind, he had been raised by monks to be fluent in many languages, and this was not the first time that particular verse from Proverbs had been quoted to him. He could easily translate the verse in his head, *Whoso loveth instruction loveth knowledge: but he that hateth reproof is brutish.*

The good brother had just called him stupid. Maybe Luke was right too. But unlike the virtuous monk, Core had no desire to accept rebuke and change his ways.

Core climbed down the ivy vines as quickly as he could and strode around the keep to the kitchens, where he hoped to find Jyne. As he walked, he remembered another chore he must do, and hoped Jyne would actually not be present, for it would be easier to complete without her asking questions.

He entered the back door to the kitchens with some caution. Cook bustled about, with several children attempting to assist but more often than not getting in the old woman's way. Jyne was nowhere to be seen.

"I need a ration o' food, if ye please," he said.

"Help yerself, laddie," said Cook, trying to show a young girl how to prepare beans. "Stew's in the pot, trenchers are on the sill, and ale is in the cask."

Core prepared a generous portion and snuck out the side door leading to the courtyard. He needed to get to the storeroom, preferably without being seen. Fortunately for his interest in stealth, the courtyard was filled with the thick Highland fog that settled heavily in the low places in the morning. From what he could tell, the courtyard was deserted. Most of his men were either still sleeping after the long night or too afraid to leave their cells.

Core moved quickly across the courtyard, the mist swirling around the edges of his kilt as he strode through the thick haze. He reached the other side of the courtyard, relieved to have met no one. His hand was on the latch to the storeroom when a familiar voice bade him stop.

"Core!" Jyne emerged from the refectory with light, quick movements and warm eyes. She glanced around to ensure that they could not be overheard and came up close beside him. She looked up at him with a seductive smile that made his heart stutter. "Thank ye for last night."

Core's mouth went dry. He wondered what part of last night she was thanking him for. He hoped she appreciated the way their bodies had melted into each other and their kisses had burned like sweet fire on their lips.

Core forgot to respond. He possibly forgot his own name.

"Why are ye taking food into the storeroom?" she asked, as if just noticing what he carried in his hand.

Core cursed himself for giving her a moment to be observant. "This is some food," he replied, his mind spinning to devise a plausible rationale. "I took note o' one o' the elders who is too frail to come to the table, so I am taking him some food." More lies.

"Ye're truly a kind man, Cormac. Och, but what am I doing, keeping ye from yer errand o' mercy. Here, let me help carry this for ye. I can speak with the elder and see if he needs any other care."

"Nay!" That would not do at all. "Forgive me, but Cook had need for ye in the kitchen. 'Tis difficult to teach the young ones."

"It is. Poor Cook is trying to entertain them, but 'tis hard for the young ones no' to run about. We dare no' let them go for fear they would antagonize one o' the warriors."

"Mayhap I can help?" asked Cormac.

"I warrant ye're rather obligated after last night." Jyne came closer and looked up at him through her long eyelashes in a way that made his temperature rise. There was precious little he could do about it, though, while holding the food.

"I shall do my utmost."

"See that ye do!" Jyne turned to walk away, then twirled back to him and kissed him on the cheek. Before he could respond, she scampered off, skipping across the cobblestones of the courtyard.

Core smiled after her, watching her leave, until another figure came into view. The black-robed monk. Seeing him reminded Core of everything he so desperately wanted to forget. With a grumble, Core turned back to his work.

Core entered the storeroom and walked to the trapdoor in the wooden floor. He had worried at first that someone would open the door and explore the crypt, but he was sure after last night none would do so now.

He carefully climbed down the ladder, holding the trencher and a crock of ale. A lantern illuminated the cavern with a pale light. The cave was hewn into the rock, crystals twinkling in the light of his lantern. Core followed a passage to the left, revealing an iron lattice and a locked iron gate. A man stood on the other side, glaring at him.

The large, bearded man was the runner Core had saved from his men when he took the abbey. Locking the man in the crypt seemed like the best thing to do with him. Over the past few days, Core had fed him and gotten to know some basics about the man. His name was Donnach. And the Campbell warrior intended to kill him.

"Care for some food? The stew smells good," said Core mildly.

"Go to hell, ye bloody bastard," snarled Donnach. "If ye hurt her, touch her in any way, I shall rip yer head off yer skinny body and dine on yer liver."

Cormac had heard much coarse language in his life and took the man's ire in stride. He had locked the man in the abbey crypt, so Donnach was justified in his anger. Core placed the food within reach of the man and stepped back. Donnach glared at him with murder in his eyes, but grabbed the food and drink through the bars of his prison and ate hungrily.

"I must thank ye for last night. Ye had the entire keep believing there are ghosts down here," said Cormac, still pleased with how things had transpired.

"Saw it off," grumbled Donnach.

"Ye have enough candles? Are ye warm enough?" asked Core.

"Let. Me. Out." Donnach spat out the words. Captivity did not agree with him.

"I would like to, and I tell ye the truth, I plan to. Trouble is, ye ken who I am, and it all gets terribly complicated. Besides, I need yer help."

"Why would I do anything to help ye?"

"Because by helping me, ye help yerself and others too. Allow me to tell ye my troubles, and then see for yerself if ye're willing to lend yer aid."

Donnach shrugged. "I have nowhere to go."

"Red Rex is under the impression that there is treasure here at Kinoch Abbey. I have been sent to retrieve it. If I dinna return wi' something, Rex will kill all the monks at the nearby monastery. If I can find a treasure of some sort, all my men and I will leave ye and Lady Jyne in peace."

"Why would Red Rex believe there be treasure here?" asked Donnach.

"Because Cormac told him that lie to save my life." Brother Luke stepped forward.

"Brother Luke?" Core was not sure why the monk had followed him to the crypt.

"Ye were right about another thing," Luke admitted to Cormac. "I need to get off my...*arse* and do something to help. What can I do?"

"I was going to ask Donnach to search the crypt to

see if there be anything within that might serve as a treasure. I've heard the caverns go back a ways."

"They do. I confess, I have never been eager to explore this place, but I must do what I can to save my friends." The monk squared his shoulders. "Let me in."

"Ye want him to lock ye in here wi' me?" Donnach asked the monk, the lines of a frown etched deep on his forehead.

"I cannot stand by and do nothing while the brothers' lives are at risk."

Donnach stepped back, away from the gate, and Core unlocked it, allowing Luke to enter. He locked the gate again, sealing the men in the tomb. He felt like a veritable lout to do so, but he knew if he didn't, Donnach would flee, and that would be disastrous for him.

Luke took a candle and nodded to Core and Donnach with a grim expression. He turned and walked boldly into the dark passage leading to the caverns that contained the crypt.

Donnach growled at Cormac, but grabbed a candle and followed the monk. "If it must be, I will see it done."

"Thank ye," said Core, not knowing what else to say. His effort earned him an over-the-shoulder glare from Donnach.

Core returned to the storeroom, unsure about his own response. He should have been pleased, for now he had two men—men he trusted more than his own warriors—looking for something that could pass for a treasure while he spent the afternoon with Jyne. He should have been happy.

Brother Luke's admonishment against lying still rung in his ears. He was playing Jyne false. Sooner or later, she would discover the truth. Core cleared his throat. He was a ruthless warlord, just like his father wished. The thought weighed heavy on his soul.

Seventeen

HER PLAN TO SCARE OFF THE FIRE LORD AND HIS ill-kempt followers had not worked, but Jyne was not as disappointed as she thought she should be. In truth, she was not ready for her time with Cormac to end. As long as they fought against the Fire Lord and his brigands, they were together. Once her brothers arrived and they left, so would Cormac. And she wasn't ready to say good-bye.

When she found Cook, the elderly matron insisted she did not need help, but Jyne could easily see that the burden of watching the wee ones and trying to get meals on the table was a taxing one. Jyne felt something pulling at her skirts and looked down into the wide eyes of Ina.

Jyne crouched down to her level. "How are ye doing, my wee friend?"

Ina said nothing but put her small hand on Jyne's cheek and sighed.

"Have those bad men frightened ye?"

Ina nodded. It broke Jyne's heart. She must find a way to protect these wee ones. She suddenly remembered something Cormac had said to her. Maybe if she could not get the brigands to leave, she could get the children somewhere safe.

"Here, stay with Cook," said Jyne, transferring Ina's small, tight fist from her skirt to Cook's. She needed to talk to Core. She entered the courtyard, mist swirling around her pale blue gown as she walked.

"There she is! It's her!" yelled a voice in the mist.

Jyne froze, unsure who had spoken.

"Come here, ye big coward. Here is yer ghost. 'Tis only our ghost story–telling hostess." Bran emerged from the swirling mist, his eyes accusing, pulling Dubh, his large companion, along behind him.

She had been instantly frightened when she saw the men, but something in the warrior's dismissive tone struck deep. How many times had she been disregarded and discounted, even by her own family? She squared her shoulders and stood up straighter. "Did ye see the White Lady?" she asked Dubh, purposefully playing into his fears.

"Aye—" Whatever he was going to say was cut off by a sharp jab in the ribs from Bran.

"I will ask ye now," demanded Bran, glaring at Jyne, "to tell this fool that all yer nonsense last night o' the ghost was merely a child's story."

She had gotten to them. She suppressed a smile and instead pasted on what she hoped was a look of pure innocence. "I dinna ken if it be real or no'. I wasna here a hundred years ago. Mayhap the ghost has moved on."

"But last night—" Dubh received another harsh jab.

"There is no such thing as ghosts!" thundered Bran.

"But what o' Robert the Bruce?" asked Jyne. "I ken many who swear they've seen him riding at night."

"Aye, so I've heard tell," agreed Dubh. "He roams the land because his dying wish was that his heart be taken to the Holy Land and buried in Jerusalem."

"But Lord Douglas died trying, and Bruce's heart was taken back to Scotland," said Jyne, continuing the well-known story. Every child in Scotland knew the tale.

"Where 'tis buried under the high altar at Melrose Abbey," continued Dubh.

"And now the Bruce canna rest, wi' his dying wish left unfulfilled, and rides the moors at night!" Jyne finished the story. It was strange that she had found common ground with this thief of such bulbous proportions.

Bran glowered at both of them, but did not refute the story. It was so well-known and so widely believed, it would have been pointless of him to do so.

"'Tis too bad the postern gate has been destroyed," sighed Jyne, thinking fast. "I would sleep better knowing that the wall around us is not breached. We have enough to worry ourselves here wi'out any new ghosties roaming in."

"Aye, we should fix the gate, we should!" Dubh bounded off, calling for men to help him in the process. Bran glowered at her, but turned and stormed away.

Jyne smiled after him, pleased with how she had been able to hold her ground. A cold hand touching hers made her jump.

"Are they gone?" Ina held Jyne's hand in her icy one.

Jyne breathed a sigh of relief. Perhaps she also was being affected by her own imagination. "Aye, they've gone. But yer hands are like ice. Now go back to the kitchens and get warm." Jyne ushered Ina back and continued her quest to find Core. They must get the children someplace safe.

❧

Cormac returned from the caverns feeling distinctly unsettled. He had not gone far into the courtyard before he met Jyne. They snuck back to talk alone in the storeroom.

"Good morn to ye again." Jyne gave him a wide smile that made his toes curl in his boots. "I've been thinking on how we can get the wee ones to safety. Ye said ye knew a place we could go to stay safe from the warriors. Could we take the young ones there instead?"

"A place to go?" Cormac was confused.

"The first night, ye wished to take me away."

He still did. "Aye, there be a few abandoned crofters' huts a few miles away."

"Could the bairns stay there?"

Core considered it for a moment. "Would be tight, but aye, they could."

"Would these men let them go?"

That was another question. Sometimes Red Rex liked to keep hostages; sometimes he cared not. "I doubt they would notice, as long as there were still enough people left to wait upon them."

Jyne shook her head. "Those bastards."

Cormac smiled at such a word emerging from such sweet lips. "Be best to leave wi'out drawing attention. Sneaking out the postern gate, or what's left of it, should'na be a problem."

"Och, it may be. I convinced Dubh to repair it to keep out the ghosties."

"Ye did?" Core was impressed. Jyne was not one to be underestimated. "Well now, let me think on this. Gather the people, and we'll meet in the kitchens after the main meal."

He watched Jyne disappear into the mist of the courtyard and thought hard on how to make Jyne's wishes come true as he dashed away to don his Fire Lord attire once more.

A short time later, he had donned the bearskin robe and idiot horned helmet and faced the men in the great hall. "I heard some o' ye are afeared o' a little ghost. Cowards!" he thundered. Or at least he tried to. His voice did not quite carry as his father's did. Still, he was attempting to resemble his father as best he could.

"Aye, there is no such thing as ghosts," chimed in Bran.

Core turned on the man. "No such thing as ghosts? Are ye daft? Why, even Red Rex has seen them. But he's not afeared o' them. Nay, them ghosties are afeared of *him*!"

Some in the hall laughed, and Cormac felt as though he was finally being accepted as one of them, maybe even as their leader.

"We need some o' ye to go on a hunt," commanded Core. "We need meat to fill our bellies, since we've eaten through the stores. We need others to join Dubh to repair the gate."

"And what o' this treasure we were sent here to retrieve?" demanded Bran.

Core took Bran aside, though he was careful to

speak close enough that others could hear him. "I may ken where the treasure is. I dinna want to announce it to all the men, because the less who know where it is, the better. I found some clues that it is hidden near a tree wi' two trunks at the far side o' this valley."

"Ye want us to search for it?" asked Bran.

"Nay, let me research it a bit more. No need to race out. I will examine the scrolls and let ye know if it's worth the effort."

Bran had a greedy glint in his eye that told Core that soon, many of the men would be searching the valley several miles in the opposite direction of where he wished to take Jyne and the children.

"Well, I shall be in my chamber should anyone wish to consult wi' me." He doubted anyone would. He marched off to his solar, which commanded a fine view of the valley before him, and watched in satisfaction as small groups of men left the keep, walking or sometimes riding to the other end of the valley. When most of the men had left as the gossip spread, Core knew it was time to act.

A few minutes later, he had shed the trappings of the evil warlord and stood in the doorway of the kitchen. He had brought his bow and a quiver of arrows for the trip, just in case.

Jyne was surrounded by children, who all seemed to be talking to her at once. She was answering them patiently and responding to every cry for attention, every bumped knee, every plea for assistance. He paused a moment just to watch her.

She was dressed in a pale blue kirtle with a cream sleeveless surcoat. There was nothing particularly extraordinary about her gown or her simple linen head covering, but he could not take his eyes from her. Her bright eyes gleamed blue, and her pink lips tempted him to take another taste.

She caught him from the corner of her eye and turned toward him, a smile spreading slowly across her face. Her eyes warmed in a manner he hoped was for him alone. Lady Jyne Campbell was simply the most beautiful lass he had ever met.

Except she was a lady.

And he was the son of a warlord.

"We should get moving," said Core gruffly to hide the disappointment of his thoughts. "There are some abandoned crofters' huts a few miles away. I'm guessing the occupants moved along wi' the monks when they left."

"Verra good. Some o' the women will go wi' the young ones," replied Jyne.

"I wish ye would stay there too. This is no place for ye," said Core, stepping near to speak quietly.

Jyne shook her head as he knew she would do. "Kinoch Abbey is under my protection. My place is here."

"I dinna wish for ye to be in danger. 'Tis no' good for my constitution."

Jyne laughed. "Yer constitution?"

"Aye, for my heart pounds to see ye at risk." He leaned close and spoke softly in her ear. "In truth, my heart pounds whenever ye're near."

"Pray tell, why might that be?" she asked, though her heightened color told him she knew very well what he meant.

"I wish to show ye, but ye're surrounded by miniature chaperones."

Jyne laughed again and gestured to the children. "Ah, my wee ones. They shall keep me safe from untoward advances."

"But on the way home…" Core returned her smile. They might have much company for now, but on the return trip, they would be alone to do as they pleased. And it would please him greatly to do a lot of it.

"On the way home, ye may have to watch ycrself, lest I do something untoward," said Jyne with a saucy grin.

"By the saints, lass, I do hope that's a promise!"

They rounded up the children and several of the matrons, along with baskets of provisions to tide them over until, hopefully, a rescue could be mounted. Alasdair Ranald came on his skinny legs to wish them Godspeed.

Core snuck ahead to ensure that their path was clear. The inner courtyard was empty, and he motioned for everyone to follow him. He hoped to get the children out of the keep without notice, for hostages were not often let go, due to their occasional usefulness. Besides, getting caught in front of Jyne would lead to conversations that would most certainly reveal him.

He peeked out of the main door to the outer ward. It was mostly empty, but gate guards were still at their posts.

"How are we going to get past?" asked Jyne in a low voice. She had walked up beside him and was standing so close, he had to force himself to focus on the meaning of her words instead of the overpowering desire to kiss her once more.

He shook his head, trying to devise a plan. The gates

were open, since most of the keep was on the other side of the valley. Getting out was not a problem. Getting out without being seen was another thing altogether.

"They seem interested in something," noted Jyne.

Cormac noticed it too. While the gate guards had not abandoned their post, they were staring out toward the far end of the valley. No doubt they had heard word of the treasure, and though they remained on duty, their attention was fixed several miles away.

He smiled at Jyne. "If we can be verra quiet, I have a plan."

A few minutes later, they were quietly edging their way out the main gate, hugging the wall of Kinoch Abbey literally under the noses of the guards. As long as the children remained quiet and the guards remained focused on the other side of the valley, they could pass unseen. Core's heart pounded, for it was not just a matter of staying quiet himself; he had to depend on over a dozen bairns to keep quiet as well. Jyne had been clever, though, and turned it into a game to see who could be the quietest.

Slowly, cautiously, they slid along the wall. Core was accustomed to being quiet, but the children and matrons were not. Several times, a scrape or rustle sounded like a ringing gong in his ears, and he feared the guards would look down. The wind was brisk, however, and provided some background noise to cover their exit. They were almost out of sight when one of the children tripped and fell with a splat. There was no way the guards could not have heard that.

In an instant, Core threw hard a rock he had been carrying, far and fast. It bounced off several boulders on the other side of the guards, drawing their attention. Jyne rushed over and picked up the tot before he could cry. Core motioned for everyone to run, and they scampered up the hill on the side of the abbey. Once they were on the far side and out of sight of Kinoch, Core breathed a sigh of relief.

"Ye did it!" Jyne set down the child and placed a hand on her chest, breathing deeply.

"*We* did it," he returned with a smile.

They quickly climbed a wooded hill out of the valley to some wild fields beyond. Once they were out of sight of the abbey, Core began to enjoy himself. He walked beside Jyne on a narrow path through the swaying purple heather. The mist had finally dissipated, leaving a sunny day in the Highlands. The sky was a bright blue, but it was nothing compared to the fire he saw in Jyne's eyes.

The children, having been admonished every minute of every day since the keep was taken to remain still and silent to avoid raising the ire of the brigands, were happy to run about. They screeched and ran ahead or frolicked in the heather. The matrons who cared for them tried to run after them, calling out admonishments that went largely unheeded.

One child, however, seemed to be permanently attached to Jyne's skirts. Jyne introduced the child to Core. "This is Ina."

"Hello, Ina," said Core. He had always interacted with adults and felt awkward around children. He was not sure how to talk to little people, though he could see that her small legs were not well equipped for the journey. "Would ye care for a ride, Miss Ina?"

The child peeked at him with wide eyes from behind Jyne's skirts. She looked up at Jyne, then toddled toward him with both arms upraised. He picked up the tot, and she clasped her arms around him and snuggled her head against his neck. He was surprised, and his face must have shown it, for Jyne laughed out loud.

"Ye're no' accustomed to wee bairns, are ye?"

"Nay. Am I doing it wrong?"

"Ye're doing verra well indeed. I hope you like yer new friend, for she winna let ye go easily." Jyne smiled, and that made the effort worth it, though in truth, he did not mind the snuggling tot. The day was a fine one, giving him hope. He was very glad to have the young ones removed from Kinoch, for now he had one less thing to worry about protecting.

"Do tell me more about yerself," said Jyne, plucking a strand of heather and running her hand along the tops of bushes. "I hardly ken much o' ye, except that ye roam the moors, looking for people to rescue."

"Ye're correct, m'lady. My sad job is to roam and assist as I may be needed."

This drew another smile from Jyne. "And I can ne'er tell ye how grateful I am to ye. But what o' yer clan? What were ye doing out in the moors?"

Core was ready for this question. He knew she would eventually ask about his history and had a ready answer. "I was on my way to a position with the Steward of Scotland. I was to work as a translator and scribe." It was the life Core wanted.

"That sounds fascinating. What clan do ye hail from? They must be verra proud."

Core gave her a tight smile. He thought it would be easier to lie to her. Instead, he had a growing tightness around his chest. "I am from the clan…" He had a story ready. It was a good one too. He was the son of a wealthy merchant and was an honorable man, but when he looked into Jyne's beautiful, trusting eyes, he found he could not continue. She was more than just a bonnie lass; she was a lady he respected, a lady he liked a little too much for his own good.

"What is wrong?" asked Jyne, confused by his silence.

"Och, what's wrong is I'm a base creature that doesna deserve to speak to ye."

"Whatever do ye mean?" A little crease formed on her forehead.

"I have studied, and I do wish to be a scribe, but I have no position."

"'Tis naught to be ashamed of. Many a young man needs to find his footing before making his way in the world. I warrant the Steward would be happy to hire ye."

"Nay." Cormac sighed. "None will ever hire me. No' wi' my family connections." Core shook his head. The Laird MacLean had banished Red Rex and all his descendants forevermore from the clan. Core had been about six years old when his clan had forever rejected him.

"But that is unfair! Why punish ye for yer clan?"

"Not my clan, my father to be exact. He has, I fear, embraced a sinful path. Ye asked for my clan, but unfortunately, I have none to tell ye, for my father and all his kin were banished." Core had not wished to see her face when he made his confession. Now he stole a look and was relieved to see something of compassion in her eyes. It gave him reason to hope.

"So ye see," he continued, "ye find me in between clans at the moment."

Jyne said nothing but reached out and briefly touched his shoulder as they continued to walk on the dirt path through the heather. It was more compassion than he had expected. It was more compassion than he deserved.

"I'm sure when my brother, Laird Campbell, hears what ye've done to protect me and the vulnerable ones, he will offer ye the opportunity to swear yer allegiance and become a member of clan Campbell." Jyne spoke with confidence.

He stifled a sigh, because he knew how wrong she was.

They walked a little farther before Jyne asked one more question. "Will ye no' tell me who yer father is?"

"Would it matter to ye what his name might be?" he hedged.

"Nay. I shall no' judge ye for the sins of another."

"If only the world felt as ye do," Cormac said with a sigh. "And yet, if ye met my father, ye would no' think so highly of me."

"Ye winna trust me wi' the name o' yer sire?" she asked softly.

"Ye'd think less o' me."

"Nay, I would'na," she insisted.

"If it truly matters to ye not, then I ask that ye give me leave no' to tell ye."

Jyne frowned, but shrugged her shoulders. "As ye wish, but I hope someday ye will trust me wi' yer name."

"Here we are. The abandoned huts I found are just over this rise," Core said, changing the subject. He wanted to tell her, wanted to be honest with her. He wanted to believe she would understand. But he knew better. She would hate him, and he could not bear the thought.

They had come upon three short huts, half built into the ground. They were modest dwellings at best, but it was a safer place for children than a keep inhabited by murderers and thieves.

"Come now, children, let us prepare these lovely new homes for ye." Jyne marched off and quickly and efficiently organized the children and matrons into groups for each hut, managing sleeping arrangements and dividing food stores appropriately. Core returned his new little friend to the ground. She patted him on the cheek before she let go and then ran off to join the others.

A commotion down the road caught his attention. A lady was riding hard in their direction, with a man in close pursuit.

"Everyone stay inside," commanded Jyne, noting the riders coming toward them fast. "What is that?" she asked, coming to stand beside him.

"I dinna ken…wait…" Recognition flashed through him as the riders drew close enough to make out their faces. "Get in a hut. I'll deal wi' this."

"Ye are always one to rescue strangers," said Jyne warmly.

"Not in this case," said Core, grabbing his bow and drawing an arrow. "That is my sister."

Eighteen

Sister? Cormac had a sister?

Despite Jyne's reassurances that nothing could diminish her positive regard for him, Cormac's confession that he had an unsavory character for a father planted within her a seed of doubt. What sort of man could be so terrible his mere existence would cause Cormac to feel he could never find work as a scribe? He was obviously well-educated, and thus, must have come from some family of means.

Truth was, she did not know much about Cormac… except that he had certainly gone out of his way to render assistance to her. Without him, she might still be stuck in a bog. With the appearance of a sister, Jyne felt sure she could learn more about her enigmatic helper.

"Get back!" commanded Cormac, motioning for her to hide in one of the huts with the children. She stepped back, but would not hide the way she might have done even a few days ago. No, she was learning to hold her ground.

Cormac ran out to the dirt road and nocked an arrow. He stood to the side and allowed the lady to pass, then blocked the narrow road and drew on the approaching man. "Stay back, or I will let fly!"

Jyne's heart swelled as she watched Cormac in action. Truth was, she did not care who he was or where he was from. She knew in her heart he was a good man. He was the man for her.

The man slowed but did not stop. "Stand aside, or I'll run ye down!"

"I said stop!" commanded Core.

"And I said move aside, ye whelp! Who do ye think ye be, giving orders to me!" The man spurred his charger as if he was going to run Core down.

Quick as lightning, Core let loose an arrow that flew with precision, taking off the man's cap in flight.

"Whaaa?" The man pulled up hard on the reins and felt his bare head where his tam used to be.

Core nocked another arrow and drew back on his bow. "Next one goes between yer eyes."

"Hold up there. Hold up." The man came to a stop before Cormac. "Ye needn't be that way about it. I was just doing what I was told, is all."

"Ye were trying to take me to hell!" yelled Cormac's sister on horseback, who had circled around and was now standing behind her brother. She was a beauty of a girl, with smooth, pale skin and flashing eyes. She looked to be in her late teens and had a wild appearance, with bright red hair flowing free. Jyne assumed she must have lost her veil and hairpins in flight.

"I was taking ye to yer future husband," roared the man.

"I'll not go! I'll ne'er wed that bastard!" shouted the fiery-haired lady.

"Not for me to say, is it?" the man appealed to Cormac. "Yer father arranged the marriage."

"Ye mean my father sold me to the highest bidder!" shouted Cormac's sister. "How much in gold was I worth, eh?"

"It wasna my doing. I canna say I like the man either, but it's no' my concern. I'm just doing as I'm told, I am," complained the man.

"I understand," Cormac said, lowering his bow. "Ye've done yer best, but I'll take it from here."

The man scratched his bald head. "But I was told to take her to her husband. The gold arrived yesterday. She's supposed to be his now."

"I ken what needs to be done," said Cormac softly.

"But what will I tell yer father?" asked the man.

"Tell him to take himself to hell!" screamed Core's sister.

"I canna say that," objected the man with true fear in his eyes.

"Tell him I met ye on the road and will take care of what needs to be done," said Cormac. "And ye might wish to take yer time in going back. Here's a coin for ye. If ye keep going down this road, in a few days' time, ye'll come to a tournament. Ye'll no doubt find many amusements." Core walked to where the man's tam was pinned to the ground by the arrow and gave it back.

"Well now," said the man, staring at the coin and his cap in his hands. "Well now," he repeated and put on his cap. "That sounds verra good. That's right nice o' ye, Cormac. I dinna care what they say about ye, I think ye're all right, always have." He tipped his hat and continued riding down the road, whistling a tune.

"Ye'll no' take me to that devil man, will ye?" asked the flame-haired lass as Cormac helped her to dismount.

"Nay," he sighed.

"I was trying to find ye. I knew ye'd help," said his sister.

"Aye, but ye've come at a difficult time."

"What kind o' difficult time? It canna be worse than being forced to marry that craven, boil-brained codpiece. Who is that?"

"Aye…well…Lady Jyne, please allow me to introduce my sister, Breanna," said Cormac in a slightly strangled voice.

"*Lady* Jyne?" Both of Breanna's eyebrows went up.

"Good day," said Jyne, stepping forward. "Unfortunately, my dower lands and keep have been overtaken by a vicious warlord who calls himself the Fire Lord. Cormac has been helping us considerably."

Cormac's sister tilted her head slightly to one side. "Fire Lord?"

"He is the son of Red Rex," explained Jyne.

Breanna opened her mouth to speak, but Cormac responded first. "Aye, ye've had yerself a trying time. Please take a moment to quiet yerself." He spoke fast, taking his sister by the elbow and leading her away, drowning out whatever she was about to say. He glanced back at Jyne. "I think we should leave, go back to Kinoch. Well, we should get moving. Canna stand around. M'lady, why do ye no' say yer farewells to the elders and bairns, and I'll get Breanna settled."

"Aye, that is verra considerate o' ye," said Jyne. "I am pleased to meet ye, Breanna."

Jyne walked back to say her farewells to the matrons and the young ones, giving Ina a warm hug. Yet all the while, her attention was captured by Cormac and the sudden emergence of a sister. Whatever answers about his past Core was reluctant to share, she hoped Breanna would be more forthcoming. Their father must surely be a dreadful man. She felt sorry for them to have suffered such a sire.

Jyne attempted to attend to what an elder matron was saying, probably thanking her for seeing to their safety, but she could not help but continue to glance at Core and his sister, who were standing a bit away, having a conversation in fierce whispers. They appeared to be fighting about something. It seemed Cormac wished her to do something, for his was a pleading look, while Breanna frowned and shook her head. Were they disagreeing about where Breanna should go now? Surely, Core would not be trying to persuade his sister to marry a man who would buy her for gold.

Jyne rushed through her good-byes and attempted to nonchalantly move close enough to hear what the siblings were saying to each other without appearing to be eavesdropping, which of course she was.

"Please, Breanna, 'tis for the best for us," Core whispered to his sister.

"Nay, 'tis the best for ye. I'll no' be a party to it," responded Breanna.

"I canna help ye if ye dinna help me."

"But…" Breanna's voice lowered, and Jyne could not hear the rest.

Core answered in a low rumble. Jyne walked to the

horse and pretended to be interested in petting the soft nose, while she strained to hear what was said next.

"But I've got nowhere else to go!" said Breanna clearly.

"Wheesht!" hushed Core, saying something else too softly for Jyne to hear.

"Fine then, have yer own way," said Breanna in a disgusted tone.

"Ah, Lady Jyne, I dinna see ye there," said Core, looking in her direction and giving her a tense smile. "We should get back to Kinoch Abbey. Why do ye no' ride? I'm sure my sister would like to walk instead."

Breanna made an incensed gasp.

"Nay, I would'na dream o' taking yer sister's horse. We Campbells are a sturdy lot. I can walk back fine."

"Campbell?" Breanna appeared to choke on the name. "Ye're Lady Jyne *Campbell?*"

"Aye, my brother is the Laird Campbell."

"Och…Cormac…" She shook her head at her brother.

"Would ye no' like to walk, Breanna?" asked Core with a pointed look.

"Aye, take the mount, m'lady, I insist. I much prefer to walk." With that, Breanna took off down the road on foot in the direction of the abbey.

Jyne ended up on horseback, feeling rather awkward riding slowly down the path after Breanna and Cormac. Neither one turned to speak to her, and they proceeded in uncomfortable silence back to Kinoch. When they were close enough to see the structure, they took care to remain hidden behind some thick brush. Cormac helped Jyne dismount, his hands lingering on her waist. Her eyes met his.

Breanna cleared her throat, and Core stepped away.

"Ye two keep out of sight, I'll go see if it is safe to proceed. I'll take yer mount, and if it's clear, I'll put him in the stables. We'll hope nobody bothers to count." Core snuck ahead to see if they could return safely without drawing the attention of the ruffians.

This was Jyne's chance to talk to Cormac's sister. But what should she say?

"I am sorry ye're in such a difficult position," began Jyne.

Breanna looked around as if she was not sure Jyne could be addressing her.

"I mean to be betrothed to a man o' poor character."

"Betrothed?" Breanna gave a snort. "More like sold. That ruttish, flea-bitten boar-pig!"

Jyne blinked at her colorful turn of phrase. "I am sure Cormac will protect ye."

Breanna slowly shook her head. "Seems to me, Core's got his hands full just protecting himself."

"He has certainly tried to protect these poor people here."

Breanna stared at her, her expression inscrutable. "He tries to do right, I'll give him that, but he often ends up in the suds. Dinna judge him too harshly, m'lady."

"Why would I judge him? He has been nothing but kind and has gone out o' his way to extend to us assistance in our time o' need. He did share that his father is...of poor moral character."

"Our father is the verra devil, he is."

"I am sorry for ye." Jyne truly was. Her own father had died when she was young, but he had earned the reputation of being a very good man and had raised good children. Her eldest brother always strived to do right by the clan. She could not imagine having parents whom she could not admire and respect.

"Come wi' me," gasped Core, running up to them. He appeared to have sprinted back to them. "The postern gate is clear."

They moved quickly back through the gate, which to Jyne's satisfaction was in the process of being repaired. Core led them a roundabout route back to the base of her tower.

"Ye go back to yer chamber, quick now, and stay safe," said Core in a whisper. "I'll take Breanna to the refectory, where she can hide with the elders."

"Nay, would she no' be safer to stay wi' me? I should be glad to welcome her," pronounced Jyne.

"Nay!" Core almost shouted. "I mean," he amended, lowering his voice, "I would'na wish to inconvenience ye."

"It would no' be an inconvenience. 'Tis the least I can do, for all that ye've done for me." Besides, she could not lose the opportunity to question his sister.

"But what o' the Fire Lord? What if he returns to find her there?" asked Core.

"Och, I had'na thought o' that. I would'na wish to put ye in danger," Jyne said to Breanna.

"I have no fear o' him, m'lady. In truth, I ken I should be there, to protect ye. Aye, 'tis settled then." Breanna gave her brother an overly sweet smile. There was an undercurrent passing between the siblings, but Jyne could not figure out what. She had so many siblings, she was familiar with making benign comments with pointed meanings, known only to another sibling. Jyne had never experienced it from an outsider's perspective.

"Breanna…" Core's voice was low with warning. Both ladies looked at him "I…I feel we should no' linger here. The men may return at any moment."

"True," said Jyne. "There should be some unused pallets in the refectory now that the children have gone. Do ye think ye could bring one up wi'out being seen?"

Core nodded with a desperate look but paused and watched them walk up the stairs. Jyne led Breanna up the stairs to her chamber. Cormac was a puzzle, but in his sister, she might just have the missing piece.

◈

Cormac watched helplessly as Breanna followed Jyne up the spiral stone staircase. Breanna turned back to him and gave him a smile of pure malice. He pointed at her and then placed a finger to his lips to remind her to hold her tongue.

All he could do now was hope his impetuous, impulsive, fearless half sister would somehow keep his secret.

"I'm dead," he moaned. "What have I ever done to deserve this?"

And then he remembered he had locked Jyne's clansman and a monk in the crypt.

Nineteen

CORE RAN ACROSS THE COURTYARD TO THE KITCHENS to retrieve something to eat. He was sure the men he had left in the crypt would not be pleased with him, especially since they had been locked in there all day. Bringing food and more candles would be essential.

Core took care to ensure he was not seen and slipped into the storeroom and down the ladder of the trapdoor.

"Brother Luke? Donnach? Ye there?" he called, walking to the locked gate.

"O' course we're here," growled Donnach. "Where else would we be?"

Core turned the tight corner of the basement corridor into the cavern that was the opening of the crypt. The air was cold, and the only light shone from a lantern and a few flickering candles casting dancing shadows on the rough-hewn rock walls. Donnach and Brother Luke were dirt-smudged and weary, leaning against the bars of their prison.

"Did ye find anything?" asked Core, hoping that somehow their grim expressions were a ruse to hide the good news they were waiting to tell him. He had to hope for something.

"Nay, we dinna find anything," said Donnach. "Unless a rotting corpse is yer idea o' treasure."

"Ye found naught? It doesna have to be o' real value, just something that looks like it might be." Cormac was desperate.

Brother Luke shook his head. "It is just a burial place for the departed."

"This tunnel seems to go back a ways. Is it just tombs? I hoped there might be something else too."

"This cavern connects with a series of natural tunnels," Brother Luke said. "The tombs were hewn out of the rock in one area, but other tunnels are untouched. There used to be a passage to the outside, but a cave-in has blocked it."

Core was about to ask another question, when the meaning of Luke's words became clear. "Do ye mean to tell me there is another way out o' these caves?"

"There was. The way is blocked."

"And ye dinna think to tell me? Master Donnach could have escaped."

Luke gave him a slight shrug of one shoulder. The good Brother Luke did not approve of locking people in crypts.

"I see I am not among friends," conceded Cormac. "Hate me as ye will, but help me save the monastery."

"That I will do, and indeed, though Donnach does hate you, he did help me search. The caves were either empty or filled with tombs."

"Were they not buried with anything?" Core was desperate.

"Ye'd rob the dead?" asked Donnach with censure, his brushy black eyebrows low over his eyes.

"My good man, if it is a choice between *robbing* the dead and *joining* the dead, then aye, I shall divest them o' their unneeded worldly goods." Morals were a luxury Core couldn't afford.

"Some of the dead were laid in their tombs wearing armor, but other than that—"

"Armor! That could be something."

"It dinna seem anything of worth," disagreed Donnach. "It would'na fool anyone into thinking it was o' value. Besides, ye'd have to be a desperate man indeed to rip the helmet off a corpse."

"But why are monks wearing armor?" Core turned to Luke.

"Some of the Knights Templar fled to Scotland after their order was condemned and some of its members executed. They hid their allegiance in life, but in death, it appears they once again wore the armor and the red cross of a Templar."

"The Templars had treasure, did they no'?" asked Core, stepping closer to the locked iron gate in excitement.

"Some say they did," agreed Luke, even as he shook his head. "But there is no evidence to suggest this is anything more than a burial crypt."

"Is that food in yer hands for us, or have ye found a new way to torture me?" grumbled Donnach.

"Och, aye, I brought this for ye both." Core handed food to each of them, trenchers and hearty venison stew, courtesy of a recent hunt by the marauders. "This one is for ye, Brother Luke." Core handed him a wineskin. "And this is for ye. I brought ye new candles too." Core handed a crock of ale and some candles to Donnach, who accepted them with a grudging snarl. He didn't blame the man.

Cormac began to pace the dimly lit cavern as the men ate. "There must be something. There is always a way out. Always. We just need to figure out a way to bring my father a treasure. Then he winna attack the monastery."

"Let me go," growled Donnach. "I'll get Laird Campbell and his men. They will make short work o' Red Rex."

Core shook his head. "Dinna underestimate my father."

"Father?" Donnach's eyes opened wide.

"Aye," replied Core. "That is the point o' this exercise. He wants to make me like him, whether I wish it or not. My aspiration to earn a living as a scribe dinna fit in his plans." Core laughed, but the men behind the locked gate did not join him.

"You must break free of him," admonished Luke.

"Ye think I hav'na tried? I've tried to get away." Core shook his head. "And every time, anyone who's ever helped me got hurt."

Silence fell in the dark cavern, the dim candlelight flickering off the rough stone walls. The gravity of their situation fell heavily in the cold, dark space.

"Let me go," Donnach repeated. "The Campbell will put an end to it."

"He might as well put an end to me," countered Core. "Can ye guarantee I also winna be sentenced for my crimes?"

Donnach slid down the gate to sit on the floor.

He appeared exhausted, his eyes half-open. "I canna guarantee anything. Ye have much to answer for."

"Aye, I winna debate ye there. Perhaps it is the scoundrel in me, but I verra much want to avoid paying for the cost o' my sins."

"In this life or the next, ye'll pay." Donnach's voice was deep, and he punctuated the statement with a yawn.

"I fear ye may be right, but I dinna wish to face judgment any sooner than I must," said Core.

Donnach appeared to struggle to stay awake.

"Are you well?" asked Brother Luke, coming to Donnach's side.

"Aye…och…the bastard tainted my—" Donnach collapsed onto the monk.

"What have you done?" asked Luke, helping to ease the unconscious man to the ground.

"Sleeping potion in the ale," admitted Core. At Luke's fierce scowl, he added, "How else was I to unlock the gate to get ye out? I feared he would charge the gate and make short work o' me."

"That was his plan," admitted Luke.

"And ye dinna tell me that either?"

"Apparently, there was no need," said Luke, motioning to the sleeping Donnach.

"I am beginning to think ye a poor friend indeed."

"I never said we were friends," said Brother Luke in an even tone.

Core looked down to fumble with his sporran to retrieve the key. He did not wish to admit that Luke's words stung. He liked the monk. He had certainly gone to great lengths to help him. It was good to know where he stood, though it did not remove the twinge of pain.

"Thank ye for making yer position on the matter clear." Core unlocked the gate and dragged over the pallet he had brought Donnach the first night he had been locked in the cavern. "Help me move him to the pallet so he doesna catch his death."

"Why would you care if he did?" asked Luke, but he did help move the large Highlander onto the pallet.

Core turned to Luke. "Because I am trying to get out o' this wi'out anyone dying. Now, are ye coming out o' the crypt, or would ye prefer to stay?"

Instead of answering, Luke asked another question. "Why would you set me free and not him?"

"Because ye wish to save the monastery and everything and everyone in it as much as I do. I ken ye dinna find me worthy to be called 'friend,' but I think in our desire to save the monastery, we are in agreement. And ye must realize that fighting Red Rex is not a risk worth taking." Core's eyes met Luke's. For once, he was being completely honest.

"In that, we are agreed." Luke cast one more glance at the sleeping Donnach and walked out of the gate. Core swung it shut and locked it, leaving Jyne's kinsman behind.

Core escorted Brother Luke back to the tower to ensure he was not accosted by the brigands now making themselves at home in the great hall. Core had lifted the ban on whiskey for fear of mutiny, and his men were feeling decidedly braver with their liquid courage.

"I do not believe you are an evil man," said Luke suddenly, as if he had been pondering the question.

Core stared at him. "Well, I thank ye for that. I'm no' evil, but no' good enough to be yer friend."

"I never said you were not my friend. I simply said I had not answered the question."

"Thank ye for the clarification." It irked him how much Luke's approval or lack of it meant to him. He had many people who disliked him. Why should the opinion of one monk matter?

Luke pressed his lips together as if weighing Core's worth on a scale. "Why are you here? You could simply run away from this. Instead, you are trying to save everyone."

"Not that I can," Cormac said with a sigh.

"Have you tried praying for guidance?" asked the good monk.

Core gave a snort. "I used to pray when I was living with the brothers. Ye see it all came to naught."

"*Habeatis in mundo pressuram*," Brother Luke quoted from the Book of John.

"Aye, in the world, we will have tribulation. That much the Bible got right."

Luke continued to quote the next line of the verse. "*Habetis sed confidite ego vici mundum.*"

"Be of good cheer, for our Lord has overcome the world? Is that a reference to a heavenly reward? I imagine heaven would welcome me as much as the university did." Core scuffed the toe of his boot along a crack in the stone stair. Heaven's doors would not open for him.

"Heaven is not for the good, but for the forgiven. Good night." Luke left him and walked up the stone stairs.

Instead of walking up the stairs to his solar, Core stepped outside and leaned a shoulder on the doorway. He had always managed to stay one step ahead of disaster, but how was he going to get out of this one? His mind spun, but he could not think of an escape this time. How could he protect the monks and the books and his sister, and somehow be able to stay with Jyne?

Oblivious to Cormac's tenuous situation, the setting sun was putting on a show, casting orange streaks across the sky, dotted with clouds of pink and amber and gold. Many a time when he was a lad, Core would watch the sunset before vespers and think on God's great love to create such beauty.

Those had been better days. It had been hard when Cormac first came to the monastery near Edinburgh, dumped there unceremoniously by his father. Abandoned and rejected, the monks had taken pity on him and showed him a form of kindness, reserved, but more than he had ever known before. They had taught him simple pleasures, like reading and writing, and even encouraged Cormac to attend university. There had been a time when Core had felt that God was good and guiding him toward a bright future. Unfortunately, he had failed to realize the sun was setting, not rising.

Once Cormac's unfortunate parentage came to light, the monks had asked him to move along. Core had attempted to attend university, but again, it lasted only until his identity had become known. He was soon expelled and forced to flee the city. He had prayed for help, but the only one who had found him was Red Rex. That was when he knew God either hated him or simply was not there to care.

"Where's the treasure?" Bran demanded, his voice suddenly behind him.

"T-treasure?" gasped Core in surprise, spinning to face the warrior. For a big man, Bran moved silently.

"Ye had us searching all day, but there was naught to be found." Bran was streaked with dirt.

"I told ye no' to go searching."

"I've been patient wi' ye, but I'm not a patient man."

"Then ye'll get the opportunity to improve yerself. These things take time," Core hedged.

"Where is the treasure?" growled Bran.

"If I knew that, would we still be here?" asked Core, utterly exasperated.

"Maybe ye be trying to steal away wi' the treasure and not give us our share." Bran narrowed his eyes.

"If ye think that, then ye dinna ken me at all."

Bran frowned at him, but his expression was more one of pondering a question than anger. "Ye're right. I dinna ken ye. Ye're no' one o' us."

"I'm the son o' Red Rex. How much more one o' ye can I get?"

Bran shook his head. "Ye're different." Bran stepped closer, glaring at him with black, gleaming eyes. "Ye'll ne'er be like yer father. I just hope ye dinna make up some fool lie."

"There is treasure here," said Core emphatically, trying to cover the falsehood. "I just need to find it."

"Ye best find it soon." Bran turned and strode back into the main hall. It was an unnecessary reminder.

Cormac put both hands on his hair and pulled, as if

he could somehow pull out an idea to save them all. Jyne, Breanna, Brother Luke, the Ranalds, the monks, the books—all were depending on him. How was he going to get out of this?

Help! It was all he could think of to pray. *I ken ye have little regard for me, but, Lord, ye must love the monks, no? I just need a treasure. Or at least more time. Please, just a little more time?*

Suddenly, an idea flashed across his mind.

A short time later, Cormac emerged into the great hall, wearing his bearskin robe and horned helm, the trappings of ruthless power. His men were up to their old antics, feasting on venison from a successful hunt that day and engaging in all sorts of wild play.

He threw down a Templar shield on the wooden table with a great clatter, gaining the attention of the men. Though it was old, the long, rectangular shield still bore the markings of the Templars, a white field emblazoned with a red cross. Core had taken his own tour through the caverns while poor Donnach slept and found a shield that was no longer of use to its owner.

"Behold, men, the Templar shield!" announced Cormac.

The men cheered and gathered around him.

"Did ye find the treasure?"

"Where is it?"

"How much is my share?"

"The treasure is no' in hand yet," said Cormac. "But the shield is a sign we are growing closer!"

The men were disappointed for a moment.

"Let us celebrate wi' another round o' whiskey!" shouted Core.

The men cheered again and went back to their sport. Core caught Bran's eye. The man crossed his arms and gave him a nod. Core had bought some time. What was he going to do with it?

Twenty

Jyne smiled at Breanna, who returned it, albeit a bit tentatively. Cormac's sister was of tall, statuesque proportions. Her bright red hair fell in wild ringlets, cascading down to her waist. She wore a simple brown gown of homespun. Despite the plainness of the gown, she was a beautiful girl, with fine porcelain skin, a spattering of freckles over her nose and cheeks, and sharp green eyes.

Breanna chewed on her bottom lip in a manner that would have brought Jyne instant reproach from any number of her female relatives. Jyne guessed Breanna had not had the benefit or burden of the constant commentary on behavior that Jyne had always known.

"So ye are Cormac's sister." It seemed a safe topic to start. Jyne now had an opportunity to find out more about Core. She was not about to let it pass by her.

"Aye." Breanna spoke slowly, as if cautious to admit to it. "He is my half brother."

"Ye share the same father, I understand. He seems a hard man."

"Aye, he is at that." Breanna chewed harder on

the maligned lower lip, and Jyne feared she might do herself harm.

"Och, where are my manners? Ye've had yerself a trying day. Please sit here at the window and rest yerself. I fear ye must have lost yer veil in flight," said Jyne, changing tactics. She wished to put Breanna more at ease. "Let me get ye one."

Jyne opened her trunk and pulled out a silver-handled brush and a clean white veil. "I hope ye will allow me the honor of attending to yer hair."

"Ye, m'lady?" Breanna's eyes opened wide. "Och, nay, it would'na be right. Anyone what owns a brush made o' silver should'na be tending to my hair."

"Dinna be silly. I have done my sisters' hair many a time." Jyne began to fight her way through the tangled mass of curls, removing twigs and bits of debris as she went. Breanna must have truly had a difficult day. "Have ye been traveling long?"

"Nay, no' long." Breanna sighed, giving in to Jyne's gentle but determined attempt to tame her wild hair. "I was hoping to find Cormac."

"Has yer brother helped ye in the past?" Jyne tried to keep her tone neutral, as if she was merely being polite and not hanging on every word Breanna said.

"In little ways, as he could. He's not been present any more than he can help. Everyone kens he'd rather have his nose in a book."

"Why seek him out?"

"Where else would I go? He's no' like the rest. There're none that I would trust to help me but him."

Jyne smiled at this description of Cormac. It was very like the man she knew.

"He's different than our father," said Breanna, turning to Jyne with a solemn expression.

"Considering what ye've told me about yer father, I ken that to be a good thing."

"Aye. And nay. The more Core is different, the more Father tries to make him more like his own devilish self."

"Perhaps in time yer sire will learn to accept Cormac for who he is?" Jyne suggested.

Breanna snorted in return. "He winna stop until Core conforms himself to Father's image or one o' them is dead."

Jyne assumed Breanna was speaking metaphorically. At least, she hoped so. "What sort o' business does yer father wish to bring Cormac into?"

"Business?" Breanna snorted again and abruptly changed the subject. "Thank ye, m'lady, for the veil." Breanna smoothed her hands down the sides of the linen veil where Jyne had just pinned it to her unruly hair, forcing it in place.

"There now, dinna move about. Let me finish plaiting it." Jyne busied herself in finishing Breanna's hair, disappointed she had not shared more about the mysterious father both Breanna and Cormac seemed to despise. Who could he be? Cormac had clearly been educated, so the man could not be a simple crofter or thief in the night. Perhaps a rich merchant gone bad? A disgraced lord? Whoever he was, it was clear neither Breanna nor Core wished her to know his name.

"Och, I'm certain my hair has ne'er looked so fine," said Breanna with a smile when Jyne had finally tamed the last of her defiant curls.

"Yer locks did put up a fight." Jyne's arms were tired from the effort. "I do apologize. I'm sure I pulled ye something fierce."

"Aye, but it was needed. Ye're verra kind, m'lady."

"Will ye no' call me Jyne? I have missed having some company around my own age."

"As ye wish, m'lady. But what are ye doing here wi'out yer kin? Core told me the others were o' the Ranald clan."

"I came to inspect my dower lands. The Ranalds were left here to fend for themselves after the great plague ravaged their clan. I found them and was here to help until the keep was taken by the Fire Lord."

"But what can ye do to help?" Breanna tilted her head a bit to one side. "Ye're only one lass, and a thin one at that."

Jyne pressed her lips together. She had always been coddled and passed aside because of her size. But not anymore. "One person can make a great deal o' difference. I can help by bringing organization, fresh ideas, and even hope. One person can change the world."

Breanna stared at her, openmouthed. "I ne'er heard anyone speak that way."

"I only wish," admitted Jyne, coming back to earth from her lofty heights, "that my kin will arrive soon. I hope that perhaps they might arrive tomorrow, though it could be later, assuming my guard was able to return home safely. Then we could drive out this Fire Lord and get the planting done. These poor folks will need the crops if they are to survive the next winter." Jyne walked to the window, opened the shutter, and stared out over the green valley. The boundaries of fields could be seen, but they had none strong enough to do the plowing.

"The ground has yet to be tilled," observed Breanna, standing next to her.

"Aye. 'Tis getting late in the season, and wi' those men about, there's no hope o' trying. Not that I believe the elders could till all this land in any event." Jyne sighed and leaned a shoulder on the stone window opening.

"I'm sorry," mumbled Breanna.

"Forgive me. I should'na be burdening ye wi' my troubles when ye have enough o' yer own." Jyne brushed her hands on her surcoat and noted that Breanna's gown was well-worn and thin in places. The fields may be beyond her ability to fix, but ladies' attire was certainly within her scope.

"Here now, we're no' done wi' reviving ye from yer ordeal. Why dinna ye don this surcoat?" Jyne rummaged through her trunk and held up a silk sleeveless surcoat of a mossy green with golden embroidery around the trim.

"Oh, I could'na," gasped Breanna, but she did not refuse when Jyne helped her put it on. Breanna twirled with delight in her new surcoat and respectable white veil.

"Ye look right bonnie," said Jyne in all honesty.

"We must show Core!" said Breanna, skipping to the door.

"Nay, ye mustn't go out," reminded Jyne, hastily moving between Breanna and the door. "Ye canna be seen."

"Och, aye."

"I shall go and—wait, I'm sure I hear Cormac on

the steps." It had not been long that she had known him, but already, she believed she could identify his quick, light step.

Jyne opened the door, expecting to see Cormac, but instead, her blood chilled; her heart stopped.

Before her stood the Fire Lord.

She was afraid for a moment, but then it turned to something else. She needed men to till the land. He had strong men. She had managed to convince them to fix the postern gate. Maybe she could persuade him to plow the fields too.

It was worth a try.

❧

Jyne stood on the landing of the stone staircase with her hands on her hips, her blue eyes sparkling like blue flames. She was so bonnie when she was angry, Cormac considered what more he could do in order to raise her ire.

"Where were ye today?" he thundered, or at least tried to with the helmet over his head. "Ye left yer chamber wi'out permission."

"Ye ne'er said I needed to ask permission," she countered, which was true.

"We made an agreement that ye would stay here and do as I please, and in return, no harm would come to the people here. Are ye going back on yer word?"

"Nay!" Jyne lifted her chin in a manner he found endearing. "I was taking the children somewhere safe. Somewhere far away, where ye'll ne'er find them."

"They're in the crofters' huts a few miles away." Cormac could not help but show off his superior knowledge before her. He wanted to impress her.

Jyne inhaled sharply, her eyes wide. He had surprised her.

"Nay," she lied. Her voice had a slightly different twinge to it, and he knew it to be fear.

He had taken it too far and had frightened the one person whose good opinion most mattered to him. He was about to say something conciliatory, but she spoke first.

"We have no need o' the wee bairns. How can they be o' service? No, what we need are strong lads, but I dinna ken where to find them."

Cormac had the feeling he had just entered into a conversation already in progress, but he was reasonably sure he had been standing with her on the landing the whole time. "Strong men?" He did not follow.

"For the planting. 'Tis past time to put in the crops," said Jyne with a purposeful tone. Strange, but fear in her eyes looked a lot like determination.

"I dinna care for yer crops, m'lady."

"Ye'll care when there's no food left because there were none fit enough to plant it."

"So have some o' yer elders plant the fields."

"We can plant, but we need someone to turn up the soil, for there are none here who have the brawn to do it. Tilling the fields takes a verra strong man indeed."

Cormac stared at her. Was she truly trying to convince him to plant her fields? He suddenly realized what he interpreted as fear was actually the cold, calculating machinations of a lass trying to figure out how to get him to do her bidding. She was trying to manipulate him.

He had never found her more attractive.

"So ye think we have the brawn?" he asked slyly.

"I know ye do." She spoke it in a matter-of-fact tone, but stepped forward and boldly put a hand on his shoulder, feeling down his arm. His jaw dropped, fortunately unseen in the helmet. Something in her eye glinted. She was good, this lass.

"Are ye trying to sweet-talk me, lass?"

Her arm dropped back to her side. "Just speaking the truth. The fields need to be planted. These people canna do it. So if it is to be done, it must be done by yer men."

He put a hand on her shoulder and ran it down her arm, just as she had done to him. "And what will ye give me in return?"

Her eyes narrowed. "Ye'll get the joy o' eating the harvest when it comes in and the gift o' no' starving in the winter."

He shook his head, a painful act with such a heavy helm. "No' good enough. We'll be gone long before the winter."

Jyne folded her arms before her. Her lips parted as if to say something, then she changed her mind and closed her mouth again. She tried a second time, only to pause once more. He was fascinated by the little flash of white teeth, the supple pink bottom lip, and the slight flash of her tongue. He had missed kissing her today, and his body ached for her. He was glad she could not read his expression, for if she could, she would know he was hers to command.

"What is it ye want?" she hedged.

"Make me an offer." He was enjoying himself too much to ever again consider himself a decent person.

"I could…I could…" Her eyes flicked between him and someplace on the ceiling.

He leaned forward, not wanting to miss her next words. "Aye, lass?"

"I could make ye a meal."

"Nay, I've seen what yer special brew can do. Ye'd have me wooing a milk cow and falling to sleep in a dung heap."

She pressed her lips together in a vain attempt to suppress a smile. Her eyes danced as she tried to stop mirth from bubbling up. He had thought she was fetching when angry, but this was beyond anything he had yet seen. She was radiant when impishly trying not to give in to laughter. Core wished to take off the helmet, but knew if he did, all would be lost.

"I could play wi' ye a game," she suggested.

"A game?" He liked games. Especially games with her. "Chess?"

His father did not play chess. He did.

"Ye think in return for plowing the fields to offer me a game o' chess?" He'd do it for less.

"I know it's no' much to offer. But what else have I to give?"

Now he was getting somewhere. "Dinna underestimate yer appeal." He spoke low in a voice he hoped was seductive. Though how seductive could a man be while wearing a ridiculous helmet with two large, protruding horns, as if desperately trying to compensate for something lacking under his kilt?

"I…I dinna ken." She looked away, took a deep breath, then turned back to face him. She flushed pink, and he loved to see it. He had put those roses in her cheeks. "What is it ye want from me?" Her piercing blue eyes struck him between the slats of his helmet. In that moment of courage, she was not afraid of him. But he was of her.

"A bath." The words were out of his mouth before he could consider what he was saying. He was under her spell. She was in control here, and he hoped she would never find out.

"A bath?" Her eyes opened wide.

"Aye. Ye are chatelaine o' this keep, are ye no'? I've traveled far and am weary from the road. I wish for a bath." With her.

She glanced away, thinking hard. Her mouth opened and closed as it did when she was censoring her words. She ran her tongue along the inside of her bottom lip. Sweet heaven, he might have seen stars. "If ye wish to bathe, I shall arrange it."

"Nay, ye shall attend me and none other." They would be in the bathing room together. It was perfect. It was…impossible. How was he going to bathe with a helmet on his head?

"Ye shall see to it the fields are plowed?"

"I swear to ye, it will be done."

She scowled at him, and he knew his word was worth nothing to her. She was no fool.

"Then as soon as it is completed, ye shall have yer bath."

"Nay—"

"Ye'd no' wish to do such hard, dirty work after bathing. Nay, after shall be better." She was quite confident. And she was right to demand proof before payment.

It was his turn to scowl. Of course, that would give him more time to figure out how to bathe without being seen by her. He would not sit in a tub of water wearing this ridiculous helm. "Ye're as shrewd as a fishwife, my lass."

"I'm no' now nor will I ever be yers!" Jyne's eyes flashed, and she returned to her chamber, slamming the door behind her.

Cormac sighed. Truer words had never been spoken.

He slumped back down the stairs. Now how was he going to convince his men to become farmers?

Twenty-one

BREANNA WAITED UNTIL JYNE'S BREATHING WAS EVEN and she was certain the lady was asleep. She had managed to avoid talking as much as she could, but Jyne was curious, and Breanna didn't blame her. Trouble was, Breanna wasn't sure what she was supposed to say and what she was not. Fortunately, when Jyne returned from her encounter with Cormac as the Fire Lord, she spent a half hour pacing and expressing her deep dislike for the man, and Breanna found all she was required to do was agree.

After Jyne had several wide yawns, Breanna suggested she get some sleep, for the poor lass appeared exhausted. Jyne confessed she had slept very little in the past several days, and upon crawling into bed, was almost immediately asleep.

Breanna smoothed her hands down her borrowed silk surcoat and the proper linen veil. She felt fresh and shiny in her new clothes. Lady Jyne was a very good sort of person, and it made her feel all the more wretched for keeping her brother's secret from her.

Breanna opened the door to the stairs a crack. She

needed to have words with her brother and figure out more of what he was trying to do. She had agreed to keep his secret for now, but needed to be further convinced to maintain that falsehood. Of course, she was not at liberty to be too demanding. If Cormac refused to help, there was nowhere else for her to go. Just once in her life, she wished to be the one in control. Then she could take care of herself and her younger sisters.

Breanna walked up the stone stairs on silent feet. From below, the familiar whoops and hollers of Rex's men assaulted her ears. She doubted her brother would be among them. She knew he disliked their company as much as she.

She rapped lightly on the oak door that led to the solar her brother had indicated he was inhabiting. The latch was not barred, so she opened the door and slipped inside, closing it behind her. "Cormac?" she whispered out of habit. Staying in the company of her father and his men, she had learned to be discreet.

The solar was long, with walls rounded from the curve of the tower. It was sparsely furnished, but at least it was neat and clean, a step up from their usual dwellings.

"Cormac?" she called a bit louder.

A man appeared from around the corner.

It was not her brother.

"Och!" She stared at the man dressed in the black robes of a monk. "By the saints, who are ye?"

The monk stared back at her, apparently as surprised to see her as she was to see him. He was a young man, perhaps in his late twenties, with short, curly black hair. The hair on the very top of his head was shorter than the rest, most likely because he had shaved it in the manner of monks, and now it was growing back. He held himself straight and tall, with a certain aura around him of one accustomed to being in power. His eyes were a slate blue-gray in color and had such a solemn reserve to them, it seemed he was staring straight into her soul.

"I am Brother Luke. I was not aware that there were any other young ladies present."

Lady? Was he referring to her? She had never been referred to as a lady before. "I was looking for Cormac. I must have gone to the wrong chamber. I apologize."

"Master Cormac is currently residing in this chamber. He has not returned this evening."

"I see." She did not see. Why was there a monk standing in her brother's chamber? And why did he look so familiar? "Och, I ken who ye are! Ye're the monk that Core saved from getting his head lopped off. Ye're lucky t'be sure. I've ne'er before seen a man be sentenced to death by Red Rex and walk out alive."

The monk raised his eyebrows, forming wrinkles on his brow. "You have me at a disadvantage, for I still do not know your name."

"I'm Breanna, Cormac's half sister."

"Greetings, Breanna. Would you care to be seated while you await your brother?" The monk motioned to a bench beside a square table.

Breanna could not help but laugh at the formal manner in which he spoke. No one had ever asked her to be seated. *Sit yer arse down* was more likely. "Where are ye from?" she asked, accepting the offered seat.

"I am originally from Florence."

"Ye're a long way from home."

Brother Luke gave her a half smile. "That was the point."

"Running from someone, are ye? What fer? Steal something? Kill a man? Long way to go."

Brother Luke tilted his head slightly to one side. "What would make you think I was a murderer?"

Breanna shrugged. "'Tis why most men join my father. Done something so bad, they can ne'er go back. Did ye kill someone?"

"Only in my heart's desire."

It was Breanna's turn to tilt her head. "I doubt that's a crime."

"The good Lord knows if we commit murder in our hearts."

"Och, then I'm done fer!"

"Fortunately, the good Lord offers grace."

Breanna gave him a tight smile. Wishing someone dead was something she was familiar with. Grace was not. "Mercy is no' found in the household o' Red Rex."

"I suppose not," said the monk, with compassion in his eyes. It took her aback. She was not accustomed to kindness, particularly from a man. "Is that what brings you to Kinoch Abbey?"

"Aye, it does at that. I'm to wed a bastard I despise, so I ran away. Hoped Cormac could help me."

"No lady should ever be forced to wed against her will." Luke's eyes turned stormy, and his voice lowered with an ominous tenor.

She was about to reply that she was no lady, but the strong feeling with which he spoke halted her words. "I agree wi' ye, but it happens often, I fear."

"Yes, it does happen much too often." Luke's fists balled, and his eyes narrowed. "Powerful men often get their way when it comes to marriage and money." Luke spoke with a cold contempt.

"Ye speak as a man of experience."

"I am." Luke's cool blue eyes stared at her, yet there was a fire of intensity within. There was no denying it. Monk or no, he was an attractive man. He was a man who clearly knew love lost. And yet, was he not a monk?

"Shall I guess yer sad story?" She tilted her head so she could gaze up at him through her lashes. She was flirting. With a monk. Her life had met a new low.

"By all means." He did not flirt in return, but neither did he banish her from the room, which was enough encouragement to continue.

"Ye were a poor farmer. Nay, an impoverished lamplighter. One night as ye went on yer rounds lighting lamps in the great city o' Florence, ye looked up at an open window, and there on the balcony was the most beautiful creature ye e'er beheld. Ye knew in one glance ye must have her, and so ye called up to her, reciting poetry and singing ballads to make love to her from the cobblestone streets. After many months, she finally returned yer love and went to her father for permission to wed ye. But o' course, it was a hopeless case, and her father refused. Crushed and determined to ne'er love again, ye joined the monastery to escape all female company and live out yer life in miserable celibacy, mourning for the lost love all yer life." She ended the recitation with a dramatic flick of her hand.

"How did I do?" she asked.

"Perfect. Every word the truth." He did not smile, but something in his eyes did.

"Nay, now ye tell me the true story."

"But you have already told it. Only I was not a lamplighter." His slate eyes gleamed.

"Not a lamplighter? A farmer then? A butcher? A baker?"

"Worse."

"Soldier? Rag picker?"

"All those men do an honest day's work for their keep. I did not."

"I was right the first time, a thief! Is that why ye're friends wi' my brother?"

"It is worse than all those things," said Brother Luke solemnly.

"I have it! Tax collector!"

"Worse. I was a duke."

Breanna stared at him. A duke? No, that was not possible. She could not be sitting across a table from a duke. "Nay, ye're in jest. No duke e'er came to the Highlands, surely. If ye was a duke, why dinna ye marry the girl ye wished?"

"Because I was not a prince."

"Ye lost to a prince? Bad luck, that."

He gave her a half smile and paused before he spoke. He seemed to be sifting through his words and would only answer once he found the right thing to say. She was a little envious of his self-control, for she was always saying the first thing that popped into her head and then realizing what she should have said a few minutes later. She was curious to know what he was filtering out.

"Yes, quite."

His response was disappointing in that it revealed nothing. What was the mysterious monk thinking?

"So because ye dinna get yer first choice in matrimony, ye gave up all yer worldly goods and became a monk? A little drastic, no?"

"I may have been. I did take all my books with me."

"Books?"

"The library at the monastery. Most of the books came from my collection."

"The ones Rex threatened to burn if ye dinna bring him a treasure?"

"Yes." Brother Luke ground his teeth. "I brought them here to be safe, and I will defend them to my dying breath."

"Ye'd defend the books to the death?" Breanna raised an eyebrow at him. Giving your life for a book made no sense. "I appreciate yer love for books... actually no' really, for I have no great affinity with any object. And if I was suffering from unrequited love, I certainly would'na give up hope of ever finding a suitable partner. Ye're overly dramatic."

A smile hung about his lips. Though she was not sure if his lips actually moved, there was certainly no broad smile or the upturned lips. And yet, she knew he was smiling at her. If he wasn't a monk...

"You may be correct. Perhaps I did forgo the chance of love too soon." Their eyes met and held together, the silent moment stretching longer.

"It is always possible to fall in love." What was she saying? She was not a believer in love. Heat crawled up the back of her neck. She was surprised, for after living with her father and his questionable compatriots, she had thought herself beyond the ability to blush, but she did anyway. She blushed for Brother Luke.

"Perhaps it is as you say." He spoke softly. His eyes were warm yet staid, as if they were the eyes of an older man. His face was clean shaven and thin. His chin was prominent, and his nose was long, which gave him a more distinguished air. The story of him being a duke was impossible, but she believed it.

Breanna looked away. She had to. She found him much too attractive for a monk. "Nay, ye probably did the best thing. Love is for poets and such, not—"

"Dukes?" interrupted Luke.

"Daughters o' vicious warlords," finished Breanna with a sigh. "When this is all over, I'll probably end up married to that sorry bastard my father picked and get naught more than a whipping fer my troubles."

"No one shall harm you." Luke reached across the table and gently squeezed her hand.

Breanna stared at him. "How could ye stop it? And why should ye care?"

Brother Luke released her hand at once. "I...I do not wish to see any lady harmed." He spoke it quickly and looked away, ill at ease. Something was there. The attraction she felt, he felt it too.

But...he was a monk. And despite being the illegitimate daughter of one of the most notorious warlords to tramp about the Highlands, she did have some moral standards, and they did not include liaisons with men of the church.

Even handsome men of the church.

Especially handsome men of the church.

"I should go," she said.

"That does seem best."

She did not move. Neither did he.

"Perhaps I shall see ye at table."

He shook his head. "I eat my meals here."

"Then maybe I shall see ye here."

"I doubt that would be wise." He picked up a scroll and examined it intently. She knew he liked her. Liked her enough to avoid seeing her to elude temptation. It was a compliment, really.

Breanna rose, and Luke jumped to his feet. She walked to the door and paused with Luke standing beside her. It was her turn to remain quiet as she considered her words. Before she could think of the appropriate thing to say to an attractive monk, the solar door jerked open.

Cormac strode into the room.

❧

Core had spent a tedious evening with his men, the only sober person in a room full of drunks. He had tried to think of a way to get them to plow the fields, but nothing came to mind. How could he convince them to become farmers? It was impossible.

He wished to retire to his chamber, but his promise to Jyne made him stay. He had assured her that the elders would not be harmed, and the best way to ensure this did not happen was to wait until all the old ones were safely asleep in the locked refectory.

Spending the hours watching men acting badly did impress upon Core one thing. He was not going to win this one. There was nothing of value in this abandoned abbey. He needed to start making contingency plans.

"Ye need to go," Core demanded as he burst into the solar. He was surprised to see his sister standing beside Luke and stopped short. "What are ye doing here?"

"I was looking for ye! And what do I find but a monk? Well!" Breanna stormed out of the room, slamming the door behind her.

Core did a double take as she left. He had never seen her attired in a proper veil and elegant surcoat. Even her hair had been tamed into something sophisticated. His sister had been in the presence of Lady Jyne for no more than a few hours, and the transformation was remarkable.

"Your sister is very…" Brother Luke's words trailed off as if he was unsure of what he wished to say. For a man who always spoke with such calculated precision, this was a disturbing trend.

"Aye, she is that, and twice on Sundays," replied Core without waiting for the monk to finish his thought. "Now, ye need to go, and look lively wi' ye."

"Where am I going?" asked Luke.

Core handed him his cloak. "To the monastery. I've saddled a horse for ye and gave leave for the guards to come to the great hall for a wee bit to have some whiskey. 'Tis time for ye to leave."

"But what about the need to find a treasure?"

"I will keep looking, but I think we both ken there's none here. I will stall them for as long as I can. Ye get the monks to safety. Eventually, Rex will come, and they need to be clear."

Brother Luke paused in the doorway; his steely

eyes searched Core's face. Core stilled. There was something noble in the brother's wise eyes.

"I would be pleased if you would consider me a friend," said Luke with solemn reserve.

Core swallowed down a lump in his throat. It was absurd how much Luke's words meant to him. Perhaps Luke reminded him too much of the monks who had raised him, the only ones who had ever shown him kindness and then rescinded it when they discovered who he was.

"It would be an honor." Core's voice wavered in a manner he feared revealed too much emotion. He cleared his throat. "Now ye need to get going. Warn the brothers to flee."

"And the books?" asked Luke.

Core shook his head. "Take what ye can."

"But we would need wagons. And where would they go?"

"I dinna ken."

"We need to move the books somewhere safe." It was Luke's turn to have his voice tremble. Clearly, the books meant more to him than anything. Core did not fault him for the judgment.

"I canna leave tonight, but tomorrow morn, I will come to help." Core took Luke's hand. "I promise."

Core watched Luke leave, ensuring he escaped safely. After a long day, he wanted to do nothing more than sleep, but he knew things were going to go badly very soon. And before they did, there was something he must do.

Twenty-two

JYNE WOKE WITH A START IN THE WEE HOURS OF THE night. She had a dream of trying to hide children from ghosts wearing horned helmets. She took a deep breath, trying to calm her racing heart. Ever since she had left the familiarity of her own castle, she had known one difficulty after another. It was one thing to think about adventures while sitting with family around the fire on a cold winter's night with a warm mug of cider in her hand. It was much less comfortable to live through one.

She pushed back the blankets and got up, relishing the cold stones on her feet. She needed something to snap her out of the bad dream. Breanna was sleeping on the pallet beside her bed, snoring softly. It was nice not to be quite so alone. Jyne wrapped a blanket around herself against the chill and sat in the window seat. She opened the shutter, breathing deeply of the cold night air. She needed the refreshing air to chase away the fears that had plagued her since the marauders had taken over her keep.

She closed her eyes in the moonlight and leaned

against the cool stone wall, allowing the tension that had crept into her shoulders to release, and smiling as the wind played with her hair. It was a clear, crisp night, with a bright moon high in the sky. The moon and stars were the same moon and stars her brothers and sisters might be looking at right now. The thought was comforting.

She had longed for her own adventure, but now that it had been granted, she wanted nothing more than to see her family again. A pang of homesickness left a lump in her throat.

She turned her thoughts back to her current situation. She needed to find a way to oust the Fire Lord and his men or send for help. The Fire Lord himself was a puzzle. Why did he wear that hideous helmet? He must truly be a repulsive sight for him to never take it off. She had expected much more marauding and ruination, and she was a little surprised to see the men be raucous, but not terribly destructive.

She closed her eyes, and her thoughts naturally drifted to Cormac. He had stood with her against the wild men, helping her with every plan, and all for a kiss. Many wonderful kisses.

Instead of running from the danger, he kept coming back, helping where he could. He was tall and strong and had square shoulders and warm eyes. He had more than proven his worth in her eyes, so maybe her brother would accept him.

She had heard many a story of her elder siblings falling in love. They all had romantic tales that had made her long for one of her own. But to fall in love with the wrong person—that would be horrible.

How could she know if Cormac shared her feelings, whatever those might be? He enjoyed kissing her, that much was clear, but he had also said he would not remain when her brother arrived. Perhaps he feared that because of his father, David would not accept him. Maybe he was right. But maybe he was wrong. If David would accept him, would he wish to remain by her side?

Jyne stared out over the valley below. The meadows, grasslands, and fields were illuminated in the bright moonlight. If only they could plow the fields so they could be planted, her newfound people would not starve come the fall. She had tempted the Fire Lord, but she had no confidence it would come to fruition.

A shadow of movement caught her eye. She strained to see what was moving in one of the fields. It was a man, working the fields, plowing long rows. Could it be the warlord fulfilling his promise?

She stared harder. No. She knew his face. This was a man who must hold her in very high esteem to be working her fields in the middle of the night. Warmth flushed through her all the way to her bare toes.

It was Cormac.

❧

Hunting he could make them do. Repairing they could be tricked to do. He could convince them it was in their interests to leave the elders alone and not interfere with them. He might even be able to persuade them to be a little less repulsive at the table. A little. But the one thing Cormac could not get his men to do was to be farmers. They were Highland warriors, not crofters.

Cormac worked by the light of the moon. It was a mild night for spring, and if the wind was brisk at times, at least it was not raining. He was trying to make the best of it, for in truth, it was hard work. He had found an old plow in the corner of the stables and harnessed it to one of their packhorses. An ox would have been better, but he didn't have an ox.

He struggled to turn the pack animal and line up the plow behind the beast to till a new row. He was a strong man, but still, his hands and arms were fatigued from grasping the wooden handles of the plow, worn smooth from years of work. His back ached from being jarred by every rock hit by the plow.

He would have given up a long time ago, but the promise of a bath with Jyne Campbell was a temptation he was not able to resist. He would claim his prize, even if it broke his back to do it. He just hoped that nobody would see it being done.

The horse tugged the lines, and he tripped over his newly plowed rows. How did the crofters do it? He struggled to lift the heavy plow back into line to continue tilling down the length of the field. He feared instead of straight, neat lines, his rows looked like the product of a drunken blind man.

Core adjusted himself somewhat, leaning back to allow the horse to do more of the work, and instead of pushing the plow, he guided it. It was still hard work, but after twenty rows, he had learned how not to trip over his own feet, and after thirty, he was beginning to feel like he might have the hang of it. There was something almost peaceful about plowing the fields that night, watching the moon rise silver in a sky filled with the tiny points of stars.

He glanced over at the bulky bearskin cloak and the horned helmet he had discarded by the side of the field. They were much too impractical for the work he was doing. Fortunately, Breanna had assured him that Jyne was fast asleep. The men had drunk much and gone to bed, Cormac himself releasing the watch, saying he would do it himself, so there was none to see him as he worked. This was fortunate, for he did not know how he would explain why he would leave the gates unbolted so he could plow the fields by the light of the moon.

The plow hit something hard and jarred to a sudden stop, giving him a jolt through his body all the way to his teeth. The horse kept going, pulling him forward and causing him to trip over the plow.

"Whoa there!" He pulled in the reins, and the beast came to a contented stop, lowering his head to take a mouthful of something he found enticing on the ground. Cormac examined what had put a halt to his progress and found a large rock.

Cormac sighed. He suspected the Scottish soil grew rocks. He pulled out a small handled shovel and got to digging, working around the edge of the rock until he could pull it up. It was heavy, and wrenching it from the ground took considerable effort, but he was not his father's son for nothing. With a grunt and a groan, he was able to pull the rock, a particularly massive one, from the rich black earth. His back complained while his arms strained, and he knew that, come morning, he would pay for these efforts.

He turned to trudge the boulder to the side only to come face to face with Jyne Campbell. She wore nothing more than a white chemise and a red plaid draped open around her. The golden locks of her hair flew loose, and her mouth was open, her eyes wide and dark in the moonlight.

"Jyne!" He dropped the rock.

"What are ye doing? Why are ye plowing the fields?" She ran up to him and placed her dainty, soft hands in his calloused ones.

He struggled to come up with something to say. She wasn't supposed to see him; she was just supposed to wake in the morning and find that the work had been done.

"I...I..." He couldn't think with the wind blowing her shift about, pressing it to her body and then billowing out again. It gave him ample evidence of the perfection of her petite form. A gentleman would not have looked, but he did. Oh, did he look.

"Ye should'na be out here at this time o' night. 'Tis cold. Ye'll catch yer death." He was at once concerned for her to be outside in such a thin garment and reticent to encourage her to cover her perfect form.

"Aye, but when I saw ye, I was so surprised, I just ran out to the fields. Why are ye plowing them?"

An excellent question, one he was sure he would come up with an answer for, probably tomorrow, which would do him no good.

"Let me take ye back to the tower. Truly, ye should'na be out here." *Focus on her; keep the conversation off of what you're doing.* Maybe she wouldn't notice the horse or the plow. He glanced around to note where he had discarded his cloak and helm. He spotted the bearskin cloak next to the horned helmet, the large curved horns bleached pale and stark white in the moonlight. There was no denying what that was. If she saw it, all was lost.

"Och, ye're a dear sweet man. Ye knew that false warlord would ne'er help me, so ye came instead to do it at night, the only time ye could do it wi'out fear o' being hindered by those evil men. Ye're the dearest, kindest man I've ever known." Admiration shone in her eyes, and he felt himself drowning in it.

No one had ever looked at him the way she did. Most saw him only as the odd son of a warlord, despised on one side for his tender heart and penchant for book learning, or on the other side as the demon spawn of the hellion warlord. No one had ever looked at him with admiration. He drank it in—drank it down to the dregs like a man dying of thirst. It didn't matter that she was completely wrong about him.

Except...it did.

What would he do to be worthy of that genuine admiration? He shook his head. He would never be worthy of her. There was nothing he could do to gain her true admiration, so he must steal it from her by playing her false.

"Nay, do not shake yer head and deny yer true nature. Ye canna deny that ye've been plowing these fields for me, for my people." She caught herself on that last statement, but she was right the first time. Though he did wish to help the Ranalds and felt guilty for eating through their stores, Jyne was the main reason he was standing next to a plow in the middle of the night.

"I did it for ye."

"Thank ye." Her fingers closed around his, and she gave his hand a squeeze. "Thank you so much. Ye dinna ken what this means to me."

He smiled at her, basking in the warmth of her compliments, and placed a warm hand over her cold ones. He could not say anything, for he knew if he spoke, the spell might be broken, and she would see through to the wretchedness of his soul.

"Look how far ye've gotten." She began to scan the fields, turning her head toward the discarded helmet.

He quickly reached an arm around her, blocking her view from the incriminating horns. "'Tis naught."

"Och, but it is!" She tried to turn again, and he knew he had to stop her somehow, or he would be discovered.

He drew her close for a kiss. At first, he only meant to distract her, turn her away from the pile of shame on the side of the field. Then she kissed him back.

Everything changed. Warmth spread through him, chasing away every ache, every pain, until he felt he could fly. She wrapped her arms around him and pressed closer. Her perfect body, shielded only by the thinnest of chemises, was revealed to him in a manner that made him weak in the knees. He slid a hand down her back and cupped her beautiful, rounded backside. He was taking generous liberties, and he knew with every fiber of his being that her brother would kill him for it, but the knowledge only emboldened him. If he was going to die, he might as well make it worth his while. He drew her closer and deepened the kiss. He had never experienced anything so beautiful, so passionate, or so tender.

He was completely undone.

"Oh," she said when she was finally allowed speech once more. She trembled slightly in his arms, but her cheeks blushed pink, and she no longer felt cold.

"Forgive me, my lass. I take advantage."

"Aye, ye do, my lad." But she did not look terribly disappointed by it.

"I'm not a good man, I tell ye the truth. Ye should have naught to do with me, and that's the truth too."

"I shall decide on that count, if ye please. And it pleases me to bestow upon ye a token o' my affection for the service ye're doing for myself and these poor people."

"If that's just a token, I canna imagine what a full measure of yer thanks would be." Actually, he could imagine it, was imagining it, and probably would be imagining it for the rest of his life.

A slow, determined smile spread across her face. "Since ye're the one who has done the work, 'tis only fair that ye receive the promised reward."

"Truly?" He was going to get that bath after all. He suddenly remembered that he was not supposed to know what the promised reward was. "And what might that be?"

"Come to me this evening when ye've completed yer task, and ye winna be disappointed." She gave him a coy smile, and he knew he would plow his way from here to Edinburgh if it meant a chance to be with her.

"As ye wish." He noted that the reward was the same for him as it was for the warlord—payment after the job was done. She was no fool, this Jyne Campbell.

"I do wish," she whispered. She gave him a chaste peck on the cheek, but one that promised more.

He watched as she ran barefoot back to the tower.

Twenty-three

"WHAT ARE YE DOING?"

Core jerked himself up. He must have dozed off over the plow. He had wanted to complete the plowing in one night, but it was an impossible task, and he was only half done. He stared at the face of Bran, slowly coming into focus. He had been up all night, and now the sun's rays clearly illuminated his actions for all to see.

How was he going to explain this?

"What are ye doing here? Get back to the keep," demanded Cormac to the utterly unimpressed Bran. Behind him, more of the men were emerging from the gates of Kinoch and wandering into the fields to see what he was doing.

"Has she turned ye into a crofter, ye milk-livered fool?"

"Nay!" True, the plow looked incriminating...but if Bran knew Core had made up the story about the treasure and now was helping Jyne by tilling the soil, Bran would march back to Red Rex, and everything, literally, would be lost.

Bran folded his arms before him. "What. Are. Ye. Doing?" He could not be any clearer.

"I...I..." Core's mind went blank. What was he to say? *Help, Lord, help!* Suddenly, inspiration flashed. "I wish ye would'na bring all the men out here."

"Why?" Bran narrowed his eyes.

Cormac leaned closed to Bran and lowered his voice. "I dinna wish so many about when we find it."

Bran's face registered disbelief, but still there was a glint of interest. "Find it? The treasure, ye mean?"

"Aye. The Templars buried it. Most likely in one of the planting rows. I'm turning over the soil so I can find it. And I wish to do it alone, so if ye'll excuse me." Core flicked the leads, and the tired horse began to plod forward once more.

"Hold, now. Ye're no' thinking o' keeping all the treasure for yerself?"

"It belongs to the one who finds it," called Core without looking back to see what color Bran had turned.

"Nay! If there is treasure to be found, I'll be here to find it." Bran rolled up his sleeves.

Dubh came up behind Bran. "What are ye doing?"

Bran said nothing. More men came around.

Dubh grabbed the plow with one massive hand, holding it still even as the horse pulled. "What do ye think ye're doing?" demanded the large man.

Cormac sighed as if being pressured into an unwanted confession. "Bran is helping me search for the Templar treasure, which may be buried somewhere in these fields."

"Ye heard that lads?" shouted Dubh. "The treasure be here!" He began to lift rocks and look underneath.

The men cheered and ran forward, looking through the freshly tilled dirt.

"Nay, no' like that. We need to search in a systematic manner." Core smiled. Within a few minutes, another plow had been located, and teams were carefully tilling the fields in neat, straight lines while other men followed behind, looking for treasure by poking sticks down into the freshly tilled soil. Had there been treasure in Kinoch, Core was certain they would have found it.

Core smiled at his success, though he could barely keep his eyes open. He staggered back to his solar. He would get a few minutes nap and then go help Luke hide the books. Finally, something was going his way.

Thank ye.

⤜⤏

Where was he?

Luke paced back and forth in the morning light. He had stayed up all night. First, he made sure that his fellow monks were warned to take flight. Then he determined to rescue his precious books, scrolls, and manuscripts. He could not let them see the flames. Impossible.

The monks had taken what they could, but much remained. Luke had borrowed a cart and loaded it up to take his precious cargo to safety. But where could he go? And where was Cormac?

Luke prided himself on excellent self-control. He had dedicated himself to learning and faith, away from the trials of life. Yet here he was, all because he refused to let two of his precious scrolls go to a thief. A thief who had now put his entire collection at risk. A thief who had lied to save Luke's life.

A thief who was not here when he promised he would be!

Luke's regard for Cormac shifted back and forth as swiftly as the swirling wind. He could not afford to wait any longer. He needed to get the books to safety. But where?

Hours later, Luke crouched in the brush, watching Kinoch Abbey. He had approached from the side, hoping to avoid detection. But how was he to get inside?

A lone, cloaked figure appeared at the postern gate. Luke crouched down farther in the brush and hoped the horse and cart would be hidden where he had left them behind a thick copse of trees. The figure looked both ways, then ran straight for him. Luke pulled his knife.

The figure drew closer, and the cowl flew back, revealing Breanna. Her face was flushed from the exercise, and her red ringlets flew behind her as she ran. He stood up in surprise.

"Breanna!"

"Brother Luke! Whatever are ye doing hiding in the bushes?"

"I am trying to find Cormac without drawing attention. Have I been seen?"

"Only by me. I was on top o' the tower, watching the men. They're all in front. Ye'll ne'er guess what Core's got them doing."

Luke was not sure if telling him he could not guess was an invitation to speculate or not, so he paused, unclear of the social convention.

She smiled up at him with bright green eyes and continued. "He's got them plowing the fields!"

Luke was sure he could not have heard correctly. "Plowing fields for planting crops?"

"Aye! Is that no' strange?"

"Quite. I wonder how Cormac managed it."

"I had to know, so I went and asked one o' them, and he said there was treasure buried somewhere in the fields, so they were plowing to find it!"

"That was very clever," admitted Luke. "But where is Cormac now?"

"Sleeping. Jyne's in the kitchen, happy as a lark because o' what the men are doing. But why are ye sneaking about?"

Luke paused. He was not sure he could trust Breanna. She was beautiful, it was true. He was a little surprised he found her so, for after his lost love, he had not so much as looked twice at another lady. Breanna was bold, vivacious, impulsive—many things he was not. But could he trust her? Did he have a choice?

"I have some things I need to keep out of the hands of Red Rex," he began.

"And ye thought to bring them here?" She raised her eyebrows at him.

"Red Rex will surely go to the monastery, so they cannot remain there. The brothers took as many of the books as they could, but they needed to flee quickly. A cart would hold them back. I needed somewhere close I could hide them. I thought this would not be a place Red Rex would look for them."

"By the saints, ye're a clever one, ye are. But where are ye going to hide a cart load o' books where my father would'na stumble across them?"

"I thought to hide them in the crypt under the

storeroom, but it is a bit far from the postern gate. I fear I will be seen making so many trips."

"Crypt?" Breanna wrinkled her nose in a manner he found rather adorable. "Nay, I have a better idea."

Luke followed Breanna through the postern gate, hoping he had not put his faith in her erroneously. He could not count the number of tales he'd heard of lovely women who lured men to their death.

"Here!" She pointed to the chapel, which had an exterior entrance right on the other side of the postern gate. He could load the books in there without even having to enter Kinoch Abbey farther than the chapel.

"Your father would not be likely to visit the chapel?"

Breanna just laughed at him, a lively, warm sound. How long had it been since he had heard a lady laugh?

Luke cleared his throat. What could he be thinking? He needed to focus back on his current dire situation. "Thank you. That is a helpful suggestion, indeed."

Breanna smiled at him, free and bright. "Shall I help ye?"

"That would be appreciated."

After a brief debate on tactics, it was decided that Breanna would stand guard and Luke would haul his precious manuscripts into the chapel. It worked well, and she was able to signal to him when to hide and when to continue. In truth, he could not have done it without her.

More than once, he caught himself looking in her direction, not only to check for a signal but also because he enjoyed the view.

But no, that was not a path open to him anymore. He had tried once and had lost in such a manner as to wreck a man. He would never again have love in his life.

Twenty-four

"GET UP! ARE YE GOING TO SLEEP ALL DAY?"

Cormac rolled over in bed and groaned, ignoring his sister. Everything hurt. His back hurt, his legs hurt, his arms hurt, his hands and feet hurt. Places on him that he wasn't even aware he had hurt. Of course, he had never worked so hard in his life. He had pleased Jyne, but at a price.

"I see you have enjoyed your rest," accused Brother Luke.

Cormac opened one eye to face his detractors. Brother Luke and Breanna stood at the side of his bed. It was the second time he had seen them together. Both had a determined look about their mouths. Luke in particular did not appear as neat as usual; his eyes were dull and his robes rumpled.

"I was up all night," defended Cormac as he slowly pulled himself up to a sitting position in the bed. He wondered what made Luke look so haggard. "Ye look tired yerself."

"I've been up all night and all day, moving the books and scrolls, no thanks to you. I see getting your rest was more important to you than keeping your promise to me."

Core's heart sank. He had truly intended to help Luke. "Och, Luke, I meant to come help ye. What time is it?"

"'Tis dusk. Ye've quite slept away the day," said Breanna without mercy.

The sharp realization that he had broken his promise to help Luke protect the books brought an avalanche of guilt. How could he have been so thoughtless?

Cormac knew how. He would do anything for Jyne. As much as he admired Luke, the monk didn't have eyes like Jyne, or smell like Jyne, or look like Jyne.

As if reading his mind, Luke narrowed his eyes further. "Do not tell me you were with Lady Jyne Campbell."

Cormac froze, trying to figure out how to deny this without actually having to lie to a monk.

"By the saints, Cormac, ye're going to get yerself killed," exclaimed Breanna. "When the Campbell comes, and he will, will he not take vengeance against ye?"

"I plan to be gone long before he arrives." Cormac yawned to show that he was not concerned at all. Or at least to pretend he was not concerned.

"Who will be gone?" asked Brother Luke in a solemn tone. "Cormac or the Fire Lord?"

Cormac looked away. Luke had touched a nerve, and Cormac did not wish to let him know. Plowing the fields through the night, Cormac had begun to think as if he would be staying at Kinoch Abbey with Jyne. He had begun to plot out what he would plant in the fields and how they would celebrate the harvest together. He had imagined himself and Jyne sitting around the hearth through the winter, telling tales and eating their fill of the food they had stored. In this shiny dream, his father did not exist, her brother did not exist; it was just him and Jyne.

Core glared at Luke and Breanna. He did not appreciate the intrusion of reality into his desires. "I have a plan." He was going to get a plan. Somehow.

"Ye canna possibly think that somehow ye could keep her?" gasped Breanna. "Whether as Cormac or the Fire Lord, she will ne'er be wi' ye. Ye must know that."

Cormac shrugged. He was regretting bringing Breanna to Kinoch. He should have left her to care for the bairns in the crofters' huts.

"Have ye gone mad?" exclaimed Breanna. "Ye ken who our father is, and so does Laird Campbell. What do ye think Jyne will say when she discovers ye've been deceiving her all this time?"

"She'll never find out," said Core testily. "That's the point of lying." He was being goaded into positions he did not truly believe. He wanted to be honest with Jyne; he just couldn't figure out how.

"I see," said Brother Luke. "You lie to Lady Jyne. You break your word to me. This is all part of your plan?"

"I'm sorry I dinna come today. I dinna mean to break my word. I was exhausted," defended Cormac. "And what are ye two doing together?" He needed to change the subject.

"Your sister helped me move the books."

"Ye went all the way to the monastery?" Core sat up farther, glaring at his sister.

"Nay, Brother Luke brought the books here."

"Here?" Core almost jumped out of bed, but realized he had taken off his plaid, so he remained beneath the blankets.

"They are in the chapel," said Luke.

"Well, that would be the one place Rex would'na go," admitted Core. "But 'tis a terrible risk. Someone might tell him."

"I had not the benefit of assistance in finding a better spot," returned Luke archly. He attempted a glare that ended in a yawn.

"Ye need some sleep. And, Breanna, ye need to get back to yer chamber. Where's Lady Jyne?"

"In the kitchens, I warrant."

"Ye left her unprotected wi' our father's men?"

"Nay, ye did that when ye invaded this place," she replied tartly. "What are ye going to do when Rex comes? Ye promised a treasure, but there is none."

Cormac stilled. "He is coming here?"

"Rex has spoken of it. I dinna ken when. What does he wants from ye?"

"He wants me to be like him."

Breanna snorted. "He's in for disappointment, he is."

"I have a plan," said Cormac. This time, both Luke and Breanna were silent, waiting to hear this plan. "My experiments, they finally worked. I can call down thunder and lightning!"

"Nay, ye jest," dismissed Breanna.

"Actually, he is correct," said Luke in a grim tone. "I fear his studies have led him to create and unleash the destructive power of black powder. He used it to rip a hole through the postern gate."

Breanna's eyes grew wide. Finally, someone was

impressed. He forgot his earlier desire to send her away and was back in charity with her.

"Truly? I thought yer boasts were naught but fancy," she admitted.

"Cormac is not the only one to experiment with this power," informed Luke. "The English have already advanced their understanding of this artificial thunder and lightning to create cannon, which they used to great effect at the battle of Crecy in France."

"The English have this knowledge? Not a pleasant thought," said Breanna.

"Aye. Rex will be so impressed when he sees what it can do," said Core. "He will forget all else to have me create this powder for him. With my skills, he shall be invincible!"

"Ye would give this power to our father?" Breanna's eyes grew wider still.

"Aye. He will finally see the benefit of book learning." This was Core's hope and dream.

"Nay, ye mustn't." Breanna sank down on a chair by the bed and grasped his hand. "Ye mustn't let our father control such power."

"I agree," said Brother Luke. "You cannot allow such a man to use this weapon against others. Just think of the misery that would bring."

"Promise me ye winna give Rex this power." Breanna squeezed his hand. "Our father can do enough damage as it is."

This had always been the problem with his plan to find respect in his father's eyes. Core had justified it, telling himself the black powder would only accelerate the inevitable. When Rex attacked, he won.

Core ran his fingers through his hair in a distracted manner. They were right. Red Rex would be unstoppable with such a weapon. He could not allow it. Cormac sighed and rested his forehead on his bent knees.

"I hope that wasna the plan," said Breanna softly.

That was his last card to play, his one way out if he could not find a treasure. His shoulders sagged with defeat. He had the one thing that might actually impress his father, and it was the one thing he could not share. Now how was he going to prove himself? His father would not stop until Core had been turned into some version of a warlord.

"I thought I told ye to get back to yer own chamber," growled Cormac at Breanna, defensive to the last. He had been thrilled this morning at having tricked his men into plowing the fields. Now his happy dreams shriveled into dust.

"Ye're just saying that because ye ken I'm right!" Breanna stood and flounced out of the room.

When the female audience had left, Core hauled his aching body out of bed and belted on his plaid. It was time to face the day. Or what was left of it. What was he going to do now?

"You should tell Lady Jyne the truth. It is not fair to her to deceive her," said the monk as he sat down on his pallet.

Another problem. Core hastened his pace. He needed to leave the solar before he was reminded of any other complications. But Jyne...Jyne was the one person Core never meant to hurt. "I winna hurt her."

"You will. Eventually, her brother will come. And if

he doesn't kill you for being the son of Red Rex, he will kill you for taking liberties with his sister."

"I will figure out something when the time comes," grumbled Cormac. Truth was, he was not sure what he was going to do. "And I've no' taken liberties," he added. His conscience pricked him. Yes, he most certainly had. "Well, no' too many," he defended, even as the memory of their kisses hung on his lips. He would remember them until the day he died, which he hoped would not be soon.

"Liberties enough," said Luke.

"Go to sleep now, my friend. I am sorry I wasna there to help ye." Cormac needed to escape.

Luke struggled to remain sitting up, fighting against the fatigue that was overcoming him. "Breanna said you deceived the men into plowing the fields for Lady Jyne. Is that true?"

"Aye," said Core with a smile. Finally, Luke was recognizing the good he had done.

"Why would you go to such trouble, especially if you do not intend to stay? You have not lost your heart to Lady Jyne, have you?"

"Nay, dinna be absurd." Core couldn't look at his friend for fear the truth would be revealed. For once, he longed for the stupid helmet to protect him from the truth he feared was evident on his face. An uncomfortable silence fell over the chamber.

"You have. You love the young lady." Luke shook his head. "I am sorry for you. That is the worst thing you could have done."

"Good night," said Cormac, walking to the door. He was not interested in reality. He was interested in claiming his reward from Lady Jyne.

"Do not tell me you are going to see Lady Jyne again?"

"As ye wish." Cormac's hand was on the door latch.

"You are going to see her," Luke accused. "Can you not see that it will end in disaster?"

"Aye, well, that's a cheery thought."

"You are the worst kind of fool. One who knows he is doing something foolish, yet still goes and does it anyway."

Core ground his teeth and turned slowly to face his accuser. "I am my father's son."

"You cannot help having a bastard for your father, but you can decide not to act like one yourself."

Anger sparked within him. "Just because ye gave up on finding love to hide away as a monk doesna mean everyone else should."

Luke's eyes widened and then narrowed immediately into small slits. "Do not speak of things you cannot understand."

"Oh no, it is only for you to lecture me. All ye've ever done is hide away wi' yer books. Ye've ne'er experienced anything but the safe walls o' yer cell. Ye've always had someone else to feed ye and clothe ye. Ye canna possibly understand what it is to live in this world."

Luke jumped up from his pallet, his eyes blazing, his calm exterior shattered. "You know nothing!"

Silence fell in the solar. The last of the sun's rays had melted away, and the room had grown dim. With a sigh, Cormac sat at the small, square table. Brother Luke sat opposite him. "What happened to ye?" Cormac asked.

"Prince Claudio."

"Who?"

"He was the sod who married my Elena."

"Ye set yer sights on a lady who would marry a prince?"

"I am a duke, or at least I was."

"Ye're a duke? Truly?"

"Was. Not anymore." Had anyone else made such a claim, Cormac would have laughed it off as absurd, but Luke had such a bearing that he believed it.

"Why did ye no' win the heart o' the one ye loved?"

Luke shook his head and sighed. "I was from a Ghibelline family. She was from a Guelph. Despite the fact that our houses were at war, we fell in love. I loved her more than my own breath, more than the beat of my own heart. When her father denied us, we decided to force his hand. We ran away and found a priest to marry us. When we told her father what we had done, we thought he would be angry, that he might disown her, but we never thought that he would send mercenaries to kidnap her and drag her back to his house, only to force her to marry that dreadful prince."

Cormac frowned. "But she was yer wife. Did ye no' fight for her?"

Luke gave him a sad smile. "Of course I did. I gathered my forces and attacked. I besieged their castle. My thought was only for her, to get her back, to protect her from her own father and the bastard who called himself her husband. I thought she would be inside, protected and safe until I could get to her. But she was not. She ran to the castle wall, and a stray arrow struck her…struck her through her chest."

Silence once again fell in the solar as darkness

gathered in the corners and crept closer, slowly overtaking the room.

"Did she die?" Cormac asked softly.

"Yes."

"My condolences to ye."

Luke looked down and swallowed hard. "I am only trying to save you from the pain that I have endured."

"I am sorry for yer loss, but…"

"You still want to go to her tonight."

"If Elena was here tonight, would ye no' go to her?"

Luke's shoulders slumped, and he nodded his head in defeat. "Go to her then. But be prepared to pay the cost, for when your account comes due, I fear the reckoning will be very dear indeed."

Twenty-five

BRAN WAS WAITING FOR HIM WHEN CORE REACHED the bottom of the spiral stairs. "There was no treasure."

"There was none?" asked Core. He knew how unhappy his men would be once they realized they had worked all day for no reward, but he had decided the risk was worth it.

"Ye're no' surprised. After we had plowed up seven different fields, I realized what ye'd done. Ye made us farmers!"

"Nay, I thought the Templars would have buried—"

Bran's fist struck fast, catching him on the chin and sending him sprawling. "Enough o' yer lies!" roared Bran, looming over him with malice in his eyes. "I thought yer father was the master o' deceit, but ye win that prize, boy. There ne'er was any treasure, was there? Ye just said that to save the life o' some fool monk. And ye had us out there today playing crofter because ye're sweet on that Lady Jyne."

"I did what had to be done." Core rubbed his jaw and stood back up. It was not the first time he had been knocked down.

"She's a bonnie lass, but I canna believe ye put us through all that, all for a piece o'—"

In a flash, Cormac lunged at Bran, knife in hand. "Dinna insult the Lady Jyne," he snarled, the tip of his knife pointing into Bran's throat. Core had endured Bran's abuse for years, but never before had he fought back.

Bran stared at him, wide-eyed with surprise. Core dug the tip of his knife into the man's throat, drawing blood, and Bran's face hardened. "It's like that."

Cormac stepped back and returned his knife to his boot. "It's like that."

Bran put a hand to his neck where he had been pricked and stared at the blood on his hand. When Bran looked back up at him, it was with a new respect. "Well then, I'm sorry fer ye, but it doesna change anything. It's over, Cormac. It's time to face Rex."

Core leaned against the stone wall, fearing the meaning of Bran's words. "How much time do I have?"

"I already sent a runner. Yer time's up."

Core felt a weight crush down upon him. His dreams shattered. It was all over. Core gradually became aware of music streaming in from the great hall beyond the doorway, dissonant with the desperation he felt.

Happy voices could be heard. "What's that?" Core walked to the doorway of the great hall, Bran by his side. They looked inside, and Core was astounded by what he saw.

The elders had emerged and had formed a band of a harp, lyre, and lute, playing a jaunty tune. Instead of the bitter ruffians he expected to see, they were eating and drinking with the elders in a friendly sort of way. Dubh was even doing something that might be considered dancing with a plump matron with a wide smile.

Core turned to Bran, confused.

"That old feller, Alasdair Ranald, greeted us like heroes when we returned." Bran shook his head. "Said we had saved them from starvation. Said he wanted to thank us and started this celebration. Probably touched in the head."

"Nay," said Core softly. "Ye did save them."

Bran cleared his throat. "I warrant ye're right."

"The men seem…happy."

"Aye. They're no' accustomed to being welcomed. I figured they could enjoy it before Rex comes."

"Dinna tell my father about Lady Jyne. Please."

Bran gave him a quick nod. "I winna say anything. I like her. Got courage to her. But ye need to get her out o' here."

"I understand."

It was all over. He needed to think of Jyne's safety. And she deserved to know the truth. She would discover it someday. Though the mere thought of revealing himself to Jyne made his heart groan with pain, she should hear the truth from his lips. She would hate him and move on. It would be for the best, for her at least.

One thing was for certain: as long as Core lived, he would put anything and anyone he cared about in danger. He needed to separate himself from Jyne to keep her safe. His father would not stop, not ever. Unless…unless Core was dead.

He knew what he needed to do.

❧

Jyne wandered about the kitchens with a smile still on her face. It had been there ever since she woke up with the memory of Core's kiss on her lips. When she woke to find the marauders plowing the rest of the fields, she was astounded. She ran to the kitchens, where she heard the rumor being spread that the treasure was buried in the fields. She guessed Cormac must have had someone start the rumor, and since then, she could not stop smiling.

Even the elders had been thrilled by the turn of events and decided to reward the hardworking men with music and dancing. Possibly because they were all too tired to do anything else, the men seemed to enjoy the music, and as improbable as it sounded, the groups appeared to be getting along fairly well. It was a day of miracles!

Though she was pleased about the fields, her smile was for Cormac alone. She could not stop thinking about him. He was simply the most wonderful man she had ever met. This was the adventure she had been yearning for her whole life. After years of waiting, it was finally her turn to find romance.

Now she just needed to convince Cormac of that fact.

Jyne dressed in her nicest silk gown, taking a bit of extra time on braiding her hair just so and arranging her gauzy veil to frame her face in what she hoped was an attractive manner. Breanna had been helpful in the effort and assured her that she was looking quite bonnie. She smoothed the veil, feeling the edges to ensure it was straight. She wanted to look her best, for she knew she would be seeing Core.

She was not sure how long it would take to bring her clan to her rescue, but it could not be too much longer. If Core still intended to leave when her brothers arrived, she needed to act now, or all would be lost.

"Ye look right fine, m'lady," said Cook, stirring a pot that hung over the fire. The other elders had gone into the great hall to celebrate with the renegades, leaving Cook and Jyne alone in the kitchens.

"Do I?" asked Jyne in a careless manner, as if it didn't matter to her.

"Ye've only fussed wi' yer veil now a half dozen times," commented Cook. "He'll like what he sees."

"To whom are ye referring?" asked Jyne in feigned nonchalance.

"Ye ken who. That Cormac fella what's been helping us against the Fire Lord. Not that I blame ye. He's a braw one, or he will be once I fatten him up a bit." Cook winked and went back to her roast, a new addition thanks to the continued hunting efforts of the men.

Jyne wisely held her tongue but could not hide the smile. She was finally getting her turn at a real, true romance. No wonder her siblings had done strange things for love. She felt as if she could fly!

Wait...love?

Was she in love with Cormac?

"I think I may be in love with Cormac," Jyne confessed to Cook.

"O' course ye are, dearie," replied Cook with the straightforward confidence of a woman who knew about the world.

"I am in love wi' Cormac," Jyne repeated, getting used to the sound of her words.

"That's right, dearie, ye are. But ye ought no' to be."

Jyne stared at the elder woman. "Why ever not?"

"What's a man doing wi'out a clan? Who's his people is what I want to know." Cook gestured in the air with an iron spoon.

Jyne leapt to his defense. She could not believe anyone would voice complaints about him. "Cormac has helped us tremendously! We are deeply in his debt. What would we have done wi'out him?"

The woman shrugged. "Just a question, m'lady."

"Well! I shall no' be made to think ill o' him."

"Ye do what ye please. But if it please ye now, could ye help me wi' this pot? I dinna have the strength I had in my sixties. Those were some good years." A small, knowing smile came to her lips.

Jyne grabbed a cloth to protect her hands and lifted the other side of a large iron cauldron of hot water away from the flames. Jyne could not help thinking on Cook's words. Perhaps she had a wisdom that Jyne, with her paltry twenty years, did not possess. Jyne realized she did not know much about Cormac's clan, except that he did not wish to share the truth with her. Her brothers would certainly see this as a reason for concern.

And yet, whoever his people may be, he was a good man. A bad man would have left her in the bog. Instead, he had helped her, protected her, and now had acted to care for everyone around him. Besides, she had no interest in being cautious. She had done that for twenty years. She was done being the overprotected baby sister. It was her turn to embrace her destiny. Even if it meant making mistakes, she would not turn from it. Cormac was her friend.

More than a friend.

Much more.

"M'lady?" As if drawn by the fervor of her thoughts, Cormac entered the kitchen by the outside door, having to duck his head to enter the low doorway. He stood before her in his Highland plaid, belted at his trim waist and thrown over one shoulder. His hair was an unruly brown mess as usual, but tonight, he appeared wild and slightly dangerous with a bit of a bruise showing on his jaw. His face was unshaven, revealing black stubble that only seemed to enhance his appeal.

"Cormac!" Her heart thumped its greeting. "Ye've done it!"

"What did I do?" He gave her a worried frown.

"Did you think I would'na find out?" she demanded.

"I…I can explain," stammered Core.

"I overheard the men talking."

"Ye did?" Core's eyes were wide. "Lady Jyne, I—"

"Ye're the most wonderful man in all the world!" She rushed to him and wrapped her arms around him, pinning his arms to his sides. He stood still, his face one of utter confusion.

"I heard the men saying that someone started a rumor that there was treasure in the fields and got the men to plow them up. How were ye able to talk to them? Ye must have pretended friendship. Och, ye're so clever!"

She hugged him again, but he seemed too stunned to move. "Ye've saved the good folks here. Ye saved them."

"Whatever I did, I did for ye," returned Core, wrapping his long arms around her, engulfing her in his embrace. She rested her head against his chest, warm and content.

"Ahem." Cook cleared her throat. "Begging yer pardon, m'lady, but in absence o' yer brother, I feel I should speak up against such goings-on in my kitchen."

"Aye, o' course," faltered Jyne, stepping back. She must be truly affected if she engaged in displays of affection in the kitchen. "Ye must be verra sore," she said, sympathizing with Cormac. He had worked hard last night.

"A wee bit," he admitted and sat slowly on the wooden bench. He moved like every muscle in his body ached.

"Then ye must have the reward I promised to that wicked false warlord."

"Reward?" Suddenly, he didn't look quite so exhausted anymore.

"Aye, but he may come and spoil things. I dinna ken where he is. I hav'na seen him all day."

"I found what is left o' yer sleeping potion and poured it in the wine he called for," said Core. "He's locked in his chamber wi' that monk."

Jyne smiled. "Then we are safe until he awakes. Come to the ground-floor chamber o' the tower. Be there in an hour, and there ye shall receive your reward. Since I am the chatelaine o' this keep, 'tis right for me to express our gratitude." She said this in part for the benefit of Cook, who shot her a glance from behind Core's back that said she was not fooled in the least.

Core, for his part, smiled at her with wide eyes. A moment later, a shadow passed over him, and his countenance fell. He stood and walked close to her, his voice low. "M'lady, may I beg an audience wi' ye alone?"

"O' course, if ye will call me Jyne."

"My Lady Jyne." He spoke slowly, as if savoring the taste of her name on his lips.

She followed him out the side door to the outer ward between the keep and the outer wall. The rising moon hung low on the horizon, large and bright. Little frogs in the nearby creek croaked and chirped, making a soft humming sound.

"I am sorry, but I need to tell ye something." Cormac's shoulders slumped. He began to pace back and forth on the grass. "I need to tell ye who I am."

"But I already ken who ye are," said Jyne. She could tell whatever he felt he must tell her was not going to be good.

"Nay, ye dinna." Core stared at the ground and shook his head.

"Was it ye who pulled me from the bog?" she asked, boldly stepping forward and taking his hand.

He looked up at her, surprised by the question. "Aye."

"And it was ye who helped me try to oust the brigands from my keep."

He shook his head. "I knew it would'na work."

"But ye helped me anyway," Jyne pointed out. "And it was ye who found a safe place for the young ones, and ye who protected yer sister, and ye who tricked those sorry knaves into plowing the fields."

"Aye...but—"

"Whoever yer father is, it doesna matter. What

matters is who ye are." She placed her open palm on his chest.

He stared at her, his dark eyes searching hers. "Do ye mean that?"

"Aye, I do." She hoped she did. In truth, she feared what he was going to tell her *would* matter, and then the dream would die. She wanted to live that dream, to fall in love. She needed the dream more than she needed the truth.

"Thank ye. But…I still need ye to leave this place."

Jyne frowned and dropped her hand to her side. "This is my home, my dower lands. I winna leave."

"'Tis no' safe. I've heard from some o' the men that Red Rex will arrive soon."

Red Rex. The name was synonymous with death and destruction.

"I canna leave these people."

"I will work to get them out too. But ye must flee."

"Nay! These are my lands. We just got the fields plowed. It will be worth nothing if we dinna plant them. We canna leave now. Things are finally starting to improve."

"Any improvements will be destroyed when Rex comes. Please, Lady Jyne, I'm begging ye, please. Ye need to leave. I need to know ye'll be safe."

"Nay, this is my keep and my land. I'll no' be chased away. No' by the Fire Lord, and no' by Red Rex either! Besides, I sent my guard back to find my brothers. The Campbells will be coming soon!"

He opened his mouth as if to speak but closed it again. He was clearly struggling with something, unsure of how to proceed. If he was unsure, she was not.

"Meet me in the ground-floor chamber o' the tower in one hour." She turned and walked back into the kitchen, conscious of his heated gaze watching her as she left. It was her turn. She was in control now. Life was hers for the taking, and she was not going to miss it.

Twenty-six

IT WAS ALL PREPARED. JYNE REQUESTED THE WATER BE heated and brought to the small chamber containing the wooden bathing tub. She was accustomed to Innis Chonnel, where they had a separate bathing chamber designed for that purpose. At the smaller Kinoch Abbey, they did not have the luxury of a separate chamber.

Jyne had found a large, wooden bathing tub in a small chamber on the ground-floor storeroom of the tower. Calling the room a "chamber" was a bit optimistic, for it was most likely designed to hold spices or other valuable commodities. It was small and had a locking door. The wooden tub was so large, it took up the majority of the space. It had taken many trips and a good many disapproving looks from Cook to fill it full of hot water.

The pieces in the storeroom were a hodgepodge of things. A wobbly bench. A broken spinning wheel. A stack of dented shields and crooked spears. Things ill-used and shoved out of the way and out of view.

She moved the unwanted items from the small

chamber to the larger storeroom. How often had she felt like those discarded items? The youngest daughter of a large family was easily overlooked.

It was just because she had suffered so many ill-nesses as a child that everyone saw her as weak. She saw herself as weak. Well, maybe they were wrong. And maybe she was too.

She pushed her shoulders back and stood a little straighter. She was a Campbell after all. The same fearless blood that ran through the veins of her siblings ran through hers. It must, for she was about to do something very bold.

Jyne lit a few more candles and tested the temperature of the water. Now well after sunset, the air was a bit chill, but the water was hot. She had brought a thick robe, some lavender soap, and a jar of a particular balm that Isabelle had taught her to make, which was quite effective in soothing aching muscles. She sprinkled lavender and chamomile into the water, releasing a pleasant aroma into the room.

She smiled as she thought of Cormac. He had been remarkably supportive of her and all the people here. And yet…Cook had brought doubts to mind. She knew his father was not a good man and that he had attempted to tell her something earlier that she was not sure she wanted to hear. But what if it was something she needed to know? Did he have a wife? Was he betrothed?

Surely not. He would not have kissed her had he been married. Yet what if his secret was that he had a bride? He would not be the first man to steal a kiss from a lass who was not his wife.

Her feelings toward him darkened and became confused. She liked him. She liked him quite a bit. But if he was married, those feelings would sour quickly.

A soft rap came at the door, and Cormac stepped in to the dim, moist room. He had shaved since she had seen him last. The effect of the clean-shaven Highlander in the flickering candlelight was enough to get her heart to pound.

"Should I return another time?" he asked tentatively.

Jyne realized he had walked in when she had been contemplating the presence of an unwanted wife, and her face surely would have revealed her displeasure. She forced her expression into something more welcoming. "Nay, do come in wi' ye. Ye've worked verra hard and deserve this reward. I have prepared a bath for ye."

Cormac entered the small chamber cautiously, as if not sure he belonged there. "It smells verra nice in here."

"Some herbs to soothe the muscles. As chatelaine o' this keep, I…I…it is my responsibility to serve ye." She stumbled over the words. Probably because she was attempting to give justification to something that deserved none. "I can either leave ye to yer privacy or stay and…tend ye."

"Stay."

Heat shot up the back of her neck at his simple reply. His eyes met hers, and no one spoke or moved or even breathed as they regarded each other in the flickering candlelight.

"As ye wish," said Jyne softly, as if someone might hear her and rush in to put a stop to it if she spoke any louder.

Cormac shut the door behind him, and she noted that he drew the latch. "Thank ye, for I confess my back is unaccustomed to plowing."

"Oh? What kind o' work are ye accustomed to?" She wished to know more about him…as long as they were the answers she wanted to hear.

Cormac bent down to remove his boots, replying after a moment, "If I had my way, I'd be a scholar." He gave her the wistful smile of a dreamer. "And read books all day long." His face relaxed into a faraway look.

Jyne had never seen anyone so enraptured with book learning. It was not that her brothers were against it, per se, but she would hardly call any of her Highland brood scholars. But here was a man who held a passion for books.

"Do ye have anything else that has met wi' yer fancy? A wife, perhaps?"

He looked up at her with a quick jerk of his head, and she knew she had been much less subtle than she had intended. "I have no wife." Amusement sparkled in his eyes.

"Oh?" Jyne busied herself in arranging the already arranged jars of herbs and oils.

"I have me no wife, no betrothed, no one." He answered her unspoken question.

"I'm sorry ye've found no one who has captured yer heart," she said, pretending to be a neutral party in the affair. At least he had not been trying to tell her he was married. As long as he was a bachelor, she felt she could handle anything else that might be in his past.

"I would'na say that." Cormac leaned lazily against the wooden tub.

She went back to focusing on the jar of soap, hoping the light in the room was dim enough that he would not notice her blush.

"And ye? Have ye a husband or a man to whom ye are betrothed?" he asked, though he did not sound concerned that her answer would be anything but a denial.

"How can ye ask me such a thing? O' course not."

"I am glad we have that settled." He smiled at her; she could hear it in his voice.

She glanced at him, and his warm eyes captured her. She could not help but smile in return. After a while, the smile became strained, and Jyne wondered what to do next. He also seemed unsure. She knew he was supposed to get in the tub now, naked, but how was that going to happen? Even the mere thought of him removing his plaid made her cheeks burn. And yet she did wish very much to see what was underneath the wrappings. He was her special present.

She paused a moment more until she realized that he would not be the one to push her into anything. He would wait until she took the lead. This was an unusual place for her, for she was accustomed to being told what to do. Having a tall, strong Highlander patiently wait for her command was something utterly foreign to her experience.

She liked it.

"Perhaps ye'd like to get into the water?" she asked, hoping she would not seem timid. She felt timid and bold, both at the same time, if such a thing were possible.

"I would like that verra much. Shall I remove my…" He gestured to his plaid and tunic.

"Aye, that would be best, since ye are to bathe. I shall turn around to preserve yer modesty, and when ye're within the tub, let me know." She turned around slowly, though in truth and to her shame, she did not wish to. What she wished for was a way for him to think she wasn't looking but still to look anyway. She shooed away such treacherous thoughts and waited until she heard movement in the water.

"Are ye decent?" she asked.

"Nay, but ye can turn around."

She spun to face him. His clothes—his shirt and plaid—were folded neatly on the bench. He was seated in the large wooden tub, his upper chest and arms visible above the dark waters. He was a trim man, but bare-chested, the definition of his muscles was clear. His chest was smooth and defined. He might be lean, but he was strong.

He did not smile, but his eyes met hers, gauging her reaction. She realized that between the two of them, he was the one stripped naked, and he was watching for her response. A new sort of confidence spread cautiously through her, if confidence could be cautious. He was waiting for her approval. When had anybody waited on her approval?

She enjoyed the novel sensation of power.

The only thing she did not like was the fact that she could not see him except for the parts that were above the water. If the parts below view were as appealing as the parts she could see, she was in serious trouble.

It wasn't as if she'd never seen a naked man. Living with so many brothers and so many cousins and so many clansmen wearing nothing under so many plaids, it was inevitable that what was underneath would not remain secret forever. Yet she wanted to see his, and the thought made her blush again.

A slow smile spread across Cormac's face. He must have interpreted the blush as approval of what she saw. And he was right.

"Ye must be sore after so much work. Would ye allow me to rub some ointment into yer muscles?" She picked up the jar and walked around the tub toward him. She kept her eyes on his face, though she did wish to look down.

"Aye, lass, for I confess I am a wee bit stiff today."

Stiff? Did he mean…of course he didn't…did he? She grabbed the jar of ointment and walked around behind him so he could not see her blush again. She took a bit of the ointment and began to rub it on his shoulders. She thrilled to be touching him, working her fingers into his muscles. He was a strong one, though she could feel those places where his muscles were knotted and sore.

"Ohh…ahh…" Cormac gave a satisfied groan.

She was tremendously pleased to have produced such a reaction and continued to massage away the pain of sore, tight, overused muscles. It gave her a chance to run her fingers up and down his arms and back. She moved closer and peeked down his front. The water was dark in the dim room, and she could not see exactly what she wanted to see. Her heart beat faster at her own curiosity. Her own desire.

When had she ever known desire? She had not known she could burn with a strong, powerful longing. And her burning was for Cormac.

She focused back on her work with renewed vigor, finding the knots of tension in Cormac's back and applying her elbow to them until the muscles began to release. Core's groans turned into something closer to whimpers.

"How does it feel now?" she asked, trying to stay focused on her task.

"Och, lass, I've ne'er felt anything so good nor so painful in all my life." Core sank deeper into the water, and Jyne feared he might submerge, which he did.

"Come back! Are ye all right?" Jyne tried to pull him up, but he emerged on his own and turned around to face her, resting his arms on the edge of the wooden tub. Water ran down his face, catching on his long eyelashes and dripping down his angular face to the tub.

"If ye were not already the lass o' my fancy, I'd sure be smitten now."

"So ye fancy me?" She blinked at him, coy as could be.

He responded by placing two wet, warm hands on either side of her face and kissing her long and deep. If she had any doubts as to the man's interest or intention, that kiss put to rest any question. He liked her. He wanted her. She knew that for an absolute fact.

So what was she going to do next?

"Come join me," he murmured as he nuzzled her neck.

"I'd get wet." It was a painfully obvious thing to say, but she didn't know how else to respond.

"That's the idea," he purred. "Most o' the baths I've taken, I've gotten wet."

"But it is improper. I could'na bathe wi' a stranger. A male stranger." As much as she wished to be bold, her proper upbringing held her back.

"Aye, 'tis improper. And if I had any chivalry to me, I'd not ask it. I confess it is not a good idea for the likes o' ye to be associating in any way wi' the likes o' me." He gave her a seductive smile that negated any argument he might have raised. "But I swear it will feel good to yer bones to soak in this tub, and I owe ye the same treatment to yer back as ye gave me."

She had never wanted anything more in her life. Steam rose softly from the hot water and the gleaming, smooth skin of the man leaning on the edge of the wooden tub. It would take considerable effort to resist. But she could not. What would her brothers and sisters say? And yet, was this not exactly what she had wanted all along?

"I'll ne'er tell. It will be our secret." Cormac rested his chin on his arms on the tub.

"But…" She was at war between her desire and her convictions. "I could never be…unclothed with a man." A steaming-hot, dripping-wet man.

He merely smiled. "Come, join me."

Well…would she?

Twenty-seven

"LEAVE YER CHEMISE ON. PERFECTLY PROPER," tempted Cormac.

Jyne knew it was anything but proper, but it was enough to soothe her internal objections so she could act the way she wished. His eyes glinted in the candle-light. "Turn around and let me loose yer kirtle."

She turned around. His hands deftly loosed the ties, and before she knew it, he had drawn the gown up and over her head. She ended up with it bundled in her arms, wondering how that happened. She knew she should be running from the room, but also knew she was not going to do anything of the kind.

She folded her gown neatly, feeling quite ridiculous, but of course, this was her nicest, and she did not wish to see it ruined. She placed it on the bench next to his plaid and unpinned her veil, putting it on top of her gown. When she turned back to him, he stood up, and she feared her jaw dropped.

The tub was deep, and his manhood was still covered, but the waterline lapped along the muscular line of his abdomen, several inches below his navel. His modesty was maintained, but barely. Water ran in rivulets down his perfectly toned chest, his muscles chiseled perfection. Everything on him was tight and firm.

He held out a hand to her, and she took it. She stepped up on the stool and gingerly climbed into the tub, trying not to look ungraceful. Her thin linen chemise hit the water and pooled up around her as she stepped in. The warm water surrounded and soothed her. She stood next to him, the water a few inches above her waist.

Core took her hands and sank down into the water, taking her with him. There was a stool in the tub that he had been sitting on, but only one. The tub was large, but with both of them, the water splashed over the sides.

"Here, sit." Cormac turned her around and positioned the stool in the middle of the tub for her to sit. He stood behind her and began to slowly massage her shoulders. Her muscles released as he eased away the tension. It was so wonderful that she leaned back against him, relishing in the seductive warmth all around her.

He slowly wrapped his arms around her, and after a bit of positioning, he was once again sitting on the stool in the warm water, and she was sitting on his lap, reclining back against him. It was so delicious; she never wished to move. It was so enticing; she wanted more.

She turned to him and boldly initiated a kiss. He responded in kind and kissed her deeply until she laid her head back on his chest. This was the way she wanted to spend the rest of her life, with Cormac. Her brothers would be coming soon, and they would chase off Red Rex, the Fire Lord, and all the unwanted brigands, until none were left but her and Cormac, whom her brother would naturally wish to reward. And she had a good idea of what, or whom, his reward should be.

"Lady Jyne, I wonder if I could be so bold as to ask o' ye a favor?" asked Cormac, holding her close and warm.

"Please call me Jyne. It seems a bit presumptuous for formal titles whilst sitting in a bathing tub together." Jyne giggled. She could not remember when she had felt so good.

"My Jyne, will ye grant me one boon?" asked Cormac.

"What is yer request?" She was inclined to give him anything he wished. Truly…anything. A ripple of excitement coursed through her.

"I wish for ye to leave Kinoch tomorrow wi' Breanna and Brother Luke. They will take ye back to yer people."

Jyne struggled to sit up so she could look at him. "I'll no' be run off. Kinoch is mine, or at least it will be when I marry. 'Tis mine! I'll no' have anyone take it from me!"

"I need to see ye safe."

"Safe! I'm tired o' being safe. Safe means ye ne'er leave the protection o' yer own walls until yer home becomes yer prison. Safe means being swept aside from every important decision because ye're too young and inexperienced. Safe means always being shunted away and forgotten. Safe is no' living!"

Core stared at her and made no reply. Water dripped from the edge of the tub to the stone floor, making a soft tapping sound.

"Is that how they treated ye?" His voice was soft with understanding.

"Aye." Jyne sighed. "I was a sickly child, small and weak, not like any o' my brothers and sisters. I was also the youngest sister, so I stayed home while everyone else went off and fought battles, and found treasures, and fell in love. I never had any adventures...until I met ye."

"I am sorry if ye dinna care for yer childhood." It was Core's turn to sigh. "But it seems to me, to live in a castle, surrounded by family who care enough no' to let ye get hurt, it is a goodly life. Did ye have books in that castle o' yers?"

"Aye," she admitted.

"Then it sounds like heaven to me. Dinna be so eager to find adventure when ye already have everything ye need at home."

"And if ye had such a home, ye'd be content to stay in it forever?"

"Aye, I would."

"If ye wanted to go out riding, ye'd no' complain if they sent ye to help make bread instead? And when yer brothers and sisters went to tournaments and festivals, ye'd be happy to be left behind? And if someone threatened yer borders, ye'd stay content by the fire, while others protected ye?"

Cormac paused before finally responding. "Ye have a point, I grant ye. But not all risks are worth taking. And this one is not. Ye must go."

Jyne raised her chin. "I will stay."

Cormac lowered his mouth to hers and whispered on her lips, "Ye will go." He kissed her until she forgot what they were arguing about. He slowly stroked up and down her side and then moved up until he was cupping a breast. He trailed his fingers across the wet material of her chemise, which hid nothing from his sight, teasing her until she arched into his hand.

"I should'na take liberties wi' ye," he whispered.

"I give ye leave to do so," Jyne whispered back. In truth, if he did not continue, she would be most put out.

He responded with a sort of guttural noise and slipped a hand down her wet chemise. He circled her breast with his thumb, sending shivers down her spine. The sensations he built within her were something she had never experienced before. When he trailed kisses down the hollow of her neck to pay even greater homage to her breasts, she felt as if she might come undone. Never had she felt anything so sensuous than to be adored in a tub of warm water.

Sitting on his lap, she felt his affection rise. Finally, she was able to get a good look.

"Do I pass inspection?" he asked, noting her interest.

She smiled in response and ran a hand up his shaft, amazed at her ability to make him jolt.

"Ah, lass, ye've undone me, but I warrant there are things we should'na do," he said, moving her hand.

"Ye fear my brother?"

"More than Red Rex, if ye should return to him no longer a maid."

Jyne rested her head on his wet chest, snuggling deeper into the warm blanket of water and closer to Core. "I suppose it would be unkind of me to ask for something that would seal yer doom."

"Ye're kind to think o' me. But perhaps there is something I can do for ye."

Jyne looked him in the eye. "Show me."

Cormac gave her a tentative smile. "I…" He leaned forward to touch his forehead to hers. "I confess my experience wi' women has been…limited. Ye must tell me what ye like, for I wish to please ye."

Jyne kissed his cheek. "Ye are verra sweet. I confess, I have no experience wi' men, so we are a hopeless case."

He kissed one cheek, then the other as he ran his hand up her leg to her thighs, easily moving the floating chemise out of his way. He kissed her lips, and he stroked his fingers up between her legs.

"Oh!"

He stopped. "Oh, bad?"

"Nay, oh, good."

He continued. It was surreal to be caressed under the warm water, but it felt so good, she could not bring herself to stop him. He paid close attention to her and continued to gently explore until he found a spot that made her gasp.

He caressed her, building up in her something like winding a coil tighter and tighter until she feared she might explode.

He stopped.

"Core!"

He continued building up the amazing sensations. "I would ask from ye a boon. A gift o' whatever I wish," he whispered in her ear.

"What?" She could hardly make sense of what he was saying, with his hand between her legs.

"I want something from ye. Will ye give it to me?" he purred in her ear, teasing her with his fingers.

"Aye." She would agree to anything.

"Anything?" He slowed his hand, toying with her.

"Aye, anything." She pressed herself closer to him, aching for him to continue.

"Promise?" He flicked a finger back and forth, sending jolts of sensation through her.

"Aye, promise!"

He continued his clever work in earnest, and she felt the tightness suddenly explode within her, pulsing through her in waves of bliss. She collapsed back against him in the warm water, her head on his shoulder.

"Was it acceptable?" he asked, tentative again.

"Nay. It was…och, I hav'na the words. It was… wonderful."

His smile was open and vulnerable. "Truly?"

"Aye. I have never…I dinna ken…I do adore ye."

"Well, now." His dark green eyes glinted with pride. "I am glad to have pleased ye."

She snuggled into his embrace. "Verra, verra pleased."

"Thank ye for offering me a boon in return."

"Aye, what can I do for ye?" She had some ideas.

"Leave tomorrow wi' Breanna and Brother Luke."

Jyne raised her head up and gasped at his smug face. "Ye tricked me!"

"Aye, lass, I did."

"Ye're no' the man I thought. Ye're no' nice at all." She splashed water in his face, but he just grinned at her.

"I fear 'tis true. I am not a nice man."

"I despise ye! Why would ye be so unkind?"

Cormac shrugged, unrepentant. "I must keep ye safe. I fear I love ye too much to see ye hurt."

Silence fell on the dimly lit chamber as both of them realized what he had just said.

"Love?" asked Jyne in a voice barely over a whisper.

All traces of humor vanished from his face.

"Love."

Twenty-eight

CORMAC HAD PLANNED IT OUT. HE WOULD SEDUCE Jyne in the tub to get her to agree to leave Kinoch Abbey. It was a dirty trick, but he was desperate. Short of tying her up and forcibly removing her, this was his next best plan. The fact that it allowed him to live out his fantasies with her was purely coincidental.

What was not part of the plan was confessing his true feelings. No, that was not in the plan at all. It was the truth though, and now that he had confessed it, he would not deny it.

"Love."

It was all he needed to say. Apparently, it was all either of them needed to say, for Jyne stared at him in stunned silence. Not exactly the response he was hoping for.

He removed himself from the tub and helped Jyne out, wrapping her in the robe she had brought for him and grabbing the plaid for himself. Now for the hardest part. The farewell. If everything went according to plan, he would never see her again.

"Brother Luke will be leaving in the morning. Ye'll allow him to return ye to yer people," he said.

Jyne frowned at him. "I'm only leaving because I made ye a promise."

"I would ask ye for yet more."

"Ye dare ask more o' me?"

"I would ask that ye allow my sister to accompany ye back to yer clan. If ye would provide her sanctuary, it would be a blessing to her. And to me."

"O' course I will. I swear she will be safe. But what o' the Ranalds?"

"Aye, I've thought o' them. If things go according to plan, they will be safe too."

"But what will ye do?" she asked.

Core stared at the ground, the words stuck in his teeth. "After this is over, I'm leaving."

"Leaving? Where?"

"I dinna ken. Somewhere far away where I might start over."

"But what about…me?"

"I'm sorry, m'lady. Where I go, ye canna go. And where ye go, I canna be. We have no place together. We are too different."

Jyne's lips parted as if he had slapped her. The look of betrayal cut him to the quick.

He tried to explain. "Please, believe that if there was any other way…I need to keep us both safe."

"Safe!" She brushed away a tear with an impatient hand. "I dinna want to be safe. I want to be wi' ye!"

"I canna be wi' ye, if it puts ye at risk. I canna do it."

"Coward!"

"True."

"When are ye leaving?"

"Tonight."

Jyne blinked, and more tears fell.

He would have rather cut off a limb than watch her cry, but this was the only way to get her out of harm's way. At this point, her safety was the only thing that mattered to him.

"I'm sorry," he said softly. "I am so sorry."

"I hate ye."

"Good, then ye winna spend any time missing my sorry presence. Come, let me walk ye back to yer chamber."

"I can do it alone."

He walked her back anyway. There was not far to go, for her chamber was only two stories above the makeshift bathing room. She reached her doorway, stepped inside, and slammed the door in his face.

Cormac stared at the wooden door. Was that how it was going to end? From within, he could hear the muffled sounds of crying. A lump formed in his throat, and he hastily wiped away something that had gotten in his eyes.

This was all part of his plan.

It truly was a horrible plan.

And it was about to get worse.

❦

It was fortunate that Core had gotten sleep during the day, for he was certainly not getting sleep during the night. He gathered his experiments, the bottles of saltpeter, sulfur, and other ingredients, and mixed them carefully to create more of the black powder. He laid out small charges in the courtyard. If he was going to do this, he might as well make it memorable. In truth, he was counting on it to be memorable, and for all to tell his father the grim tale.

After the courtyard was prepared, he went down to the crypt. It was almost dawn, and he needed to get everything prepared. He began to carefully mix the exact proportions of saltpeter and sulfur, taking care to stay well away from the torch he had brought.

"What is this ye're doing?" asked Donnach, waking up. He sat up and stretched, pushing back the blankets from his fresh pallet.

"Alchemy," returned Core over his shoulder.

Donnach washed his hands and face in a basin of water and prepared himself for the day. Over the past few days, thanks to Core and Brother Luke, Donnach's cell had been transformed. It now boasted all the amenities of any good chamber, except a key to turn the lock. Core had ensured that Donnach was well supplied with food and drink, and even emptied his chamber pot.

Donnach sat on a chair and began to leaf through an ornately engraved book, no doubt courtesy of Brother Luke. "What are ye doing wi' alchemy? And when might I expect my breakfast?"

"Sorry, too busy to serve ye today." Core set the charges, making sure the powder was just right. "I'll be showing everyone the power o' the Fire Lord."

Donnach snapped the book shut. "Fire Lord? Ye're no' fooling about wi' that thunder and lightning sacrilege that ripped a hole through the postern gate, are ye?"

Core turned to him. "How would ye ken about that?"

"I heard it, dinna I? And Brother Luke told me o' the damage. I dinna want any o' that here. Take it away!"

"It will be fine. Just dinna toss any sparks this way."

Donnach jumped up and rattled the bars on the gate. "Ye let me out now! If ye care to kill me, come do it like a man!"

"I'm no' trying to kill ye," soothed Cormac. "I assure ye, I'll let ye go at the right time, so ye can run away. Ye're right. 'Tis time for ye to fetch the Laird Campbell." He turned back to his work. "I think there will be enough time," he muttered.

"Ye think? Ye're not sure? Let me out!" Donnach rattled the cage harder, the loud clanging echoing off the cavern walls.

"I will, I will. But if I let ye out now, ye'll just hurt me."

"I swear I'll rip ye apart!"

"Well, ye're going to have to wait. Now remember—no sparks." Cormac left Donnach hollering and threatening and banging on the bars of his cage.

Cormac quietly crept back to the tower. The sun's rays had not yet broken over the horizon, but he needed to move quickly to get everything prepared. Despite his haste, he paused on the second floor, outside the door to Jyne's room. Was she sleeping? Did she still hate him?

Core forced his feet to move up one more flight of circular stairs to his own solar.

"'Tis my turn to wake ye." Core shook Luke.

The monk blinked a few times in the predawn gloom. "What are you about now?"

"I have a plan. I need ye to take Breanna and Jyne back to her clan. Jyne has agreed to ask her brother for sanctuary for Breanna. She should be safe there. Ye need to leave this morn."

Brother Luke sat up straight. "And what of you?"

Cormac sighed. "The Fire Lord needs to die."

Luke stared at him. "What are you saying?"

"My father is determined to see me become some ruthless warlord like himself and will destroy anything and anyone I care for to make me serve him. Ye're right. Once he learns o' my power to destroy, he winna stop but use it to harm others."

Luke frowned at him. "What are you going to do?"

"If I am dead, it all stops. The monks are safe. The books are safe. Jyne is safe."

Luke rose with a deep frown etched on his face and put a hand on his shoulder. "My friend, to take your own life, it is not right. There must be another way."

Cormac shook his head. "There is no other way. The Fire Lord must die. Though…if I do it right, I hope to live to die again some other day."

Luke's frown turned to confusion. "I do not follow you."

"I plan to set a blast that will convince all that I am dead."

"But you will not be?"

"I hope not. Then I will run far and fast. Mayhap Florence will suit me better than it did ye."

"And Jyne?"

Cormac took a breath. "Jyne will return home wi' an adventure to rival her siblings'. In time, I hope she will remember me fondly. But the important thing is that she will be safe."

"And the truth about you?" asked Luke.

"Tell her," said Cormac firmly. "She will not suffer heartache if she hates me. But wait till ye get her safe."

"As you wish," said Luke with a nod.

"Hurry now. Red Rex may come at any time. I've met wi' Ranald and told him to get his people moving, at least the ones who can travel. The sooner ye leave, the better."

"But my books…"

Core shook his head. "We must hope for the best. Will ye leave the books to protect the lives of—"

"Of course I will," interrupted Luke. "What do you take me for?" He thrust his feet into boots and prepared himself for the day. "Though I may be able to take a few in flight—"

"When Red Rex arrives, there will be naught here but stories o' my glorious death. Bran has already told him my story about the treasure was false. He will come to take out his vengeance on me, but with me dead, there will be little point. I warrant he will leave the Ranalds and the books alone. I fear he may put the monastery to the torch, but at least the monks and the books will no' be inside. Later, when he is gone, ye can return for yer scrolls."

Luke nodded slowly. "I hope ye're right."

"Just leave now. I've said my farewells to Jyne. Convey to Breanna that I wish her well."

"I wish for you the same." Much to Cormac's surprise, Luke embraced him warmly, then kissed both cheeks. It was more affection than he had ever displayed. It was more emotion than Cormac thought Luke capable of feeling.

Cormac grabbed the large cloak and horned helm, the trappings of the Fire Lord. He would not be sorry to see them go. He nodded a farewell to Luke and went back downstairs. He had not made it far before he was accosted by the enraged figure of his sister.

"What did ye do to her?" Breanna demanded, standing before him on the stone stairs, her hands on her hips, her eyes blazing like fire.

"Is she no' well?" he asked with true anxiety.

"She cried herself to sleep, that's what. Now what fool thing did ye do?"

"I tricked her into agreeing to leave. Rex is coming. She needs to be gone before he arrives."

Breanna's face sobered in an instant. "Aye, she does. I would'na wish to see her hurt."

"Aye. Ye both need to be gone. Brother Luke will take ye both to the Campbell. Jyne has agreed to ask for sanctuary for ye."

Breanna stared at him and blinked back emotion welling up in her eyes. "Ye did that for me? I always thought in the end, I'd have to marry that old fool."

"O' course I did that for ye. Why would ye doubt me?"

"No' doubt ye. I just know our father. I wish I could find all my sisters and protect them in the same way." Breanna took a deep breath, as if a great weight had been lifted. "I canna believe ye did this for me."

"Ye're my sister," Cormac said with a shrug.

Breanna shook her head. "Half sister. Yer mother was a lady. Mine was…well, she wasna a lady, I can tell ye that. I'm just the bastard child of a warlord."

"Ye're my sister," Cormac said firmly.

"And a fine lady," added Brother Luke, coming down the stairs.

"Take care o' them, and get them clear o' Kinoch as soon as may be."

"What shall I tell Jyne?" asked Breanna.

"Tell her…tell her I love her. Nay, tell her I'm sorry. Nay…I dinna ken. She doesna understand the danger she's in. Just, dinna tell her anything. The sooner she forgets me, the better."

"Will ye forget her?"

"Nay. I will never forget."

Twenty-nine

"CORMAC TOLD US TO MOVE QUICKLY," SAID BROTHER Luke, grabbing another armload of books.

"Aye, but would ye leave these behind? Red Rex loves to burn books," said Breanna, carrying out a load herself.

"Does he?" asked Jyne, seizing more books to carry.

"So I've been told," said Breanna quickly.

Jyne hustled out of the side door of the chapel where all the books had been stashed and carried them out the postern gate to where the cart was hiding. Leaving brought mixed emotions. She did not wish to abandon her post or the Ranalds, but she was a Campbell and would honor her word. Besides, somewhere out there was Cormac, and she still held hope that somehow they could be together again.

She had met with Alasdair, who was already helping to pack those who could travel to join the children. He would stay with those who could not leave. She said a tearful farewell to Alasdair, Cook, and the others. She did not wish to leave them, but she knew she had no other choice. Also, they may be better able to avoid notice if she was not among them.

"What about the children we took to the crofters' huts?" she asked Breanna and Brother Luke. "Should we take them wi' us?"

"Do ye ken yer brother would be open to helping them also?" asked Breanna.

"O' course he would!" exclaimed Jyne. "We've never turned aside a person in need, and none in our clan ever know hunger, at least not when it is within our power to prevent it."

"Ah, then let's take them wi' us," said Breanna with a wide smile.

"They would slow us down considerably," warned Brother Luke. He shook his head. "I probably should not take the books, but to leave them here…"

"Nay, the books must be moved. Red Rex will burn them," said Breanna firmly. "I doubt he will care about orphans living in huts a few miles away. They can mean nothing to him. Taking them wi' us might put them at more risk."

"Agreed," said Jyne reluctantly, for she knew Breanna was right. "When we tell my brother where Red Rex is, he will certainly ride here with his warriors to put an end to him. I hope we can return here soon, for my brother canna be far." The thought that Donnach had not been able to deliver the message was one too terrible to entertain.

"He can certainly try," muttered Breanna. "Red Rex is as slippery as an eel."

They were almost finished loading the books when loud popping pierced the quiet dawn, shattering the calm and sending hundreds of birds loudly squawking into flight.

"What in the world was that?" cried Jyne.

"'Tis the Fire Lord up to something," grumbled Luke.

"Finish what ye're doing. I'll go check." Jyne grabbed her bow and a quiver of arrows that Brother Luke had managed to return to her for her journey home.

"Nay, m'lady!" cried Breanna.

"Please, stay here!" insisted Brother Luke, but Jyne paid them no heed. If the Fire Lord had decided to hurt her friends, she would stay and defend them, promise or no promise.

Jyne ran into the chapel and out the door to a passage that led back outside or to the sleeping quarters of the marauders. Something was happening in the inner courtyard; she could hear it.

Not wanting to be seen, she slipped into the old passageway of the converts and ran down the dark, narrow passage, trailing her fingertips to the wall to prevent herself from crashing into anything. She crawled out the other side and dashed into the east storeroom. From there, she could peek from behind the door to see what was happening.

The Fire Lord, in his bulky bearskin cloak and his monstrous horned helm, stood with his back toward her in the middle of the once-peaceful courtyard. He held a torch high in one hand. His men and the few elders left were gathered on the other side of the courtyard, watching him.

"I have heard ye doubt my knowledge and my power!" the Fire Lord accused. "Some o' ye doubt I know where the Templar treasure is. To these, I only have one message." He lowered his torch for a moment, and something on the ground began to sparkle and spit, running along the ground until it flashed lightning with a huge clap of thunder.

Jyne clapped her hands over her ears in surprise at the loud noise and stepped back farther into the storeroom.

"Dinna ever doubt me again!" roared the Fire Lord.

Jyne was inclined not to. He was truly a wicked demon. She could not wait to have her brother put an end to his existence.

A sudden banging sound from below her feet, followed by the wail of the undead, filled her with a gripping fear. Had the Fire Lord awoken the ghost of the old tower? She frowned at herself. She had created that story. She could not let it terrify her. But something was making quite a racket in the crypt.

"I will go now and show ye the treasure that has been sealed in this keep. Prepare to be amazed!" shouted the Fire Lord. More bangs and roars of his particular demonic power rang in her eardrums and shook the very stones around her.

She grabbed a lit torch from the wall and wrenched open the trapdoor in the floor, revealing a stone staircase leading down. The banging and hollering was louder now, almost sounding like a man.

She carefully made her way down the stairs and around a bend in the passage, which opened into a larger cavern. The cave had been hewn from the stone in sharp, angular strokes. Minerals in the rock sparkled in the light of her flickering torch. On the far end was an iron-bar gate, and within stood a man.

"Donnach!" She ran to her clansman, who was

locked behind the gate. Donnach was here? Then nobody had run for help? Her heart sank to her shoes.

"Lady Jyne!" he exclaimed in surprise. "Are ye well, m'lady? Ye should no' be here."

"Och, Donnach, did that bastard lock ye in here? I swear to ye, I will avenge ye."

"Nay, lass, ye must go. 'Tis no' safe here."

"Jyne!"

Jyne spun around to face the Fire Lord himself.

"How dare ye!" she demanded. "How dare ye lock my kinsman in a crypt! I will see ye hanged for this and all yer other crimes!"

The Fire Lord held up his hands, showing her that he was holding a key. "Ye're right. I am a wicked, horrible man. I will unlock the gate now." The Fire Lord spoke slowly and calmly, as if trying not to spook her. The torch in her hand flickered, its orange light dancing against the walls of the cavern.

Jyne backed away from the gate to allow the warlord access to unlock the door. Why would he agree so readily to her demands? Something was wrong. Something was very wrong.

"Ye need to get her out o' here," the Fire Lord said to Donnach, who nodded in return. He slowly placed the key in the lock and turned it, unlocking the iron-bar gate.

"Now back away and let him go," demanded Jyne. She dropped her torch and grabbed her bow to make sure the Fire Lord did not hurt Donnach. Something behind her began to crackle and spit.

"Run!" commanded the Fire Lord.

Donnach sprinted toward her and grabbed her

hand. "Run! Make haste!" He pulled her toward the stairs even as several more black lines on the floor began to sparkle and hiss.

She tried to run after Donnach, but he pulled hard, yanking her off her feet. She fell to the ground, and something flashed before her eyes. She rolled over and backed away from the spitting, crackling fire, but it was now between her and the stairs. The strange sparkling and popping fire was racing toward a black lantern sort of contraption.

"Get away!" shouted the Fire Lord, emerging up from behind a large rock formation, his horned helmet casting grotesque shadows on the rock walls like an emerging demon.

She backed away from him toward the hissing lantern. "Ye stay away from me!"

"Get away from there! Run!" He jumped over a large boulder and sprinted toward her. She shrieked and braced herself for the impact, for he looked as if he would run straight through her, but instead, he dashed past her toward the hissing lantern and kicked it to a far wall, then spun quickly and tackled her to the ground, covering her with his body.

She opened her mouth to scream in protest, but a loud blast ripped through the cavern, silencing her with an ear-splitting explosion. A thunder of rocks shattering, falling, cascading down, gripped her with a nameless fear. They were going to be crushed. She opened her mouth to scream but choked on the dust. They were plunged into total darkness, the inky blackness of a tomb.

She was buried alive with the Fire Lord.

Thirty

THE DETESTABLE WARLORD PRESSED HIMSELF CLOSER ON top of her as rocks and debris rained down on them. The man suddenly went heavy on her, and she gasped for breath, coughing and sputtering in the thick dust.

As suddenly as it began, it was over, a few pebbles continuing to slide, and then all she could hear was the ringing in her ears in the darkness. She blinked her eyes against the grit, but could see nothing. She struggled to get free of the crushing weight on top of her. Was the man dead?

She grasped at him, trying to push him off of her. His helmet was gone, and he was trimmer than she had imagined under the bulky bearskin cloak. He suddenly gasped for breath and coughed, rolling himself off her. He groaned and remained down, his shoulder touching hers. Nothing could be seen in the inky blackness, the gaping void of nothingness that had fallen over them.

She sat up, coughing from the dust, her head spinning, her ears ringing. She was shaking from shock and fear. "What have ye done?" Her mouth was filled with grit, and her words came out low and hoarse. She coughed from the dust and debris. Her heart pounded in her chest. She had almost been killed.

The form next to her lay silent for a moment, and she would have thought him dead were it not for the raspy breathing. This was her chance. The Fire Lord was incapacitated. She should defend herself before he could attack. She scrambled up to her hands and knees and felt around for a rock. She found one and lifted it up with trembling hands. Was she truly going to kill him?

She held the rock tight, unsure what to do, her pulse pounding in her ears. She could kill him now. She should kill him now.

He moved, scraping the floor of the cave covered in sand and grit. "Are ye hurt?" he asked in a low, throaty voice.

She said nothing and instead held the large rock at the ready. This might be her last chance to protect herself. To protect all of them.

"Jyne?"

She lifted the rock higher and turned in the direction of his voice. Her hands shook, and she dropped the stone with a crunch on the mass of other stones. She could not kill a man unaware in the dark.

"Jyne!" His hands fumbled at her.

"Leave off! Dinna touch me!" She scrambled away from him and put a hand on her table knife that hung from her belt. She was ready to defend herself should he attack.

Instead, the hands withdrew. "I...I thought ye were hurt."

"What have ye done?"

"Och, my head," mumbled the warrior. The ringing in her ears had turned to pounding behind her temples. Since he had been above her when the thunder struck, she did not doubt his head was aching something fierce.

Jyne began to fumble around at the wall of rocks. She could see no crack of light. She could see nothing at all. She felt around with a growing sense of panic. How was she going to get out? She must escape!

She climbed up the pile of rubble, trying to toss aside the rocks. Beside her came the noise of scuffling and scraping, and she assumed the Fire Lord was also searching for a way out. She moved along what should have opened into the tower stairs, but all she could feel was a cascade of rock.

"There is no way out." The Fire Lord's words were grim.

"Nay!" cried Jyne, her breaths coming short and quick as terror stuck in her throat. "Nay, there must be a way out." She began picking up rocks and tossing them aside.

"The whole corner o' the keep most likely collapsed," said the warlord. "We canna escape this way."

"I must get out o' here!" Terror blossomed into panic. She redoubled her efforts in tossing aside rocks. She had to get out. She had to see light. It was getting difficult to breathe.

"We canna get out that way," repeated the warlord with a sigh.

Hands touched her arms, trying to stay them. She flinched and flailed back, hitting something hard. The warlord gasped in pain.

"Are ye hurt?" she asked, trying to catch her breath. He remained silent.

"Good! I'm glad ye're hurt!" she pronounced and grabbed another stone. It was too heavy to lift, though she tugged at it with all her might. "I should have knocked ye on the head with a rock when I had the chance."

Despair settled on her, and she sank to the sandy floor of the cave, blinking back tears in the stifling blackness. Where was Cormac? He had always been there to rescue her. But no, not this time. He was already gone and believed her to be safe with Breanna and Brother Luke. Core would not come to save her. She was on her own.

She was trapped with a man she despised. A man who might attack at any moment.

And yet…he had saved her. Had he not kicked aside the fire lantern and thrown himself over her, she would probably be dead. "Why did ye protect me from yer unholy blast?"

"I could'na let ye be hurt," he answered in a gravelly voice, as if it was obvious. But it wasn't clear at all. Why should a warlord, who had come to conquer them and take a treasure he seemed convinced was buried here, want to save her? Especially since saving her put him in harm's way.

"Well…thank ye for saving my life. But why would ye place those…what was that thing that ripped the rocks apart?"

"A blast o' black powder."

"Is that how ye broke through the postern gate?"

"Aye. I've been studying alchemy and the principles

o'…och, never ye mind." He broke off his train of thought, probably realizing he was sharing too much. Her interest was piqued.

"Ye've been studying?" For some reason, she had assumed all warlords were illiterate, ignorant, and downright unappealing. This one was not fitting the mold. "Why did ye set that…that…thing down here in the first place?"

"I…I had a plan."

"A verra bad plan!" she cried with feeling.

"Aye, it seems that way," acknowledged the Fire Lord, sounding defeated.

"Did ye wish to kill Donnach? Ye're truly an evil man!" Jyne scrambled to her feet, not wishing to sit beside him any longer.

"Nay! If I had wanted to kill Donnach, I would have done so days ago." Boots scraped on the gravelly floor, indicating the warlord had also stood.

"Then why did ye use yer unholy magic to destroy the cavern and trap us in here?" She was trembling again and decided it was anger. Anger was better than fear.

"First, 'tis alchemy, no' magic. And second, I was no' trying to lock ye in here. Just me!"

"Ye were trying to trap yerself in here?" Jyne was confused.

He gave an audible sigh. "I was going to make it look like I was crushed in a cave-in. Then I was going to travel down the tunnel to where it collapsed a long time ago and rip another hole to escape out the back gate."

"There's a back gate?" Hope sparked.

"Aye, but I wasna ready when ye dropped the torch, and the other charge I had to blast through the back gate exploded wi' the first."

"Why did ye wish to pretend death?" asked Jyne. Nothing was making sense.

"I had my reasons."

"I want to hear them," she demanded. "If I'm going to be trapped wi' ye, I'd like to ken the reason for it. Why attack this abbey, making the poor elders wait on ye, then feel ye need to fake yer own death to run away?"

"I...I..."

"Nay, I ken why. Ye promised those men a treasure, and yet there is none. Instead o' facing the truth and admitting ye were wrong, ye put everyone in danger by blasting yer alchemy and running away from it all!"

"Aye," said the warlord in a tired voice.

"And that is how ye behave? Ye take what ye want, wi'out care for anyone, and then take flight when things are difficult?"

"Thought ye'd be pleased to see me go."

"But what o' the elders left in at Kinoch wi' yer men? What will happen to them? Ye think o' naught but yerself!"

"Naught but myself? Did we no' plow the fields? Have we no' provided food for the table?"

"We were fine wi'out ye!" Jyne yelled. A few pebbles fell and scraped along the floor of the cavern. "Ye're a hateful, horrible man." Jyne would have gone on, but she began coughing.

"Saints give me strength," he muttered.

"The saints? They canna hear the blasphemous prayers o' the likes o' ye."

"'Tis the truth, and I know it." He spoke slowly, with such a forlorn tone, she almost repented berating him. Almost.

The sound of more pebbles and rocks dislodging and falling from the ceiling or walls gave way to a new fear. The entire cave might collapse on top of them.

"We should move farther into the caverns. I fear this place may further collapse," said the warrior in a deep, gravelly voice that sounded like it was affected by the air thick with dust and debris.

Jyne wished to argue, but she instantly saw the wisdom in his words. She moved forward with the new fear of being crushed alive. She shuffled in the darkness until she hit a wall, then followed it along until she came to an opening. It was just as dark, but the temperature was cooler. They were proceeding into the crypt.

He shuffled along beside her, his boots scraping on the floor of the cavern. The reality of her situation settled on her even as the dust settled on the floor of the cavern. She was trapped in this underground crypt with her enemy. The man who had attacked and taken Kinoch from her. The man who had risked his life to save hers. What was she to do now?

"How are we to get out?" She was almost afraid to ask the question. Was there a way out? If not…if not, she would spend the last days of her life slowly starving to death with the man she despised.

He was slow to respond. "We shall find another way out." It was sheer bravado, for she knew he had no idea how they were going to escape, but she appreciated the courage it took to speak the words with confidence.

"I shall pray ye're right."

"Aye, do pray, lassie. For the good Lord canna hear my prayers, and we surely do need some divine intervention."

Jyne felt the squeeze of guilt in her chest for her words of judgment. This was not the time to get in poor graces with the Lord. "I should'na have said what I did. The Lord does hear the prayers o' the penitent." Jyne almost hated to admit it, since she did not wish to extend grace to such a man, but she knew it to be true.

"Does he?" It was an open question, honest, without the film of sarcasm.

"Aye, he does. We all are in need of grace."

"Some o' us more than others."

She was surprised by his easy and honest admission of his need for forgiveness. She had not supposed a warlord to be so self-effacing. "Did not Brother Luke remind us that our Savior came no' for the healthy but for the sick?"

"*Non est opus valentibus medico sed male habentibus*," quoted the warlord.

Though her Latin was not as good as it might be, she was certain he had quoted the verse from the Gospel of Matthew correctly. Why would a vicious warlord quote scripture?

"Ye ken the scriptures?"

"Nay!" he denied. "Well, aye. Heard it enough."

"Have ye? Where?"

Silence met her again. She strained her eyes, trying to make out his form in the blank nothingness.

"We should look for a way out." He had changed the subject, and she decided to let it drop. They had much more pressing concerns.

"Truce?" he asked.

She considered the matter. She did not wish to join forces with such a man or be anywhere near such a man, but if there was any hope of escape, they would need to work together.

"Truce."

Thirty-one

"THAT IS THE LAST O' THE BOOKS," SAID BREANNA, placing her load in the cart. "As soon as Jyne returns, we can all leave."

"Yes," said Luke, throwing a sheet over the precious cargo and tying it down securely. He wore a frown and cast several glances back at Kinoch Abbey.

"What is it?"

"There is something I left here when I thought I would leave all my worldly goods behind. Considering our situation, it may prove useful."

"Where is it?" asked Breanna, her interest piqued.

"The quarters where the men have been sleeping."

"They are all in the courtyard now. If we are quick, we can get it." She had to know what this man had left behind. Something of his old life as a duke?

They crept quickly into the abbey and took an immediate left into the quarters where the cells for the monks had been. In the courtyard, they could hear Cormac giving a rousing speech to the men about finding treasure and him being the Fire Lord or some such rot. Instead of figuring out what her brother was doing, Breanna preferred to follow Luke.

Luke entered a small cell. "This was my room," he said, glancing back at her with his blue eyes. It was unusual to meet a man with black curly hair and bright blue eyes. Unusually attractive.

She caught herself once again lusting after this monk. She really needed to get herself under better regulation.

Luke tossed aside the cloak of the man who was using the room, revealing a wooden chest. Breanna leaned closer to see what might be in the chest. He opened it, but no, it was empty.

"O' course whatever ye left, they would have stolen," said Breanna with a sigh.

Luke turned back to her and flashed a knowing smile. He drew a knife and edged it in between the bottom of the chest and the sides. With a bit of effort, he pulled out a board, then another. Breanna leaned in. It was a false bottom.

"Och, ye're a clever one," she praised. "What did ye hide?"

Luke carefully pulled out some folded clothes of fine linen, silk, and velvet.

"Lovely," said Breanna, slightly disappointed.

Then he drew out an ornately wrought sword with an elaborate crest engraved on the hilt.

"Holy Saint Andrew! Ye really were a duke!"

He met her eyes. "I was. I left it here because I thought once I took my vows, I would not have any need for it, for I was denouncing the world."

"I am sorry ye got pulled back into it."

"Do not be sorry. The past few days have shown

me much. I realize I had become quite closed to my fellow man…" He glanced over at her with eyes that seemed older than his years. "I cannot use the monastery to hide. I am glad to have learned that before I took my vows."

"Before?" asked Breanna, confused. "I thought ye were a monk."

"I am a postulant. I have yet to take my vows."

Breanna smiled. "I see." What she saw was a gorgeous man who had yet to take a vow of celibacy.

A loud boom crashed through the quiet moment, so loud and unexpected that Breanna jumped toward Luke in fright, and he wrapped his arms around her. The blast was so thunderous, it shook the very stones of the building in which she was standing.

"What was that?" she gasped, holding a hand over her chest to keep her heart from leaping out of it.

Luke shook his head in disapproval. "Cormac."

"By the saints! He actually harnessed the power of thunder and lightning?"

Luke nodded. "That shook the foundation. I hope things have not gone amiss."

"We should go see." She turned and fled from the room. She ran into the courtyard, with Luke following behind. She passed the stunned men and the elders, to the smoking hole where the storeroom and the entrance to the crypt used to be. It was now nothing more than a pile of rubble. The storeroom floor had collapsed, falling into the crypt below, filling it with debris.

"W-what happened here?" gasped Breanna.

Luke came up after her, his sword strapped to his side. Even he appeared stunned at the destruction.

"This is larger than anything I have ever seen him do before."

"Where is my brother?"

"I think, perhaps, this was his plan," reassured Brother Luke, though his brow wrinkled in worry.

A faint movement caught her attention. It was someone trying to grasp and pull their way to the top.

"Core!" She rushed forward to the male figure, who was coated entirely in gray dust. She helped him out of the rubble, with Luke assisting him on the other side. Core stood up, brushing himself off...except he wasn't Core.

"Who are ye?" she demanded of the tall man with a bushy black beard.

"This is Donnach Campbell, Lady Jyne's guard," said Luke, his face impassive.

"That's the man we caught on the first day!" said Dubh, moving forward. "I thought Core killed him."

"Apparently, he did not," replied Bran with his usual cool demeanor.

"Ye were going to kill me?" Donnach accused Dubh. Dubh gave him a shrug.

"Perhaps I owe Cormac an apology," muttered Donnach.

"Where is Cormac?" asked Bran.

Donnach shook his head. "He's down there. Where is Lady Jyne? She was down there with us."

Everyone looked around, but she was nowhere to be seen.

"Lady Jyne?" called Breanna, walking to the edge of the rubble pile. "Lady Jyne!" she called as loudly as she could, her heart pounding in fear. No one answered.

"Jyne!" shouted Donnach even louder. No reply.

Breanna looked at Luke, searching his face for answers. He seemed to know Cormac had been planning something. Was this possibly part of the plan? Luke joined her in looking down into the smoking hole, his face one of true concern. Something had gone terribly wrong.

"Jyne and Cormac have been buried alive. Quick, we must help them." Breanna grabbed a stone and tossed it aside. She could not lose her brother and Lady Jyne in one day. She swallowed down dread. How could anyone survive this?

She heaved another one and realized she was the only one working. "What are ye waiting for?" she demanded.

Bran stood with his men on one side, glaring at Donnach, Luke, and the elders, while they glared back. She strode boldly in between them. "Did ye daft fools no' hear me? We need to get them out!"

"Stand aside, Breanna," growled Bran. "I see ye got a verra nice sword there, Brother Luke. Ye'll hand it over to allow me a closer look."

"This sword bears the crest of my family. It will be taken from me only upon my death," said Luke, stepping in between Breanna and Bran. Behind him, Donnach, still pale gray with dust, appeared to be a ghostly figure bent on vengeance.

"As ye wish," said Bran, reaching for his own great sword.

"Nay! Ye're being foolish," said Breanna, though she was more than a little impressed by the way Luke faced down Bran. Not many men had the courage to do that. Yet nothing good could come from confrontation, so she put herself between Bran and Luke once more. "Stop this. Everything we want is down there." She pointed to the pile of rubble. "Core, Jyne—"

"The treasure?" chimed in Dubh.

"Aye, mayhap that too," agreed Breanna, though she had no idea if any riches lay below. "We need to work together to get it."

"Lady Breanna is correct. Cormac and Lady Jyne need our help. We must try to rescue them," said Luke.

"And find the treasure!" said Dubh.

"Red Rex is on his way. There will be a reckoning, Breanna," warned Bran. "Ye may want to leave now," he added in an undertone.

"He is right," said Luke, surprising her by agreeing with him. "We should leave."

"Nay! Lady Jyne has been naught but kind to all o' us." The elders nodded in agreement.

"She done gave us a sleeping potion," complained Dubh.

"Be grateful she did not give you poison," countered Luke.

"She would no' rest if any one of us was buried alive. Ye ken it to be true. I will no' be the one to let her down. Who is wi' me?" cried Breanna.

"If you are determined to stay, I will stand with you," said Luke. His support made her slightly giddy. She felt she could conquer any foe.

"I winna rest until I free Lady Jyne," declared Donnach.

"Aye, us too," said the leader of the elders.

Bran pursed his lips and frowned. "Fine. We will help search for Lady Jyne and Cormac and, aye, Dubh, I know, the treasure."

Before anyone could change their mind, Luke organized them into work crews to excavate the rubble. This was a new side of Luke that got Breanna's heart thumping more than it already was.

She needed to focus on the work at hand. She glanced over at Luke with a smile. Now if only they could reach Jyne and Cormac in time.

Thirty-two

Jyne struggled against the imposing nothing, which felt poised to swallow her whole. It was hard to tell whether her eyes were open or shut, because it was just as dark with them opened as closed. She put a hand up to her face to feel her lashes so she could tell that indeed her eyes were open.

She shuffled forward, tripped, and stumbled.

"It's so dark." She had never been entirely comfortable in the dark. Now she was trapped in a darkness so impenetrable, it felt like it was closing in on her.

A warm hand touched her shoulder, and despite whose hand it was, she welcomed the connection. He slid his hand down her arm and attempted to hold her hand, but she pulled away. He was her enemy. She may have accepted a truce to find her way out, but that did not mean they were on friendly terms.

He released her hand, and she immediately tripped over a rock and wished she was with someone whose hand she could hold. She needed connection with another human being to know that she was not alone, trapped in the darkness—just not a connection with the man who unfortunately walked beside her.

They made their way slowly forward, feeling their way into the cavern leading to the crypt. Jyne tried not to think of it. They shuffled along, tripping over rocks and stumbling forward as best they might.

Her head pounded from the thunderous blast, and her eyes ached for some form of light. The total darkness was unnerving. At night, the stars shone, and the moon gave its light. Even on nights when the clouds covered the moon and stars, there was usually some point of light, a red ember in the hearth, a glow of the lantern, something for her to know that the world around her still existed and she had not fallen into nothingness. Despite her intense dislike for the man beside her, she shuffled nearer to him. To be entombed alone was unthinkable.

"Do ye have a name, Fire Lord?" She did not wish to speak with him, but the silence was even worse. She had to talk to someone, and he was the only someone available.

"Ye can call me MacLean, though I doubt the clan would wish to claim me." His voice was low and gravelly from the dust.

"So how does one become a warlord?" she asked as if inquiring about the weather. She needed conversation to distract her mind from the terrifying reality that grasped at her chest, making it difficult to breathe. She needed to know something of this man, something that would make him more human and less a nameless, faceless monster. How did a man who studied alchemy, could quote scripture and work wonders, albeit destructive ones, use these gifts for evil?

"'Twas requested I continue the family business."

"Family business?"

"My sire is Red Rex, perhaps ye've heard?"

"Aye, I've heard." Red Rex, the scourge of the Highlands. He had a nasty reputation for being cruel, destructive, and utterly wanton in his desire to inflict pain and suffering on others. Clans that could agree on nothing could still work together to rid their lands of such a man. "When I was a child, my nursemaid used to frighten me into eating my morning gruel by telling me Red Rex would come for me if I dinna eat it all."

MacLean chuckled beside her. "My father would be pleased his name was used to terrorize small children. Did it work?"

"I learned to feed it to the dogs when she wasna looking. I was always the smallest o' my siblings. I dinna think my nursemaid ever forgave me for being weak."

"Someone thought ye weak? 'Tis hard to believe."

"My sisters and brothers are all of a hearty constitution. I was verra small at birth and often unwell as a child. Out of all of us, I was the only one prone to frailty. There are fifteen of us, ye ken."

"How many?" His feet scuffed on the ground.

"I am the youngest daughter o' fifteen siblings." She paused, allowing him time to process the number. It was not unusual to have many siblings to start with, but to have them all survive to adulthood, that was unique to her clan.

"That is a goodly number o' siblings."

"It's a goodly number o' people telling me what I'm to do." For some reason, being in the complete dark made it easier to speak to MacLean. Easier to try to forget what he was.

"Ah, ye wished for more freedom."

"Aye," said Jyne, surprised he understood her so readily. "I was overprotected and coddled, and nobody expected much from me. Mayhap, I dinna expect much from myself."

"This description o' yerself doesna match my experience of ye. For ye have been a formidable foe."

Jyne could not help flashing a smile in the general direction of MacLean. "No one has ever said that about me. In truth, I am known as the runt of the litter."

"Then they are fools, for there is no weakness about ye."

Jyne felt her step grow lighter at the unexpected praise. If she could only escape, it would be her turn to tell tales around the fire.

They both stumbled at the same time, tripping over a rocky ledge in their path. She lurched forward, but he caught her before she hit the ground and righted her back to her feet.

"Careful o' yer step," he said, still holding her upright. His arms were warm around her.

"Aye." She took a deep breath, trying to stop her heart from pounding. She desperately wished to be free of the cave, to see the light again. She lingered in the comfort of his arms for a moment before she realized what she was doing. It had all felt so natural. What was wrong with her?

She cleared her throat and scuffled back. "Ye said

there was a back gate that was blocked by a cave-in. Where is it?"

"I am no' certain. I only heard of it from Brother Luke."

"If he said it was here, then it must be some-where." Though how they would find it, and what they would do even if they did find the right place, she hardly knew.

It was hard to say how long they stumbled their way through the darkness. Was it a matter of minutes? Was it hours? She no longer cared to know. Whatever it was, it was much too long.

"How is it ye came to quote scripture?" she asked when she could no longer stand the silence in the oppressive blackness.

"My father was not one for children, so I was raised by others who taught me well. I even attended university."

"Ye went to university?" She could not prevent the surprise in her voice. This was not what she expected.

"Aye. Two years at the University o' Edinburgh. Until they found out who I was. The lads at school were sons of lairds and wealthy merchants. The son of a notorious warlord was no' welcome."

"Perhaps ye should'na have revealed it," she suggested.

"Aye. I told a lad I thought was my friend. I was wrong. Before the end o' the day, the news had spread through Edinburgh. The next morn, I was called before the chancellor and told to leave school immediately. I had not the correct moral fiber for a university student. Where'er I went, people turned their backs, grabbed their purses, and watched to see what mischief I might do."

"And did ye?"

"Did I what?"

"Did ye do mischief?"

He paused, and there was a low chuckle. "Aye. I fear wi' everyone waiting for me to do something deplorable, I could hardly disappoint."

"What did ye do?"

"I had been studying alchemy. Many had told me it was impossible to bottle thunder, but I proved them wrong...in the dining hall. Och, ye never saw such whooping and running about over a few small pops. Then I took off on the master's own horse."

"Ye destroyed the dining hall?" Jyne was horrified.

"Nay, I had only been able to make loud noises, not destruction at that point."

"Oh." She was somewhat mollified but still could not condone it, though she suspected her brothers might have seen the humor. "But ye ought no' to steal." She felt the need to return the talk to something more moral.

"The master o' the boarding house where I lodged owned a very sweet mare. She was a lively stepper, fast but skittish. She caught sight o' something and threw him, so he beat her until the blood ran down into the cobblestones."

"That's horrible! I am glad ye stole her. That man had not the right to keep her."

"Oh, he had the right. But he did not keep her." She expected him to sound smug, but instead, he spoke the words in a matter-of-fact tone.

"Do ye still have her?" she asked.

He took a deep breath before answering. "Nay. My

father saw I favored the mare, and he believes affection is a weakness. He was determined to cure me o' the affliction. Made me watch while he killed her."

Jyne gasped and placed a hand over her mouth, a pointless gesture in the pitch-black of the cavern. "Red Rex is truly evil."

"I know none who would disagree wi' ye."

"Ye as well?"

"Me most of all," he said with a sigh.

MacLean was not what she had expected, and while she was relieved not to be stuck in the underground tunnels with a true monster, his strange behavior kept her unbalanced. It was easier to hate him.

"And yet even knowing what he was, ye still joined him. Ye were so hurt over yer unfair expulsion that ye inflicted yer vengeance on the world by joining the most bloodthirsty, notorious warlord the Highlands have ever seen." She attempted to reestablish the moral high ground and felt better for it. Her bravado made her take too large a step, and she tripped over a rock and fell to the ground, skinning her knee. She hissed in pain.

His hands were upon her instantly. He felt along her head, where she had long since lost her veil, to her arms, and lifted her to her feet before she had time to protest. He held her close, helping her keep her footing.

"Ye think my expulsion was unfair?" he asked. He was so close, she could feel his breath on her cheek. His question caught her off guard, for he spoke like nothing untoward was passing between them though he held her in his arms.

"No one should be judged by the sins o' their father." It was strange in the dark, but she felt a strange attraction to the man. A pull toward him that defied explanation. It was as if, in the dark, he was no longer her enemy but a different man altogether.

He said nothing but continued to hold her close, chest to chest. She could feel him breathe, short and quick. She had no doubt he must be able to feel her heart beat through her kirtle.

"Even if their father is Red Rex?" he finally asked.

She paused. She did judge him for his father, yet her feelings and her beliefs were not in concert.

He let her go. "I thought so."

"Nay, ye should'na be judged by yer father. Ye should have the chance to be the man ye wish."

MacLean made a sound of derision, something like a snort. "That is one thing I have never had."

"Why did ye return to yer father?"

"It was not my choice."

Silence fell in the darkness. Jyne could not stand it for long. "I am sorry."

"We should move on."

"Aye." They began to shuffle along, Jyne with her arms out in front of her. She took a few steps and ran into his arms, which were also extended.

How could she escape when she could see nothing? A lump formed in her throat, and tears pooled in her eyes. She might spend hours walking in circles and not know it. Her bottom lip began to tremble, and she wrapped her arms around herself as protection from the chill of the cave. She was going to die here, slowly, trapped beneath the earth, buried alive.

She sniffed and blotted her eyes with the back of her sleeve. It did not matter now what she did. A wave of despair crashed down on her.

His hand found her once more and rested on her shoulder, warm and comforting.

"We will escape this place," he said with confidence.

"How?" she whispered.

"I dinna ken, but we will."

She shook her head in the endless dark. "There is no hope. We shall be trapped in here forever." Her voice cracked. All the fear and doubt and worry that she had been pushing aside finally caught up to her, winding its icy tendrils around her chest, making it difficult to breathe.

He ran his hand down her arm until he grasped her hand. "We will not die here."

She took comfort in the firm assurance of his tone. If only she could believe him. "I fear there is no hope."

"Did ye no' tell me earlier that there is always hope?"

"I said there was grace enough for everyone."

"Well, if the good Lord can forgive a sinner like me, then He can certainly help ye find yer way out of a cave." MacLean spoke with such authority, Jyne almost could believe him. Almost.

She squeezed his hand. In that moment, she did not care who he was or what he had done. She was on the edge of desperation and grief, and he was there, comforting her when she needed it most.

They began to shuffle forward together, still holding hands. She should have let go, but she didn't. She needed him now like she had never before needed anyone. "Thank ye."

"Ye're welcome."

Like it or not, their fate was sealed, quite literally, together.

Suddenly, her hand before her touched rock. He also stopped beside her. They released each other's hands to feel along the pile of rocks they had found. They had reached a dead end, the cave-in they had sought, yet there was no discernible way out. They were stuck in the cavern.

Sealed together.

Thirty-three

CORMAC MACLEAN SEARCHED DESPERATELY IN THE dark for some escape, but it was a dead end. This was the cave-in Luke had spoken of. Now they needed to dig their way out.

"Let us move some rock and break free. I am sure with some effort we can manage it." He spoke with much more confidence than he felt, for he wished to provide some comfort to Jyne.

"Aye," she responded, and they both began to dig through the rubble.

He picked up a large rock and threw it behind him, careful to listen to where Jyne was to avoid hitting her. He picked up another, then another, and another. They worked silently, their work too hard for speech. More than that, he did not know what to say. He became hot with the strenuous labor and tossed the bearskin cloak aside.

He lost track of time and continued to work long after Jyne had exhausted herself and sat to the side, breathing hard. He cursed himself for putting her in such misery, albeit unwittingly. He struggled against the rocks until he came to a large boulder that had crashed down, blocking the tunnel. He felt along it to find its ends, but there was no way around it and no way to move it. There was no escape.

His heart pounded in his chest. What had he done? What had he done to Jyne?

"Is something wrong?" she called, for his work had halted.

"There is a boulder here. It blocks the passage. There is…there is no way to move it."

"I see." Her voice was small and low.

They were truly trapped in the cavern. There was no hope.

And it was all his fault.

Ye should have the chance to be the man ye wish. Her words echoed in his head. How he wished they could be true. Even now, when they were trapped together in their final hour, he still clung to secrets. He would not tell her who he was.

He couldn't.

He had tried to tell her before, but she had not wanted to hear. To reveal the truth to her now just seemed cruel. She liked Cormac. She needed that. He needed that. He could not stand to have it taken away, even if it was false. She had even been kind to MacLean, the Fire Lord. But if she was ever to discover they were one and the same, she would hate him. Both of him.

So he continued to disguise his voice, not terribly difficult with all the dust and grit making his voice sound like gravel. He hid his identity, yet everything else he told her was the truth.

"Is there any way out?" came the voice of Jyne. She sounded small in the echoing cavern.

He did not have the heart to say the words. He did not have the heart to tell her many things. He sat down on the cold, sandy floor of the cavern, his legs unwilling to move further. All his plans, all his good intentions to keep her safe, to keep everyone safe, were for naught.

Somehow, he had thought that once he came to the cave-in, he could find some way out, some small hole from which he could escape. But no. There was none. He was going to die here in this cavern with the lady he loved.

And it was all his fault.

Please, Lord, show us a way out. I confess I am not worthy, but please save the Lady Jyne. Cormac waited for some answer to prayer, some grand revelation, some miracle, but there was only silence.

"MacLean?" Jyne called.

"I am here," he answered.

She moved toward him, her feet shuffling closer. Soon, two hands ran into him and grasped his shoulder. He put a hand on hers and realized she was very cold.

"Here, ye must wear this." He crawled around until he found his cloak and brought it back to her, wrapping her up in the fur. He sat beside her on the ground, and they leaned back on the boulder that prevented their escape.

She was close, and he breathed deeply of her. The faint scent of lavender brought back memories of their time together in the tub. Had that been only the night before? How could it have gone so terribly wrong?

They sat in silence, both aware of their doom. His mind spun for some new plan, some way out, but this time, he could think of nothing. He wanted to say something, do something to make it better, but what could he possibly say?

"I'm sorry." The words were woefully insufficient, but they were all he had to offer. "For everything."

Jyne took a deep breath and blew it out again. "I am called as a Christian to forgive ye."

"I dinna deserve it."

"But I do. So ye will have yer forgiveness, deserved or no'."

It was Core's turn to take a deep breath. "Ye are the kindest lady I have ever known."

They sat in awkward silence before Jyne changed the subject. "Have ye a Christian name? What did yer mother call ye?"

"My mother died at my birth. She never called me anything, unless it was to curse my existence." He cursed his own existence.

"I'm sorry ye grew up wi'out yer mother. That must have been difficult." She was being kind. Even to him.

"Ye canna miss what ye never had."

"I dinna think that is true."

"Perhaps not. Sometimes I wonder what it would have been like had my mother lived."

"What do ye know o' her?"

Core took a breath and thought back. Jyne was keeping them talking about anything other than their dire predicament, and for that, he was grateful. They must speak of something to avoid the horrible reality of their situation.

"My mother was o' the Cameron clan. She and my father were married in—"

"Yer father and mother were married?" Jyne interrupted with surprise. She must have assumed that he would be a bastard son. It was a safe assumption, for what father in his right mind would give his daughter in marriage to such an evil man?

"This may be hard to believe, but there was a time before my father was the devil he is now. He was always a big man, my father, but he saw my mother at a tournament and fell instantly in love, or at least that is what I heard. She was a small, delicate thing, and her father initially refused the marriage. But Rex was determined, and ne'er in my life have I ever seen him foiled when he sets his mind at something. He badgered my mother's father, demanding he be allowed the opportunity to win her hand. He was given multiple tasks, each one more impossible than the last. Each time my father completed it, expecting his reward, her father would ask for something more."

"What kind o' quests was he sent on?" asked Jyne, resting her head on his shoulder. It felt natural, though he knew it was a poor sign that she had given up, even in fighting him.

Core thought back to remember the story. It had been a long time since an old washerwoman, who had seen these things in her time, had told Core the story. "A rock from the top o' the highest mountain. One thousand head o' sheep, probably stolen. The removal of all the stumps in his field with naught but his bare hands."

"We could have used that skill for our fields," commented Jyne.

"Aye," agreed Core, laughing to himself at the thought of his father clearing fields, yet he had done it for Core's mother. "Eventually, my grandfather relented, and Rex and my mother were wed. By all accounts, they were happy together, though they must have made an odd couple. My father is such a massive man, and my mother was a petite lady. I have often been told I favor her, not my father." It had not been a compliment. His father had never forgiven him for not growing as massive as he was.

"What happened to yer mother?" Jyne asked softly.

"It was close to the time o' my birth. My father had gone away to attend to something, I dinna ken what. While he was gone, some other clan attacked our stronghold. The defenses fell, and the raiders stormed in. In all the chaos and confusion, my mother went into labor, early. She died in the process, and I was born too soon, too little, too sick, not expected to survive."

Jyne did not say anything, but a small hand closed around his, giving him comfort.

"My father returned, and his fury was unrivaled in all of human history. He killed the warlord whom he blamed for killing his wife, and hunted down every member of the raiding party and killed them all. He then took the fortress in which they had lived and set it to the flame. That which did not burn, he ripped asunder, casting away the stones, toppling the walls. He did not rest until there were no stones still standing. Then he plowed over the crops and poured salt in the fields, ruining it for anyone who might try to use it. From that day forward, he became what he is now, a warlord wi' no home, no humanity."

"So he is what he is because he lost his love?"

"'Tis hard for me to imagine he ever once loved, but it is true. I canna account for what happened to him."

"He turned his pain into hatred—hatred for everything. He would be a pitiable creature if he was no' so horrible," said Jyne with more charity than his father deserved.

"I am certain my father would rather be reviled than pitied." Core knew that for a fact.

"What happened to ye? Ye said ye were no' expected to live."

"Nay, I was not. Everyone expected that I would die soon, so my father wished to have naught to do with me. One of the serving women bundled me up and brought me to a wet nurse, who agreed to feed me until such time as I died, for no one expected that such a tiny baby could live."

"And yet ye lived."

"Aye, though sometimes I think it would've been better if I had not."

"Ye must no' say such things," chastised Jyne.

"Why ever not?" From his perspective, trapped in the cavern, Jyne and everyone around him would have been better off had he never been born.

"Ye must believe that if ye're here, 'tis God's will. Perhaps there is a plan for ye, yet unknown."

"I'm trapped in a crypt wi' no way out. I am reasonably certain the plan for me is to starve to death. I have lived a sad life, and I will die a sad death; there is no more planned for me than that. I'm only sorry that ye, who deserve so much more, are trapped here wi' me. I deserve this, but ye do not." Bitterness sliced at his soul. He could accept his fate, but not hers.

She was silent for a moment. He had spoken the truth neither of them wished to hear. "All my life, I wished to do more than I was given an opportunity to do. In truth, I never thought I could do much, but fighting against ye and meeting...a new friend have been the best few days o' my life. "

Core lifted his bowed head. A new friend? Best days of her life? This was interesting. "Ye met a friend?" he prompted.

"I met a man who helped me fight against ye. It brought us together, so I suppose I have to thank ye for that."

"This man, tell me about him." His voice caught, and he hoped she did not notice it.

Jyne sighed; it sounded happy. "He is a wonderful man. He helped me and encouraged me and even plowed the back fields, and then tricked yer men to plow the rest so that the people here could plant."

"He sounds...helpful."

"Oh, but he's more than that." She warmed to her topic. "He is the most handsome man I ever met. He never once told me I could'na do something. He makes me laugh. He is my...friend."

"A friend. Just a friend?" he could not help but ask.

"More than a friend," she replied with warmth in her tone. "Much more."

"How much more?" He was pushing, he knew it, but he could not help himself.

"Is it really so important that we talk about this?"

"Aye, naught could be more important. Did this handsome man ever try to…press his advantage?"

"Would stealing a kiss be considered pressing his advantage?"

"I…I am no' the best judge o' that. Was it unwelcome?"

"Nay, it was quite welcome." The smile in her words was clear.

"So his kisses, ye enjoyed them?"

"And why is this of importance to ye?"

"We cannot sit here in the darkness wi'out conversation. It will drive us mad. So, ye were discussing this man's kisses. They were acceptable to ye?" Those kisses had rocked him to his foundation and beyond. What had they meant to her?

"Aye, they were quite acceptable. More than acceptable. When he held me in his arms and kissed me, I felt… I dinna ken how to describe it, but I felt like I could fly."

"Aye." He smiled at the memory of those kisses. He also remembered more that they had shared, but Jyne wisely held her tongue. From the heat in her tone, he guessed she had enjoyed all of their time together.

"Sounds like this man took liberties wi' the sister o' the Laird Campbell." He tried to sound stern.

"Aye, he did." She gave another happy sigh. "But it is no' taking liberties when the feeling is reciprocated."

"And what is this feeling?" He held his breath. How did she truly feel about him?

She paused again. "He told me he loved me."

"And do ye return his affection?" he asked softly.

"Aye. I love him more than anything else." Her voice lowered. "Though we quarreled last we spoke, and I never got the chance to tell him."

"I warrant he knows." A flood of joy swept through him. He was finally loved. Loved by someone whose good opinion was worth earning. Of course, if she ever found out who he was…

The happy cloud he had been floating on burst, and he smashed back to the ground. She loved Cormac, the side he had shown her, not the side he had not. It was good, though, to be warmed by happy memories. She needed this story to remember and give her comfort for the long days of misery ahead.

She deserved this story. He would not be so cruel as to strip it from her with the unwanted truth.

"I'm glad ye found someone who brings ye joy," he murmured.

"And ye? Have ye a wife?"

"A wife? Nay, that is a laugh. Sons o' warlords dinna get married."

"A lass o' yer fancy, then?"

"Aye. There is a lass, a lady, mind ye, that I adore above all. But obviously, we could never be together."

"Perhaps if ye tried to change yer ways?" She was being kind.

"Nay, I would have to change more than my ways. I would have to change my name, my face, everything about me, and I could ne'er let her ken the truth. Do ye think that would be fair to her?"

Jyne took a deep breath, as if thinking hard on the subject. "Nay, I think ye should tell her. Just maybe not right away, and not all at once."

"Ye give good advice. When we find a way out o' this cave, I shall do as ye say." They would not be getting out of the cave, and they both knew it.

"Why did ye go back to yer father after ye left Edinburgh?"

"I dinna intend to. Nay, I hoped to ne'er see him again," Core confessed.

"Then how…?"

It was Core's turn to sigh, though not a happy one. "I saw my father but rarely when I was young. When I did, he would tell me I was a pathetic weakling who would'na amount to anything, and as soon as he sired a true son, I would ne'er see him again."

"That is a horrible thing to say to one's own child."

"Were ye no' called the 'runt o' the litter'?" he queried. No one should ever have made his Jyne feel small.

"That was…that was different," she defended. Though he could not see how.

"As ye wish. After my father abandoned me and I ended up at the monastery, I assumed he would sire a son and leave me be. Unfortunately, Red Rex was plagued wi' naught but daughters."

"So yer father remarried?"

"Nay, he swore he would never marry again, but that dinna mean the man was celibate."

"So he decided ye must be his legacy."

"Aye, except I tried running from him. Several times. Every time, he'd send someone after me, and every time, innocent folk who did naught but give me aid got hurt. I stopped trying to escape my destiny. I thought if I could win his approval, he would let me be."

"And did ye?"

"That is why I continued to study alchemy, so I could make the powerful weapon o' the English. I thought he would finally approve o' me and let me be. But my work has gone too well, and Brother Luke is right. Red Rex should no' gain such a weapon."

"How are ye acquainted wi' Brother Luke?"

"I stole a scroll from the monastery. Brother Luke caught me and tracked me all the way back to my father. Unfortunately, my father caught him and was going to kill him, so I told Rex that Luke was the key to a treasure at Kinoch. I thought Kinoch was abandoned. I had no idea ye were here."

"Aye, I thought it abandoned too," she concurred.

"My father let Luke live, but said if I could'na produce a treasure, all the monks would be killed."

Jyne gasped. "Nay!"

"That is why I tried to find a treasure. And that is why, when I failed, I planned to pretend I was dead, so hopefully my father would feel no need to make good on his threat."

"Och, I have misjudged ye." There was self-recrimination in her tone.

A warm hand rested on his cheek. He closed his eyes and enjoyed the sensation. Jyne had shown him more compassion in a few days than he had ever before experienced.

"I always blamed myself. If I had been more the son he wanted, then he would'na have had to go to such lengths to change me and hurt anyone standing in the way."

"That is rubbish. Ye're no' responsible for the

poor choices of yer father. And there's naught wrong with the way ye are. Just because ye're different from what he expected doesna mean that ye should hold yerself with any less value. In truth, it is the ways in which ye're different from yer father that prove yer worth."

Her words echoed down the cavern's walls. He was stunned by her defense. He had never had anyone defend him in such a manner. It made him wish to do the same for her.

"We, neither of us, fit the mold set for us by our family," he said softly, reaching over to hold her hand with both of his.

"Aye," she whispered. "We have strengths they canna understand."

He gently squeezed her hand, marveling at this new view of himself.

"Ye're not as bad as I thought ye were," she confessed.

"And ye have a more generous heart than I could possibly deserve. I am so sorry for the trouble I have caused ye. I have earned none o' the grace ye've shown me."

"As Brother Luke quoted, 'tis not the well who need the doctor but the sick.'"

"Aye, thank ye. I just never thought it applied to me."

"O' course it does."

"There are few as lost as me," admitted Core. Perhaps he had misjudged Jyne's ability to forgive. Perhaps he was not such a bad fellow after all. Maybe he could tell her the truth of who he was, and she would understand. He had always lied to protect himself. Telling the truth was strange, but it would also be an amazing relief to reveal himself completely, if only he would not be rejected for it.

"Jyne, I feel I must…ye have the right to know, though it will make ye hate me."

"I dinna hate ye anymore."

He sighed. "Ye will." Though he hoped maybe she would not. Maybe she would understand. He did not want to hurt her with unwanted revelation, but she had the right to know. His heart beat in his throat as he tried to find the right words.

"I'm no' sure how to say this." He released her hand and stood up. If he was going to make such a confession, at least he could do so on his feet. His knees might be a better choice, but she could not see him to appreciate the gesture.

A scraping sounded beside him, and he guessed Jyne had also regained her feet.

"The truth of it is—"

"Wheesht. Stay still," she suddenly hissed.

"What? Why?"

"I think I feel the breeze."

"A breeze?" Hope leaped in his heart. He turned around. "Where?"

"Here!"

He walked toward her, hands outstretched, and met with something soft.

"Oh!"

"Sorry," he said, though he wasn't sorry in the least.

She grabbed his hand and held it up at a certain angle. "Do ye feel it?"

He stood still, moving his hand slowly to try to feel what she felt. Was this an actual breeze, or was Jyne so desperate that her mind had started to play tricks on her? Ever so slightly, he felt it. A breath of something cool on his palm.

"I feel it. I feel it!" Core grabbed Jyne and lifted her off her feet in a great embrace. He pressed her tight to him, needing to feel her warmth, needing to feel that they would escape. He remembered himself and relaxed his grip, holding her in a loose embrace. He expected her to pull away; she did not.

He stroked a hand down her silky hair. She had lost her veil, so he twirled a lock of her hair around his finger and dropped his other arm around the small of her back, pressing her ever so slightly closer to him. He should let her go, but he couldn't. He needed her.

The breeze softly floated across his cheek. "I feel it," he whispered.

Thirty-four

JYNE STOOD MOTIONLESS IN THE ARMS OF HER ENEMY. She should pull away, but she gave in and wrapped her arms around his shoulders, drawing close to him and resting her cheek on his chest. He was a tall man, trim and strong. And he smelled nice. Familiar even. Like lavender.

Like Cormac.

She pushed herself away. What was she thinking? She must be light-headed due to lack of food. Perhaps she was losing her faculties. She needed to focus. She needed to stay strong if she was to escape this tomb.

She reached up her hand to feel the gentle wisp of fresh air. "I believe it is this way."

They shuffled forward slowly, both feeling for the air current until it grew stronger. Jyne's hopes soared. Maybe they would not die in this cavern after all.

They shuffled forward until they came to the area of rocks blocking their path, yet the breeze continued to tease them, floating through cracks in the rocks that they could not pass.

"Let us follow this faint current," said Jyne. She let

go of his hand and stumbled forward. She got down on hands and knees and climbed slowly, blindly, up the pile of debris. She found a large boulder blocking the path, but the air was coming from the side.

Following the faint breeze like a lifeline, she climbed higher, until her head bumped against the ceiling. She moved along the edge of the rocks and ceiling, carefully picking herself along. She found a small ledge at the ceiling, from which the air was flowing.

A scramble of rocks drawing nearer told her that MacLean was following her up the rocky pile. "Did ye find anything?"

"I found a small ledge. The air is coming from it. I think I might be able to fit into it." She lay on her stomach on the ledge and inched her way forward. She feared she might be high up and, for the first time, was glad she could not see. She hoped the ledge would hold her.

"The air is definitely coming from this direction," said Jyne. "Saints be praised, I feel a hole. If we could make it bigger, we might be able to get through."

"Let's do it!" cried MacLean.

Lying on her stomach on the ledge, Jyne pulled and scraped at the rocks and debris until her fingers ached and her back screamed in pain. It didn't matter. Every small rock she pulled was one rock closer to freedom. Nothing could be more motivating.

She pushed whatever debris she could down the ledge, and MacLean reached up beside her and scooped it away. Since the work was done by feel, there were times his hands brushed against her legs. She assumed it was accidental. There seemed to be a lot of accidents. Sometimes if he "accidentally" rested a hand on her ankle, she would "accidentally" toss a stone in his direction and be rewarded with a thump and an "Ow!"

After a while, MacLean took a turn, sliding in on his stomach. The man was leaner than she had thought, and a good thing too, for a hefty man could not have fit.

MacLean somehow managed to move his stones without hitting her, for which she was appreciative. It was hard to gauge the time without any light, but she knew they had been at it for quite a while. Every time she felt like stopping or possibly collapsing into sleep, she would feel the tantalizing breeze again, and she would redouble her efforts. She kept hoping to see even a pinprick of light, just a speck to let her know their efforts were making progress, but she saw none, and they continued to work in complete darkness.

After a while, MacLean stopped his work. "There is a large rock here, hard to move. Can ye hand me my *sgian dubh*? 'Tis in my boot."

She felt for the knife and drew it, sliding it up to him. Scuffing and scraping echoed through the cave as MacLean worked on the rock, stirring up the fine dirt. Dust filled her nostrils, and she sneezed.

"Bless ye," said MacLean absently.

Jyne knew at that moment he was not the hardened warrior he pretended to be. She sat back and leaned on the rocks, thinking of how much she had learned about him and how he was not at all what she had expected from a Highland warlord. She was very glad too, for otherwise, it would have been very unpleasant for her.

MacLean grunted and swore under his breath. With some surprise, she realized it was the first time she had heard him swear. Unlike her brothers, who, as good-natured as they were, could roll off a curse as easily as taking a swig of whiskey.

"Can ye move it?" she asked, more than a little anxious to know if they could be successful.

He did not answer. Jyne crawled closer, hearing the sound of her gown tearing, again. Her kirtle must be a complete loss, but it would all be worth it if they could escape…and it would not matter if they did not.

Another grunt greeted her, and then nothing but the sound of him breathing hard in the darkness. "Nay, I canna move it."

Fear gripped her heart and squeezed hard. They were trapped. Trapped forever.

No, there must be a way out.

"Mayhap if we try together." She crawled forward on top of his body into the small tunnel they had dug. This was one time it was beneficial to be slight of frame, for it was a tight squeeze, even for her. They had to find a way out. They just had to.

Heat flushed through her to be pressing herself forward on top of MacLean's back. She could feel every breath he took. She was sure he could feel hers. She wriggled forward until her head reached his.

"Good day to ye," he said in a cheeky manner that made her smile. "Friendly sort o' lass ye are."

"Let us just move this stone." She felt forward and found his hands wrapped around the hilt of his knife, the blade of which was jammed beside the rock like a lever to break it free.

MacLean gave the word, and they both began to pull as hard as they could. MacLean grunted. She wrenched on the handle with all her might.

Suddenly, the knife in her hands moved slightly. It was working!

"Harder!" cried MacLean and grunted louder.

Suddenly, the knife flew back, and the rock fell forward with a rumble of rocks and debris. Jyne tried to scream in fright of being buried alive, but her mouth and nostrils filled with fine dust, and she shut her mouth immediately, breathing into MacLean's tunic. It was a familiar, comforting smell.

As suddenly as it started, the rumbling stopped.

"Are ye hurt?" he asked anxiously.

"Nay, I thought we were going to be buried, but naught fell on me. Are we free, or buried further?"

"Let me see," he said with a cough. Jyne hoped he could see, for even the smallest glimmer of light would give her tremendous hope. "I canna see light, but I can feel the breeze. 'Tis stronger now. I think we have broken a hole through the wall."

"Truly?" She scrambled up over him a bit more, impatiently pulling aside her skirts, ignoring another rip. She felt a fresh breeze on her face. She breathed in deeply. The air was still filled with the dust of the cavern, but it was a cool, moving breeze, such a relief from the deathly stillness of the crypt.

"We must have opened into another tunnel," said MacLean. "But the moving air means that it opens somewhere to the outside."

"Is the opening big enough for us to get out?"

"If it's no' now, we will make it so," said MacLean with raw determination.

She quite agreed with him. She flushed warm, which must have been the result of her excitement at finding freedom and had nothing to do with the man on whom she lay. They both pulled themselves forward to dig at the small opening and make it larger, tossing the rocks and debris down into the open hole.

Despite her desperation to get out, she was constantly conscious of how her body was pressed against his. If she had any shred of dignity left her, she would not continue to lie on him, but she was near frantic to escape. They both clawed and scraped at the rocks until the opening was large enough for a person to shimmy through.

"I believe we've done it. The hole is big enough for us to get through," he said.

"Aye," she said, resting her head on his back.

It was one thing to want to escape the cavern, another to contemplate lowering oneself through a hole in the wall into the black unknown. They did not know what lay on the other side or even how far down the drop might be.

As if reading her thoughts, MacLean stilled, and they both listened in silence, trying to hear what might be on the other side. "Let us see what kind o' fall we might have." He scraped along the rocks, and Jyne guessed he was choosing one. She remained quiet until she could hear the slight plunk of the rock hitting the ground. Of course, she did not know when he had released the rock, so she had no way to judge whether it was a far or near distance.

"Is it far?" she asked.

"Nay, I think it will be fine. As much as I appreciate yer company, I may need ye to back up so I can turn around. Close quarters in here wi' ye."

Her cheeks burned at the mention of her lying on top of him, though it was all done in the effort to escape. She scooched her way back down his body, growing ever conscious of his form. His plaid had rucked up in the progress of their escape, and she was very aware of sliding down over his naked thighs.

When at last she was free of him, she could hear the scrapes and shuffles of him turning around in the narrow space.

"Be careful," she called out as she heard him knocking loose stones about, and she knew he was positioning himself to drop into the unknown.

"Better to break my neck trying to escape than slowly starve to death," said MacLean reasonably. He was clearly a pragmatic man.

"Still better to proceed carefully and not break your neck at all," she countered even more reasonably.

"Aye, I like yer plan. Let's do it yer way."

Jyne crawled forward once more until she reached his arms. She recognized that he had put his legs through the hole and was now holding on to the edge of the hole, about to let himself drop. "Can ye feel the ground?"

"Nay. Shall we see what happens?"

She leaned forward and, using her hands to guide her, planted a kiss on his cheek. It was a sudden impulse, and she was not entirely sure why she had done it. "For luck." She hoped she had some luck to bestow to him.

"Wi' ye, I do feel lucky." He let go.

Jyne heard him land down below, but she could not tell how far he had fallen. "Are ye well?"

"I'm all right. 'Twas no' far."

Jyne released the breath she had been holding. They were at least escaping one of the tunnels, and she entertained hopes that they could find a way out entirely. She sent a prayer of thanks to her Maker, with an additional plea for help.

"'Tis yer turn," he called up to her.

She felt for the opening of the hole and then moved around so that her legs were exiting first. She was glad it was pitch-black in the cavern, for her gown got stuck on rocks and hitched up in a most unladylike position. She squirmed her way out through the hole and felt a cool breeze across her bare backside. She wriggled some more to try to arrange her skirts to cover what they ought.

"Are ye all right?" MacLean's hands clasped her ankles.

"Aye, I am fine," she exclaimed, trying once more to rearrange her skirts so they hung appropriately. She no longer felt the incriminating breeze, but she was certain had anyone been able to see her, she would be decidedly less than decent.

She lowered herself down, and his hands ran up her naked legs.

"Oh!" she exclaimed.

"My apologies. I canna see what I'm doing."

"But ye can certainly feel!" she chastised, hanging on to the rock, her legs dangling in midair.

"Aye. Ye're right as always. I am a bad man." But he said it with relish.

"Ye quite enjoyed that!"

"Aye. I did." There was a smile in his voice.

"Ye're a horrid man, and I will tell ye more o' what I think o' ye after ye help me to the ground."

"As ye wish." His hands ran up her legs once more, this time on the outside of her skirts. "Let go."

She clung to the rock. Did she trust this man to catch her?

"Let go o' the rock. I winna let ye fall."

"Are ye sure?"

"I swear to ye, I would ne'er hurt ye."

"Just take my home, steal the verra bread off my table…"

"Aye, all that and more. But I winna hurt ye. Let go, Lady Jyne. Ye shall no' fall."

She let go and landed softly in his arms. She wrapped her arms around his neck instinctively. And they stayed there. He cradled her in his arms and held her close. All the stress and strain of the day overcame her, and she laid her head on his shoulder. They remained there much longer than they ought. She could not get herself to move or to demand to be put down. She felt good in his arms, like she fit.

"Are no' yer arms tired?" she finally asked.

"Ye're no' heavy. Such a light little thing." He did put her down, but his arm remained around her shoulders.

Once again, she relaxed into him. He smelled good, with that familiar scent of lavender. With a snap of her head, she jerked back and out of his arms. What was she thinking? This was her enemy! Even if she had determined that he was not too horrible, still he was not deserving of her affection. Besides, she was in love with Cormac. Perhaps he had heard the sound of the blast and returned to Kinoch Abbey. Maybe even now, he was trying to rescue her. And how did she repay him? By embracing their enemy!

"Ye did no' fall," he said softly.

"Nay, but…but we ought not…"

"We have escaped a chamber o' certain death. I think we can share some gratitude."

Jyne relaxed her shoulders. MacLean was right. Their embrace was simply the natural reaction to their harrowing escape. It meant nothing, other than neither of them wished to slowly starve to death.

"Where are we now?" she asked. It was time to get back to the business of escaping the cave.

"I dinna ken, but I do feel the breeze. Shall we follow it?"

"Indeed!" Fresh air meant freedom. Nothing else mattered right now.

"Take my hand." Somewhere in the darkness, he was extending his hand to her. She reached out toward his voice and found his hand. His fingers wrapped around hers, and she could not squelch the sense of safety that accompanied them. She wished she did not trust him so implicitly, but she did. Despite everything, she knew he would protect her. He might be a thief and a scoundrel, but he seemed to be an honest one.

They began to scuffle forward, both with their hands before them. Her fingertips brushed across something made of stone. She felt what it was and found it was something of a shelf carved out of the rock.

"I've found something. A long shelf of some sort. It was made by human hands," she reported.

"I've found something too." His tone was unreadable.

"What did ye find?" she prompted.

"I think it is a…skeleton."

"What?" Jyne's right hand squeezed his, and she snatched her other hand away from the stone shelf lest she touch something she ought not.

"This must be part o' the crypt."

"We are in a tomb?" She swallowed hard.

"Aye, but there must be a way out." His low, gravelly voice resonated with confidence.

They shuffled forward, Jyne trying not to think of the decayed corpses lying on the stone alcoves. If they did not escape, she could find an empty one and lay herself down onto it to save her people the trouble of having to bury her.

It was not a comforting thought.

They stumbled forward until she gradually began to notice that the absolute blackness around her was beginning to turn to a dark gray. She could not see much at first, but gradually, she could make out the difference between a wall and a corridor. MacLean was nothing but a dark blob, but she could tell where he was.

Her heart beat faster as they continued on. She probably no longer needed to hold his hand, but she held on anyway. They moved faster now, toward the faint light. They must escape. They must.

They rounded a corner, and the light was brighter. She dropped his hand and ran toward the pale light, craving light more than anything in her life. Light meant freedom; it meant escape from being buried alive.

"We've found a way to get out!" Jyne ran forward with increasing speed until she came to a metal lattice gate. Pale light shone through, and the bright full moon was perfectly framed in one of the holes of the iron lattice. She shook the gate, trying to open it.

It was locked.

"Look! Here! I can see the moon, but the gate is locked. Come quick! We are almost free!" Jyne called to MacLean, wondering why he was not right behind her. Surely, he must be as anxious as she was for escape.

His footsteps echoed down the cave. She waited with anticipation for him to come into view. She had never seen him without the ridiculous horned helmet and wondered what he looked like.

He slowly came into view, walking hesitantly, and stepped into the shaft of moonlight. His boots were revealed first, his legs, his plaid, his plain tunic, and finally…

A helmet.

"Where did ye get a helm?"

"He wasna needing it anymore." He walked up slowly and stood next to her, tall and mysterious.

"Ye took it off a dead man?" Her stomach turned. "What is so wrong wi' yer face that ye'd rather wear a dead man's helm than show me?"

"Ye would'na care for me if ye saw me."

"Do ye truly think me so shallow that I would think poorly o' ye because o' yer visage? If I am to think ill o' ye, it will be for yer actions in thieving my keep. Though I confess, ye've acted wi' perfect chivalry wi' me in the cave."

"Perfect chivalry?"

"Well…" She paused, remembering his "accidental" wandering hand. "Almost perfect."

"I dinna suppose ye have the key?" he asked, abruptly turning the conversation.

"Nay. Och, we canna have come so far only to be trapped here." Tears sprung to her eyes. She was so tired. They could not have worked so hard for nothing.

"What will ye give me if I can free us?" he asked.

"Anything!" said Jyne recklessly.

"Dinna fear. We shall no' die here." He drew his narrow knife and began to work the lock until she heard a friendly click.

With a loud groan and sharp creak, the gate swung open.

Thirty-five

CORE DEFTLY PICKED THE LOCK AND SWUNG OPEN the gate.

"We're free!" Jyne rushed past him into the cool night air. She ran up a small grassy rise and twirled in the light of a full moon. Her hair was loose, her gown was torn, and every part of her from head to toe was covered in a gray film of dust. Still, she had never looked more beautiful. She laughed out loud, her blue eyes twinkling like stars. Her kirtle had been ripped, revealing a tantalizing amount of cleavage. She was wild and free, and oh, so lovely.

"Aye, we're free," he said gruffly, walking up the rise to stand next to her. And yet...he was not free. No, he was wearing a dead man's helm because he would never be free. His father was still coming, and he was still lying to her. No, he was definitely not free.

"Are ye no' pleased?" She looked up at him, the moon reflected in her eyes.

"I am pleased to be out o' the crypt, but naught has changed."

A crease appeared on her forehead. "Nay, I am

changed. Why do ye hide from me? Do ye no' think I could accept yer visage, no matter what it might be?"

"If ye saw me, ye would truly hate me."

"Nay! I would'na judge ye based on yer appearance. There is naught ye could show me that could make me hate ye."

"Ye dinna mean that."

"I do. I truly do. I understand ye better now. I dinna condone everything ye've done, but I think I understand why ye did it." She gave him a tentative smile. How he wanted to believe her.

He shook his head. "Ye would'na like what ye see." Could she understand? Could she forgive? Impossible.

"What have ye to lose?" she asked, her face open. She had no idea what it was to live a lie. What had he to lose? Everything.

"Did ye truly mean what ye said about the sick needing the physician?" he asked, not sure if he dared to hope.

"Aye, I do believe in grace. And if anyone needs it, ye do."

"Ye're verra right, m'lady. But I doubt I'll ever find it."

"I canna speak for all, only myself, but I think if ye give people a chance, they may be willing to forgive ye. I have told ye I forgive ye."

"Do ye? Truly?" Core held his breath.

Jyne pursed her lips, as if considering the matter. "I do forgive ye. But I would ask ye to live a better life."

"If only I could," he muttered.

She walked up to him and reached out a hand, and he took it. "Ye asked me to trust ye and let go when

I was hanging on the wall. I did. And ye caught me. Trust me now, and let me see the face o' the man who, while no' perfect, did get me out o' the crypt alive."

She was so brave and so beautiful and so good, it made his heart hurt, literally. He felt a painful squeezing sensation in his chest at the recognition that Lady Jyne Campbell was much too good for him. He could never be with her. She was good. He was bad. Nothing could change that.

Nothing but grace.

"What o' the boon ye promised?" he asked.

"The boon?" She tilted her head in confusion.

"Aye, ye promised to give me anything if I would free ye." His heart squeezed harder. He feared he was making another bad decision, but he did not care.

She raised an eyebrow. "What do ye wish?"

"I claim a kiss." He was breathing fast, and his heart beat loudly. This was his last chance. His last chance to kiss her. He could not pass the opportunity to steal one more kiss from the woman he adored. If this talk of grace was real, then she would forgive him that too. If it wasn't, at least he would have one last kiss.

A shadow passed over her eyes. The wind blew her long, straight hair around her like a rippling halo. Her face was unreadable. "As ye wish."

"Close yer eyes."

This earned him a glare. "Only because ye saved me from the caverns." She closed her eyes.

"Dinna open yer eyes. Promise me." He wanted her kiss. Needed her kiss. Even if he had to steal it from her.

"I promise ye, I winna open my eyes."

He paused, knowing he had no right to kiss her, but drawn to her with a force he could not deny. He stepped to her and lifted the visor, revealing his face. Her eyes remained closed.

He took a deep breath of the fragrant field, relishing in the cool, crisp air and the light fragrance of the heather. Maybe he could finally be free. Maybe his life could be different. Maybe there was a God in heaven who loved and forgave him and sent him an angel here on earth.

Gently, he wrapped his arms around her and pressed her close to his body, brushing his lips against hers. He kissed her softly, slowly deepening the kiss, relishing in her soft lips, her warm mouth. He slid one hand up her back until it came to rest on her neck, gently pressing her closer to him.

To his surprise, she reached up, wrapping her arms around his neck, pulling herself even closer. It was she who deepened the kiss, and he responded. Maybe she could forgive him. Maybe…

"Och!" She turned away suddenly, her hand over her mouth.

He slammed the visor down over his face to shield him from her view. She turned back at him, her eyes wide. "Ye're the verra devil."

"Ye dinna care for the kiss?"

"I agreed to kiss MacLean and ended up kissing Cormac." She reached up and snatched the helmet from his head.

"Jyne, I—Ow!" She smashed her fist into his nose. He doubled over, holding his nose as it began to drip blood. For a small thing, she certainly knew how to level a punch.

"How could ye?" she cried, brushing away tears with the back of her hand.

"I…I…"

"How could I be so stupid? Och, I am the worst o' all fools. I believed ye. Not only as Cormac but as the bloody Fire Lord too!"

"I am so sorry. I ne'er meant to hurt—Ow!"

She kicked him in the shin. "Was it not enough that ye captured Kinoch and forced these poor people to serve ye? Why deceive me? Was this all a cruel jest?"

"Nay! I lied about who I was, but everything I said to ye was the truth."

"Truth? What do ye know o' that? I thought I had misjudged ye. I thought ye were misunderstood. I thought ye were no' the monster I believed ye to be. But now I ken the truth. Ye're more evil, more despicable than I ever thought. Why would ye do this?"

"Because I had to!"

"Had to? *Had to?* Nobody was forcing ye to lie to me!"

"Nay, but if I was honest wi' ye at the beginning, when I first pulled ye out o' the bog, would ye have ever spoken to me?"

Jyne opened her mouth for a retort but closed it again, glaring at him.

"I ken I've done ye wrong. But I have to lie to everyone I meet, or they are either scared o' me or want to hurt me."

"I thought we were friends," she said in a small voice. "I thought I could trust ye."

Her pain hurt him more than her anger. "The more

time I spent wi' ye, the more I liked ye, and the more I dinna want to lose ye. I...I liked ye too much to lose ye."

"Ye were only thinking o' yerself, trying to get something from me by trickery and deceit."

He felt the truth of her words as if she had struck him again. She was right. He had been selfish. And wrong. He hung his head, not knowing what to say.

"I canna believe ye would do this to me after all we shared. Why deceive me so? Why toy wi' my emotions?"

"Because I love ye!" he blurted out.

She stared at him in stunned silence, then squared her shoulders and looked him straight in the eye. "Ye dinna ken the meaning o' the word."

Her words cut him to the quick, stabbing him with a pain crueler and deeper than even the sharpest knife.

"I am sorry." It was all he could say.

She turned on her heel and began to walk through the tall grasses back to Kinoch Abbey.

He watched her go. It was all how he had predicted. If she knew the truth, she would hate him almost as much as he hated himself. There was no grace for him. No heaven above. No God who cared. And definitely no angel on earth, at least no angel that was sent for him.

He put a hand to his chest, trying to stop the awful, empty, hollow pain. It was no use. Maybe his father was right all along. Human emotions were an affliction, a disease that must be destroyed.

There had been a moment, just a moment, when she had assured him that no matter what he revealed, she would not despise him for it, that he had believed her. Maybe she could discover the truth, see him for who he truly was, and find a way to forgive. But no, his sins were too great for grace. Forgiveness was for folk who didn't really need it. Not for him.

Once she knew the truth about him, she hated him. That was why he had concealed it from her for as long as he could. Could she not see the logic in that? And truly, what right did she have telling him that she would not think less of him no matter what, if she had no intention of actually following through on her bold claim?

He realized he was beginning to blame her and stopped himself. This was not her doing. No, this was entirely his fault. He had done it. He had been selfish and cruel. He knew there had never been a chance of a future together. Their fate had always been inevitable.

Cormac trudged after Jyne back to Kinoch Abbey. He reached a rise and paused on the top of a hill, looking down into the valley of Kinoch. The sky was lighter in the east, revealing the first glimpse of the coming dawn. They had been in the cave all day and all night. Core shook his head. Dawn might break for others, but it would forever be night for him.

He realized he had hurt more people fighting his father than if he had simply given in. All his plans and good intentions had caused everyone nothing but trouble. He needed to give up, for everyone's sake.

A bit of movement in the distance caught his eye. Core could make out riders slowly winding their way down the steep path toward the far side of the valley. They were still a ways away, but they were heading toward them.

Core squinted at the figures, trying to make them out. One was larger than the others riding with him. Core's blood ran cold. Only one man could so dwarf his companions. Cormac coughed and tasted bile.

Core sprinted toward Kinoch, panic rising within him. Jyne was in danger. He needed to ensure his father never discovered his true feelings toward Jyne, or her life would be cruelly forfeit. His father demanded that he be a warlord. If he had any chance to save Jyne, it was time to become the only thing he ever could be.

It was time to join Red Rex.

Thirty-six

JYNE WIPED HER EYES WITH AN IMPATIENT SWIPE OF her hand. He was not worth her tears. Grit got in her eyes, and she blinked back more tears from the sting. She must be filthy from crawling around in the crypt for a day and a night. All of which was Cormac's fault.

She hated him. *Hated* him!

She had trusted Cormac. She had even begun to trust MacLean. But it was all a farce, all some cruel joke at her expense.

She picked up her pace, striding over the freshly tilled ground. How she had praised Cormac and thought him so brave for risking capture to plow the fields. Of course he got the ruffians to plow the fields; they were his men!

Things started to piece together in her mind. She had unwittingly shown him the postern gate, which he then blasted through with his unholy doings with alchemy. She had warned him about the sleeping draft, but why had he played along? Why not stop her? If this had all been a mean jest, why try to force her to leave? None of it made sense.

The sky was pink in the east, and the sun's rays began to peek over the horizon, casting the outer walls around Kinoch Abbey in a rosy hue. It would have been a welcoming sight had she not been so hurt and so angry.

How could she have been so blind? And yet… looking back, there were signs. Could she not have suspected it? No wonder she had felt a strange attraction to MacLean; it was none other than Cormac himself. Why had he deceived her? And yet…as the morning chill cooled her anger, she realized maybe she had deceived herself.

Core had tried to tell her something, and she had not wanted to know. In truth, MacLean also had tried to reveal something, and she had cut him off too. She hadn't wanted to have her dream crushed. She did not want to know the secrets he kept. She did not want to see the truth.

She strode boldly up to the gate of Kinoch Abbey. It was not even locked. She pushed it open as it groaned in complaint. She walked across the dark outer ward to Kinoch. She expected the house to be asleep, but she could hear voices from inside. She stopped short, realizing that the entire southeast corner of the keep had collapsed. She swallowed gall at a sudden realization. Had Cormac not rushed to save her, she would have been crushed.

She hurried into the inner courtyard and was arrested by the sight. The entire corner of Kinoch Abbey where the storeroom had been had fallen into the crypt below. Even more shocking than that, a line of Cormac's men and elders were passing along rocks and buckets of debris out of a crater in the ground. They appeared tired, their eyes all but closed, their shoulders slumped. Some people were even sleeping on the ground or benches in the courtyard. They had clearly been up all night.

"Dubh, lend Donnach a hand there with that rock. It's a big one," commanded Bran.

"Here, use this spear as a lever," said Luke, jumping into the crater.

"Any sign yet?" asked Breanna in a weary voice as she leaned against a shovel and looked down into the hole.

"What are ye looking for?" asked Jyne, coming up behind Breanna.

"We're looking for—Jyne!" Breanna turned around and cried out, dropping her shovel and giving her a wild embrace. "By all the saints! It's Lady Jyne!"

Donnach, Luke, and others climbed out of the crater, and the line of people with the buckets suddenly came alive.

"Lady Jyne!" She was instantly surrounded by people, all wanting to embrace her and ask questions of her.

"How did ye escape?"

"What happened to ye?"

"Och, ye look a sight!"

"Are ye hurt?"

"Quick, bring her food and drink!"

"Where is Cormac?"

"Cormac MacLean, the *Fire Lord*, and I dug through the other end of the cavern and escaped." She pinned a significant look on Breanna and Brother Luke.

"So ye know," said Breanna in a small voice, her joy draining into an expression of contrition.

"Aye, I know. Ye certainly kept his secret well." She glared at those she had thought her friends.

"I am sorry. Cormac convinced me to keep his secret. I do apologize for no' being a better friend to ye," said Breanna.

"I also wish to convey my apologies," said Brother Luke. He had set aside his monk robes for a tunic and breeks.

"Well, it does seem ye all have been trying verra hard to save us," conceded Jyne, looking around at how they had worked hard to try to dig her out. "I forgive ye and thank ye. But what does this new attire mean, Brother Luke?"

"He is not actually a monk. He was just a postulant," Breanna answered for him.

"More secrets?" Jyne said with a sigh.

"Please, eat and drink, m'lady," said Alasdair with a warm smile beneath his wrinkles as he and Cook brought her beef broth, trenchers, and drink. "We've been so worried over ye."

"Aye, we have," agreed Cook, handing her the drink with a motherly smile.

Jyne's stomach growled with longing. It had been much too long since she had last eaten, and she gratefully accepted their offerings, finally soothing her dry throat with a long drink of weak ale. "Thank ye," she said between bites of bread and sips of broth.

"Please forgive me, m'lady," rasped a penitent Donnach, coming up to her with his head bowed. His black hair and bushy beard were covered in gray dust, giving him the appearance of being much older. "I canna express my shame at leaving ye behind. I shall present myself to our laird for judgment."

"Nay, ye will do nothing o' the sort. I forgive ye, my friend. The only one who deserves judgment is Cormac MacLean."

"Where *is* my brother?" asked Breanna.

"I am here." Cormac strode up to the crowd. A cheer went up for him as well, but died in people's throats at the fierce look on his face. He was covered in dirt and grime. Dried blood was smeared on his face. His great kilt, belted around his waist and thrown over one shoulder, produced clouds of dust as he strode forward through the morning mist, giving the impression that he was smoking.

Cormac stormed toward her, his men and the elders giving him a wide berth. He glared at them as he passed. Core had never struck her as a fighter, but the look on his face was something she had never seen before.

"Cormac? Brother, is that ye?" Breanna seemed a bit unsure. Jyne was unsure herself. She had never thought she had anything to fear from Cormac, but of this creature before her, she had no idea.

"What are ye all doing about the courtyard?" he demanded.

"They were working together to free us," explained Jyne to this new, strange iteration of Cormac MacLean.

"Waste o' time," he pronounced.

"Waste o' time?" she repeated. "These people have worked day and night to find us. We owe them our appreciation."

"We owe them nothing for acting like fools. Where is the gate guard? Go, now, to yer posts, ye lazy dogs!" Several of his men trudged to the gate.

Jyne gasped at his harsh words.

"Ye should have fled this place while ye could," continued Cormac. "Red Rex is upon us, and none o' ye will wish to be here when he arrives. Ye ken this better than anyone, Breanna."

"Yer sister was verra brave and verra kind to forgo her flight to try to save us," Jyne said, defending Breanna.

"And now ye must resign yerself to the consequences, Sister, for I canna help ye anymore. I canna help anyone anymore. I canna save the monks or yer books, Brother Luke. I canna save Breanna from her bastard betrothed. And I surely canna be the man Lady Jyne deserves. Nay, I grow weary to the point o' death o' trying to be someone I can never be."

"What do ye mean?" asked Jyne, her heart sinking.

"It means ye're right. I am the verra devil, or the son o' one to be sure. I dinna ken the meaning o' love or decency. I am the son o' Red Rex, and it's time I start to act like it. 'Tis time for me to take my rightful place as his son and heir."

Breanna's jaw dropped. "What are ye saying?"

"I'm saying ye better resign yerself to marrying that knave."

Breanna gasped, and Luke put his arm around her shoulder, lowering his eyebrows at Cormac. "It seems you have experienced a disappointment in the catacombs, but there is no need to upset your sister. Perhaps you should sleep, and we will talk about this further when you are fed and rested."

Core grabbed the wineskin from Jyne's hand and took a long drink of the ale. He grabbed the bread too, and took a healthy bite. "Aye, that would be a wise and prudent decision, but what would it change? And why are ye still here, Luke? I thought I told ye to take Jyne and Breanna and leave early."

Luke tightened his lips.

"Ah, ye could'na leave the books. I should have known," said Core, taking another lengthy drink before handing it back to Jyne. "Too late now. We might as well start a bonfire now, for those manuscripts are as good as ash."

"How can ye be so cruel?" asked Breanna.

"'Tis no' cruelty, 'tis reality. Ye ken that better than anyone, Breanna. Red Rex will always win in the end."

"Ye ne'er believed that. Ye always found a way around him. Ye ne'er gave in to him." Breanna wiped a tear from her eye.

"I was a fool," said Cormac, biting off another piece of bread. "The sooner we recognize who we are in this human tragedy, the better. Red Rex will have his way. He always does."

"Ye're just like our father." Breanna stood tall, her green eyes blazing. "And I hate ye for it."

"What happened to ye?" asked Jyne, shocked at the sudden change in demeanor in Cormac.

"I'm done pretending. Ye're right about me. I lied to ye. Used ye. And now I'm done wi' ye. Get ye gone. I hope to ne'er see ye again."

Jyne gasped. Before she knew what she was doing, her hand flew out to slap him, but he caught it before she could strike. He grasped her arm and pulled her to him with a sudden jerk, whispering in her ear. "Red Rex is upon us. If he discovers the depth o' my regard for ye, yer life will be forfeit."

Heat crawled up the back of her neck, and she was painfully aware of everyone staring at her and Cormac. His eyes were stormy, but standing so close to him, she could see fear, not anger. She remembered the story of how Red Rex had killed Core's horse, simply because he cared for the animal. Despite everything, Core was still trying to save her.

The faint sound of a horn, mournful and warbling, shot through the early dawn. "Riders approaching!" called a man from the wall.

Cormac released her and strode away without a second look. His lips tightened into a thin line. "Too late for us all."

Red Rex was coming for them.

Thirty-seven

WHEN JYNE HAD BEEN TRAPPED IN THE CRYPT, SHE HAD thought things could not get worse, but they had. Then when she discovered Cormac's duplicity, she had thought she was as devastated as anyone could be, but she was wrong. Seeing Cormac give up all hope and surrender to his father, that was lower still.

At the sound of the battle horn of Red Rex, everyone flew into a panic.

Cormac shouted commands as he strode to the wall. "Bran, take Lady Jyne and Breanna and lock them in their chamber. Anyone over the age o' fifty, find a place to hide. Men, prepare yerselves."

"Corc, wait," said Jyne, but Bran grabbed her by the arm and escorted her and Breanna to their tower chamber in a very determined fashion. He pushed them both inside.

"Stay!" Bran commanded and slammed the door shut, locking it behind him.

"What did ye do to Cormac?" demanded Breanna, her green eyes accusing.

"Nothing! Besides, he lied to me," defended Jyne.

"Because he loves ye!" declared Breanna. "And ye broke his heart. Congratulations, for ye've done something my father could ne'er do. Ye turned him evil." Breanna's bottom lip quivered with emotion.

"Nay," said Jyne. "He is feigning disregard to protect us from yer father."

Breanna's mouth was already open to continue her attack, but she paused, realizing what Jyne had just said. "Aye, if Rex knew how Cormac felt about ye..." Breanna shook her head. "Rex hates affection. Hates love itself. That is why he sold me in marriage to a hateful creature. Said he was doing me a favor by forcing me to wed a man I would despise. Said I was better off hating the man."

"Yer father...he is not well."

"Nay. He's not."

What would it be like to have such a man as a father? Jyne knew what Cormac had done was wrong, very wrong. But he had been unfortunate in his sire, which had not been his choice at all. And even after Jyne had rejected him, he was still trying to protect her.

If he discovers the depth o' my regard for ye, yer life will be forfeit.

He had said he loved her, and she suspected that much at least was the truth. Jyne collapsed on the stone bench cut into the tower wall and opened the shutter to look out the window. Men were riding across the valley toward Kinoch.

Jyne closed her eyes, fatigue setting in. She leaned her head back on the cold stones. She knew her reaction was entirely justified, though she did feel a twinge of guilt about one thing. She had promised Cormac grace for whatever he revealed but had not shown it. But then again, she had had no idea he was going to reveal such betrayal. Surely, she was right!

Is there a limit to grace?

Jyne stilled at the sudden thought. A limit to grace? Why…no.

"Och! Breanna. I need to get to Core!" exclaimed Jyne, suddenly realizing that she had been called to show the man forgiveness. "Before he lets in Red Rex, there is something I must say."

Breanna shook her head. "Ye canna go down there. 'Tis no safe for ye, truly."

"Red Rex will kill me." Jyne could not keep the tremor from her words. She held her hands together to keep from shaking.

"Aye, if he knows ye mean anything to Core."

"Core is going to join him because of me. Yer father will gain Core's power with alchemy. We canna let that happen. At least, I feel I must tell him something first." Jyne strode across the room and rattled the door.

Breanna drew her table knife. "Then let me pick the lock. I hope ye ken what ye're doing."

Jyne hoped so too.

❧

The sound of his father's mournful horn rattled through Kinoch Abbey, bouncing off the stone walls and smacking him with almost physical force. Core's stomach clenched and turned, threatening to expel the bread he had just eaten. If he wasn't already feeling sick after his rejection from Jyne, the plaintive wail that announced the coming of Red Rex certainly would have made him ill. His fear for Jyne thrummed with every beat of his heart.

"Donnach. Luke," Core called to the men who were helping the elders from the courtyard. "I've no quarrel wi' ye, but my father will. I have no ability to keep ye safe this time, so stay from sight. As soon as ye can, take them to safety." He motioned with his head to the tower where the ladies had been taken.

"We will," said Luke, and Donnach nodded.

It was the best he could do. Core ran out of the keep to the outer wall to witness the arrival of his father. Red Rex had reached the far side of the valley and was riding toward them. On impulse, the elders had barred the gates and then run for a place to hide. Not a bad strategy, but not one that would stop Rex for long.

His men followed him out to the outer ward, standing in the field between the keep and the outer wall. They looked up at him, their faces grim. Even the strongest of them appeared a bit anxious, and all checked to make sure that their leather armor was strapped securely and their weapons were at hand. One did not appear before Red Rex without being prepared to fight and do his bidding.

Cormac realized that unlike in the past, when Bran had given the commands, this time, he was silent, and all were watching Core. For the first time, he felt that these men might actually follow him.

"Prepare yerselves. 'Tis time to meet Red Rex," said Core, hoping he was prepared himself. The wind in the outer ward was brisk, and he welcomed the cold wind on his face after such a long time in the crypt. At least if he died today, he would die in the open and not under the ground like a rat.

"Open the gates!" Cormac shouted to the guards on the wall. They looked down at him for a moment before complying, as if to ask in a silent plea if they must. Core's only hope was to appease his father by convincing him he was willing to become like him, and no further manipulation was necessary. Core feared it would not be enough to keep Jyne safe.

The portcullis was raised with a groan, mournful and long, as if even the iron gate itself was complaining at being opened to the warlord. Cormac stood in the gateway, looking out over the fields and watching as his father rode for the keep.

This was the monster everyone feared. The monster he feared. And yet, as the large man rode toward him, Cormac realized a strange thing. He wasn't afraid anymore. What could his father possibly do to him? Kill him? Jyne had already ripped out his heart, so that was not any great loss. He had already been buried alive, lost his love and anything else he ever cared about. It did not matter now. He would join his father, become whatever he wanted, and pray that it would be enough to save them.

"Cormac!"

He turned and saw Jyne hurrying toward him. His heart squeezed in pain at the sight of her. What was she doing down here?

"Get back! 'Tis no' safe!"

"Nay, ye must hear this. I was wrong. Ye can be forgiven. Dinna give up."

"Ye forgive me?" He stopped short, forgetting his facade of disregard.

Jyne paused, for she was an honest lady. "I'm still really, truly angry wi' ye, but ye are no' yer father. I believe ye can be a good man."

Jyne believed in him. She knew what he was, *who* he was, and she still could see some value in him. He stared at her in mute surprise. This was not anything he had expected. Everything else, he could have predicted, but not this. His understanding of the world shattered.

He took a step toward her. She was still covered in gray dust, but nothing could diminish her loveliness, for it shone through from the inside. He loved her more now than ever.

And everyone watching them in the courtyard knew it.

"Close the gates!" he shouted. His father had picked up speed and was almost upon them. If Red Rex got his hands on Jyne, she would be dead. Core might not be able to prevent it from happening, but he would surely die to defend her.

"What?" called down the confused gate guard.

"Ye heard me, ye bat-brained fool. Close the damn gates! We'll no' let this bastard in wi'out a fight."

The man shrugged and began the slow process of closing the rusty gates.

Jyne smiled at him with an approval that shone in her eyes. He felt like he could soar. His men reacted in quite the opposite manner. Bran's eyes bugged out of his head. Dubh dropped his jaw and stared at him.

"Listen well, ye followers o' Red Rex," Core addressed his men. "I choose this day to no longer serve my father. If ye wish to continue under his service, go now, before the gates close. If ye will serve me against my father, then stay. If ye have any fear in ye, go now, for where I am about to tread, few men go and live to tell the tale."

A few men stirred and glanced at the gate as it groaned in protest at being disturbed once more after being moved so recently. The thunderous sound of approaching horses rumbled on the ground. Red Rex was almost to the gates. Dubh shifted his feet, as if preparing to run if any of the others did. The men stared at their feet, glanced again at the gate, and then back at Cormac.

Cormac held his breath. Would the men stay?

The gate slammed closed with a tremendous thud and a clank. Men ran to bar the door.

"We will stay and serve the Fire Lord," declared Bran.

"As ye wish. Ye have chosen freely, and time will tell whether ye have chosen well," said Cormac.

"We will serve ye too, if ye'll have us." Donnach and Luke stepped forward from the keep, both armed.

"Aye, and welcome to ye," said Core. "But ye, go now!" He shooed away Jyne. He was not surprised when she crossed her arms and shook her head.

"Open this gate!" thundered the voice of Red Rex from beyond the gate. It had closed almost on his very nose.

Cormac ran up the stone steps, leading to the wall walk, with Bran right behind.

"I hope ye ken what ye're doing," muttered Bran.

"I've no idea," confessed Cormac with a half smile.

"That is what I feared." Bran sighed. "It shall be an interesting day."

"I hope to see ye at the end of it," said Core.

"This side o' hell," grumbled Bran.

Cormac looked down from the wall to his father and the men, warriors all, who followed him. His father looked up at him, and even with the height and the wall between them, he could feel the heat of his father's glare. He wavered for a moment. What was he thinking? How could he stand up to the one man no one could defeat? He knew better than to think that his father would spare his life. Red Rex had destroyed everything he loved; he would not think twice about killing him too.

"Open this gate! Yer master has arrived!" Red Rex's voice thundered across the outer ward and no doubt the very valley itself. The gates may have been barred to his physical body, but his voice certainly slashed through.

Cormac's pulse thundered in his ears. He had spent years being afraid of this man, trying to run away from him or avoid his ire. Not today. He was done running. Whatever this was between him and his father, it needed to end here. Now.

"I am the master o' this keep. The gates open for none but whom I choose." Cormac's voice rang out over the hills, sounding almost like somebody else's voice. He had never, ever spoken to his father that way.

"What's he doing? He's gonna get us all killed!" Dubh's voice could be plainly heard, along with furious whispers from his men to remain silent. Cormac agreed with Dubh. He was certainly venturing down a course that got men killed.

Red Rex was silent for a moment, perhaps too shocked to make a reply. Cormac held his breath, waiting for the response. Even the wind had died down, as if it too was holding its breath to see what the notorious warlord would do in the face of such flagrant defiance.

"So my son has finally decided to become a man." Red Rex laughed. "Do ye hear what my boy just said to me?" He turned to his compatriots, and they nodded cautiously, unsure which way this unpredictable and dangerous man was going. "Looks like my boy has found his manhood today." Red Rex removed his helm and laughed again in an angry, scornful tone, his coarse red hair sticking out at all angles around his head, like he was on fire.

Cormac was slightly relieved at his father's response, for he had expected blind fury.

"Now ye listen here, boy," Red growled, his laughter ending in an instant. "I am the master o' ye and anything ye think ye possess."

"Nay, sire. I choose this day to be my own master."

Rex's voice was low and ominous. "I own ye, boy. If ye want to be yer own master, ye have to kill me to do it."

The wind blew like cold daggers against Core's face. If he ever wanted to be free of his father, he would have to kill him. The only surprising thing about the realization was that Cormac was not surprised. Somehow, he'd always known it would come down to this. He would have to face his father in combat.

And his father would win.

Everyone knew this. There was no way Cormac could hold his own against his father. He either needed to accept defeat and serve his father the rest of his days, or he would have to fight and die.

Cormac knew his father too well to think that he would show him mercy. His father had shown him many times his willingness to kill things, regardless of whether his father liked them or not. Cormac wasn't exactly sure which camp he fell into, but either way, if he fought, his father would kill him.

Cormac felt the eyes of everyone on him. His father and all his warriors glared at him. Behind him, he could sense his men staring at him. He turned around slowly to look at the only one who truly mattered to him.

Jyne Campbell stood on the other side of the courtyard. She was still the small, thin, ethereal creature who had captured his interest from the moment he had seen her. His eyes met hers. Even from a distance, he could see how they blazed.

She glided toward him, crossing the courtyard with such fluid movements, it almost appeared that she floated. He also moved toward her, ignoring his father at the gate. Jyne reached the stone staircase and stood at the bottom, looking up at him.

"What will ye do?" she asked.

What would he do? It would be senseless to try to fight his father; everyone knew that. Everyone except Jyne Campbell. In her eyes, he saw determination. She had not let her size or insurmountable odds stop her from fighting against him.

He took a deep breath of the cold, fresh air. "Ye make me want to be a better person."

"I know ye can be. I know ye are." Her words melted away the pain and bitterness. It was time to let it go. It was time to break the chains and claim his freedom.

"Has all the bite gone out o' my son? He is so scared, he canna even answer me!" his father roared from beyond the gate. The man did not like to be kept waiting.

"If ye would excuse me for a moment," Core called back. It was the kind of polite statement that would set his father's teeth on edge. Cormac didn't care. He was going to be the man he wanted to be, and if that meant using correct grammar and social politeness, then so be it.

"Thank ye, Jyne. Ye've changed my life, for as many minutes as I have left me. I want ye to know that."

"I trust ye shall have many minutes to string together yet," said Jyne with shining eyes.

"Now if ye have any compassion for me, please run from this place. I will face my father, and barring some sort of miracle, I will die. Please go."

"Dinna die," she commanded, her shoulders back, her eyes flashing. She turned and ran back across the outer ward to the keep, with Donnach following behind as her personal protector.

Core returned to the wall walk and leaned against the battlements, looking down at his father. "Then we will fight. For no man owns me."

A small smile spread across Rex's face. The man respected courage. But he would still kill him. "So today, my son becomes a man. And today also will be the day he dies. But at least, Son, ye shall die a man."

Thirty-eight

CORMAC HAD FINALLY EARNED HIS FATHER'S RESPECT. After years of attempting to placate his father, all Core had ever gotten were insults and blows hurled at him with rapidity and soul-wrenching accuracy. Apparently, the only way to earn his father's respect was to kill him.

There was something very disturbing going on in his family.

"Open the gate," commanded Core.

No one moved.

"I said, open the gate," he shouted.

With great reluctance, the portcullis was slowly raised once more, moaning its complaint along the way. Cormac ran down the stone stairs to be the first to meet his father at the gate. If his father lunged at him now, there would be little for him to do but die bravely. He swallowed down gall. He really didn't want to die bravely.

"Welcome, Father," said Cormac as the gates opened and his father strode through on mighty legs like tree trunks. His father was a giant of a man, and

Cormac feared he may have grown a few inches since he had seen him last. Often, as children grow, their parents seem to shrink in size. In the case of Red Rex, his magnitude only seemed to increase.

"I'm glad ye finally grew to be a man." His father slapped him on the back so hard that Cormac stumbled forward. "Wish ye were stronger, so this would be more of a fight, but at least ye can die a man."

"I would ask for the honor o' choosing the weapons," said Core, trying to think of some way to survive. Jyne had demanded it of him, and apparently, he was hers to command. He doubted his father would accept a rousing game of chess instead of swords.

His father laughed. "Choose whate'er ye like. The outcome will be the same." Could his father kill him with a chessboard? Yes…yes, he could.

"Ye must be tired from the road. Come, eat, drink, and then we shall proceed," said Cormac, trying to give himself time to devise a plan. There was no way he could face his father in any form of combat and emerge the victor. He was not particularly pleased with the prospect of having to kill his father, but he was less pleased with the prospect of being killed himself.

"I need no rest. Ye can sleep when ye're dead," his father growled at him.

"Please do accept my hospitality. The last request of a condemned man."

"Och, ye talk too much. I'll have a whiskey to whet my appetite, and then we'll see this through." His father glared down at him and shook his head. "Damn, but ye look like yer mother." It was not a compliment.

Core gestured toward the great hall, and his father

brushed past him into the keep. The rest of his followers passed Cormac, not one looking him in the eye. You should not look too closely at the condemned.

"Feed them, and get Rex as drunk as ye can," whispered Cormac to Bran as he passed him on his way into the hall.

"I've seen yer father drink kegs o' whiskey and no' so much as slur a word," replied Bran.

Cormac knew it to be true. His father must have whiskey running through his veins, for the man drank steadily without noticeable effect. "Do the best ye can to keep him distracted for a while."

"What are ye going to do?"

"I dinna ken," answered Core honestly. "I need time to think."

"Ye best come up wi' something, or we may face yer same fate."

"Probably should'na have thrown yer lot in wi' me then."

"Aye, but I did, and I stand by it. Someone needs to stand up to that man," Bran muttered. "I've seen strong men go at it, only to be laid waste. I've seen the clever, the skilled, the brave, and the utterly foolhardy, and Red Rex has killed them all. But what I've ne'er seen is ye stand up to him."

"And ye reckon I can succeed where others have failed?" Hope blossomed within him. If Bran thought it was possible for him to defeat his father, maybe it actually was.

"Nay." Hope crashed back down. "I just meant I've ne'er seen it."

"That is not at all helpful."

Bran shrugged, his face impassive. He clasped Core's shoulder for a moment, then filed in to the great hall with the others, leaving Cormac to fight his own battles.

Instead of going into the hall, Core turned to go up the stairs to the tower. He needed to escape the chaos below and think.

"Have ye gone mad?" Breanna rushed down the stairs, her eyes wide, her face pale. "Our father is going to kill ye!"

"Nay," said Jyne confidently, coming down the stairs behind her. "Core will think o' something. He always does."

"I thought I told ye to run away," cried Core, dismayed to see her there.

"I believe ye can overcome him."

Core stared at her, incredulous. He shook his head at her confidence in him, false as it was. "Thank ye. I just need to think of a plan."

"I shall no' distract ye then." Breanna sighed and put a hand on his shoulder. "Farewell, my brother." She slowly trudged back up the stairs to the chamber.

"Stay wi' Luke, my sister."

"I will," she answered over her shoulder.

"I am sorry, m'lady. For everything," said Core, turning back to Jyne. He held out his hands, and she took them.

"Ye are forgiven. For everything." Jyne returned his smile, though her eyes were moist. She was fighting against tears.

"I hope the Good Lord can be as forgiving as ye."

"If ye pray for forgiveness, ye can be assured of it!"

She wrapped her arms around him and gave him a warm embrace. It was her good-bye to him, and he knew it. He truly was going to die.

"I shall be sure to say my prayers before—" The slaughter? The murder?

"Good. I shall pray for ye too." Jyne held him tighter. "I wish things were different."

"I wish my biggest problem was to convince yer brother to allow me to marry ye."

"Ye wish to marry me?" asked Jyne, looking up with wide eyes.

"More than anything," sighed Core. He did not care anymore about hiding his feelings. If he was going to die today, he might as well tell Jyne the whole truth.

"I…I would like that too."

It was Core's turn to stare down at her. "Truly?" Joy rose in his heart.

"Truly."

Core drew her closer and kissed her firmly on the mouth, all his fears and hopes and dreams and worries crashing together into one last passionate kiss. When their lips finally parted, he was feeling a bit light-headed. Jyne gazed up at him with an unguarded passion that made his heart skip a beat.

"I canna lose ye," murmured Jyne.

"At least ye're no longer angry at me."

"Not angry at ye? I am furious! But ye're mine, and none should kill ye but me."

Cormac grinned at her ferocity. He would willingly submit himself to her hand.

"If only there was a way for ye to face him wi'

something ye know well," said Jyne. "Too bad the Fire Lord canna go in yer place."

"Wait…" The wheels began to spin in his mind. What if he used alchemy? "I think I have an idea."

Jyne kissed him on the cheek. "For luck."

"I wish I could tarry longer, but och, I must go. If ye would help me, bring to the kitchen the box from my room wi' the alchemy equipment and jars. Be careful wi' it!"

"I will!" Jyne hiked up her skirts and sprinted up the stone stairs.

Core ran off to the kitchens. He did not have long. His father would drink a while once he started, but still, that left him only an hour or two. In the kitchen, he began to search for something that might work. He picked up an iron kettle with a long, narrow neck and a thick bottom. It might just work.

Jyne ran in, carrying a crate from his room. "Is this what ye need?"

"Aye, thank ye. Will ye help me?"

Jyne's eyes shone. "O' course I will."

Two hours later, Cormac stood in the outer ward, facing down his father. People lined up on either side of the ward, giving the combatants a wide berth.

"Kettles?" His father laughed so hard, he almost fell over. "Ye wish to conduct mortal combat wi' kettles?" He snorted, and his men mocked and howled.

Cormac held a short spear with a modified iron kettle affixed to the top. His men stared at him in horror. Only Lady Jyne gave him a nod of courage. He had told her to run away and hide, but she had clearly refused.

"If ye dinna bring yer war kettle, ye may use a sword," conceded Core.

"War kettle?" His father began to laugh again. "Och, I thought ye had finally become a man. But nay, ye've ne'er been anything but a weakling, and ye'll die a weakling."

Core did not respond to his father's taunts but held his ground.

"At least I had found a funeral pyre prepared for ye." Rex motioned to some men behind him, and they dragged out the cart full of precious, rare texts, books, and scrolls. His father had found the books.

"No!" shouted a voice Core knew to be Luke's. It was all going terribly wrong.

At a signal from Red Rex, a man stepped forward with a torch.

"Wait!" cried Core. His heart pounded to see a torch hovering over the irreplaceable texts. "Ye can do whatever ye wish to me and the books, but ye have to kill me first."

"That is no great feat," growled Rex.

"If ye had any sense, ye'd submit to Cormac now," cried Jyne, fierce in her defense.

"Shut it, wench! Who do ye think ye are?" thundered Red Rex.

"Dinna insult her!" cried Cormac.

"Ah, so ye have found yerself a lightskirt, eh, lad?" Rex gave him a cruel smile, and Core knew he had made a mistake. "I will take a turn wi' her after ye're dead!"

Core's heart pounded in his throat. Jyne was in grave danger. He had been afraid before, but never had he known such dire panic. If he failed, Rex would assault and murder Jyne. The books would be burned to ash, and everyone around him would be hurt. He had to stop this man.

"Ye'll no' touch her." Core knew there was only one way to prevent it.

"Have ye developed feelings for this wench?" Rex sneered.

Core paused, but only for a moment. It did not matter now if he denied it; Rex would not believe him. The only way to protect Jyne was to kill his father. Since that was unlikely, Core wanted his last words to be the truth. Jyne deserved that much at least. He squared his shoulders and stood tall. "I love the Lady Jyne."

"Love is for the weak!" roared the warlord, all trace of humor drained from his face.

"Then as a weakling, it is for me!" Core thundered back in a voice he had not known he had.

"This ends now!" His father drew his sword and charged with a fierce battle cry.

Core leveled his weapon and lit the fuse in the spout. He prayed it would work, or he and Jyne were both dead. His father sprinted toward him, sword upraised. Core braced himself, his heart pounding against his chest, waiting for his experiment to work. Nothing happened. His father was almost upon him, arms upraised. This was the end.

A powerful blast tore through the outer ward. The force of it knocked Core against the stone wall of the keep. His vision grew hazy around the edges, and he saw pinpricks of light. He lay on his back, his head spinning, his ears ringing. He closed his eyes, wanting to be claimed by the nothingness that seduced him. He wondered if he had died in the blast instead of his father.

But what of Jyne? His eyes flew open again. He needed to protect her. Was his father still alive? Was she in danger even now?

Slowly, he struggled back to his feet and stepped forward into the haze of smoke and dust. All was quiet. Perhaps all were stunned, or maybe he could not hear anyone speak over the ringing in his ears. What had happened?

He staggered forward until he found the still-smoking kettle on the ground where he had dropped it. Hand-carrying such a weapon was not the best option. But where was his father? As the dust and smoke settled, he could make out the forms of people standing on either side. They were all silent and all staring at one spot on the ground. Only one person was looking at him.

Jyne ran forward. "Are ye hurt?"

"I still stand, but what o' my father?"

"He does not stand." She turned in the same direction that everyone else was staring.

A few more steps forward brought into view a large black form on the ground. It was his father, lying on his back. Was he dead?

Cormac stumbled forward. His father lay with his eyes closed, blood pooling around him. His sword lay abandoned several feet away. Still clutching it was his arm…an arm no longer attached to his body.

Cormac knelt by his side. "Father?"

The big man's eyes opened wide. "What was that power?"

"Alchemy," said Core. "What I was studying in university."

"They taught ye that in university?"

"They taught the principles. I figured the rest."

Rex glared at Cormac. "Too smart for yer own good."

"Too smart for *yer* own good," Cormac retorted.

His father snorted in response. "Finish me off, boy. Ye canna do anything right."

"I will do things the way I choose," countered Cormac.

"Ye disarmed me, boy, literally. Now finish the job. Kill me quick. 'Tis yer duty."

"I will choose what is my duty and what is not. This reign of death and misery ends today. Though ye have hated me, Father, I choose no' to hate ye in return." Cormac experienced a lightness when he spoke the words, as if he had been shouldering a heavy burden and, finally, it had been removed from his back. He glanced up at Jyne, who gave him a watery smile.

"I dinna hate ye, boy." Rex spoke in a low, gravelly tone. "I only wanted to make ye tough, for a weakling in this world knows naught but pain."

"Weak or strong, all men know pain."

His father searched his face, looking at him as if he'd never truly seen him before. "True. When did my son become so wise?"

"When he went to university," answered Cormac in a practical tone. He looked up into the misty eyes of Jyne Campbell, who stood by his side. "And when I heeded the counsel o' those wiser than me."

"Enough talk. Finish the job."

"Ye loved her verra much, did ye not? My mother?"

"Ye winna speak o' her."

"I have a right to know."

"Nay, the only thing ye must do is attend to yer business here and finish me off!"

"I want to know o' my mother. I want to know what turned ye into a demon."

"This is how ye exact yer revenge? Ye wait till I lay dying and then demand answers? Ye're a cruel bastard, ye are."

Coming from his father, Core took it as a compliment. "Aye, tell me o' my mother."

Something between a sigh and a gasp escaped the large man's lips. It was surrender. "She was the most beautiful creature in all the world, and she was more kind than beautiful. When she died, she took my heart wi' her."

"And me?"

"Ye were the worst reminder o' her. When I looked in yer eyes, I saw her. I tried to kill ye many times, but something always stayed my hand. So I sent ye away, hoping ye'd die. When ye dinna die, I determined to be hard on ye so ye could have a heart o' stone that would ne'er break."

"Then ye've failed me, for my heart belongs to another."

"Ye're a fool."

"True. If someday we are parted and my heart breaks, I would'na trade one moment o' her love, even if it meant the end o' pain."

"Then ye're a stronger man than I. Hear this, all ye who will listen. I yield to my son!"

Thirty-nine

JYNE PUT A HAND ON CORE'S SHOULDER AS HIS father breathed his last. The man closed his eyes and drifted away. Red Rex was dead.

"I killed my father." Core looked up at her, raw pain in his eyes. Jyne had expected him to be relieved, but all she saw was grief.

"I'm sorry," whispered Jyne. She was not sorry for the man's death but for all the circumstances around it.

Core rested his hand over hers and said a prayer for his father. While Core was engaged with saying farewell to his father, everyone in the courtyard was silently staring at him. What would the warriors his father brought with him do now? Would they attack at the death of their leader? The air around them crackled with danger.

"Core," she whispered, getting his attention.

He looked up at her and recognized her concern. He stood to face his father's men, who looked like they were considering a fight.

"Men o' my father," Cormac called. "I have

defeated Red Rex. Ye have a choice before ye. Leave now, or swear yer allegiance to me."

The men looked around at each other, grumbling and muttering. With sudden inspiration, Jyne ran to where Core had dropped what was left of his "war kettle" and handed it to him. The iron was mangled, but it was a grim reminder of Cormac's power. He held on to the pole of the war kettle like a staff of power and stared down his father's men. The men all stepped back and looked at Core with a wary respect.

A few men slipped out the gate, but most shouted, "We swear our allegiance to the Fire Lord!"

Chaos had erupted around her, but all Jyne saw, all she heard, was Cormac.

He gave her a weary smile. "Thank ye, m'lady. I could'na have done this wi'out ye."

She looked up at him with pride swelling in her heart. Her eyes filled with tears for quite another reason than earlier that day. "I love ye, Cormac MacLean."

He gaped at her. "Ye do?"

"Aye, I do." This was the man she loved. He was not perfect, but he was hers.

"I dinna have the right to ask ye, and this is hardly the proper time or place, but my heart demands it o' me. I have naught to offer, not even a name, and as yer friend, I can only advise against it, but Lady Jyne Campbell, will ye consent to be my wife?"

"Aye!" Joy flashed through her.

"Aye?" His eyes opened wide.

"Aye, ye daft fool. I will marry ye!"

Core dropped his staff and wrapped her up tight in his arms. In another moment, he was kissing her, hot and demanding. She gave back to him in equal measure. It was all over. They had won. They could be together forever! The crowd around them cheered and then grew suddenly quiet.

"Unhand my sister!" commanded a stern voice.

Jyne jumped back from Cormac with a gasp and a small shriek. Her brother, Laird Campbell, stood before her, his hands at his waist, his feet planted for battle. His broadsword was strapped to his back, and Jyne knew how quickly her brother could draw it.

"David! How did…? When did…?" She quickly looked around and realized that her brother's men and the former men of Red Rex were glaring at each other from opposite sides of the field. She had been so focused on Core that she had not noticed the sudden arrival of her brother.

"I have been tracking Red Rex for the past week. Seems I've found him." David glanced at the unmoving form of Red Rex.

Jyne looked up at Core, but his face had shuttered and was unreadable. Everyone in the outer ward was silent and still, waiting for the fight to begin. It was the calm before the storm, but a battle was inevitable.

"Gracious, Jyne, what happened to ye?" asked David, his face one of concern, and she realized her gown was torn, her veil gone, and she was still covered in dust from her sojourn in the crypt. Before she could answer, David turned to one of his men. "Take her out where it's safe."

"Nay!" she cried.

Her brother raised an eyebrow. "What did ye say?"

Jyne grasped Cormac's hand with her trembling

one. She had never stood up to her brother. Never. Why should she? He was a good man, a kind brother, and a powerful laird. He also ruled his clan as an absolute monarch. His word was law.

But no more. If Cormac could stand up to his father, she could stand up to her brother.

"I said, I will no' go wi' ye. Kinoch Abbey is my home, and here I will stay!"

David leveled a glare at her that made her mouth go dry and her hands sweat. "Kinoch Abbey is my property, which may or may no' be given to ye on the day of yer marriage, if I should ever decide ye shall wed."

"That was not particularly charitable, my dear." Lady Isabelle, David's English wife, walked up from behind him and put a staying hand on his shoulder.

David turned to his wife with irritation. "I told ye to remain in the back, where it's safe."

Isabelle gave her husband a calm smile. "But I am always safe when I am with you. How are you, my dear?" Isabelle turned her question to Jyne.

"I am well, thank ye," Jyne responded, appreciating her sister-in-law's support.

"It looks like you have had quite an adventure," commented Isabelle with enviable serenity. "And made a new friend." She gave Cormac an appraising sweep of her eyes.

"Isabelle, take Jyne and get ye back where it is safe," said David through gritted teeth in a tone that brooked no argument.

Isabelle stretched out a hand to Jyne to escort her away. Core released her hand. Jyne would go back to her people, while David decided what would be done. There was going to be a fight. And Cormac was not even armed. Why had she thought she could make a difference? She was just one person. She was…just Jyne.

She glanced back at Cormac. In his eyes, she saw a reflection of herself that was different. In his eyes, she was formidable, powerful, and resilient. In his eyes, she was never small.

"Nay!" She stood her ground.

"Nay?" David stared at her in shock. Even Isabelle raised her eyebrows, and her hand fell back to her side.

"I winna go wi' ye. I will stay here. Ye may have bought this land, but I have fought for it, and I shall keep it." Jyne grasped Cormac's hand once more. He stared at her with a surprise rivaled only by her brother. Not one person in the outer ward said a word.

"What's more," continued Jyne, taking advantage of the moment of silence, "I will marry Cormac MacLean. Son o' Red Rex though he may be!"

"Nay!" thundered David. "Ye marry the son o' a warlord? Never!"

"I'm not asking yer permission. I'm telling ye how it will be. I will marry Cormac MacLean, and I will live here wi' him. And that is the end of it!"

"Impossible!" bellowed David.

"As impossible as an English countess marrying a laird?" Isabelle reminded David of their own unlikely history.

"That…that was different. And ye need to get behind our men," growled David, taking Isabelle by the arm.

Jyne was about to object, but realized that the

Campbell warriors and Cormac's men were growing hostile. Swords had been drawn. They were going to erupt into battle at any moment.

"Core, yer men. Do something," she hissed.

His eyebrows shot up in sudden understanding. "Let us welcome our friends," he called to his men. "Go into the main hall, and tell Cook to prepare a repast to refresh our friends, who have traveled long to arrive at our gates."

His men stared at him in surprise, then looked about at each other with a low rumble of dissent. Jyne held her breath. Would they follow his commands?

"Ye heard the Fire Lord," commanded Bran. "Into the keep wi' ye, look lively. Ye would'na want him to take a kettle to ye."

The men returned their swords to their scabbards and strode into the main hall with some haste. No one was laughing at the kettle now. Bran marched them in and gave a sharp nod to Core as he passed. Only Luke and Breanna remained in the yard, standing apart from the Campbell warriors.

"Laird Campbell," began Cormac, "I understand yer reticence, but I tell ye true that I love yer sister. I dinna deserve her but—"

"Aye, ye dinna deserve her. Let's leave it there," said David. "Now, I appreciate the welcome, but this is my holding. Ye and yer men must leave."

"Nay, Brother," Jyne jumped in. "Cormac has conquered Kinoch Abbey. 'Tis his now."

David turned a maleficent glare on Cormac.

"But then she conquered my heart, so the scales are even between us," said Core quickly.

"This man is a warlord, a raider, and a thief!" roared Laird Campbell.

"Cormac has defeated Red Rex," defended Jyne. "He killed his own father to defend me and others."

Her words stayed whatever David was going to say next. He took a few steps closer to the monstrous form of the fallen warlord. "Ye went up against this man in single combat?" David raised an eyebrow. Even with Red Rex on the ground, the difference in size was considerable. And everyone knew the notorious reputation of Red Rex.

"Aye," said Core. "He threatened everything I hold dear, in order to turn me into a warlord like him."

"Looks like ye did some damage," said David. He respected courage. More than that, he respected results.

Cormac gave a nod.

"To go against Red Rex and emerge the victor is something few could boast," admitted David to Jyne. "But that doesna mean he would be a good husband for ye."

"Ye canna judge the man by the sins o' his father," said Jyne, pleading his case. "Besides, he killed the man. What more can ye ask o' him?"

"Actually," said Isabelle, calmly interrupting the debate. "The man still lives."

"He lives?" gasped Cormac, turning to stare at the man on the ground.

"In my experience, dead men do not usually still breathe." Lady Isabelle glided forward to the body of Red Rex. "He must have lost consciousness due to the shock. His wound will need to be cauterized, or he will soon bleed to death."

She turned back to David, Jyne, and Cormac, her eyes asking the question. Did they want her to save him?

"I am certain he would rather die here. But if ye can save him, I would show him grace," said Core. His eyes met Jyne, a smile in the glance.

"He doesna deserve it," commented Laird Campbell, which was true.

"Nor do any of us," replied his lady wife, which was also true. "Bring me my smock, boiling oil, a bone saw, a red hot poker, needle and thread, and a priest." Several Campbell men jumped to heed her request.

"Ye fear he winna make it?" asked Jyne.

"The priest is for you, my dear."

"For me?"

"Yes. I believe you said you were getting married." Jyne smiled at Isabelle. "Thank you."

"MacLean may have proven his valor, but he's no' the groom o' my choice," said David with finality.

"Nay, he is the groom o' *my* choice," replied Jyne with defiance.

"There will be no wedding!" hollered David with growing frustration.

"Then we will say our own vows before God," returned Jyne. "And if ye want Kinoch, ye're going to have to fight me for it!" Her pulse pounded in her ears. She had never defied her brother, Laird of the Campbells. Behind her brother, several of the Campbell warriors were staring at her with open mouths. No one spoke to Laird Campbell in such a manner.

"What did ye…? How could ye…? Now ye listen here," sputtered David.

"I'd no' oppose her," warned Cormac. "She is

a fierce enemy. Defeating Red Rex, I could do. Overcoming Lady Jyne, I could not."

"Overcoming Lady Jyne?" David repeated in an incredulous tone. "Ye could defeat Red Rex but no' Jyne?" David stared at Jyne as if seeing her for the first time.

"You Campbells are in the habit of marrying the wrong persons," commented Isabelle in an offhand manner as she accepted the smock to protect her gown and knelt by her unconscious patient. "Cait married a McNab. Gwyn married an English lord. And I hardly need remind you that I myself am English and entirely unsuitable."

"I thought I could'na dislike any groom more than a McNab," David grumbled to his wife. "I expected something like that from the likes o' Cait or Gwyn, but no' my little Jyne. She never caused me a moment's worry, except when she was sick. What has gotten into her?"

"She's a Campbell, David," said Isabelle without looking up from her work.

"True. And Campbell ladies are ferocious creatures. I know that too well. Ye heed me, lad?" He directed the comment at Core.

"Aye, sir."

"Why do ye want to marry this lout?" David asked Jyne.

"Because I fell in love," answered Jyne. "'Tis what all Campbells do. 'Tis yer fault if I want a love match, for ye and Isabelle have shown me what it is to be in love. How can I no' wish that for myself? Would ye truly deny me, Brother?"

David raised an eyebrow at Jyne and turned back to

his wife. "I blame ye for being such a loving wife and filling my days wi' endless joy."

"If being in love is a crime, then you have been a complicit partner," returned Isabelle as she tended to her work.

David sighed. "I do wish ye every happiness, Jyne. I suppose if ye truly feel this man is the one ye love—"

"I do!" shouted Jyne.

"Then I shall give ye my blessing." David smiled at Jyne, then turned to Cormac. "If ye cause my sister a moment's grief, I shall disembowel ye." He was deadly serious. "And ye'll need to join the Campbell clan and swear allegiance to me."

"Aye, sir," said Core, putting his arm around Jyne. "It would be my honor to do both."

"I suppose we should find that priest," muttered David.

"I may know a priest or two who would be willing," said Luke, putting his arm around Breanna. "Especially if there was more than one wedding to perform."

"More than one?" asked Breanna, with expectation in her green eyes.

"I thought I could never feel this way again," began Luke. "I planned to hide away forever. I have given away everything, but—"

"Aye! I will marry ye!" Breanna sealed her acceptance with a kiss.

"Congratulations!" cried Jyne. "I am so happy for ye both!"

"I dinna even ken who these people are," complained David to his Isabelle.

"Sorry, dear, busy with an amputation," returned his wife, holding a bone saw.

"What is all this?" Jyne's brother Rab chose that moment to return to Kinoch Abbey. He saw David and paled.

David narrowed his eyes at his youngest brother. "Ye were supposed to watch over yer sister. Ye and I are going to have words."

"Och, David, dinna be too hard on him. It was my idea for him to go to the tournament," said Jyne.

"Tournament?" thundered David.

Rab shot her a glance to tell her to stop helping him.

"What do ye want me to do wi' the gold?" Dubh wandered back outside to ask his question, drawing everyone's attention.

"What gold?" asked Cormac.

"The gold we found in the big hole ye made. The gold ye said would be in the crypt. Found it just like ye said."

"Gold?" gasped Jyne. She looked at Luke and Breanna, who both nodded and smiled.

Core stared at Jyne in shock and then laughed until tears ran down his cheeks. He held on to her like he was never letting go.

Forty

KINOCH ABBEY WAS A FLURRY OF ACTIVITY. JYNE TOOK a few minutes to inform David and Isabelle of all that had transpired, and she could not miss the look of surprise in David's eyes. He was impressed by her, and she was gratified by his stoic praise. All the while, food was being prepared for the large gathering, the children and elders who had left were called to return, and most importantly, the gold they had found in the crypt continued to be recovered.

Core oversaw the process, and all watched with eager eyes as more and more was pulled out of the crater and piled on a large sheet in the middle of the courtyard. Many hands were eager to help, under the watchful eyes of Bran and Luke, who directed the activities and ensured no stray coin ended up in someone's pocket.

Core's men grew restless, helping haul stones and watching the treasure being brought forth. Not even the procession of Red Rex being carried on a litter by ten men to a chamber to recuperate from his ordeal could reduce their ardor for gold.

Jyne feared that the tenuous truce between the ruffians and the Campbells might break any moment in a brawl for the gold. While all other eyes were focused on gold, she ran to the kitchens and found another long-necked iron kettle to bind to the pole and bring out to Cormac. All eyes watched the strange contraption, particularly the former men of Red Rex, who knew the power Cormac could wield. They may wish for gold, but they respected the Fire Lord.

When it became clear that they had recovered all the loot, they stood around to stare at it. Who did it belong to? What was going to be done with it?

"This gold is yers," said Core to Laird Campbell. "This is yer holding, so it goes to ye."

Several of his men gasped and grumbled at the pronouncement, but he held up his deadly staff, and they glared at him in sullen silence.

David Campbell looked surprised at the statement, as was Jyne. Would he really give it all away?

"Ye would give it to my brother?" exclaimed Jyne.

"It is naught to me, compared to ye," Core said boldly.

"It means something to me," grumbled Dubh loudly.

Again, Core held up a staying hand, and again, his men obeyed him. They had clearly taken heed of the unconscious form of Red Rex, and no one wished to stand against Cormac MacLean.

"Ye are correct," boomed Laird Campbell to the crowd who gathered around the pile of gold. "Kinoch Abbey and all within belong to the Campbell. As such, it is my right to distribute its wealth as I see fit. First, I would reward the elders here who helped dig to rescue the Lady Jyne. I accept the oath of allegiance ye swore to clan Campbell wi' my thanks for the protection o' my sister. Let every elder o' clan Ranald, heretofore to be known as clan Campbell, come forward to claim one coin each."

People gasped and cried out, either in joy or dismay, as each of the elders stepped forward to claim their prize. In one minute, they went from being the poorest of people to those of comfortable means.

"Since my men have also assisted in this quest, I would grant them the same boon," said the Campbell, allowing his few dozen soldiers to claim a piece of the prize. The men of Red Rex grumbled louder.

"The rest, along with Kinoch Abbey and all the lands therein," called David for all to hear, "I give to my sister, the Lady Jyne Campbell, today, the day o' her wedding." David nodded to the priest, who had been hustled to Kinoch to oversee the event.

"Thank ye, David," said Jyne, blinking back emotion. She looked up at Cormac. "I trust ye to do what's right."

"I hope I shall no' disappoint," he said to her under his breath. Jyne smiled at him with confidence. He had more than proven himself to her.

"First, to my wife, I give a goodly portion for her comfort and the comfort of our children." He scooped up two handfuls and gave them to Jyne, who struggled to hold them all, shoving the heavy gold coin into pockets, which strained under the weight.

"Next, I give a portion to Brother Luke and my sister Breanna. I understand it was Breanna who called ye all to dig to save our lives and, in doing so, found the treasure. We all owe her a debt of gratitude, which I hope this will compensate." He handed them a large portion.

"Next, to each o' the men o' Red Rex, I offer ye the following accord. Each o' ye has earned a coin for yer service."

Men began to scramble forward to claim their reward, ignoring whatever else Cormac might say.

"Wait!" hollered Cormac, slamming his staff down on the linen sheet containing the gold. "Listen to what I will tell ye. Ye all have lived a life deserving of retribution. And yet, I would like to offer ye the chance for redemption that I have found. I put this question to Laird Campbell. Ye are laird here and have the right to measure judgment against us. Instead of the punishment we deserve, will ye accept one gold coin as compensation for our crimes that we may find pardon in yer eyes?"

David raised an eyebrow and looked at Cormac with a slight smile. Jyne knew David was pleased with Core's request, and she was pleased to have fallen in love with a man who could show such wisdom.

"Aye, I will accept one gold coin as restitution and offer any who choose it pardon. Any who would accept it must also swear allegiance to me and serve the house of Campbell."

Core stooped down to grab one gold coin. He walked to David and handed him the coin. Core kneeled before him and swore allegiance to clan Campbell. Jyne's heart soared, and she had to wipe away a tear more than once before the oath was complete.

"Welcome, Cormac, to clan Campbell." David offered his hand to Cormac, who shook it heartily.

Jyne found she needed to wipe away another tear and was grateful for Isabelle's offer of a handkerchief.

"Now, men who have served my father. Ye may come forward and collect yer coin. If ye will turn away from this life and accept pardon, offer yer coin to Laird Campbell, swear allegiance to him, and begin a new life."

Bran stepped forward first. He picked up a coin and stared at it, turning it round in his hand as if savoring the feel of the coin in his hand. Jyne held her breath. What would the warrior choose?

Bran strode forward to Laird Campbell, offered the coin, and took a knee. Jyne found she was getting a lot of use out of the handkerchief and blew her nose.

"Ye best keep that one," said Isabelle dryly.

Jyne smiled at her.

More of the rough men came forward to give their coin to Laird Campbell and swear their allegiance. Not all though. Many of Rex's men who had arrived that morning took their coin and ran.

After all the men had made their choice, Cormac gathered the edges of the sheet, forming a pouch with the remaining gold coins within. He shook the bag, causing the coins to jingle in a tantalizing manner. Jyne assumed this was Core's portion, but her betrothed was not quite finished.

"This I would claim as my portion. And yet, since ye are a righteous and forgiving man, Laird Campbell, I would beg yer pardon for one more undeserving soul—my father, born Reginald MacLean."

David's eyebrows clamped down into a stern

frown. It was one thing to forgive those who served
Red Rex. It was another to pardon the man himself.

"None can change the crimes that my father com-
mitted, but I hope that within this bag, some solace
can be found to compensate those he hurt for their loss
and restore the property of those from whom he stole."

"Red Rex has twenty years of sins to atone for,"
said David, shaking his head.

"It can never be enough, but let this serve as restitution to the victims." Core handed the sheet and all
the remaining gold coins to Laird Campbell.

David accepted them but said, "Why would ye seek
pardon for such a man?"

Core looked over at Jyne. "Because I have been
shown mercy. And because God commands it of us
and grants it to us."

David acknowledged the truth of the statement
with a slight nod.

"My father allowed his grief to poison him. Losing
someone ye love can feel like a pain that will never
end." Core looked over at Luke, who nodded and
reached out to take Breanna's hand. "But I hope that
love can heal too. My father has shown me naught but
cruelty and neglect. Today, he intended to kill me.
And yet, I winna give him power over me. I hope to
live a better life." He looked back again at Jyne. "For
now I have a reason for it."

Core smiled at her, and Jyne returned a watery
smile of her own.

David jingled the bag, as if weighing the contents,
along with Core's arguments. "And if he lives and
starts causing trouble again?"

"I shall blow off the other arm."

David smiled at the thought. "We have reached an accord. I accept this payment as restitution."

Jyne rushed to Core's side, who dropped his staff in favor of holding her in a warm embrace. Their lips met until the loud sound of David clearing his throat reminded them to wait for their vows.

"Ye are so clever!" cried Jyne.

"Do ye approve o' how I have distributed it?" queried Core, apprehension in his eyes.

"Aye, verra much! But ye've left none of the treasure for yerself."

"I suppose I shall have to be content with marrying a rich wife," said Core with a gleam in his eyes. "I wonder where I might find one."

Jyne smiled in return. "I am happy to perform the office."

"Ye're verra kind, Lady Jyne."

Whatever she was going to say was captured by his kiss.

"Well now, good thing Luke was able to secure a priest. Let us get ye ready for a wedding!" cried Isabelle.

Isabelle took over preparations for the wedding and insisted first that the bride and groom be made presentable. Jyne soaked in the tub, relieved to be clean once more, though it was not quite as good without Cormac. With Isabelle standing guard outside, there was no chance of that. She ensured that all people heading toward matrimony were properly and separately bathed.

Isabelle saw to Breanna's transformation, lending her one of her own silk kirtles in sage green. With her red curls pulled back and a gauzy veil, Breanna looked a very bonnie bride.

Isabelle also fussed over Jyne's appearance, putting her in a pale blue silk with silver embroidery. A sheer veil was pinned on her hair, and Isabelle stood back and nodded in approval. Despite all the excitement and lack of sleep that made her slightly giddy, Jyne was more than ready to say her vows.

The brides were led out by Isabelle, Cook, and the other matrons to the doors of the chapel, where the priest stood to bless their union. When she saw Cormac standing there, her knees went weak. He was clean and shaven, his angular features appearing noble and true. He had been clothed in the Campbell plaid and wore it to perfection on his trim, muscular body. This was the man she would marry. This was her husband.

Oh, what an adventure she had to tell!

Epilogue

JYNE WOKE TO A TRAIL OF KISSES BEING PLANTED DOWN her cheek.

"Sorry, did I wake ye, lass?" asked Core.

Jyne stretched in the warm blankets in a luxurious manner. After five months of marriage, waking up in the arms of her husband was something she still found a delightful surprise.

"Aye, ye did. Do it again."

"As ye wish." He began to kiss her again, this time running his hand up her thigh to the place that made her groan with pleasure.

"Ah, ye're just doing that because ye ken I can deny ye nothing when ye do. What do ye want now?" she asked, wrapping her arms around his neck.

"I have everything I want, everything I need. Except mayhap…" He nuzzled her neck, warm and tender. This was her lover, her husband, the future father of her children. He was far from a perfect man, but he was hers, and she was more than content.

Her clever husband had been quick to learn the language of her body, understanding whether a gasp meant stop or more. He rolled on top of her, caressing and massaging intimate places until she pulled him closer, desiring him above all else. He joined with her, building up a cascade of delight until she found sweet release in his arms.

"I love ye," he murmured in her ear when he was capable of speech once more.

"I love ye too," said Jyne, happy on such a sunny summer morning. "Och, but look how high the sun is already. We need to get out o' bed, or there'll be talk."

"Talk? What talk? That I am hopelessly bewitched by ye? I think everyone already knows it by now."

"I need to get dressed to meet wi' Breanna. We are going to talk more plans for their new home."

With their generous portion of the Templar treasure, Luke and Breanna had decided to build a large manor house on the other side of the valley. Breanna had searched for all her younger sisters who needed a good home and had brought them to her. She also took on all the children who had been left behind at Kinoch Abbey. The resulting cacophony of children seemed to make her and Luke very happy.

Dubh had decided to become their personal protector and enjoyed playing games with the children even more than they did. Dubh had a particular affinity for ghost stories, to the delight of his young friends.

There was one little girl, though, who left their happy home. One morning, Jyne felt a tug on her skirts and found Ina standing there, a handful of her skirt bunched in the tot's tight fist. Jyne had smiled at Ina, and Ina had returned it. And so Ina remained with Jyne and Core, sliding into life within the keep like she belonged there, for so she did.

Jyne rolled out of the warm bed and chose a gown for the day. "Breanna and Luke are thinking of adding another tower and additional chambers."

"The more rooms they plan, the more children they seem to obtain," commented Core. "I think the rooms breed them."

Jyne laughed. "Would ye like children, my love?"

Core propped himself up on an elbow and smiled at her. "I think Ina would enjoy a little one to play with, if we are so blessed."

"Well then. I believe we may be so blessed." Jyne smiled.

"Truly?" Core's eyes opened wide.

"Truly."

Core whooped and jumped from the bed. Jyne laughed at the amusing sight of her naked husband dancing about the room.

"Is everything all right in there?" Bran pounded on the door.

"Aye, we are well," responded Core, diving back under the covers in case their new captain of the guard should decide to enter the room. "We are more than well. We are expecting!"

"Expecting what?" asked the gruff captain. "Oh, aye, well then…carry on."

Core snuggled back under the covers, and Jyne cuddled into him, warm and happy. "Shall we tell yer father the news? I hope he shall make a better grandfather than he did a father."

"Could hardly miss," said Core with a snort. Red

Rex had been quite put out when he woke and realized they had not let him die. He was utterly amazed when he heard of what Cormac had done for him, giving up his share of the treasure to pay restitution for him. Perplexed by these events, Rex took on the name Brother Reginald and decided to become a hermit. Core built a lonely hermitage for him, where he remained, weak and humbled. Jyne had made sure it was equipped with a long-necked kettle, to be a daily reminder to behave himself.

The elders had encouraged more of their clan to return and, with their wealth, had built up a small village around Kinoch Abbey and had indeed gotten the crops in on time for a bountiful harvest. Jyne had taken a few of the coins to furnish her new home comfortably for all who lived in it, even splurging on a growing library, to the delight of her husband, though he insisted her stories were always his favorites.

Core placed his ear to Jyne's tummy, as if to hear his unborn babe. "I think I hear him!"

"I think I'm hungry," replied Jyne.

"He shall be a strong lad."

"Or a strong lass," reminded Jyne.

"Och, nay, the lasses in this family are no' strong; they're ferocious!"

Jyne laughed. "Come here then, if ye dare!"

Cormac was a very daring husband indeed.

Keep reading for an excerpt from

the HIGHLANDER'S *Bride*

France, 1359

SIR GAVIN PATRICK SPURRED HIS DESTRIER AND RACED into the rising tide of English soldiers with the full knowledge they had already lost. Gavin was a bright lad by all accounts, but even one slow with his sums could readily see that the small force of French and Scottish allies was grossly outnumbered. Again.

A more practical person may have considered a tactical retreat, but the French would fight for honor, and Gavin, being a Highlander, would fight the English any chance he got. Besides, if he led a charge now, he could prevent a rout.

Unfortunately, the French were honorable only to a point and fled as soon as it became clear their advance was a failure. Without order, the knights turned and ran for the protection of the forest, leaving their retreating flank unprotected. It was the worst thing they could have done. One noble continued the fight and was quickly surrounded, unable to flee.

"Hold the line!" cried Gavin to the retreating men. It was a pointless command. The soldiers could hear nothing above the din of their own panic.

Gavin pushed ahead to the surrounded noble. The man was still mounted and fighting hard, but it was a matter of seconds before he was captured or killed. One of the English soldiers grabbed the bridle of the French noble's mount and forced it down. The end of the nobleman was near.

Gavin gave the howling war cry of the charging Highlander. It succeeded in momentarily arresting the attack of the English soldiers, who turned to see what demon was approaching them. Gavin charged forward, scattering the foot soldiers. He grabbed the gauntlet of the nobleman and in one bold move pulled the man onto his own horse.

Gavin spun and galloped back across the field of battle toward a large stand of trees, full of the dense green leaves of spring. The man behind him was leaning precariously and Gavin attempted to hold him with one arm as he urged his mount faster. They must reach the tree line before the English soldiers caught them.

He crashed through some low brush into the forest. The English pursued them into the trees, but here Gavin had prepared a surprise. Arrows rained down from the treetops and the English soldiers dropped and howled. The first wave of English soldiers turned and ran into their own charge, halting their advance.

Gavin smiled, though more in relief than from success. They had turned the English for the moment and prevented them from marching farther, but they were outnumbered and everyone knew it. Without reinforcements, their small force of French soldiers and volunteer Highland warriors would eventually fall.

The man behind him could hold on no longer. Gavin jumped off his horse just in time to catch the falling nobleman. He laid the man on the ground and removed his helmet. The nobleman appeared to be middle-aged, with a well-trimmed, dark beard in the style of the day.

The man gave him a wan smile. "You have saved me, Sir Knight. Pray tell me to whom I am indebted."

"I am Sir Gavin Patrick, of the clan of MacLaren," Gavin responded in French, a tongue he had learned well over the past few years he had spent in France.

"A Scot, are you?" The man's smile grew. "Tonight, you will accept my hospitality. If I do not reward you richly, I do not deserve the name of duc de Bergerac."

❧

Lady Marie Colette, the only daughter of the duc de Bergerac, sat sedately in the ladies' solar with her ladies-in-waiting. By tradition, her four ladies, Marie Claude, Marie Jeannette, Marie Agnes, and Marie Philippe, were there to tend to her needs, but they had been her mother's ladies-in-waiting and had adopted an instructional role after her mother died. They were all old enough to be her mother or her grandmother, and had distinct opinions as to how a lady such as herself should behave.

Colette had hoped when a fifth lady had been added to her entourage, she would be more of a friend to her. Marie Suzanne was indeed young, but at twelve years of age, almost a decade her junior, Suzanne was hardly a bosom companion. The young girl spent most of her time staring wide-eyed about the room and agreeing with anything her elders said.

All the ladies were at work on their embroidery, one of the few useful arts acceptable for ladies of court. Colette gathered a large sheet of linen about her. She had chosen to embroider a bed linen due to its bulk. Surreptitiously, she pulled a leather-bound book from her workbag, placing it behind the gathered sheet, out of sight from her ladies.

Colette quietly opened her book, careful to take a stitch now and then so as not to raise suspicion. Her ladies would be most displeased if the illicit text were discovered. They did not approve of a lady being taught to read, for everyone knew books would overcome a lady's delicate sensibilities. Colette's educated mother had embraced a more expanded view and once Colette had been taught, nothing could stop her from reading everything in her father's priceless book collection.

Pressed on by a sincere desire to read, Colette had become fluent in many languages. She read stories of glorious battles, myths from the Greeks, and of course, the Book of Hours, her prayer book, the only reading condoned by her ladies. Above all, her favorite stories were adventures of amazing courage and forbidden love.

She secretly turned the page of *La Chanson de Roland*. She had read the heroic adventure so many times she could almost recite it. She longed for her own adventure beyond the reaches of her strict nursemaids, but she had rarely traveled beyond the walls of the castle, and now that the dreaded English were causing havoc in their realm, she never left the castle at all.

She often lost herself completely in a book, but today the story of Roland dying bravely against the onslaught of foreign soldiers caused a ripple of fear to flow through her. Several weeks ago, her father had marched out with his knights to repel the English. He was late in returning. Colette did not wish to consider losing the only parent left her.

A clarion trumpet call gave the signal that the soldiers' return had been seen in the distance. Was her father among them? Colette swooped her book up with the linen sheet and stuffed them both into her workbag, hidden until next time.

"My father, he has returned," she announced, rushing to the door. "Come, let us greet him on the castle walk."

"A lady does not rush about like a common servant," chastised Marie Claude. Stalwart in stature, she was as old as the lines on her face were long. As the eldest of her ladies, Marie Claude's word was law in these chambers.

"And you must wear your headdress and your cloak, my lady," said Marie Jeannette with a scandalized gasp. Her life's work was perfecting the physical appearance of her lady, no matter what Colette's preference might be. Colette was heralded as the most beautiful lady in court, and Marie Jeannette lived on such praise.

"But I am already wearing a veil. Surely I do not need a headdress to stand upon the ramparts. It is a warm day, so a cloak, it will not be necessary," reasoned Colette.

Her ladies stopped her with their shocked expressions. "My lady!" they protested.

Colette sighed. They were right, of course. Everyone in the castle looked to Marie Colette to dress and act in a particular manner. If she should be seen running about the castle in anything less than rigid decorum, it would no doubt cause pandemonium.

"Vexing, forward child, always thinking for herself," muttered Marie Agnes, whose purpose in life was to ensure Colette never forgot her shortcomings.

"Let us pray His Grace has returned safely to us," said Marie Philippe, the only one to grasp what was truly important, at least to Colette, and thus the one who received looks of censor from the other ladies.

Colette relented, allowing them to weigh her down further. "Make haste, if you please." She submitted herself to be further dressed, though she was already warm in a formfitting blue silk kirtle and a brocade sleeveless surcoat, with rich embroidery of golden thread. To show her status, it had no less than a two-foot train, the minimum her maids would allow for everyday use. To this, her maids added a large velvet cloak, lined in ermine.

Colette tried to be patient as her maids pinned on her ornate headdress, a jeweled fillet over the silk barbet, which circled her hair. Her maids were even more chaste, wearing pristine white wimples that encased their heads and wrapped around their chins. Despite the current fashion that allowed unmarried ladies to let their hair flow loose or in two braids, her maids would not allow her hair to be seen in public.

The gown and robe alone were a load to drag

around, particularly while keeping her posture rigidly straight, but the ornate golden headdress weighed enough to crush any rebellion from her spirit. It was so heavy it never ceased to give her a pounding head-ache before it was finally removed. She had to move carefully not to tip out of balance and stagger under its weight.

Finally, she was deemed acceptable to walk sedately along the corridors to the castle walls. Even if she wanted to move faster, she was forced to walk slowly, carefully picking up each foot correctly so as not to trip over her fashionable, pointy-toed shoes. It would have been easier to lift the hem of her skirts, but her maids would have been scandalized if she'd accidently revealed (heaven forbid!) an ankle to the public. Thus encumbered, it took great effort to walk down the castle corridor, her five nursemaids trailing along behind her.

Author's Note

Our modern-day divisions of the scriptures into chapters is commonly attributed to Stephen Langton, Archbishop of Canterbury, who completed his work early in the thirteenth century. The further breakdown of the chapters into verses did not come along until the sixteenth century. In the fourteenth century, the only version of the scriptures approved by the Church was the Latin, thus when Brother Luke quotes scripture, he does so in Latin. Here are the verses Luke shared in English (King James Version), just in case your Latin-English translator is on the fritz.

A false witness shall not be unpunished, and he that speaketh lies shall not escape. ~Proverbs 19:5

Whoso loveth instruction loveth knowledge: but he that hateth reproof is brutish. ~Proverbs 12:1

In the world ye shall have tribulation: but be of good cheer; I have overcome the world. ~John 16:33

When Jesus heard it, he saith unto them, "They that are whole have no need of the physician, but they that are sick: I came not to call the righteous, but sinners to repentance." ~Mark 2:17

Acknowledgments

I could not have written this book without considerable support from my husband and my children, who have learned to ask me, "Mom, shouldn't you be writing now?" Thanks to my beta reader, Laurie Maus, who has the nicest way of telling me to try again. Thanks also to my editor, Deb Werksman, and my agent, Barbara Poelle, who continue to support and encourage my growth as a writer.

About the Author

Amanda Forester enjoys writing historical romance and divides her time between the rugged Highlands of medieval Scotland and the decadent ballrooms of Regency England. She enjoys researching history almost as much as writing, and attempts to provide the reader with a glimpse of the historical reality, without the fleas. Amanda lives with her family in the Pacific Northwest. You can visit her at www.amandaforester.com